Cunning Folk

Books by
Adam L. G. Nevill

Novels

Banquet for the Damned

Apartment 16

The Ritual

Last Days

House of Small Shadows

No One Gets Out Alive

Lost Girl

Under a Watchful Eye

The Reddening

Cunning Folk

Short Story Collections

Some Will Not Sleep

Hasty for the Dark

Wyrd and Other Derelictions

Cunning Folk

Adam L. G. Nevill

Ritual Limited
Devon, England
MMXXI

Cunning Folk

by Adam L. G. Nevill

Published by
Ritual Limited
Devon, England
MMXXI
www.adamlgnevill.com

Cover artwork by Samuel Araya
Dust jacket and cover design by Simon Nevill
Text design by The Dead Good Design Company Limited
Ritual Limited logo by Moonring Art Design
Printed and bound by Amazon KDP
ISBN 978-1-8383789-1-2

For Will, Ash and Elisa.

'Certain it is that the Pagan divinities lasted much longer than we suspect ... Who knows whether they do not exist to this day?'

Vernon Lee ('Dionea')

Before the Beginning

A motionless man stands alone in the hall, the foundations of his thick legs sunk into dusty boots. Bleak electric light illumines a galaxy of emulsion, pebble-dashing the grey overalls that are stretched taut over the barrel of his middle. His fingers, stained as if by a baker's flour, droop from the weight of the tools they barely hold. A hammer within the unclenching left fist. Suspended from the idle digits of the right hand, a small axe.

Below eyes stricken wide with terror, a tear of cream paint dries upon a cheekbone. Enlarged to voids, his pupils absorb the sight of what hangs from the ceiling of the hall.

A noose.

Beneath the newly painted ceiling, below the rope's end, his own collapsible aluminium steps have also been repositioned to create a scaffold for the condemned. Folded white dust-sheets fashion a path from the kitchen door to the ladder.

DIY gallows.

Tools and the scattered detritus of plaster dust, timber offcuts and tongues of dirty wallpaper litter floorboards blackened by age. One half of the hallway is pristine and issues the sheen of fresh paint. The other half hasn't heard the whisk of a paintbrush, or felt the slop of a paper-hanger's paste, in decades. A house of halves. The present and past huddled together.

The loop and knot of the noose are fashioned from the white electrician's cable of the light fitting – *his cable that he threaded yesterday*. But this man did not tie the end of this wire into a noose. Nor does he know when it was fashioned. He lives alone. But other hands made certain that the cable intended to bring light into this reception area now serves to usher a terrible darkness into the space. And in the house he'd hoped to call home, before the threshold he's secured with crossed planks of wood, the slack loop of wire beckons him to bow for a fitting.

An urge to blink the sight away, or close his eyes, is overcome by the same compulsion that bid him leave the kitchen, walk in here and behold *this*. One foot simply followed the other before caution and restraint fired the first warning shots.

With growing difficulty, the man's lips move to ask a question of himself, or the house, or the gods. 'Inside? How . . .' And then, as if to his invisible executioners, a simple, piteous entreaty dies inches from his tongue. 'Please.'

A brief struggle commences within his frantic thoughts before his body jolts rigid. And like a man who finds himself upon ice, spider-webbing beneath his heels, he stumbles forward.

One grubby hand twitches, drops the hammer. *Bang.* From the second hand, the axe handle slips. *Clump.* And inexorably, against their own volition, his feet scuff the white path of linen and carry his heavy body onwards.

Towards the metal steps that climb to the noose, he goes unwillingly. Face bulging the purple of kidneys, he is a prisoner who strains desperately to free himself. His own will is bound by a knot of iced rope that ratchets yet tighter to tug him forward. To the noose.

Begrudgingly, he mounts the metal stairs. All three unto the summit.

Tinker-creak. Tinker-creak.

No louder than the sound of air squeezed from a valve in a rubber tube, his voice wheezes, 'Not this . . . I'll go . . . Promise.'

Under duress from his shifting weight, as he assumes the required position upon the platform, the gallows moan. And his hands, which might as well belong to another man, carefully collar his neck with the noose. They tuck the pebble of the knot under his jaw. Then tighten the cord about his bristly throat and nape.

As he powerlessly watches his first foot venture out and hover in thin air, the ladder's protests subside as if the steps themselves are holding their breath.

With one foot on and one foot off the trapdoor, a whimper escapes the man's thin lips. His first boot prods out further and plants its weight upon empty space, pulling the second boot into the very last stride these legs will ever take.

A vegetable sound of twisting fibres obliterates the silence of the hall. A trickle of plaster-dust sugar coats the scalp of the hanged man.

Screened upon the pale wall he painted expertly, his shadow kicks a jig. Steel toecaps rake the air, rubber soles run across nothing. A foot then sweeps in a half-circle and knocks the steps. And as he turns upon his throttling tether of sealed, waterproof cable, his engorged face drifts. Within what remains of his eyesight, now darkening from the pressure of the blood that cannot escape his skull, a pale smudge disinters itself from the wall near the kitchen door.

Within the shadows, inking the waters of the dangling man's vision, most of the intruder's form remains indistinct. But what can be seen steps birdlike and probing. Then stops. A thing girlishly thin and chalky in half-light. Only the head is dark. And tatty and showing too many teeth.

Standing upon one leg, the intruder points at the hanged man.

The momentum of his soundlessly stamping boots turns the hanged man about-face until he confronts the threshold once more, so recently barricaded to keep *them* out. His final kick disperses a shower of urine across the bare floor and jerks him around a second time. But this time, what's left of his sight only glides over bare walls and an empty kitchen. There is no one there. Nothing at all to see before his own light goes out.

I

Six months later

'Daddy! Daddy! Your turn!'

Gracey's head hovers, a pale orb radiating impatience at the edge of Tom's vision. Behind the tiny features of his daughter's face, a four-year-old mind is committed to this game of I Spy. A distraction initiated by his wife to counter Gracey's fidgeting.

It's Tom's turn. Again. Part of being Dad. Taking it for the team. But Tom can't think of a clue because of a preoccupation with other matters. His wife and daughter are present inside the van, sitting alongside him. But they are akin to passengers standing on a station platform, blurred into the background by a train of fast-moving thoughts, divided into multiple carriages.

His attention is split between driving the unfamiliar van, glancing at the satnav to avoid missing the turning to the village, and a mental squall of memories. Recollections threaded with imagined disasters and joyous scenarios of his family's future in their new home; all blooming, racing, fading, blooming.

Nor can he explain his distraction to Gracey. His disbelief. His failure to acknowledge the enormity of this moment in their new life that is soon to start in their own home. One they own. *Theirs. Home.* The word has not carried such power since his own childhood.

Tom doesn't feel like himself today and imagines a new persona is required to match his newly acquired status of home-owner. Only he doesn't know what the role demands.

Now he has the keys and deeds to the house, he feels as if he has stepped out of a murky room, in which his anxiety obscured every feature and detail. A room he was waiting to leave for a long time. A confined space he'd rented that belonged to someone else. A landlord who might tell him to leave at any time, or charge him even more for occupying the room's dismal confines. And yet the restless, impatient feeling of waiting to leave that room has also continued into this morning, as if he has only succeeded in stepping into another similar room, in which his anxiety will obscure every feature and detail. All over again.

Surely, he'll adjust in time. But, right now, the title of home-owner is incongruous. Comparisons with other life-changing experiences of his past are a poor fit but are all he has to go on. Like meeting Fiona, his wife, whom he'd desired for so long, from afar, before they courted. After he'd finally summoned the courage to ask her out, there had been a long wait for her to contact him and he'd ached with a ghost of abdominal pain. During their first date, when her hand folded into his unselfconsciously, he'd recognised that they were together. She'd charted a new course in his life; one much better than the route he'd floundered upon alone.

Gracey. A miracle preceded by two years of futile attempts to create a child. Almost giving up and then, nine months later, she was swaddled in white towels and nestled within his arms, blinking milky eyes at him for the first time. He'd never entirely believed he'd ever be a father.

Dreams coming true. Longing requited.

But this . . .

Somehow, owning a home and no longer renting from the negligent and unscrupulous while living in a state of perpetual compromise and dissatisfaction, had been the hardest thing of all to achieve. Because, *money.*

'Daddeee! Come! On! Your! Go!'

'How about I go.' Conciliatory, from Fiona.

'No. It's Daddy's go!'

There was an order to things, rules. Many not written down but existing. Even a four-year-old could tell you that. And in the order of things, he was never destined to be a home-owner. What he'd been through to become one had made him older and more tired than he imagined he could ever be. Just to get here, maybe he'd burned through wires that can never be replaced.

Now, with the keys in his pocket, so hot and uncomfortable against his thigh, he obsesses about what he must earn to pay tradesmen; and earn to cover the repairs and improvements that he needs to fashion with his own hands to make their home habitable. And he suspects that more of his fusebox is destined to blacken in the year ahead.

One thing at a time, mate. We're in.

Tom distracts himself from himself to make a half hearted attempt at giving Gracey a clue. 'Something beginning with . . .' He has nothing. His eyes dart behind the windscreen, side window, searching. 'Beginning with . . .'

Gracey tenses, gripped by the desperate importance of guessing before her mum.

Outside the van a vast, open spread of farmland glides by. But there's little to provide reasonable clues for his daughter to swipe at. *Grass. Fence. Cow. House. Tree. Gate. Road.* All of it has already been suggested and guessed. There is nothing else.

I've never seen a soul here. No one shows themselves in the dismal wet fields, patchworked into sections by wire fences. No one toils behind the tufted vestiges of hedgerow. Few birds mark the sky beside the desultory spectre of a crow. As for trees, only spindly copses sprout on higher ground, shorn or shattered into piteous last stands; the woods have been whittled skeletal behind the wire of internment camps, to make room for more empty fields. And cement barns. Telegraph poles. Litter in the roadside ditches. Burst animals on tarmac, smeared, further compressed. Denatured land.

Denuded. Scrub grubbed out, scraped away. Ugly and too neat. Empty. Industrial even. Blasted. Nowhere for anything to nest, take root, hide. Green but made desolate by the impact of the nearest settlement's conquest. These are factory-farmed lowlands orbiting a city. A ring of ice encircling a blackened planet.

'Daddy! Your go!'

And then they cross the border. To *their* bit.

Exactly when they pass from the bleak to the fecund isn't clear. The B road narrows and some oak branches drape the road for a stretch, darkening the interior of the cab. The route then dips, veers west. A turn, a steep ascent later and the outlook changes. Even Gracey is distracted by the carousel of shadow and sunlight upon a wilder earth and upon the windscreen.

Not so flat here either. Hills ruffle the skyline and contour the land with smooth undulations. Patches of trees extend into actual woods that you can't see the far side of from the nearest edge. A buzzard hovers. Then another. Wood pigeons flap for cover beneath them. Tonal shifts emerge. Varieties of cereal crops occult the liverish earth, combed by giants. Odd hay meadows are pebble-dashed with pastel. Hedgerows thicken to spike outwards and suggest internal hoppings and buzzings of minute life. Ancient trees instil repose, austere sentinels drowsing in the corner of fields. Below their muscular branches mooch caramel cows patched with chocolate. Above the vista, the dusty sheets of ashen cloud break apart into cumulus, plump like white cotton.

The distinction between *back there* and *here* startles Tom. As it did when he came here for the viewings. The last of his preoccupation seeps away on a cloud shadow retreating over a steep hill. *And look over there!* A village's church spire needling between ash trees, spiking the blue heavens, evoking a sense of fire-lit interiors, citrusy hops, roast pork, smoke-cured beams, owls, bats, leaping deer, chattering streams, green paths, mill wheels, rope swings and bluebells. That must be the village of Eadric.

This is practically another country and he's an immigrant, gazing over the railings of a big white ship; his mind one big eye sucking at the light, the dreamy details picked out and cherished.

'Here we are,' Fiona says, wearily, breaking her husband's reverie. 'End of the line, folks.'

Beyond the dirt-speckled glass of the windscreen, an old house darkens a narrow lane. *Home.*

The pale blur of Gracey's face closes and she pushes at Tom's shoulder to return her father to her need.

'Something beginning with H,' Tom finally says.

An inhalation from Gracey, a breathless pause. Her head swivels about. 'Hair? Hedge!'

'Haunted house?' Fiona offers.

Since leaving the flat they've rented for eight years, and all that Gracey has ever known as home, Fiona has said little beyond attending to her daughter's needs; snacks, amusements, distractions. Taking their daughter on a journey longer than thirty minutes requires a steeling of the nerves, deep breaths and moments alone with closed eyes. But Tom's wife is smiling now. Sort of.

The van slows. Tom laughs. 'Home!'

Gracey's outraged. 'Didn't gimme no clues!'

'Dufuses!' Tom rolls the van across the end of the drive and their front garden is unveiled. A rectangle of spiky weeds and unruly grasses with unkempt borders, mopping broken tarmac.

Blotched by verdigris and speckled with moss, the roof might be a moth-eaten hat atop the head of a vagrant. Its dimensions score uneven lines against the sky, as if drawn by a child as the ruler slipped. The spine of the roof is further serrated like the teeth of an old saw and corrodes into the pillar of an oddly solid chimney.

Below, two storeys of exterior wall are coated in greening stucco, holed in places to reveal the reddish bricks of the building's muscle. Windowpanes, smeared by cataracts of dust, appear indifferent to the afternoon light. Not even the sun can pierce the glass and relieve an interior of perpetual night. Bristling the ground and only parting at the porch, an ungroomed beard of shrubs extends wildly for the sun.

Directly ahead of the van's bonnet, before the lane curves and cascades down the hill and into the village, a caravan slumps at the kerb, its grubby rear panels spoiling Tom's outlook. The state of the vehicle suggests it's been abandoned in the same spot for decades. But the old caravan wasn't there when he came for the viewings and to measure up.

The cranking hand-brake functions as a starting pistol. Seatbelt clasps snap open. Fiona shifts her position and moves Gracey's snatching hand to unclip her daughter's belt from the bottom of the child seat; Gracey can't reach the buckle but never stops striving for it.

At least Fiona is smiling. He's pleased to see that, even if it's nothing more than her determination to support him and be happy for her family. 'There go the next five hundred weekends,' she says.

'What else were we going to do?'

'Something fun.'

'This will be. Transforming it. Making our future.'

Still inside her car-seat but loose and wriggling, Gracey holds up her toy penguin to see the house.

Relieved the terrible shaking of the van has come to an end, Archie, the spaniel pup, stirs from his basket in the footwell. Immediately, he channels Gracey's joy and energy and climbs into Fiona's lap as if to see outside. But then glances from one occupant inside the van to another, struggling to comprehend the suspense that lies thick about him, yet satisfied that his people are in better spirits.

'Did a witch live here?' Gracey asks now that she and Waddles the penguin can subject *home* to closer scrutiny.

Tom grins. 'Mum, what did the due diligence say about witches?'

'We didn't have enough cash for a report on evidence of the supernatural.'

Frowning, Gracey glances from Dad to Mum.

Fiona kisses the side of Gracey's warm head and dips her nose into chestnut curls. 'No, Gracey-love. Damp, rotten eaves and fascias, corroded wall ties. Plumbing and electrics are shot. New boiler and roof on the cards. For starters. But no witches. This place hasn't been looked after very well, so we're going to make it happy again.'

Gracey is delighted by the idea.

Tom throws open the driver-side door. He slides out and Gracey rolls into his arms. Tom kisses her forehead.

Eager to be on her feet, she squirms free of his embrace. Racing, then slowing to wade through the thickets out front, she chatters to her penguin and swings the toy over the weeds. In her wake, Archie scrambles out, his claws timpani as he gives chase.

Fiona is last to alight from the van. Sheltered by the open door she stares at the house, her expression long, as if the mere sight of the property is adding years to her face. Tom watches his wife and how her attention immediately sweeps to the proud neighbouring property; the first storey and unblemished roof vaulting above the tall hedge that separates the front gardens of the adjoined houses.

When Fiona's smile slips, Tom feels he is losing her in some small way that causes an anguish that is almost a chest pain.

He's seen and coveted the neighbours' house three times already. A property effortlessly exuding the charm of an English village idyll. A vision of a dream-home realised. A fairy tale cottage beyond the ungroomed hedge, sagging to earth on their side.

Across the leafy boundary, the crisp *snip-snip-snip* of steel secateurs is audible, though no gardener is visible. A patter of sprinkler water darkens the tarmac of the passing road surface, yet no one emerges to greet Tom and his family.

During his first visit, Tom had wandered next door to introduce himself to the neighbours. And though he'd sensed his new neighbours were home, no one had answered the door. Perhaps they'd been out back. But he recalls how startled he'd been by the neighbours' front garden; the lush beauty both arresting and intimidating. He'd felt scruffy and awkward as if suddenly in a place he didn't belong, among the wrong class of people, wearing the wrong clothes. And he'd sloped back to his side, relieved the neighbours hadn't answered the front door and its strange piped chime.

Gracey pauses in her prancing to thrust her penguin in the direction of the neighbours'. 'We should live in that one.'

Fiona suppresses a giggle.

Momentarily stricken by the guileless comment from a four-year old, and unable to conceal his wounded eyes, Tom forces a smile. *His own daughter too.* He winks at Gracey and playfully wags a finger. 'Hey. Once I'm done with our place, it'll be . . .' *Better than theirs? As good as theirs?* 'Better than theirs.'

Tom raises his smartphone. 'Come on. Selfie. We'll do a *before.* Once our place is fixed up, we'll do an *after.*'

Fiona raises an eyebrow. 'Here's hoping Gracey's hair won't be grey in the second photo.'

Tom and Fiona are still laughing as Gracey slams into her parents.

Tom readies his phone. 'On three, money pit. Ready? Okay. One. Two. Three . . .' Together as a family they cry out, 'Money pit!'

To reach the crooked porch hooding the front door, Fiona and Gracey disentangle from Tom's arms and step around clumps of weed sprouting from the worn path.

Tom lingers out front because of the muted voices beyond the scruffy hedge. He can't hear what is being said, so sidles towards the narrow lane; an ancient green path, furrowed by horse and cart for centuries, before the swish and glide of tyres on tarmac took ownership.

Dappled with light spots and shadows from the overhanging branches of trees, they will walk this pretty road together in the future, as a family. They'll stroll to the village. Though no shop or pub exists any more, the buildings and front gardens of the village's cottages are also beautiful. Likewise the row of semi-detached villas, further down the slope that flows into the village. Their house is the last building, set apart on the outskirts. The only property in disrepair.

Beside the lane, Tom's attention transfers to the blight that is the old caravan slumped at the verge. Within the gloom of tree cover, the weathered sidings are a pond-green. Cheap orange curtains hang behind windows blown with condensation. Any exposed metal is peppered with rust spots. A wreck, an eyesore. The neighbours must own it.

'Fi'. Have you seen this? It wasn't here before.' Tom hopes his voice will carry and prompt an explanation from the gardeners beyond the hedge. But no one appears; the patient *snik snik* of secateurs continues as if in passive defiance to his presence. Tom takes another step in the direction of next door, unsure whether to introduce himself first, or just request an explanation as to why the caravan is there.

The sound of Fiona opening the front door distracts him.

'Daddy! Daddy! Look!'

Archie barks and won't stop, and doesn't seem ready to go inside with the girls. But between the puppy's yaps, Tom is sure he hears a sharp intake of breath from beyond the hedge; the kind of sudden inhalation that is sparked by outrage.

2

*L*ike nervous guests, unsure of themselves after crossing the threshold of a stranger's home, Tom and Fiona fidget to a standstill inside the front door. And immediately, deep from the throat, the mouth of the old house breathes upon them, gusting a miasma from its mouldering innards. Damp-darkened wood and moisture-softened plaster. A chemical and custard aroma of paint. Nose-tingling spices from grey pelts of dust. A peach and ammonia tang of animal urine, probably cat. A gassy whiff of sewage; an underlying trace that is there, then not there. And too much of the outdoors indoors. Cold, composted, autumnal odours; the last spirits to slope from buildings that have lain empty.

Anxious glances flit between them as they peer up at the long white cable and empty light socket above their heads.

Fiona touches her throat, swallows, shuffles from standing directly beneath the fitting. 'I wonder if we'll ever come in. Come home. And not think of . . .'

Tom winces. 'We'll get a nice light.'

'Yeah. That'll take our minds off it.'

The previous owner's suicide has affected Fiona more than him. Gracey doesn't know anything about it and never can.

Making peace with the house's history was always going to be hard but relegating the former owner's tragedy to the bottom of his thoughts, while enduring the exhausting process of buying a property, was effortless. How he would feel after taking possession of a building in which the previous owner strung himself up in the reception and choked to death, he'd also managed to never fully consider. But an abrupt and enforced intimacy with the very space in which a stranger's heart stopped beating takes his breath away.

'It knocked at least twenty grand off the price,' Tom offers, more softly than intended, which makes his voice sound weak. 'There's always that to remember. Instead.'

Fiona looks at Tom as if she can't believe he just said that, then grins and punches his arm. 'It being nowhere near a school and having a sieve for a roof also helped. Can't believe I let you talk me into this.'

Tom smiles. 'What. Was. I. Thinking?'

They're suddenly laughing like children in the face of something terrible that contains an irresistible thread of the absurd. Fiona folds herself under his arm. Guilty giggles subsiding, they kiss, then turn to peer beyond the gallows of a simple light-fitting.

A dark gullet of bare floorboards and plain walls gapes, the sight of it settling like a cold shadow. For Tom, the walls seemed to support a heavy object that must be picked up and moved a long distance.

Gracey's feet scuff and boom against hollow wood as she excitedly bangs along the entire length of the hallway. 'Old room! New room!'

Near them, magnolia's smooth infiltration and the restored skirting are evidence of the previous owner's intentions. In the brief time he owned the property, their predecessor attempted to erase former eras but never got far, only managing to plaster and paint the stairwell, first-floor landing, living room at the rear and half of the hallway. Tools were downed when he stepped off the ladder.

'House of halves,' Fiona mutters.

'Old room. Old room,' Gracey announces.

Many earlier episodes of the building's long life still haunt the dim shell. Wallpaper patterned with orange and brown squares, a design near psychedelic in its boldness, has hung on inside the drawing room beside the front reception. Tom peers inside, at the scuffed skirting, thickly painted the colour of vanilla ice-cream; the woodwork also moustached with black grime as if the cone was dropped in dirt. A frosted-glass light switch resembles a butter dish. The kitchen, bathroom and bedrooms upstairs are no more palatable or inviting.

Everything Tom glances at stirs cyclic thoughts, his mind compulsively listing the work he must do with his own hands, at the same time as looking for freelance work that uncannily dried up the moment they laid down the deposit – their life savings, no less. To raise his spirits, he imagines laying linoleum on these bare floors, redecorating the remaining half of the ground floor and all of the bedrooms, tiling the bathroom. The bits he can definitely do. Rising damp on some ground-floor walls he'll also have to address by employing what he has learned about plastering on YouTube. He thinks he can manage.

The precious money Fiona's mum gifted them as a housewarming gift, and more than they believed she had tucked away, is just enough to pay a plumber to fit a new boiler and replace the pipes in the kitchen and bathroom that make the sounds of a submarine running aground.

A home-improvement loan, through the bank where Fiona works, must cover the roof's repair, or replacement, a new fuse-box and wiring. New windows will have to wait until they can afford them. When he's got work coming in again.

To remain buoyant, to keep his nose and mouth above the choppy surface of the deepest, most precarious waters he's ever swum – the mortgage he can't really afford on a house that needs everything *doing to it* – his focus must remain upon one task at a time. One room and then another. Or he will be consumed, will drown. He knows this and tells himself this fact over and over. *Early days.*

'There's a few long days here. Almost relieved the freelance stuff's gone quiet.'

Fiona nods an acknowledgement but looks away, troubled by the spectre of money, of only one income trickling in. She goes and fills the mouth of the kitchen, her back to Tom. 'You can see where he ran out of cash. Or gave up.' She winces, turns to Tom. 'You think he . . . it was about money?'

Tom and Fiona exchange glances. Tom raises his eyebrow in warning. Fiona returns the expression as a challenge because she objects to being warned about Gracey overhearing bad *things* about the house. She's hardly the one who'll let something like that slip.

Gracey thumps out of the living room. 'I'm going to my room. Come on, Waddles. I'll show you where you gonna sleep.' Down the hallway she races, pounding out wisps of dust from between floorboards.

'Steady as you go, kiddo,' Tom says. 'Don't want any accidents.'

Gracey clambers up the stairs, her little legs pistons, knees rising high to propel her upwards. Waddles, her toy penguin, flaps about her hand. Archie, Gracey's other constant companion, overtakes her on the stairs.

Tom smiles. 'At least Gracey can see the potential.'

Fiona snorts. 'Gracey would be happy living in that knackered caravan if Daddy called it a castle.'

At the idea of the caravan out front, the house's damp atmosphere intrudes afresh into Tom's thoughts and only the stomp of Gracey's feet upstairs returns his eyes to the ceiling. Her small voice carries down, muffled by masonry and timber but the excitement isn't tempered. 'This is where we have bath-time.'

Fiona reappears beside Tom. They grip as much as hug each other. Looking into each other's eyes, they rest their foreheads together.

'We can do it, Fi.'

'If nothing goes wrong.'

3

The sound of a powerful car engine murmurs through the open window. Followed by a satisfying *clump* of a door closing and two lowered voices.

Too preoccupied to investigate, Tom ponders the room he will decorate first. This one will be Gracey's room. At the front, first floor, overlooking the lane and its columns of trees. He'll give it the best of himself. And will need to because the room is a murky space, unchanged since the 70s. A cubicle in which it is easy to imagine an elderly man as a former occupant, intent upon a dour vigil, wincing around a roll-up. He can even smell tobacco.

Between the building's long periods of lying empty, none of the five previous owners decorated the bedrooms. Maybe because no one stayed long enough. A notion that dims his thoughts with a dread tinted the same tone as the room's pall. Perhaps there is a deep and meaningful reason why no one liked the house and it lies right before his eyes. Much like a sense of a memory that hovers just beyond full recall, it will soon and suddenly become clear.

No. Stop it.

Everything is going to change inside this house now. And in this room first; the colours, contents, the very character and spirit of the place. Surrounded by toys and walls of ice-cream pink – the colour Gracey requested, her favourite colour for three years and counting – his daughter will reclaim and enliven this space.

Plump duvet on a white bed. Doll's house over there. Bookcase here, at the foot of the bed. Glow from a night light. A place she will associate with comfort. Imaginary worlds for bears and dolls will be devised. This room will become a stage in the theatre of future play-dates, where her friends will want to come.

His little Gracey will then grow taller and cleverer inside here, the toys and posters changing to reflect her evolving interests. But always, this will be her refuge, where she will dream, think and rest; a sanctuary for his child, his girl, his teen, and maybe a young woman too. More than any other room in the house, Tom wants this one to be special. Beyond all that he is expected to earn and own and provide and be and do, at his age, he wants to know that Gracey is safe, healthy and happy. This room will be a monument to how much she is loved and cherished. The seed of their home's transformation will start here.

The voices outside hush, yet the tone stiffens as if the exchange grows serious. No words are discernible but Tom is made to think that solemn news is being exchanged. He shifts to the window, the creaks under his feet muffled by an oxblood carpet, dust-peppered and cobweb-smeared, yet unhealthily moist. At a pane of glass, near opaque with grime, he peers out.

From this angle, he is again taunted by the idea that two front gardens could not be more unlike each other. And as if the clouds have parted exclusively above the sharp pinnacle of the neighbours' roof, even sunlight blesses the garden next door, yet falls short of his dank, shaggy lawn. So neat and regular are the planes and edges of the hedge on the neighbours' side, the privet might have been shaped by a stonemason. Only a glimmer of a lawn is visible, a baize amidst a rainbow of flowers mustered like ornamental soldiers at clinically ordered verges. The explosions of floral colour even make his eyes smart. The frenzies of bees and butterflies, careening in drunken ecstasy, make him dizzy. But through their gaudy clouds, he can see two women standing at the end of the neighbours' empty drive.

The older woman must be the female half of the couple next door; she's small and wears a loose shirt folded at the elbows. Baggy grey trousers are rolled above her bony ankles. Old clothes for gardening that appear to have once belonged to a man.

Her back confronts Tom; a narrow body and hips. She's not an ounce overweight and the tiny frame is held erect by an enviably straight spine. Her slim muscular arms end in gardening gloves. Only the henna bob that crowns the diminutive figure is shaped in a way that strikes Tom as really odd, though from this distance, seen through a dirty windowpane, he can't define why.

The woman's bearing also appears stiff, with a hint of prideful confrontation, as if she is looking askance at the much taller woman before her. A visitor who has parked her black Mercedes across the end of his drive. She hasn't parked outside the neighbours' because the dirty caravan consumes that stretch of kerb. So maybe because his house has been empty for so long, next door's visitors are accustomed to parking across his drive? Though surely this visitor can see that there is now a van on the drive, a vehicle they've blocked in.

Tom's attention flits to the driver of the Mercedes. Next to his neighbour, two women could not be more unlike each other either.

The visitor presents neat and chic in two tones, black and white. Formal apparel signifying business and money. Something to do with a bank or the law, he assumes. Her raven hair shimmers and is ratcheted into a bun at the rear of a narrow skull. Her figure straddles slender and bony, her silhouette sharply defined by a second skin of tailored suit. Beneath the hem of the pencil skirt, her black hosiery discharges a sheen, the slender calves appearing wet. A texture extending to her patent court shoes.

When the exchange between the two women becomes more intense and the gap between their faces narrows, Tom leans forward. 'Nosing,' his mum would have said if she'd seen him standing there, a few centimetres back from the window.

His neighbour offers a plastic bag to the woman in black and the visitor's respectful facade abruptly melts into an excitement she cannot contain. Despite her professional bearing, an unbecoming eagerness takes her over, as well as a furtiveness that impels her to snatch the bag.

When the article has changed hands, passing from a gardening glove to alabaster fingers with nails clotted burgundy, the suited visitor seems about to weep tears of joy. She even clutches the older woman's dirty glove to express her gratitude. A hand, if Tom is not mistaken, that was proffered regally.

The visitor dips her arm inside a slim bag that hangs from her angular shoulder. She retrieves a white envelope and pushes it at the older woman.

What follows fires a tingle across Tom's scalp. A feeling akin to accidentally witnessing an erotic moment between strangers.

The elegant visitor bends at the waist and kisses the old neighbour's glove, pressing her crimson lips to the back of the grimy fabric. Nor does she hurry to break the contact of her shiny lips on the coarse material, so recently employed in grubbing the soil.

The visitor then performs a slow, deferential bow, her ankles crossed as if she's curtseying before a queen after an honour has been bestowed.

Wearily, perhaps dismissively, the neighbour merely nods her bobbed head at the obsequious display.

The woman in the suit then withdraws and teeters past the front of Tom's house to her Mercedes, her posture huddled as if afraid of dropping something precious or fragile.

Frowning, Tom leans further forward. When his forehead bumps the window pane, the elderly neighbour turns swiftly.

Blinking the shock of the collision from his eyes, Tom's vision settles upon the old woman's crumpled yet fierce face, the chin raised. In confrontation, if he's not mistaken.

Before he's thought it through, he's dropped to a squat, his face hot with the embarrassment of a spy caught in the act. It's not only shame he feels but a cramp of apprehension too; even a fear that he cannot account for.

4

Enough to make anyone top themselves.

Another dowdy, dated room with a depressing atmosphere. Filthy windows strain the pewter light in which swarms of dust particles frolic. Disdainfully, Fiona turns about and surveys again, as if in disbelief, what is to be their bedroom. An empty space imprisoned by faded yellow wallpaper, with angles that vanish into darkness at the four corners of the high ceiling.

In the distance, at the bottom of the garden, a smudgy tangle of treetops erupts. The wood – one of the reasons Tom wanted this house so much: to live close to surroundings that would enrich Gracey's childhood; where enchantment could be conjured by the natural world. Fiona wants to shriek with laughter.

Within the distant interior of the house, the muted sound of Tom's drill grinds through plaster. He's still in the bedroom at the front, Gracey's room. He wants their daughter settled first. Fiona doesn't disagree. And in the pauses when the drill whines down, Fiona uses half her mind to listen out for Gracey and the plastic wheels of her toy pushchair that her daughter is currently racing up and down the stripped floor of the hall downstairs. A pursuit the little girl has not yet tired of.

But Fiona's gaze soon returns to the plethora of latches once used to secure this bedroom door from the inside. She wonders if the previous owner was responsible, or someone who'd owned the house before him. Maybe an elderly woman, paranoid about intruders.

The skin of her bare arms and legs gooses. Moving to the radiator under the window and the suggestion of sunlight outside, she seeks warmth. Drops her armful of bedding onto the cleanest area of floor she can discern on the ancient carpet.

Around the window frame, empty screw holes in the chipped woodwork indicate where wooden boards were fixed over the windows from the inside. Two planks remain on the floor. The estate agent took them down. The previous owner had no family. She and Tom bought the unfinished house from the bank at auction. They were lucky to get it.

Fiona touches a Rawl plug poking from the plaster. 'Poor bastard.' And, right then, a wave of fatigue overwhelms and stalls her, softening her limbs yet adding weight to her bones. She wants to sit down and stare into space. A compulsion that has beset her pretty much since they came in the front door earlier.

Even though Tom will soon decorate and lay a new floor in here, she needs to make the space temporarily habitable so they'll have somewhere to sleep. And yet, now that she's in here, so slight an exertion feels too much. She sighs and craves something to lean on so she can gather herself. She places her hands on the grubby windowsill. A prickle and crunch register like a series of tiny explosions under her palms. A glance is sufficient to reveal a legion of desiccated flies and moths on the sill. They only make her think of the spiders that drained so many to dust.

She swats the grime from her hands and is picking off a small black leg when her vision is drawn to the vibrant floral palette and intense golden light that blast from over the sagging fence from the neighbours' rear garden.

Small, neat trees on the neighbours' side of the border are either holding the fence's punch-drunk wooden panels upright or are pushing them to their knees. Through the treetops, a haze of butterflies and bees hectically orbit flower beds and rock-walled islands of sprouting plumes, wild grasses, bushes heavy with regal purples, rich yellows and scarlet.

Her gaze sweeps the beautiful garden's length until the unrolling of abundant, shorn grass meets the wall of dense woodland crossing the rear of each property. Close to the treeline next door, a feature catches her eye. A circular pond, the surface a black mirror, fringed by lustrous reeds. From the obsidian water, a small stone statue rises.

Fiona leans forward, squinting to better see the greening stone ornament. A grinning imp with long ears and the legs of a fawn. It stands on one leg and plays a woodwind instrument.

And then, abruptly, her dreamy gaze is shattered by a sudden materialisation of two pale smudges. That sharpen into a pair of faces. The neighbours.

The pair stand with their backs ramrod-straight and return Fiona's scrutiny. In the middle of the garden, they simply appeared without warning, like an indigenous people in a South American jungle.

On either side of a circular rock feature, from which a vast fern shoots at the sky, the neighbours stand and stare at her. As if delighted to have caught her snooping, the man grins. Flushed with suppressed fury, the woman appears outraged that Fiona would dare to even look at their immaculate property.

Flustered, Fiona swiftly turns her head and attention to her own garden: dark, shaggy, shapeless, bereft of birds and butterflies. It looks cursed.

Gracey runs into view. Little Archie frolics at her heels, ecstatic at the scents gathering about the unkempt grass and unruly bushes. Selecting a spot, he digs. Fiona has never seen him do that before.

The neighbours' intense scrutiny continues. The bony ovals of the two faces stain her peripheral vision, the woman's chin now rising in a provocation directed at the window that Fiona wants to cower behind. She wants to watch Gracey and Archie, but the two staring faces next door are too much to bear. She turns away and withdraws into the gloom.

5

*T*om walks no further than the doorway of the master bedroom. Leaning on the frame he swats his hands free of the sawdust that also peppers his jeans and exposed forearms.

He finds his wife sitting on a plastic storage box at the edge of where a grey light appears reluctant to enter the house. She is dabbing her eyes with a tissue. Around her, bedding and folded curtains lie crumpled like articles abandoned behind refugees. She hasn't brought any of the smaller cases in.

Tom's awareness of her being in the room for some time, in silence, has steadily grown as he affixed curtain poles to the walls in Gracey's room and then in the living room downstairs. He knows Fiona only stopped crying when she heard his approaching footfall. She's been in here for ages but doesn't appear to have done anything to make the room more comfortable. That surprises him.

'Tears of joy from being inside our first family home? Or despair?'

'Somewhere in between.'

Tom sidles in. Sits on the bare floor beside Fiona. Puts a hand on her knee. 'Hey.' She covers his hand with both of hers.

'Just having a moment.' Wistful, Fiona glances at the speckled windowpane.

Tom looks around the ceiling grimly. Shrugs with exasperation. 'I get it. I really do. Daunting. We're here and I just feel winded. But this is going to be a real home. Maybe for the first time in its life.'

32

'It seems so different to when we viewed it. Even worse.'

'I'll make it good for you and Gracey. I promise.'

'I know. You'll do anything to make this work. But everything we have, and a lot we don't have, is sunk into this, mate. Think it all just hit home and got the better of me. State of it. So . . . tired. Beaten. Miserable. No one ever lived here long.'

Tom gazes at the floor between his feet. 'What happened. In the past. Has no bearing on us. The guy was depressed.'

Fiona holds up a hand in warning. *Don't. Not now.*

Tom alters his tack. 'It's what we've saved every penny for. Ten years, Fi. Two old cars and one holiday in Aberystwyth. We earned this.'

Fiona sags more than leans into his shoulder. He is a mad evangelical who led his people into a green desert. There is no going back. The decision made, forced across the line by him during frantic months when they were wracked by excitement and fatigue in equal measure, while escorted by numerous estate agents around cramped flats and ex-council properties with lawns like thickets. Their budget barely competed for the half-derelict Soviet-style blocks circling a treeless city centre.

'Life in the country. Why not us? I can see it. I will make it happen.'

A widening of their house hunt only led to greater dissatisfactions: houses cramped along the scruffy fringes of ring roads. Every single property a compromise on what they wanted and needed. As he drove away from one dispiriting possibility that they could just about afford to another within their meagre reach, his imagination would inevitably divine Gracey's childhood in these places. A young life expended on cramped patios between sagging fence panels. On streets like blocked sinuses she'd walk to school, kerbs choked with parked cars. Passing shaggy lawns and playing in tatty play-parks with him uttering the endless refrain: 'watch out for dogshit'. Endless roads and traffic lights and metal fences amidst the superstores and warehouses and industrial estates, and Gracey would have breathed air like the atmosphere around an oil refinery. She already had asthma. Diesel particulate the culprit; they were convinced.

Later in their lives. *Broken and grey. He and Fiona. Up and down the doctor's.* Gracey grown and gone but knowing nothing better than the little they'd provided; expecting the same for herself at their age. He'd imagined it all and the prospect of that future had split his timbers and hardened his heart.

Fiona sniffs, reaches for the sheets. 'I feel silly now. Don't know what happened. Just felt . . . overwhelmed. Am I being ungrateful?'

A floorboard creaks. Tom and Fiona turn their heads to the door where Gracey stands, her face as long as her mum's. 'Is it a bad house, Mommy?'

Fiona forces a smile. Tom waves his daughter in. Gracey needs no further prompt and runs into her dad's arms. When she is smothered by his embrace she's on the edge of tears. 'Is Mommy hurt?'

'Come on. Dad sandwich.'

Fiona leans across and surrounds Gracey with her arms from the other side. Their daughter's distress is immediately soothed by the contact and tempered to a self-pity that she wants indulged.

Tom speaks to them all. 'We gotta treat this as a big adventure. Bit intimidating at the start. Takes time to adjust because we've been living in a rabbit hutch for so long.'

'There was no rabbits!'

'There was. You!' Tom tickles Gracey and she squeals and laughs.

Fiona smiles, her eyes tearful but filled with love for Tom and Gracey.

'And you know what?' Tom adds. 'This house comes with a wood. Full of rabbits.' Tom kisses Gracey hard on the forehead, each cheek, the top of her head.

Gracey writhes in his lap. 'Your beard scritches!'

'Come on.' Tom helps Gracey to her feet and gently swats the dust off her bum. 'Let's get at least one mattress in, or we'll be sleeping in the van tonight.'

6

First night in their own home and like refugees huddled in a makeshift shelter, all three of them are in one room. Gracey's lying on an inflatable mattress beside the double bed but she won't be there for long. Even when so close, she's too far away from Mum and Dad, and Tom will wake up with his daughter's arms and legs splayed between him and Fiona.

Getting the mattress up the stairs and round the newel post nearly killed him that evening. He's hurt one shoulder and his neck again. And now that their tired voices are no longer whispering to each other as if they're in a library, the dark house announces its various parts. They could be below deck on an old sailing ship. Even Tom finds the sounds uncanny. If he didn't know better, those are footsteps downstairs and something is definitely scratching behind one of the ceilings. In the kitchen, he thinks, a surface is groaning as if it's taking the weight of a body sitting down.

Between these enigmatic disturbances, there is a silence so profound he imagines that the house goes on for ever into rooms, corridors and spaces they've not yet found. But at least it turns his mind away from the compulsive circling of his thoughts – where to send his CV, which contact to tap, if this wall or that needs stripping first. It goes on and on. He suspects his preoccupations have cut an actual groove into his brain matter.

He thinks Gracey is asleep. She hasn't whispered in a while.

Not that he'd know but his daughter's mind is more active than ever.

This is a strange, bright place she's passed into. Inside a circular arrangement of black trees she finds herself standing upon a grassy hill, with Archie.

Just inside the gnarly legs of the vast trunks, grey hares with old men faces struggle on their poorly legs to move around the hill in a counter-clockwise circle.

They're still coming out of the stone door in the hill and all talking in Nanny and Granddad voices before they begin the shuffling. They're speaking a different language to the one she knows. But she understands what they mean without knowing how. She doesn't like them looking at Archie with their mean, rusty eyes.

When she looks for her mommy from the top of the green hill that's as round as an igloo, she sees their new house across the treetops. And inside an upstairs window Mommy is laughing with a big red mouth. Then she goes all blurred and ties something around her neck.

Beside Tom, Fiona's breathing slurs and she mumbles. Her body is absolutely still and seems partially deflated. He always falls asleep first but now he's the only one awake in the house, he feels horribly alone.

Fiona finds herself beside a black pond, putting on blood-red lipstick and checking her reflection on the surface of the water. Her face is indistinct save for her mouth.

She isn't alone. But she can't see who is moving about on all fours beyond the enclosure of shrubs that hems the water. They're laughing. At her. Two people moving like animals. 'More bloody rubbish has blown in,' a woman announces.

Fiona raises her hands and tightens the rope around her throat.

'Where do I do it then?' she asks. 'In there?'

The house nearby is perfect enough to be a mirage: red bricks glossed by ivy, a frill of pink wisteria drooping from the guttering, white woodwork gleaming like the perfect teeth of a gloating smile.

She can't see anything inside the building. The windowpanes are dazzling. But the smell of rodent urine and damp wood, sawdust and gas that leaks from the pretty house is choking. She looks down at the floral bells hemming her legs until the colours become pins of nerve pain poking inside her eyes.

She shouldn't be here. She's in the wrong garden and tries to get up when she hears Gracey crying next door.

But Gracey isn't next door, she's beneath the surface of the water before her. Eyes closed, her mouth moving, the child is completely submerged. Her hair spreads like weed then becomes weed.

Fiona might as well be in a wheelchair because her limbs feel as if they're filled with wet sand. Even rocking forward becomes difficult and she soon stops breathing because the loop around her neck has tightened again.

Tom isn't sure he's even awake when Fiona says, 'I was in the wrong garden.' Her silhouette is sitting up in the bed next to him. She's staring at Gracey who's just climbed onto the bed.

Gracey is crying and Tom thinks she says, 'And the rabbits is being mean to him. Big one is in the house wearing a black dress and she's put Daddy's tail in a trap and Daddy's cryin' and can't get out . . .'

Tom couldn't have been asleep for more than a few seconds. But he'd sunk so deep that a fear of dying quickly forced him awake. From out of his broken rest comes a memory of being chased through the ground floor of the house by something with a white mask for a face. Half of the floorboards had been missing. He can't remember anything else.

Tom comes fully awake as Fiona settles back down, mumbling.

Gracey's warm body folds into his arms. She's half-asleep. Tom folds the duvet over her and turns onto his side. Gracey squashes herself into his stomach and nestles her head under his chin. While waiting for his own disorientation to settle, he uses a thumb to gently wipe the tears from her cheeks.

He soon wishes that he could turn over without disturbing Gracey, because he doesn't like having his back facing the open door.

7

'Oh, you bastard. Get in.' Toes scraping the floorboards from which he's stripped the dirty carpet that blackened his face and arms, Tom heaves the mattress onto Gracey's divan.

Stacked like toy bricks, plastic crates tower from the floor of her room. Toys and clothes press against the sides like tropical creatures held captive in murky tanks. But at least the floor is solid in here. They'll buy her a rug. New carpet can come later, when they can afford it upstairs.

Disruption and making do will define their lives for a long time. Meantime, Gracey will need a bed, clothes to wear, toys to play with in her own room. She slept with them again last night. None of them are sleeping well. Strange dreams and talking out loud. They keep waking up and waking each other up. It can't go on; they need to settle.

Voices drift through the open window from outside.

Taking a breather, Tom sits on the bed. The exertion of getting the bed up the stairs haunts his already sore shoulder, his back and one elbow too now. Using the back of a grubby hand, he wipes sweat from his forehead.

A fluting laugh chimes outside; forced, possibly affected. The sound of it irritates him.

They still haven't met the people who live next door, their neighbours who have had ample opportunity to swing by and make stiff, self-conscious introductions. Out of sight, the people over the hedge have simply continued to titivate their already perfect garden. He suspects a deliberate suspension of neighbourliness. Maybe there's a touch of contempt towards strangers. The bizarre transaction with the driver of the Mercedes that he witnessed two days before hasn't helped him overcome his reservations.

Adjusting his position and lying across the bed-base, so that his face hovers some distance from the window, he peers out.

Today, a silver Japanese vehicle is parked across the end of his drive. A presence that immediately annoys him more than the Mercedes. The neighbours have an empty drive and the driver is their visitor. There are opportunities for the parking of idle vehicles where the lane widens, further down the hill, beyond the neighbours' caravan. So why continue to allow your visitors to block the drive of your new neighbours? A territorial precedent?

The bobbed thatch of hair of the female half of the couple next door is the first thing he sees over the tatty hedge. She's involved in another transaction at the end of her drive. This time, a plump woman in her early sixties with greying hair pinned behind an Alice band is offering a brown envelope to his neighbour.

In return the visitor receives a bundle, the size of a loaf of bread, wrapped in newspaper. And again, while covetously clutching the parcel to her bosom, the visitor performs a deferential bow. She also concludes the exchange by pecking at his neighbour's casually proffered hand. Another servile gesture. It's as if his neighbour is wearing a Pope's ring. The performance awakens the mild disgust Tom felt when he saw all of this before. *Who would expect that kind of deference from another person?*

'Nut-jobs,' he whispers and turns away.

But his thoughts won't detach from them. Before they arrived, he hadn't spared a thought to who'd be living next door. Not knowing who they are now niggles him and makes him restless and irritable.

He hears the whoosh of the silver car's engine as it drives out of the lane. The neighbours must be running some kind of business.

The hour grows late and the daylight fades. Their first weekend is all but gone and he still hasn't even exchanged a glance with the people next door.

He's tired and dizzy. They need to fashion a meal soon. This probably isn't a good time but he wants to get the common courtesy settled. Leaving introductions any longer feels wrong and may introduce a greater awkwardness into proceedings.

'I won't be kissing your bloody hand.' Tom laughs and stomps from the room, his work boots pounding the floorboards.

In their flat, they were strict about taking their shoes off before leaving the tiny reception area. Here, they are being strict with Gracey about never taking her shoes off because of splinters, exposed nails, screws, dirt and what Fiona identified as rodent spoor. There was more evidence of *black rice* in the kitchen cabinets.

When he reaches the top of the stairs, a distant rattle of plastic wheels grows louder: Gracey's pushchair whizzing over bare floorboards in what will be the living room. She's spent her whole life in a small flat and Tom adores the sounds of his daughter relishing the space here.

He spins round the bottom of the staircase and peers down the hall. Fiona's inside the kitchen again, and appears, as usual, to be doing nothing but morosely assessing another neglected room that their predecessor left unfinished. As if cold, she's hunching her shoulders, her arms folded across her chest. 'Same in here. He boarded them all up. The windows. In every room at the back.'

Gracey clatters into the mouth of the living room. The front wheels of the pushchair strike the threshold and upset the vehicle. She's crammed her penguin Waddles inside the toy pram, in which she is also trying to transport a bag of clothes, taken from other dolls, to dress the penguin. The bag has fallen and upended on the floor. The pushchair is at a tilt.

Red in the face, Gracey explodes. 'Waddles won't stay in! He's falling out. All going wrong!'

Fiona sighs. 'It won't all fit in the pushy, love. Give me a minute and I'll help you.'

Tom raises his voice. 'Think I've just seen another drug deal go down next door. Better pop round and tell them who we are. Can't put it off any longer.'

'Pick me up some crack.'

Gracey hurls the penguin into a wall. 'Dis is stupid!' Her parents have continued to talk amongst themselves, despite the fact that her failure to transport a penguin and its baggage in a pushchair has not been immediately addressed.

Tom reaches for the latch of the front door. Raises an eyebrow at Gracey's outburst. 'I'll reassure them we're a nice, quiet family.'

Fiona giggles. 'Don't forget my crack.'

Gracey will not be left out. 'Me too, Daddy! I want some. Mommy, what's crack? Do you eat it?'

8

From his childhood until he left home at eighteen, Tom's parents forged and maintained good relationships with all of their neighbours. His family moved three times and his mum often reiterated how important these connections were. In an emergency, you might need neighbours to call the fire brigade, the police, an ambulance. Or feed your cat or dog when you were away. Maybe do a bit of shopping when you were ill. Even watch your child. Trust, camaraderie, community.

There had also been a social element with neighbours: evening drinks for his parents, barbeques, day trips with next door and their children. His mother still exchanged Christmas cards with several former neighbours who'd become lifelong friends.

He'd grown up believing that cordial connections to the people who lived on the other side of your bedroom and living-room walls, or across the street, came pre-loaded into home ownership. An automatic benefit, even entitlement. One of their reasons for getting out of the city was to find a community similar to those that had sheltered him as a child. He wants the same for Gracey. The confirmation of a safety net extending beyond her parents. So the idea that owning a home is no different from his experience of renting is unthinkable. Everyone keeping to themselves, folks coming and going with nary a nod, maybe small talk but nothing meaningful developing? Not possible, or acceptable.

Clad in his work boots and old clothes, he plods over. The dirty caravan soon looms. Another anomaly. Why would people so obsessively house-proud position the wreck outside their pristine home? The neighbouring house clearly and outwardly projects a particular set of standards. That's no accident; the house next door is a symbol, a communication of status. The caravan makes no sense.

He really needs to straighten this issue out, and his head, then move on. He has enough on his plate. Get a quick exchange over with, then get back to work on Gracey's bedroom. He wants the furniture assembled before teatime.

A sense of subtly passing from autumn to summer across the few metres dividing the two properties compels Tom to glance at the sky to establish how the sun shines here when cloud douses their home with premature autumnal gloom. And even though the neighbour is no longer out front, how does her garden feel *occupied*, even unusually alive? Maybe the frenetic insect life can account for this.

Humming bees vibrate the air and thrum the ground as if they're discharging an electric current. He hasn't seen a single bee in his own garden. Nor so much as a brown moth. Yet, here, not only do they have enough bees to furnish a rank of hives, a confetti of Peacock and Cabbage White butterflies also attends the floral banquet on offer, perpetually scattering about the heavily perfumed air.

Tom pads a pristine path laid parallel to the neighbours' drive. Lamps of flowers that encroach upon the bleached flagstones light up the sawdust and stains plastering his boots. A temptation to linger and stare at the incredible garden slows his feet. The last time he saw plants so vibrant was in a botanical garden. He wants Fiona to see this too and see what they can achieve. The soil must be exceptional.

The front windows of the house are concealed by dark curtains but the front door is open, a black space. Barely discernible walls suggest the murky silhouettes of pictures and ornaments, inviting Tom to narrow his eyes to better see what appears to be a mask with tusks.

Before he can get any closer, a shrill voice shrieks behind him, 'Yiss?'

Startled, Tom turns towards the challenge.

And sees no one and nothing save groomed shrubs, heavenly flower beds and a symmetrical hedge. Until, at the corner of his vision, a blurred figure abruptly rises from cover.

Tom starts again. 'Shit. Sorry. I . . .'

The hostile tone of voice is matched by the speaker's disapproving expression. But, at such close range, Tom is more shocked by the diminutive figure's appearance; even more so than he is by how she managed to project her voice from a different section of the garden. But two distant sightings are no preparation for the sight of the peculiar haircut framing the woman's cramped, fierce face: a severe fringe guttering a thatch of hair; a henna bulb hooding plain features, free of cosmetics. She appears to have too many hair follicles on the scalp of so small a head. She also hasn't trimmed those thickets of eyebrow nearly as well as her plants and appears to be wearing a man's clothes.

'Can we help you?' A second voice announces itself behind Tom. A man, his tone prickly.

Tom shifts his footing and as he turns to face the man, the manoeuvre blurs his vision as if he's just stood up too quickly. Brilliant, florid hues and the gauzy light drenching the garden do nothing to ease his disorientation. By the time he's blinked the glowing palette from his eyes, his vision settles upon . . .

No one.

Again, there is no one there. Only more of the garden and the lane beyond, funnelling through the oaks and ashes and beeches.

Until a second figure shoots upright from another section of the garden, contrary to where the voice originated. A man grinning triumphantly and clearly pleased with startling the visitor.

Tom's surprise immediately extends to this figure's equally absurd appearance. Earlier, he'd heard a plummy male voice murmuring beyond the hedge, but this is his first sighting of the male half of the couple next door. An embroidered waistcoat, intricately patterned an intense blue and red, covers a loose linen shirt. His tight trousers are pink. The uppers of his shoes appear woven. And the man's baldness is clownish, a shiny dome of scalp between two muffs of groomed hair that fall to his shoulders. Like a Jacobean playwright, his snowy beard has also been trimmed to a meticulous point. Thin lips, framing a set of dark and unhealthy-looking teeth, worm moistly. The default setting of the face's expression appears to be a smirk.

Bewildered, Tom glances from one neighbour to the other: the grinning man, the disapproving woman. The front garden is no bigger than ten square metres and is strictly marshalled by hedges on either side, so how did they manage to hide? Or had he been too preoccupied to notice them as they knelt and attended to the flower beds?

At least the man is smiling, after a fashion. Tom clumsily veers towards him.

'The dianthus!' the woman shrieks. 'You're trampling them!'

Tom pulls up. Looks at his feet. 'Sorry. I—'

'Where you are is fine,' her male counterpart says and minces towards Tom, up on his tiptoes between the plants. On either side of his nut-brown head, his bob flounces and sways like a sea creature in a rock pool. And when the self-regarding face confronts Tom at close quarters, the man's cold blue eyes twinkle with amused contempt.

Tom extends his hand.

Rather than accepting the shake, the man taps Tom's fingers. A gesture made with reluctance.

'I'm Tom. My wife, Fiona, and my—'

'We know who you are.' The curt reply ratchets Tom's bafflement and he futilely scratches through his thoughts to discover a reason why his new neighbours are upset. Or is this the level of disapproval they inflict on all strangers?

'Got your work cut out.' The man nods his head in the direction of Tom's house, his expression disdainful at the mere sight of the building. There's an over-familiarity to the mockery, as if he's repeating sound advice that Tom failed to heed the first time he heard it. Without bothering to acquaint himself through small talk, this ridiculous figure, with a head best suited to the stage at Stratford-upon-Avon, is genuinely taking a tone.

An unpleasant warmth flushes Tom's scalp. For a moment each hair follicle seems to bulge.

'The whole thing should have been torn down years ago.' This from the woman, the clipped enunciation again striking Tom as affected.

Tom looks at her angry face but her fierce eyes startle his thoughts into a flock of panicking birds. He lowers his eyes and focuses on her chin, which is grooved like a hairy walnut. Disgusted, he glances at the bowl-shaped thatch and recalls a picture of a knight in a childhood book, the dignitary having removed his steel helmet to reveal a foppish bob. He wonders if this pair cut each other's hair.

And now they're both staring. At him. Into him. They stare and stare with their piercing blue eyes, pinning him in place, where he silently writhes in a discomfort that is physical. His neighbours have the same eyes.

A tremor ripples his vision. He's hot, breathless, dizzy, antsy, the sensation becoming unbearable. His wounded outrage intensifies the garden's colours until they seem hyper-real.

The bald man's gleeful grin only broadens. The woman frowns, her lined mouth sagging as she too grasps an opportunity to look askance at his new home, as if it is an insult to common decency. 'Two properties could not be more different.'

Tom's throat becomes a drain clogged with wet leaves. He needs to swallow but won't because that will be visible proof of his distress at being shamed. His posture ramrods.

The man embellishes, his competitive spite matched by a viperous glimmer in his eyes. 'Always been that way. But then we've always made the right choices, haven't we, me dear. Different standards.'

Tom's cheeks smart as if from slaps. He hasn't felt this way since being disciplined by a manager in his first job, at twenty-one. A similar sense of being scolded at school revives, until exposure to the man's persistent smirk finally breaks him from the enforced deference he feels when standing on their property, their turf. 'Come again?' His voice is higher and sharper than he intended and his thoughts continue to riot. But a desire to strike back, to confront, grows hotly.

The woman throws her thin arm in the direction of her house. 'The fence at the back is the first thing you'll need to address.'

'It's that time,' the man contributes in a headmasterly tone, rising onto his toes. The performance is completed with an admonishing, pitying shake of the head, the drapery of white hair swaying above a grin twisting triumphantly. Points scored.

The part of Tom's mind that produces language remains frigid, iced over. He has no words. The curious paralysis baffles him. He's unable to release anything from behind the knot of his larynx other than 'What?' He wonders if he is more angry with the neighbours or with himself for failing to react with anything but stupefaction.

The woman's face colours a brighter scarlet, matching the absurd hood of hair about it. 'The fence. Back garden? Surely you've noticed its considerable disrepair?'

'Can't say that I have,' he squeezes out, churlishly.

Tom has noticed the half-collapsed and algae-greened mess at the back, dividing the two properties. He'd assumed the neighbours must be used to it, so has given it scant consideration. And to his eye, crucially, had the neighbours not planted a line of ornamental trees at the very border, the posts and panels of the fence would not be falling apart. And anyway, in the scheme of things facing him, the fence is a cosmetic outlier in his plans; it is beyond his budget and the very last thing that he'll be addressing during the renovation of the property.

The man is up on his toes again, his hands folded in the small of his back, appearing owlish as he remonstrates. 'Been overlooked for far too long.'

Tom stops swivelling within this ambush but remains reluctant to move his feet in case he tramples a valued flower. They're everywhere. Barely any lawn, and only one or two flat stones offer any hope of egress in any direction. He might have blundered into a minefield. The neighbours must prance between them like strange, angry birds. But he's trapped, rooted.

The slow drain of adrenalin finally loosens his limbs. His jaw unlocks. 'Look—'

'On the left. Your side. Your responsibility. A priority!' So ardent is the woman's emphasis her tongue lisps on the last word, *pwiowity.*

Tom glares at her.

She glares back. 'An eyesore! All needs replacing! Every panel and post. Use concrete posts. Wood will rot.'

On the other side, the man positively beams as his wife berates Tom. 'Your predecessor never managed it. You can afford it, I hope?'

'Come again?'

'First home, is it? Bit late in the day, eh? Hope you have deep pockets.'

Tom's dog finally bolts. 'How deep were yours when you picked that up for a couple of grand? When would that have been, 1970?'

The figure can riposte with nothing but an odious grin that, at least, is no longer so assured. But before Tom can capitalise on this subtle alteration in the balance of power, the wife chimes in, her voice more strident than ever. 'It's falling onto our trees! A disgrace! We don't have broken fences in this village.'

Regaining ground quickly, the man seizes a chance to jab low, working under Tom's first defence. 'Don't skimp on the height of the panels either. We enjoy our privacy.'

Involuntarily, Tom's left eyelid flickers and he feels a delinquency sidle into his emotions. An instability. Yet he fails to think of a reply to the double-act and what must be an unleashing of their stored grievances against the house next door. But their manner is unacceptable and he will soon have nothing to offer his neighbours but a roar of animal rage. He even feels ready to spit into their faces.

They understand how he feels too. That's the worst part. And he intuits that they are amused, even energised by his discomfort. They show no inclination to stop the taunting and the hint of their satisfaction makes Tom grow cold. And colder until he catches a welcome glimpse of Fiona approaching. She must have been listening. He'd left the front door open when he'd popped next door.

Fiona's smile is tense from restraining her own irritation. She works as counter-staff in a bank and is used to dealing with the rude, the stupid, the hapless, the aggrieved, the general public. 'Look, Mister?' She slips in front of Tom, forming a human shield before her cornered husband, until they stand united upon a tiny patch of available grass.

Immediately, the female neighbour appears scandalised by the sight of Fiona's bare flesh. She's wearing denim shorts and a vest, a pair of old trainers on her feet, in which to work in the warm grubby confines of their home.

Grinning lecherously, the male half, however, cannot restrain himself and leers at Fiona's bare legs with undisguised appetite. Brazenly, before Tom's very eyes, the freak's gaze then crawls up Fiona's body and lingers upon her chest. 'Moot,' he says, grinning at Fiona's breasts.

Brack! A gun might have exploded behind Tom and Fiona. They both flinch.

'Christ!' Fiona says.

Together, they turn to the source of the bang. The front door of the Moots' house is now closed, has been slammed shut. The female half has disappeared from the garden.

Dazed, the explosion of the front door ringing in their ears, Tom and Fiona return their attention to Mr Moot.

Who grins some more, enjoying their shock.

Tom tries to speak. 'I don't—'

Fiona interrupts. 'We'll make a note of the fence, Mr Moot.'

'Magi Moot.'

'Right. But it's on a very long list. I'm sure you can appreciate that. The place has been in a state for a long time. And after what happened . . . Yeah? You'll understand how much work we've ahead of us. So you'll just have to be patient.'

Fiona looks to Tom, then nods in the direction of their house.

Magi Moot turns his back. And so swiftly, Tom flinches as if the man is about to throw a punch. But Magi Moot, if that could possibly be his real name, casually picks his way, light on his toes like a dancer, back to where he was gardening. He doesn't look at Tom or Fiona again. Unruffled, he crouches and his secateurs resume the snipping that infuriates Tom even more than the barrage he's just endured; his rage is now augmented by the added humiliation of his wife needing to rescue him. He remains immobile and mute with his hands extended, his palms open, sharing his astonishment and shocked disbelief with his wife.

Raising an eyebrow, Fiona glances at Tom's hands and nods. 'Gracey's wardrobe's about that size. Let's crack on.'

Tom still can't seem to move his feet with so much left unsaid. Until Fiona squeezes his forearm and whispers, 'Assure them we're a nice quiet family?'

A rash of shame finally enlivens his muscles and he falls into step behind his wife. But as they leave the illusion of summer and return to the grey air and blackening greens and peeling facade of their property, a reckless tailwind of confidence suddenly invigorates him. He becomes giddy. 'What a pair of pricks!' His voice might have carried all the way to the village.

Fiona turns. 'Ssh. Don't make it worse.'

'Did you hear all that?'

'In the scheme of things facing us, Fred and Rose are a footnote. Come and see what I've found under the kitchen sink.'

'What?'

'Mouse mother-ship.'

9

One week later

Another long, noisy day has almost passed and most of the games that Gracey tries to play inside the house make her mommy and daddy say, 'Don't', or 'Put that down', or 'It's not a toy', or 'Be careful', so she's going into the garden.

Rattling wheels of Pushy the pushchair bump the floorboards. Sometimes they squish or carve clumps of grey furry dust that continually sprout into being, no matter how many times Mommy sweeps them up. 'Dust rabbits,' Mommy says and it makes Gracey think of a huge rabbit under the house shedding old fur that puffs through gaps. Sometimes she imagines big eyes peering through the holes.

Belted in tight, Waddles the penguin sits erect, Gracey's own baby alert to his new surroundings. A plushy mouse is tucked under his wing. Waddles is her toy, the mouse is Waddles' toy.

Racing past doorways. The room with the television is filling with bags previously stored inside the cupboard of their flat, with the vacuum, board games and shoes. Yesterday in 'new house', she asked Mommy if they could 'go home' to the flat and Mommy tried not to cry.

Cardboard boxes with food names printed on the side make her mouth water. Plastic storage boxes are stacked like coloured bricks and surrounded by paint tins and poisons in bottles that she mustn't touch. She's made sure that Waddles knows this too. Their settee and two chairs from the flat look as scared and lost as she did when she started school. Daddy's tools litter bare floors.

Inside this house are spaces and holes and caves and hiding places and mazes in big rooms. But she's been told not to build tents because everything needs moving again. Daddy wore a plastic suit like a spaceman when he ripped up the stinky carpets, rolled them and carried them into the garden.

She wants to see the mice. They're the last thing her mommy wants to see. Gracey's been checking the traps every five minutes. Grey plastic boxes inside kitchen cupboards.

On the first day, Mommy and Daddy were whispering about 'mice' and her daddy talked about 'traps' when he thought she was out of 'earshot'. But Gracey heard and got upset. But her daddy says the traps are only for catching the mice before he carries them into the woods so they can find new houses. 'You don't want them pooing in your crispies,' he'd said.

Across the kitchen floor she, Waddles and Pushy go whizzing. The lino is the colour of cream-of-chicken soup but smells of 'mice piss'. Waddles the penguin stares ahead from his stripy seat and out they go, into the garden, as the sun lowers onto the jungle's spiky roof.

Above her, a window cracks. The back of the house is even scruffier than the front.

Mommy shouts, 'Gracey! Stay where I can see you!' Her face is grimy.

'Am!'

When Mommy and Daddy have cheeks like tomatoes and Daddy uses rude words, she stays away. They're struggling to free a wardrobe trapped on the stairs. It's been stuck there all week since last weekend and you have to squash yourself thinner to get round it. So they've been lifting Gracey over the blockage every bedtime. When Mommy caught her finger earlier, she shouted at Daddy.

'Your side. Your side.' Now that's Daddy, telling Mommy what to do again. Their voices punch out of the darkness of the upstairs but sound closer out here in the garden like her parents are inside the kitchen.

Daddy's still in a bad mood after going to see the neighbours last weekend. When she's at school and he uses his electric saw they slap the walls on their side. The man with clown hair came round and complained about ivy crawling under the fence and into the garden next door. Next door's visitors keep parking across the drive and they blocked in a builder who came to the house to quote on the roof, and that was bad news too that made Mommy look like she was going to faint.

Mommy's mostly busy all the time and tells her to 'amuse herself' but today Mommy is still blaming Daddy for her hurt finger. When Daddy's angry, Mommy gets angry. Gracey gets tearful.

'I can't.'

'Left. Left!'

'Piss off! Bed's in the way.'

That's a rude word. Better to be in the garden.

Gracey snatches up wildflowers and weeds that look like lettuce from around the edge of the patio. It's like the deck of a ship sinking under green waves of grass.

She places the bouquet in her pushchair for Waddles to look after.

Archie is madly digging a new hole near the fence. A small crater in black soil. Worms twist. Lice scatter. He has dug three holes. No one knows why he digs them. Whenever the back door is opened to let in some fresh air, because the kitchen stinks, Archie bursts through people's legs to speed into the garden. He's been outside for ages today. When she catches up with him, Gracey threads yellow flowers under his collar.

At the top of her garden, the fence between her house and the pretty house next door, belonging to 'the rude bastards' as her daddy calls them, has broken bits. Through gaps she spies into the neighbours' garden. From here she might be looking at a page in her book of fairy tales; a scene filled with lights and colours that are brighter because of magic.

There is a statue of a Mr Tumnus from *The Lion, the Witch and the Wardrobe* but with a nastier face. He towers over a black pond that might have frogs. Maybe they all wear red waistcoats. It's a shame they're 'rude bastards', or 'funny old people', as her mommy says, because she'd like to go into their garden and pick flowers and look at frogs and fish.

For a while Gracey stands still and watches next door's garden. When she feels the flowers are looking back, she returns to the hole. Archie's been busy and has pulled out more soil.

'Treasure, Archie!' Gracey kneels. Reaches into the hole and uses both hands to pull at the dully glimmering thing in the moist clay.

'So heavy, Waddles. Help me, Archie.' Gracey drags out a metal lump that films her palms with slimy mud. It's as long as a house-brick and as thick as a big chocolate bar. Squatting, she scrapes soil from its surface with her fingers. Under the sticky mud, the surface is bumpy with letters on one side. Writing she can't read. Archie sniffs it, then breaks away and races to the end of the garden where the woods rise like waves to smash the saggy fence.

Gracey drops the metal tablet and pursues Archie until she arrives where he is winding circles before the gate that tilts. 'You mustn't hurt the rabbits, Archie. Only say hello and tell them I live here now.'

A big rusty padlock and an even rustier bracket lie in the long grass.

Gracey unlatches the gate. Hinges squeal and her bones go funny inside. The little door opens. The rotten bottom judders, scrapes weeds. She opens the shaky door wider to see if there are rabbits running among the trees.

Her attention is seized by ornaments instead, screwed to the outside of the garden gate. Like rusty scratches, the metal decorations face trees that remind her of another story in her book of fairytales. The story about a witch. It has a picture of a greenish lady that Mommy covers with a hand, so Gracey won't think of the horrible face when she's in bed at night.

Metal crosses are fixed into the gate's flaking timber. Together they shape one bigger cross like those on churches. Gracey traces her finger over a cross. The metal surface is rough. She touches another. A third. Two more. If Daddy takes them off the gate she can keep them in her jewellery box.

Archie scrabbles into the woods. A fluffy bullet, his stub of tail swiping.

Gracey looks up. So many trees. A wet, leafy smell moistens the air, tasting mushroomy inside her mouth. Old and fruity as her nan's compost. Not exactly nice. Not horrible either. A smell from winter.

Fading light the colour of tin spikes onto silvery limbs, dark green leaves, crispy brown scrub and pale nettles with fuzzy leaves that sting legs. Other parts of the wood stay in night time. Between the trunks and low boughs, blackberry vines choke either side of the track that Archie trots, nose to ground.

Her tummy prickles. Magic lives in this wood. In the distance there will be dens and clearings and treehouses and narrow paths of golden light guarded by singing birds. Foxes, rabbits, badgers, maybe lions that have escaped from safari parks live here too. She feels small and frightened and excited in the way that makes her want to wee.

Soon she will be able to come here whenever she wants. This is one of the reasons they moved here, for woods she can play inside. She'll have a den in here, with chairs, for when Ben, Avni, Amaya, Isobelle come over. Her daddy said so.

'Archie!'

Gracey takes Waddles out of the pram. His big blue eyes look as scared as she feels. Gracey reassures her penguin. 'The gate is open. We can't get locked out, Waddles.'

She takes a few steps along the track between the giant trees who peer at her. Maybe they are all holding their breath and about to speak. When she imagines being up in the top branches she feels sick.

She can't see the dog but can hear him rooting ahead. 'Archie! Archie!'

Archie barks but doesn't return. Gracey worries about getting in trouble for opening the gate and losing the dog. She stamps further along the path.

The smell of cold earth tints her mind, colouring her thoughts darker as if her head is a jam jar filled with water for cleaning bristles and a paintbrush has been dipped inside. Tunnels burrow between the trees in all directions. She believes the rabbits use these routes to hop about and visit each other, sharing food, seeing each other's babies. She's tempted to find a burrow and look inside to judge how tame the rabbits are. She wants them coming into the garden freely but doesn't want to get too mucky on her hands and knees.

A rustle and *clack clack* from above her head. She looks up and at the glossy ivy crawling up white trunks and limbs to tailor green trousers and sleeves onto the trees. Where the ivy stops, bony branches spider-leg at the clouds. The tops are fuzzy like hair blown by wind and sticking up. As many new leaves as there are stars in the sky grow and *shush* with sea sounds. Dimming light hangs mist over the world.

She looks over her shoulder in the direction of the garden and sees the house through a criss-cross of sticks. Until Daddy fixes the new house it'll be scarier than the woods. She can still hear her mommy, so she's not gone far. And now she's actually inside the trees she's not so nervous. Nothing skitters or flaps nearby. All is still. The cool air is shivery good and the smell of the woods makes her think of fireworks, roasted pork on a bun and helping her granddaddy collect slippery leaves inside a wheelbarrow.

There are no wolves or bears in England and Archie will detect anything as big as a mouse that comes near. Night time is not far away but there is only one path and that's easy to follow out.

She'll just go round this bend and if Archie isn't there, then she'll fetch her daddy so Archie doesn't get lost.

Her breath catches when she sees the snow.

On either side of the track, the scrub and nettles thin and give way to waxy leaves the colour of limes and more white spots than she could count before her tenth birthday. The white spots carpet the ground all the way into the shadowy distance. Shaggy trunks of trees pull upwards from this green and white frothy sea and lean like the legs of wading people losing their balance.

As she gets closer to this white wonder, the patches of snow become lots and lots of flowers. She bends over and her head fills with the clean scent of onions and leeks. When the filigree of minute petals grows into focus, each flower is as beautiful as anything she has ever seen.

She picks flowers until distracted by a blue fog hovering where a tree has fallen. The path will take her closer to this odd blue-purple smoke.

It's not fog but more flowers, blue flowers. Amidst waves of blue flowers, the white flowers still grow too. The ivy-furred legs of the trees now stride an ocean of teeny blue and white flowers so startling she feels dizzy. She imagines so many tiny people wearing white or blue hats, crowding the big feet of giants who are trying not to step on them.

Every little blue flower is a fairy hat. She picks some for her mommy. Then remembers Archie but is in such a big, strange space she doesn't want to raise her voice.

When the blue flowers dwindle into sprinkles of odd bunches here and there, the track gets walled again by low-hanging branches, bearded by nettles and blackberry vines. Some plump red berries look delicious on bushes with prickly Christmas leaves but must be poisonous because the birds don't eat them. The birds that live this far inside are noisier too. They yodel fire-alarm songs around the tops of trees, telling each other that she and the dog have come inside.

Not being able to see the house anymore makes her tummy busy with the fizz of drinks in cans. Around her bum there's tingling like before a poo she really needs. But she'll only go a bit further. One more corner.

She goes that far and sees a light and airy space glaring ahead. And there's Archie! Mooching round a clear bit of the woods that appears so suddenly she's confused and wonders if she has come to the end of the trees. But no, the woods are even thicker after the glade and only stop here for this moat of lawn that surrounds the perfect green dome of the hill, as big as a caravan, onto which the last of the light pours.

Gracey runs to it, then stops.

Waddles drooping from one hand, she gapes with astonishment at what exists inside this strange clearing ringed by trees. She thinks that maybe she's seen it before. But can't have.

She also wonders if someone lives inside the hill. This must be a garden inside a fence of trees. The mound has a pelt of grass like the smooth circles with flags on the golf course where she was forbidden to do handstands. And the hill is just like the 'barrow' in the story she's been read by her dad, about fairies and the boy who goes to live with them. He doesn't get any older and when he comes out, his family are in graves.

A circular track in the grass, trodden down by feet, runs round the bottom of the hill. Archie snuffles round the groove like someone has scattered dog treats.

Astonished by the hush that reminds her of the church they went in for granddaddy's funeral, Gracey steps inside the circle.

Mossy pillars of rock stand around the edge like people turned to stone just inside the trees. *One, two, three, four, five . . . ten!*

She and Archie circle the glade like they are hands on the face of a strange old clock made of earth and rocks. Round and round they go, like the little hill makes you do it without knowing why.

After three full rotations, Gracey places Waddles on the nearest stone. Then sits on the neighbouring rock, the shortest one. 'This is our wood house. These are our chairs.'

Between each stone about the miniature hill, shiny pots sprout red flowers. Gracey peers inside the nearest container and spies a small skull. She picks it out and slips it inside her pocket.

One stone, larger than the others, stands at the top of the hushy glade that is so open to the sky. The big stone reminds her of the table-thing the priest stands behind in church. The altar. Cut flowers mop the surface like a colourful wig.

Attracted by so many flowers, Gracey pads over to investigate.

The rock is flat on top and must stand here to remember someone. 'Waddles, somebody dieded here.'

Archie whines and won't follow her to the stone.

Gracey scatters flower stems and discovers that this big boulder has a bowl inside the top. Noisy flies move about the hollow like slugs after eating too much. They're crawling over black stains inside the hole.

Gracey ruffles her nose and as she steps away, she hears a voice and jumps as if someone has just crept up behind her and shouted 'Boo!'

Voice. Or her thinking? A voice, or just her thoughts?

Like a cold flannel wiped down the inside of her face, she feels the blood drain and she's dizzy as if she's just stood up after sitting cross-legged for ages.

For a while she's all shaky until the shock of hearing *the voice* subsides. The voice now feels like it was more inside her head than outside it. Gradually her fear switches to wanting to know who spoke, because it wasn't a bad voice.

There it is again, and it sounds like a lady whispering words from inside the trees. Or maybe from behind the stone, or even from inside the small hill. There might be a window or door.

She answers the lady's query; or what might be no more than an urgent feeling that she should introduce herself. 'Gracey.' And as usual she gives out the information she expects all strangers to be interested in. She gives her address. She goes on. 'I'm in foundation. My class is called Minnows. My teacher is Miss Collins.'

There's no one here and she wonders again if the voice of the lady might not be in the trees after all but inside her head and she's only imagining the words. As she tries to understand if new voices can just happen inside your head, the speaker moves further away – not drifting away through the trees but going deeper inside her ears.

Questions then come rushing to her in a babbly fountain and Gracey feels as if someone is looking at her face from inside. She knows exactly what to say because of the look in their eyes that she can sense without seeing their eyes.

Is she lost?

'No. We come to live here now. I live in the house down there with my mommy and my daddy.'

Might the little dog bite?

'He's okay. He don't bite no one.'

No brothers or sisters inside the house?

'Just my mommy and my daddy and me.'

Who makes the noise?

'My daddy. He's fixing things. He's clever.'

Another voice, from behind the small hill. This voice has no music or whispery loveliness. It is harsh and louder and rushes close. 'No. No. No.'

Gracey sucks in her breath and turns about.

And sees the old lady from next door with hair cut into a red helmet for a motorbike, creeping towards her with her hands outstretched. An old witch with a weird head.

Gracey stumbles about as if her legs are half asleep.

Thin cold fingers close on her shoulders. The old woman is not looking at her but over her shoulder, as if she's seen a ghost standing upon the grassy mound.

The angry blue eyes lower to Gracey.

And there is the man from next door too, with his strange clown hair. He's at the edge of the clearing, pacing nervously like Archie does by the front door when he needs to do 'his business'.

The man is trying to smile at Gracey. He has a small, dark mouth inside a Santa beard. His mouth looks like it's been sucking liquorice.

Gracey tears up. The strangers scared away the lady in the trees with the soft voice that she could have listened to all day. These next-door people make her feel like she's in trouble. And now she's so scared she feels sick and dizzy and airy in the head. She might just blow away like a balloon in a breeze.

'Didn't do nothing. Didn't take nothing,' she whimpers. The skull in her pocket weighs heavy as a brick. 'My mommy and my daddy,' she adds to build a little defence around her tottery feet.

The witch isn't listening. She's peering about the glade, looking for someone else.

'Not in the circle. Never go inside the circle, my dear,' says the old man with the head of the minstrel in a picture inside her fairytale book. He's wearing yellow trousers and she's never seen a man wear lemon trousers before. They distract her from her distress enough to wonder if they are girls' trousers. She has yellow trousers. Maybe he doesn't know these trousers are for ladies and has put them on by mistake. The old lady might have made a similar mistake because she is wearing a man's clothes.

The ruddy hood of the lady leans in. Her eyes are the colour of a cracked blue teacup marbled with angry red worms. Her face is as wrinkled as a wet bedsheet that's just been pulled out of the washing machine. She is as angry as Gracey's ever seen a teacher up her school.

'Come. Come. Away!' the lady says. She pulls Gracey away from the altar, along the path that goes round the mound and out of the circle.

The yanky hands and the mean face are too much and now Gracey is crying and all she can think of is Mommy and her whole skin is full of a violent need for Mommy. She can't breathe properly around sobs and she feels like the ground has disappeared and she's falling away from everything that makes her happy.

She remembers pictures and bits from the film they showed at school about talking to strangers who have sweets in their cars and men who come into your 'private spaces'. And it all feels too late now to go remembering them things and her thoughts are going everywhere like scared birds.

The man leans down, his whiskery ham-face too close and thrusting inside her panic and confusion to stir it up more. His breath smells like a pond and his teeth are brown rice, sloping backwards like a shark's. *How does anyone chew with them teeth?* He is smiling and has very twinkly eyes that might be kind.

He touches her cheek with a soft finger. 'You mustn't come into these woods, my little button.'

'They belong to someone else,' the lady says and lets go of her shoulder.

'She's very old and needs to sleep.'

Archie whimpers beside Gracey's feet and the witch-lady peers at the dog as if she's just put her foot squelching into one of Archie's curly poos that are the colour of mustard.

The man looks at the spaniel and pulls a face like he's eaten garlic by mistake, hidden in a spaghetti sauce when her daddy promised not to put it in the food.

'And I'll tell you a secret,' the lady with the bulb-hair says. 'She doesn't like dogs. This is her home and she doesn't want to be disturbed. You understand?'

Gracey nods. She'll agree to anything just so they'll let her go. It's like the time the boys on bikes came into the playground and fighted each other, knocking over some little ones.

From the distance, Mommy calls her name and her voice is all high and screechy with worry.

The old man smiles again. 'Go on. Take the dog.'

Gracey needs no further prompt, neither does Archie. They flee, racing from the grass circle, the hill and strange voice and the horrible witch people with snatchy hands, weird hair and stinky breath. Only the toy penguin, Waddles, remains by the hill and the stones and the red flowers.

Later, Gracey imagines how he must have watched her go, sat all on his own upon the stone chair, left behind.

IO

'All over now, love. Mom didn't mean to shout. She was just worried.' Eyes closed, Fiona presses her cheek on top of Gracey's head. 'Keep out the woods. You can help us sort the house and garden instead.'

Perched upon a stool, Gracey sniffles out the last of a deluge of tears. Pressed into her mother, she extracts the immense pleasure that accompanies feeling sorry for one's self after a fright, as well as a telling-off. Fiona hugs her tightly. Rubs her small back. Kisses her forehead.

Before the sink, Tom rinses the lead tablet that Archie and Gracey excavated from the garden. Raising the object into better light, he studies the surface and traces the odd markings with his finger tips, before placing the block on the counter beside the rabbit skull he retrieved from Gracey's pocket. 'This is really old.' He speaks to himself but wants Fiona to overhear.

She doesn't respond. He turns, shaking wet hands, nods at the wall. 'They don't own the woods. It's public land.'

Fiona glares at him but Tom persists, lowering his voice to speak Gracey. 'They're yours too, my Peanut. Big part of the reason we moved here. So you can grow up among trees. Breathe clean air.'

Fiona draws a deep breath. 'Think it through, mate. Not the time.'

'She's just had a fright.'

'You don't go in there again without us,' Fiona mutters into her daughter's hair, sidelining Tom.

A fresh surge of despair erupts from Gracey. 'Waddles is lost up there! He's cold and he's crying for me!' A large tear plops onto Fiona's forearm.

Wearily, Tom pushes off from the counter and stretches his back. 'Daddy's gonna find him. I'm going. Just gotta find the torch.'

As he rummages in one of many cardboard boxes littering the floor, he can't resist looking at his wife and nodding in the direction of next door. 'The fence. Ivy. Banging the bloody wall every time I use a drill. Visitors' cars. Now the woods. What next? We should ask them to write it all down. I can't keep up.'

'Ignore that pair of oddballs. Just put them out of your mind.'

'They're not helping with that.'

'Focus on the damp upstairs instead, which is much worse than it looked. The shit-box fuse-box. The leak under the bath. And how we're gonna pay for a new cooker on my salary until your phone rings. I can also make a reasonable guess at what the other builder's gonna quote, once he's looked at the roof. So I don't want to hear any more about the freak-show next door.'

Chastened, belittled, not sure whether to be angry or defer to what might be good sense, Tom looks away from his wife's incensed face. Good judgement isn't so easy when there is so much emotion bustling, trapped inside a room filled with a mess of boxes and storage crates, tools, articles of furniture, photos, pictures, implements; the disorder of artefacts that now shapes and reflects their existence. Indoors, nothing they own has found its true place yet. Their belongings swarm like outcasts in a liminal space between fleeing and resettlement. A preposterous situation he hadn't counted on lasting so long. All three of them have occupied the same bed for an entire week. He can't help comparing them to a family of peasants in a black and white film, who pray for morning while huddled in the corner of a hovel.

He's not managed to finish prepping a single room, let alone decorate one, either. He's only made them less habitable.

One thing at a time. The penguin. A story for Gracey. A drink with Fiona. Sit and sort each other's heads out. It's been a long day.

Tom peers at the window, squinting out to where he must now go, where it's dark, damp and cold. The last place he wants to be. Beyond the half-formed images of his wife and daughter, reflected in the grubby pane, he can make out the humped silhouette of the woods, inked black against a sooty sky.

He turns to put the lead tile down but realises that he has already done so, despite the sensation of still cupping the cold weight within his empty hands. There's the tile, on the window sill, beside the grubby skull.

God, he's tired. He blinks to banish an imprint of the sigils too. After-images. Smoke rings floating at the back of his vision, that soon accompany, or incite, a hideous feeling of being stranded. It squeezes his bowels.

He shakes his head and looks at the faded lino but finds himself too easily imagining the years of struggle and anxious pacing that must have lightened the kitchen floor in the past; reaching back to someone breaking the ground to dig the house's foundations, a century or more ago.

Tom rubs his face and sighs. The air escapes his body like the last of his strength.

Another woody crack from outside, from the near distance, draws him back to the present. A splintering. *The neighbours? Chopping firewood in the dark?* The noise has continued intermittently since they came inside and as the last of the daylight evaporated.

Tom pushes his face closer to the window but sees little outdoors and too much of the reflection of the kitchen behind him, funnelling his vision back to the open door and the hallway beyond; an image, burrowing like a corridor in a nightmare to the white cable hanging from the ceiling, under-lit by a new bulb.

A man hanged himself right there.

Was he so blinkered by a need to buy a house that he was able to dismiss that crucial fact? What was he thinking? Fiona's been tearful for a week and is more forlorn than he's ever seen her. The strain of it all. They live next door to cunts. And now Gracey's traumatised. This was too much to ask of them.

Stop it!

But they're so far away now from what they know, from their own time and place in the world. That dreary and unsatisfying city in which they were stuck, unfulfilled and thwarted. But at least that was known. Here, they're diminished. He's always winded, reduced to stumbling around a ruined shell of a building. All week, he's been picking things up, putting them down. Losing tools. Forgetting the sequences of renovations he'd meticulously planned, while standing idle for too long pondering grimy walls.

He's wasted so much time and energy compulsively depicting imaginary future scenes of domestic bliss; remedies for the persistent dread he feels at being a trespasser in an unfeeling place. *What's that all about?* It's not like him at all. But how can this house settle into the familiar with so many old relics oppressing him indoors? *Everywhere.* Glimpses of the past that perpetually revive in each room he drifts inside, the very atmospheres suggesting concurrence, that the building cannot change. All week, horrible notions of the transience of life have thickened his throat with melancholy. It's as if he's become sensitised into a strange awareness of the many lives scattered through the building's past. They left nothing in the world but faded wallpaper and scuff marks on the floors. Enigmatic symbols of despair.

People may only ever have abided here as a matter of endurance. Then died, perhaps engulfed by crisis, like the suicide. Each new day's weak light won't erase those scars.

To make him feel even worse, he's sure he's suffered the same dream several times now – that's how familiar it seems – of an elderly woman rooting through filth in their unlit kitchen, murmuring, her mind half gone. Around her, the lonely and isolated from other times gather too and direct their mournful gazes to the restless trees beyond the rotten fence.

Tom rubs hard at his eyes and face to try and rid himself of the awful, recurring feeling of contamination, as if he contracted something merely by crossing the threshold of this old house.

Gracey's innocent light is too frail to banish the tragedy here.
Stop it! You don't know that.

Across the room, from out of the snuffles and his wife's shushing, Gracey blurts, 'Waddles is frightened by the trees! He's all on his own in the dark!'

Tom returns his tired feet to his sawdust-peppered boots.

Beyond the back door, the cold, lightless land awaits him.

II

He's almost at the gate when he pulls up and suffers a curious sense of the garden, at the top, being more airy and open than it was during daylight.

Once he's fiddled the torch on, a mere glance is sufficient to reveal that recent adjustments have indeed been made to this section of his property. And for several seconds, Tom is incapable of doing anything besides gaping at the smashed fence panels.

He sweeps torchlight across what resembles driftwood, washed ashore on his lumpy, weedy garden. In the top corner, three fence panels have been torn apart, the timber slats reduced to scattered shards. Rusty nails extend from two felled posts. Wanton destruction. The wreckage was then tossed over the border with an intent and force that he intuits as malicious.

Standing upon a naked and more spacious boundary between the two houses than existed that afternoon, he now recalls the sounds of snapping wood he heard in the kitchen. As he'd rinsed the metal tablet and while they comforted their frightened four-year-old daughter, he'd heard someone breaking wood out here. It was his fence. A fence in poor shape and leaning on the neighbours' trees maybe, but still upright that afternoon.

Turning towards the Moots' house, he flashes his beam over their symmetrical garden, the neat hummocks draped by dusk. The red-brick house is mostly beyond the torch's range, but a few windows still manage to glimmer in the dregs of his

69

light, and a few white timbers stubbornly issue the brightness of a gingerbread house. A jigsaw-puzzle picture of a country house, glimpsed in a darkened room. Though in his eyes the silhouette of the perfect roof now resembles a Puritan's hat: solid, self-regarding, disapproving.

'Bastards.'

He suffers a recollection of the dwarfish Mrs Moot thrusting her thin arm in the air, remonstrating about broken fences in the village. This destruction of his fence is her prompt.

Tom grows breathless and dizzy. Sweat dries cold upon his brow while his innards writhe like warm serpents. He feels an urge to throw a brick at the Moots' house and even glances about his feet for a missile heavy enough to cover the distance.

The penguin. Fiona.

Addressing the destruction of his fence will have to wait. But he'll get to it. And *them*. In the morning.

He goes to take a step towards the woods but his boot catches a rusty nail concealed in the long grass. A trap set for his little girl's feet and Archie's paws. Tom's face returns to the boil and anger bulges his heart.

A significant force of will is required to move on. Even then, he doesn't get much further than the end of the garden because he's soon eying crucifixes screwed into his gate.

'The fuck?' More symbols from the impenetrable madness of his home's history. *Did the suicide screw them in? What for?*

He's been so busy stripping rooms that he's not even walked this far from the house until now. But with Waddles lost, there is no time for another distraction.

He ducks into the trees and concentrates the weak beacon of his torch on his feet, which he places carefully amidst extruding vines and nettles.

A pale dusting of his light scatters over scrub at the side of the track, frosting leaves and revealing portcullises of blanched sticks, spider-webbing maws of pitch. Deeper inside the wood and he's soon batting branches from his face, or ducking when wiry limbs appear before the tip of his nose.

No matter how long his torch sweeps and scours the muddy track for the scruffy shape of the missing penguin, he finds no sign of it. Though he eventually detects evidence of something else and is soon crouching to examine the mud where the path widens.

Here, the mire is patterned by a set of unusual tracks, encouraging him to wonder if cows or sheep, from the nearest farm, graze these woods. But then, would the feet of farm animals – *hooves* – leave imprints like this? Two commas, or tears, upside down? He doesn't know but they're everywhere in this mud as if something recently stamped through here, impressing its large feet into the soil.

In other places, he can make out the pattern of Gracey's boot soles. The prints point in both directions: where she came in and where she ran out crying. But the animal prints are fresher and obliterate most of Gracey's.

The Moots told Gracey to keep out. They must assume some sense of ownership of this wood. And if that wasn't preposterous enough, there's this too now: evidence of another invasive presence upon the perimeter of their new lives. His fence lies in ruin and an animal has stamped about at the end of their garden.

He had such big plans for this wood. Family picnics, nature trails with Gracey, dog walks, a bit of foraging. He wanted his family to roam and enjoy the green space unselfconsciously.

Pushing the torchlight further along the rut between the trees, he ambles further until he loses the animal tracks. But something on four legs definitely ran through here before crashing into the undergrowth. At the point where the tracks vanish, he drops to one knee and peers into the scrub.

And immediately detects the stench of excrement.

It doesn't take him long to spot a pile of spoor, the colour of black pudding but uncomfortably human in appearance. One end is squashed flat, beneath his knee. He's broken the crust on something meaty and miasmic that smells far worse than dog-shit.

'Oh, for the love of . . .'

There follows a sensation of moisture seeping through his jeans. And not only has he knelt in it, he's also touched it with his right hand. Tom stands up quickly and clouts his head on a branch.

'Fuck.'

Hopelessly, he stares ahead at what little of the track remains visible. Not much. The rest is engulfed by verdure spiky enough to put an eye out in this darkness.

He decides to call the search off and it is only then, when so deep inside the wood but intent on returning to the house, that his senses abruptly stretch taut with the insidious feeling of being observed. From both sides of the track.

Flicking the torch about, he seeks confirmation that he is, indeed, alone. But immediately realises that when inside unmanaged woodland after sundown, a torch will only suggest that something is in fact watching you, from beyond the furthest reach of your meagre light.

'I'll be back in the morning, Waddles.'

Slouching and defeated, Tom bumps through the back door. The scent of the damp garden clings to him like wood-smoke.

Fiona sits on a stool, tapping at her laptop. She doesn't look up as her husband fights to remove his boots with one hand, plucking, then clawing the laces. He keeps the other hand raised like a lame animal, until he loses balance, stumbles and thumps a shoulder against a wall.

Eventually, the first boot is kicked clear of his foot and skates across lino mellowed by aeons of feet and sun-fade. Ordinarily, he would remove boots deftly and place them side by side, out of the way.

At the sink, he yanks at a tap, initiating a judder from hidden pipes as if the house itself is groaning in pain.

Throughout the building, air pockets in the arterial system are restricting blood flow, causing seizures that rattle timbers and thump bricks. The plumbing is far worse now than when they arrived, a week ago.

That too now. *Just a break is all I'm looking for.*

A trickle of milky water dribbles from the spout.

Tom wrenches the tap around one full turn. The patter of drip-drops does not increase.

'Fuck it!' He jabs the offending hand, oiled with faeces, under the pathetic drips.

'Find him?' Fiona asks, wearily. She doesn't look up.

'Too dark. He could be anywhere. Goes for miles. Get on Ebay.'

'Already on it. Waddles the fourth should be here in two days. Express delivery.'

'And guess what? Guess what they've done. That pair of rude bastards next door? Mmm?'

Fiona doesn't try and guess.

From beneath the sink there is a bang and from the tap, water finally gushes.

'They've smashed the fence panels. At the end of the garden. Kicked them through!'

Fiona looks up but remains unaffected by his outburst. 'They were hanging off, mate. Breathe on that fence and it'd collapse.'

Tom jabs a wet finger at the wall that shackles them to the Moots. 'Fi. They broke them! To score some petty little small-minded point.' He draws a breath to prevent suffocation by anger, yanks the tap, cutting the flow of water. 'That was our fence . . . Imagine doing that to your new neighbours . . . I can't understand why.'

'Village life. Not like we weren't told.'

Tom closes his eyes to gather inner forces, a tiny fire brigade of reasonable thoughts that's often required to douse his blazes. He doesn't want his smouldering to escalate and spread into a clash with Fiona.

Her attention moves to his soiled knee. 'What's that smell. Is that shit?'

12

$\mathcal{A}$round the old, dim house, a great hush smothers the land. And a heavy black swaddling of a night without light pollution drapes the building as if it is a birdcage. Time itself seems to slow, while far away the world they knew before pursues a faster trajectory. Sometimes Tom imagines he can sense the other world pulling even further away, leaving them adrift.

No sound at all seeps through the wall they share with their neighbours. But it is a calm that Tom intends to shatter with the electric drill that his gloved hand grips like a murder weapon.

They despise his family. *They* know only contempt for his household. Why, he can only guess. The Moots might be snobs. When they see him and Fiona and little Gracey, they may recoil, wincing. Perhaps they judge them as unrefined social climbers with their purchase of a rural property at auction.

But his family is not loud, gaudy or garish. Not crass or excessive. Coarse? A little, but whose fault is that?

You're trampling the dianthus!

A working-class family, ordinary but educated, that drives old cars and gets by, just about. But in this status-obsessed age this might be all the prejudice boils down to: pure social competitiveness. The neighbours *need* to feel that their status is superior.

You can afford it? I hope? First home, is it? Bit late in the day, eh? Hope you have deep pockets.

Or is it something else: is this a territorial matter? Provincial prejudice aimed at outsiders with no roots here? *A disgrace. We don't have broken fences in this village.*

Whatever the neighbours' motivation for destroying the fence and frightening his daughter, Tom doubts that a discussion will ever take place in which the truth behind the Moots' aversion to his family will be revealed. Getting to the bottom of their ire will involve time, patience and an energy he lacks. And why should he placate the Moots, ameliorate, defer, doff his cap or wheedle for approval? Their last landlord and letting agency wore his diplomacy to the thickness of a cigarette paper. And they're never getting that deposit back.

He must respond to the day's infractions.

It's that time.

If you have neighbours, the hour when a drill can be used has passed. Tom knows it. And now that he is standing before the partition wall, dividing *them* from him, an innate reticence struggles to regain its hold of him; a strong, abiding sense of common courtesy that is ingrained in him and forbids such behaviour. Observing conventions so as not to trouble or irritate others has always dictated his conduct in life. It was the way he was brought up. He might wake Gracey too, so putting shelves up now is a stupid idea.

This instinctive vacillation, however, makes him feel even less substantial than he did when he came back from the woods empty-handed; his legs are somehow thinner, his heart craven. Simply one of the worst things a man can feel: a withering of fibre and seeping of sap, a lowering of the gaze, a hunching of shoulders.

No!

Weaponised, he came into the front room to do battle and battle he must do. A noisy, un-neighbourly skirmish is required. A retaliation for the fence is called for; one immediate and substantial. Etiquette will not serve him here. After the Moots strike a blow, they will grasp greater liberties in the face of his passivity. That's how they tick over, people like *them*.

A fresh and unwelcome sense of them bustles anew, crowding into his mind; their odious faces and absurd hair, their spiteful remarks that stiffen his spine, the condescension and smirking, the proprietary attitude towards the border, the insults flung at his home . . .

They made Gracey cry!

Between two loud beats of his heart, a drunken electricity courses through his nervous system. Mad, gleeful hounds, loping with a capability for petty acts of mischief, unleash into his thoughts and Tom aligns a metal bracket on the dark patch of a wall. Clenching the muscles in his forearm to prevent the drill's weight reducing the rigidity of his wrist, he takes aim.

The screw goes through the wall like a pencil pushed into soft cheese and his hands, lungs, teeth and the soles of his feet trill wonderfully from the boring, destructive power blurring his hand.

A second screw grinds in flush.

The bracket is straight. Nice job. He's making a home. This is their home.

He finds his mark and commences to screw in the second bracket.

After the third screw has spun home and the motor's whine subsides inside his ringing ears, the room is nudged from the other side of the wall.

Thud. Thud.

It quickly grows rhythmic, determined. *Side of a fist? Palm of a hand?* Perhaps a hint of a raised voice too. Yes, that was a 'Hey!' he just heard. Magi is outraged. *What a shame!*

Slap, slap, slap, from a second hand, a smaller hand. *Her hand.*

Encouraged by each other and whipped into fury, the neighbours begin to slam their hands against the wall. Muffled, inarticulate shouts chorus the fleshy blows but barely penetrate the bones of masonry, the muscle of lath and skin of plaster.

Tom grits his grinning teeth and prepares to secure the second bracket with another screw.

The door clicks open behind him. 'Hell you doing?'

Fiona stands in the doorway, arms folded. She is about to speak but pauses to listen to the commotion making itself known upon the wall.

Her expression then softens to conciliatory and Tom knows his wife doesn't care for the reckless inebriation in her husband's eyes. 'Tom. It's getting on.'

Tom shrugs. 'Just doing a couple of shelves. Then I'm done.'

'Think we've had enough grief for one day, don't you? And you'll wake Gracey.'

Tom raises the drill. Glances at the ceiling. *Silence.* 'Will be quick.'

Fiona turns away, shutting the door with a decisiveness that makes him reconsider continuing.

The slapping hands and roars have since subsided to a tense silence that he can almost feel, as if someone is standing too close and staring at the side of his face. Thrusting into his mind comes the visage of Mrs Moot, her default grimace hooded by the ridiculous mop of hair. If he stops now, the Moots will think they have won, *again*, another round.

Tom places his ruler against the wall, marks a spot with a stubby pencil, a target for the screw. Readies the drill and whispers, 'Coming at ya.'

Through the wall and any chance of peace, the spinning drill-bit chews hard.

Across the divide, the Moots erupt like captives inside a bricked-over cavity. Futilely, they drum out another messy staccato of slaps. Magi's pompous tone grows louder.

Tom laughs.

We've always made the right choices, haven't we, me dear. Different standards.

Tom obliterates the sound of his neighbours, inside and outside his mind. And why not another bracket and four more screws? It's not like he can't use another shelf in here.

When his work is finally complete, he stands before a neat row of three shelves.

Amidst the scent of the drill's oily exertions, he's unsure whether to be relieved or disappointed that the Moots never came round in person and hammered on the front door. That would have been an opportunity to let them have it about the fence and upsetting Gracey. But nothing. No boarding party, no torches and pitchforks, no rolled sleeves. And no muffled cries or patter of old hands for some time now. All quiet on the eastern wall. Tom grins. *Progress*.

Triumphant, like a man with a loaded pistol before unarmed enemies that he's surprised on the counter-attack, he raises the drill and pulls the trigger one final time.

From the distance, upstairs, a tiny voice cries out in response. 'Mommy! Why's Daddy drillin'?'

Tom releases the drill's trigger but as the noise of the motor whines down, in the room on the other side of the wall, a fresh commotion makes itself heard: what resembles a faint *bump bump bump* of unshod feet.

The Moots may have stopped shouting and slapping but they haven't withdrawn to their bed, tense and muttering, or enraged and yanking at their mediaeval thatches. They're still in position on the other side of the wall.

Tom moves closer, turning his head to the side. Doing so makes him feel ridiculous but he's too curious about the neighbours' response. This *stamping*?

There it is again: a set of feet circling a hard floor. *Bump-scuffle*, *bump-scuffle*, *bump-scuffle*, round and round. The floor surface in that room must be wood. And they're both crying out now too, though it must be the impediment of the wall, and the hard emptiness of this room, that creates an impression of the Moots' voices being akin to croaks and squeals. There's a particularly unpleasant harshness to the tone of the one speaker too, as if they are forcing cruel laughter.

No less startled than being confronted by a stranger's derangement in the street, Tom suffers a swift creep of discomfort. He tries to ignore this shift in his feelings, from triumph to alarm, and wonders anew at the acoustics in these old buildings.

Next door, the *bump-scuffles* continue but there is a longer pause between the blows of each foot upon the floor, compelling him to imagine that the circular pattern of racing feet has now lengthened into that of a figure striding. Or a figure jumping from one spot to another, beyond the wall, but at a speed exceeding the capability of all but an Olympian.

The footsteps abruptly cease and the ensuing silence swells and drags long enough for Tom to idly survey the room about himself, as if making certain the walls will hold. *Hold out against what? Don't be stupid.*

Even with a new lightbulb, little of the room's pall is dispelled. A deep murk exudes from the actual walls. Same with every room at the front of the property, even during the day. He's never experienced this kind of morbid dimness indoors before. It's as if the rooms are trapped by the austere barrenness of the world after the last war. A melancholy that has clung on, drab, joyless, remaining hopelessly dutiful to a time of need.

They were thinking of making this a dining room but you'd never see what was on your plate. In the flat, they ate on their laps in front of the television. The use of a specific room here for eating their meals had felt exciting and novel but also preposterous and anachronistic.

None of them can get used to the volume of space inside this house either. Their flat had two small bedrooms, a kitchen best suited to a caravan, a toilet that wouldn't have been out of place in a child's Wendy House. He's noticed Fiona timidly peeping inside the rooms in this house as if checking with the occupants, to whom the rooms belong, to see if she is allowed inside. Gracey cannot stop running indoors as if she's outside. But is wary of being too far away from her parents and often flees back to them, from wherever she's been exploring, arriving into their arms frantic, on the edge of tears. She says she gets 'lost'.

As if his appraisal of the room draws out the malicious inclinations of those who live on the other side of the divide, the strange noises resume. But have moved closer, near to his feet. Tom steps back from the wall.

He's sure the Moots don't own a dog, or any pet that he's aware of. They're not farmers either. But what he can hear scratching at the foot of the adjoining wall, though dulled, reminds him of Archie's claws mauling the back door when he's frantic to get into the garden. Yes, the agitation suggests that an excited animal, something large and on all fours, is trying to dig through to his side.

Tom retreats further and places the drill on the workbench. Then stands in the doorway and stares at the wall with a horrified fascination, waiting for the scratching to cease.

He remains there for some time, because the raking, or gnawing, of the neighbours' skirting does not stop. Nor does the frantic circling of the hard feet. It is as if one of the Moots is scraping the wall with a fork, while the other is wearing shoes with wooden soles and frantically circling a confined space.

He wants Fiona to come and hear this but knows she won't. Nor is it a good idea to provoke his wife any more this evening. Instead, Tom shuts the door on the scratching and the thumps of the unseen feet and shuffles off, ashamed at the glance he feels compelled to take over his shoulder. Followed by another.

At the foot of the stairs, he averts his eyes from the white cable of the light socket, dangling from the ceiling. And he also finds it necessary to suppress the horrible leap of his imagination that suggests he's just made their situation far worse than it already was.

13

$\mathcal{A}$s soon as Tom powers down the floor-sander, tipped heels strike and ricochet against the stripped stairs descending to the hall. Fiona appears a moment later, dressed in her uniform: charcoal suit, printed blouse and name tag, high heels, hair styled, pretty make-up. First day back at the bank after a week's leave to move house.

Tom whistles. With a hand turned into a gauntlet by a protective glove, he pushes his goggles over his forehead and into his hair. His face, jeans, hoodie and work boots are filmed with a powder of sawdust. 'Ever have builder fantasies?'

Fiona cocks an eyebrow, smiles saucily.

Upstairs a toilet seat slams. Fiona turns and raucously shouts up the stairs. 'Gracey! Done your teeth? And if that was a poo, you have to flush!'

Tom winces. 'Illusion dispelled.'

The upstairs toilet goes *clank clank clank*. Then produces a rinsing trickle more than a flush, followed by a chorus of groans reverberating between the bathroom floor and hall.

A *bump, bump, bump* of small feet passes through the ceiling before Gracey thumps her way down wooden stairs. Alert, Fiona watches her daughter's descent. 'Not so fast. The steps are steep. You ain't used to them, love.' Gracey fell the day before. She was unhurt but frightened herself. 'Remember what Mommy said about us being a long way from A&E. Got to be careful.'

Tom feels the sting of an accusation within his wife's good sense, as if he's been fingered for something else that he overlooked when he insisted they bought a house that will probably remain a building site, filled with hazards, for the best part of a year.

Any reminder of what is required to make the house habitable is ever accompanied by the cold spectre of their finances. 'When your boss's back is turned, fill your bag with money. Fifties. No fives.'

Gracey makes the foot of the stairs safely. 'You find Waddles, Daddy?'

'Soon, my love. Today. He's fine.'

Tom and Fiona's eyes meet briefly, conspiratorially: the express delivery cannot arrive soon enough.

'Too dirty to give you a bye-bye kiss, Peanut. So I'll blow it from here.' Tom kisses the air.

Around her smile, Gracey returns a louder kiss to her dad.

Fiona gently raises her chin and one eyebrow, catches Tom's attention, then nods at the neighbours' side. 'Don't go wrecking anything while I'm at work.'

'You have my word. It's gonna be the new cold war from now on.'

Tom suspects the Moots' tactics will continue. Probably revolving around harassment, from their side, at the border. Underhand tactics. Provocative attempts to shame and bully their neighbours into doing their bidding. Operations directed from the advantage of home turf. But he suspects they will balk at direct confrontation. Easier to bang on a wall than get into someone's face.

And yet he remains deeply mystified about the source of the sounds the Moots produced against the wall of the front room last night – the scratching, the thumping of hard feet in a circular pattern. They were the first thing he thought of after waking that morning; the sounds trapped inside his ears. Noises he now wants, if not urges, to fade.

Fiona searches her husband's face for insincerity and he thinks how lovely his wife's eyes are when stern and fully made up. 'Exactly. Radio silence,' she says in a tone he finds too similar to the one she uses when explaining things to headstrong Gracey. 'Big walls. Let the other side get on with it.' Fiona turns and motions Gracey towards the front door.

Tom watches through the window as his wife teeters down the drive. Gracey follows, dawdling, picking at dandelions. She raises a stalk, blows the seeds. Tries to catch a handful.

14

'You think I don't know what you're doing? All three! How did you do it?' A raised male voice from next door, out front again, from another visitor. Mrs Moot's affected tone is occasionally making itself heard too. What she says is impossible for Tom to hear from inside Gracey's room, though twice she's chuckled unkindly.

Tom promised Fiona he'd ignore next door and has thus far restrained himself during the exchange outside, refusing to peek while staying focused on the many tasks at hand. Around his legs, IKEA flat-pack instructions form a blanket for screws, rivets, Allen keys, his screwdriver. Veneered white bedroom furniture rises like hurricane damage filmed in reverse. They bought a dresser and bookshelf to help make Gracey's room special and to compensate for the major disruption in her small world.

When Gracey and Fiona get home in late afternoon – after Fiona has driven from a long day at work to pick Gracey up from after-school club, then driven the forty minutes to their new home – he wants his family to see that he's making progress; to know the dream is coming alive with tangible improvements, even if only inside a single room. Making one room presentable will require a full day's work with no interruptions or distractions. But when the man outside begins to shout, Tom rises with a groan, his knees cracking, and positions himself back from the window.

Below, on next door's driveway, a portly, dishevelled man with unkempt hair is pointing a finger at Mrs Moot, whose chin is vertical with defiance. Magi appears to be sheltering a few feet behind his wife, peering over her shoulder. But the spindly minstrel is half turned in the direction of the Moots' house too, as if ready to bolt indoors should the confrontation ascend to the next level.

Tom's blood immediately sings at the prospect of someone having a go at Magi in the way that he wants to. He imagines a fist smacking the pointy features, stunning the glittery eyes blank. Those muffs of white hair, which look like floppy animal ears, would sway absurdly from the impact of a blow to the smirking face. Yes, he'd pay to watch that and is tempted to record the confrontation on his phone in case there is a highlight to replay and to enjoy, again and again. He does enjoy watching the odd thief beaten up on YouTube. It makes his heart pound. He even has a favourites folder on his PC for these very acts of public revenge.

The haggard figure of the Moots' visitor appears to be sleeping as poorly as Tom did last night. His trousers and shirt may never have seen an iron. Yet a plummy accent and pompous intonation shape the man's words, as if he's standing behind a lectern in a theatre. 'Been with me for years. All gobbled up as if by some vile corporation.'

A thick forearm and pudgy hand jab at Mrs Moot, the man's shirt sleeves carelessly rolled, cuffs wafting with each gesticulation. 'You're deliberately damaging my reputation. This is scorched earth. Does your fetid ambition know no limit? And as for the other thing, I know it was you. How did you do it? Mmm? Three grave mishaps in one week. That's no coincidence. And I heard from the bank this morning. Why? Why is that necessary? Priscilla too. You've already taken our business.'

Mrs Moot replies but Tom doesn't catch what she says. In response to whatever she mutters, the scruffy visitor turns away in disgust and stalks to the car he's parked carelessly across the end of Tom's weedy drive. A vehicle at least twenty years old, once red but faded the orange of one of Gracey's sucked sweets.

Face now purpling, emphasising whiskers as if his cheeks have been sprinkled with table salt, the car's owner pauses to cast one final enraged threat over his shoulder. 'This isn't the end! Not by a long chalk!'

Tom shifts his attention to his neighbours and watches the Moots laugh, clearly mocking the man. But the woman's imperious bearing slips and the laugh that she issues, if that is what it is, evolves into a snort. An uncouth grunt of satisfaction at repelling her foe. A retort seemingly too deep to have risen from such a diminutive form.

The neighbours turn their backs on the visitor and saunter to their front door. A little triumphant march before they disappear from sight. But even though she's gone, the sound of Mrs Moot's grunt remains in Tom's ears like a black stain. Just like the clawing on the wall the night before, the echo of the noise unsettles him; this time as if he's just heard a hyena cackle with excitement.

'Mad, rude old bastards.'

Tom returns his attention to the shabby visitor, who swings his backside into the driver's seat; a much repeated but still ungainly manoeuvre that sinks the car on one side. Even from a distance, he hears the cry of protest from the vehicle's suspension.

He rushes from the room and covers three stairs per stride as he descends.

15

Casting a wary glance to the border, Tom jogs down the drive, his ears straining for any sound of the neighbours returning to their patch. Archie pads behind Tom.

Tom raises a hand. 'Excuse me. Mate. Hold up.'

The occupant of the car struggles to lower the window until a series of stiff jerks move the speckled glass. The smell of the vehicle's interior belches; an exhalation of weathered carpets, male sweat, plastic warmed by a heater. 'I'm going. I'm going,' the dishevelled figure barks. 'I've been here a few minutes! Is that such an inconvenience?' He waves a plump hand at the general area containing the drive that he's strewn his car across. 'So great an imposition? Really!' The man turns the engine over but he's left the car in gear. The engine stalls and a pained lurch jolts the old machine.

'No. It's not that. I just wanted to ask . . . It's . . .' Tom looks in the direction of the neighbours' house. 'Them. I mean . . .' Tom shrugs. 'What's the deal? With them?'

'You live here now?'

The question feels like an accusation threaded with pity. 'Not for long,' Tom says, and realises that he's distancing himself from ownership of the house, ashamed of its shabby exterior, its dreadful past.

'Then you better keep your stay short. Or they will.' Returning his attention to the ignition, the driver rattles keys until the unhealthy-sounding engine squeals and turns over again. This time, a gust of black exhaust hits the road as if a bag, filled with soot, has been upturned onto the kerb.

Desperate for more information, Tom dithers but can only haplessly watch the old car grumble away, throatily spraying particulate.

He shifts his attention to the Moots' house, taking in the straight lines, smart brick walls, the immaculate slate scales of the roof. The facade of the building no longer enchants him, though, as if it is something from a fairytale. He feels that its character has changed, or been enlivened by a previously disguised persona. The front is now a haughty, spiteful, mocking facade made of bricks, wood and paint; the windows are mirrored lenses covering arrogant eyes, narrowed to a sneer.

'Fuck it.'

Archie trots behind his master, excited to be on the move again as they head next door.

16

*I*nside the Moots' porch, shadows treacle thick. Tom can't see the underside of the conical canopy above his head. Wood painted black appears tarred and fashioned to absorb all light, to momentarily dip a visitor into night. Easier to feel consumed than welcome here.

A frilly curtain of purple wisteria droops symmetrically about the edges, like swamp grass woven by fairies then neatened by artisans. An embellishment blocking more of the daylight. Below the floral skirt, the iridescence of the garden dazzles.

Before the front door, Tom squints to read what shouts from a sign beside the doorbell. He saw it once before, when he was measuring up and called round, but never bothered to read this elaborate warning to trespassers. It's almost a novel. NO COLD CALLERS. NO SALESMEN. NO JEHOVAH WITNESSES. NO FREE PAPERS. NO PAMPHLETS OR CIRCULARS . . . The list goes on.

He's made it this far on an upsurge of adrenalin but now he's in the porch, nerves puncture his gut and drain his vigour. He also remembers what he promised Fiona that morning.

But the Moots are only people. Older than him too. Early seventies at a guess, though sometimes they appear much younger and lithe. Their aura of dismissive impatience is the best indication of their vintage; a tendency to look askance at anyone not settled in their station in life, as if the young have made a mess of things. But what are they doing here and what's the point of them? All this combing the bloody grass and shrieking about borders? Though people are also visiting regularly and taking something away. Packages. There's a mercantile element to what he's observed from Gracey's window. *What are they selling?* Something the Moots grow round the back? Tom suspects there's more to it than growing and selling veg but the major share of his mystification is occupied by the peculiar quality of the exchanges: the obsequious deference, the hand-kissing. Until the chap who just left here with a serious grievance. A visitor who claimed the Moots were ruining him.

Tom muses on what he is going to say but now he's here, his mind is opaque. He feels woozy and sun-blinded by the glare blasting upwards from the polished flagstones of the empty drive. But he can't possibly withdraw and powerlessly observes his grubby finger depress the bell buzzer.

There is a pause before a curious pan-piping chime on the other side of the black door. His takes a step back, his confidence taking an extra two steps. Annoyed at the thud of his pulse and at the rash of prickling sweat at his temples, he waits.

There is no response. Tom rings again.

Pan-pipes.

A few more seconds lapse and he's about to abandon ship when a muffled shuffle encroaches at the edge of his hearing. Moments later, a latch is scraped away on the other side. Then, as if the occupant is furious at being disturbed, the door is yanked wide.

Tom retreats another step.

Against the darkness, two grim faces probe forward: Magi's familiar mask of amusement with added disapproval, his wife's features carved from consternation. 'Yisss!' she yaps in her clipped, queenly voice.

Tom clears his throat. 'It's me. From next door.'

The Moots glare.

'I just wanted to clear the air. Don't want to get off on the wrong foot.' *Bit late for that.* Tom tries to laugh but the noise he makes is loathsome to his ears, a school boy snigger. 'We want to get along with our neighbours. Only I have a couple of problems. Things I'd like to address. Number one, I don't appreciate you telling my daughter that she can't play in the woods. They're not yours.'

The old woman's eyes flare. Probing rays of light pick out whiskers on her chin. Pubic curls. Having noticed them, Tom's recalcitrant vision won't leave them alone. His vision attaches to the bristles.

'As a parent are you not concerned with your daughter's safety?'

'That's not something you need to question.'

'A child's safety. Paramount,' Magi Moot intones, dismissing Tom's reassurance as insufficient.

Tom feels the first glow of the hot ashes smouldering in his gut. 'It's a wood. A few trees. It ain't the Amazon, mate.'

Mrs Moot is quick to counter. 'It's a very old wood. An area of outstanding conservation. Not a playground.'

The condescending tone fans Tom's coals. 'What kind of damage could a four-year-old girl do? I—'

She cuts him off. 'Children are so attuned. Their imaginations. They get all kinds of odd fancies in old woods. And that one is twelve thousand years old.'

'Fancies? That's the whole point, isn't it? And being outdoors is an essential part of a child's development. We want nature to be a part of our daughter's life. So maybe you've lived here a bit longer and developed some sort of proprietorship over that wood at the back—'

Magi inches forward. 'A sanctuary for serpents. Adders. What if she trod on one?' He's talking down to Tom again, as if to a child in some old film. The fool must think he's on stage. *A performance. They think you're thick.*

Today, the man's tight trousers are buttercup yellow.

A linen shirt gapes at the neck, the laces loose, revealing a thicket of white chest hair. So much hair that Tom is tempted to wonder if it's real. Magi must be thin under those clothes and covered in white hair, like a skinny rodent or monkey. Reluctantly, Tom imagines the Moots together in bed, naked. An image swiftly chased out of his mind by the shudder of revulsion that follows.

From Mrs Moot's hirsute muzzle, framed by that thicket of hair cut like an ornamental shrub, darts a barbed comment that finally flicks off Tom's safety catch. 'We scolded her for her own benefit.'

Tom's coals flame and he is shouting before he knows it; abruptly and wildly free of the deference that has dogged him near this pair. He even takes a step forward, emphasising his point with the jab of an index finger. 'Scolded her? You don't scold my daughter! Ever!'

Magi's eyes flash wide as he withdraws behind his wife, before retreating deeper inside the gloomy hall. But Mrs Moot's face stiffens into a mask of outraged defiance. She stands her ground and Tom pulls up.

'Look—' He tries again. 'This is getting out of hand. I didn't come here to argue. But no one can "scold" and frighten someone else's child and then justify it. What's wrong with you? From day one—'

The woman's little frame trembles. 'No! You look! That wood is not a recreational area. It is no place for children. It is a protected environment. We don't want it spoiled! Trampled over! We—' Glancing at Archie, her mouth twists with revulsion. 'We don't want it littered.'

'Own it, do you? Yours, is it? Whole village too maybe? Bit entitled, aren't you?'

'We observe boundaries here. Borders you'll learn to respect.'

'Respected the fence did you? My fence!'

'A little prompt. So address the gap. The last thing we want is an open-plan garden . . . with that mess at the back of yours.'

'It's your bloody trees that are hanging over the length of the—' The door slams in Tom's face and he's left blinking and stunned.

From behind the door seeps Magi's muffled tittering.

Tom tries to settle back into his mind as if he's just suffered an out-of-body experience. He blinks the bright shimmer from his eyes, clueless about his next move until he sees Archie. The dog is squatting on a patch of grass, groomed like a snooker table, and curling out a crap. Behind the little quivering tail drifts a hint of steam and a plop of putrescence.

Tom panics and bolts from the porch, his head scattering purple blossom. 'No. Archie. No.' Fearfully, he peers at his neighbours' windows, patting his pockets for bags. But doesn't have any. The Moots' windows are sealed by curtains.

Tom's relief swiftly transforms into a churlish glee. Perhaps he will have the final word after all. 'That's my boy. Squeeze it out, lad. All of it.'

He trots down the drive and whistles to Archie, who crashes through the flowers and groomed plants like a drunken oaf. Only then does the drapery twitch behind the Moots' front window. Fingers and a dim suggestion of Mrs Moot's face become visible in a slit.

Tom turns the corner and jogs onto his property, failing to suppress laughter. Archie, excited by this change in his master's demeanour, pads alongside, smiling.

From the neighbours' side comes the sound of a front door yanked open. Followed by a scuffle of feet on the smooth path before Mrs Moot's regal shriek pierces the air like a burglar alarm. 'The . . . dog!'

'Disgraceful! Remove this! You hear!' From Magi, stentorian.

'Spread it round the bloody dianthus,' Tom calls back and calmly strolls home.

17

Fitting his thoughts like a metal skullcap, from the day they arrived, the tightening sense of futility has, finally, loosened its iron bands. His work in this room acts like a shrive upon the burden of anxiety that's swung from his thoughts like a goitre. He needed a win; a salve for a persistent fear that the house's debilitated state would dwarf any skills he's picked up over the years, mostly from his dad.

On entering Gracey's room now, the explosion of the candy-pink paint is startling. Matching the smooth ice-cream palette of the walls, a matching pink alarm clock and lamp pose on the newly assembled chest of drawers. Sweetly complementing the woodwork of the unit, shelves, wardrobe and toy-tidy, the ceiling and skirting boards gleam white. Three framed pictures of Gracey's artwork form a gallery of rainbows: big-shoed people, a unicorn that looks like a bear, and a small hill with Gracey and Archie standing on top.

Tom never found Waddles in the woods but he did pick wild garlic and has arranged the flowers inside a white teacup on the freshly painted window sill. Satin curtains, the colour of new steel, will remain tied up until the paint dries.

Paint thinner and the pungency of the first coat have added a giddiness to his perception, so Tom swings wide the bedroom window. After lacing the hinges with oil, even the frame glides soundlessly open. He reminds himself to add a child-lock just in case Gracey is tempted to lean out.

Standing back, he surveys his handiwork. Again.

Dust sheets conceal the spattered floor boards but this one room now offers a glimpse into their future home. One down, another three bedrooms to go, plus the bathroom. Then he'll do the front room, kitchen and the unfinished half of the hall downstairs. A family home feels possible again.

The familiar purr of Fiona's car announces itself outside, turning then parking on the drive with a skiddy crunch.

Tom peers through a windowpane he's cleaned to near invisibility. Since the morning, he's even stopped looking next door each time he passes the window. There's been no new parlay with the Moots. He's even tempted to presume that a sullen acceptance of having met their match has descended next door. A quiet resentment, perhaps settling into a reluctance for fresh hostilities. The last sign from them was the sound of a trowel scooping Archie's mess from their lawn, followed by the rattle of a bucket handle.

His big hands covering her eyes from behind, Tom leads Gracey along the hallway. 'No peeking!'

The girls are late home. Fiona hit traffic on the way to after-school club and Gracey's just clambered from the car hot and soporific. But his daughter is alert now and completely engaged with seeing her surprise. 'Want to see!'

Fiona follows in her uniform, her tired eyes smiling at the pair of them.

In the doorway of Gracey's transformed room, Tom finally removes his hands. 'Da-da! I did your room first, Peanut. Pink like you wanted. First coat. I'll lay a floor next. Get you some big fluffy rugs too.'

Gracey's face splits into a crazed, excited grin. She races into the room.

From the door, Fiona leans in, peers at the ceiling, the corners. Lowers her gaze to the neat stripes of skirting.

'Now, I want you to keep this tidy,' Tom says, trying to look serious.

Gracey reaches ramming speed as she hits her dad's thighs and wraps her arms around his waist. 'Daddy! Daddy! My daddy!' Tom folds his arms around her, laughing, his eyes betraying a glimmer of moisture.

Fiona winks one carefully painted eye. 'About those builder fantasies.'

18

All Gracey can taste in her mouth is paint, the taste of *mungolia*. All weekend, Mommy and Daddy have been painting more walls and another ceiling. Daddy let her have a go with the spongy roller but she made a mess and got the paint all over the floor and her hands, and got bored anyway. Even when Dad used chalk to draw a hopscotch grid on the floor of the hall, so that she could 'amuse herself', she was bored of that after two passes.

And now her mommy and daddy are standing on the sanded floor and looking round a room watching paint dry. Watching them do that is so boring the boredom aches. But her dad never stops talking about the things he's fixing and her mum says 'Mmm' and 'yes' a lot.

Her parents each have a hand on the stepladder that she is not allowed to climb up and down, so the boredom in her belly burns redder. New Waddles is bored too and just flopping about in her hand.

Gracey scuffs her feet over bumps on the floor to the little woodland house that she's built in the corner of the room. An empty paint tin under the dust-sheet forms a hill. Coloured blocks, stacked like columns, erect standing stones around the mound. A king and queen sit on top. She's used her pig and rabbit. She wonders what might happen next in the woodland house game.

And then, she understands.

She closes her eyes and sees how many times she can circle the hill, walking backwards without losing her balance. She throws her arms into the air and completes three ungainly circles. Then she stands on one leg and points at her daddy, before realising that she's hungry and ready for another snack. Before she can think about what kind of snack she wants, she hears her name called from afar by the same lovely voice that she heard among the trees at the real woodland house. The sing-song voice is inside the faraway distance of her head again. Maybe it's outside too, rising from the bottom of the garden by the tilting fence.

Mum and Dad don't hear the voice. She asks them if they hear it but they're not listening and her dad is pointing at the corner of the ceiling saying, 'It's an old stain. Been painted over.' Her mum says, 'Still needs looking at. Might be water coming from the roof into the loft.'

There it is again, the lady's voice travelling from far beyond the garden, drifting like the music of the ballet about swans she watched with her mommy. This is the sweetest song that she's ever heard too; far, far prettier than Mrs Baxter's voice in school assembly.

The voice opens a space in her thoughts as warm and inviting as a sunny garden filled with bees and rabbits. A golden and secret space. The lady in the trees offers to show her where to find such a place.

Gracey races for the stairs. She'll hear the lady's voice much better in the garden. 'Archie-bear!' she cries out as her feet thump down the wooden stairs. And, on cue, she hears the tinkle of a collar and the woolly flapping sound of Archie shaking himself awake in his basket. When she sees him, he'll be looking at the kitchen door. She knows it.

Outside, Archie starts digging a new hole in the lawn; his third this week. Though Gracey was worried that he was digging through the ceilings of rabbit houses, what he was actually doing was finding metal bricks. Two dug up so far, all with funny writing on the sides. She hopes he'll find a box of gold coins soon, so that her daddy will never run out of money again.

Archie's eager scraping at the soil throws dirt on her feet while she stares at the bottom of the garden and listens hard for the lady's voice to start up again. The wood is strange and tense like an empty room in a game of hide and seek, waiting to be searched. Further out, above the bushy roof of the wood, a wisp of smoke drifts. The sun is sinking and might have set the red and apricot sky on fire in places too far away to see.

When the lady of the wood's voice rises once more, as high and thin as the smoke, Gracey nods her head, a smile playing around her mouth and eyes. 'Yes. Yes, please,' she says to the heavy fringe of branches overhanging the broken fence; those twisty arms with spiky hands, always groping inside to fumble at the weeds.

The whispering voice inside her ears, and inside the wood at the same time, tells her that lost Waddles is safe. But he's noisy and never stops dancing. Gracey giggles, then looks to the rear of the house. Squinting in the silvery light of the sun, now finishing its arc from east to west, she scans the murky panes to make sure her parents aren't watching. The open windows are black holes and she sees no faces.

Frowning her forehead into a scribble, she turns back to the trees. She doesn't know what to do, so just listens to the lady of the woods some more, singing her song about the place inside the trees where friends and animals play. Lost Waddles is up there. A place that might seem far away but isn't really when you get going. She imagines having two Waddles penguins. Twins on her new bed tonight.

'Archie. Let's go get the other Waddles. Lady's got him. But we gotta be quick.'

A few steps from the garden gate and she is swallowed, the wood closing its scaly lips behind her heels. She's crossed over, is inside now.

Today, more birds than she's ever heard anywhere call out and answer each other inside the canopy that shields her from the red sky. Acres of scrub and trees, skinny and fat, shutter most of the light. The air is wet. Mulchy and muddy. Freshwater smells from wet bark and cold leaves fill her nose and chill her cheeks.

Passing from the dusty house and packing crates, paint stink, the blurting radio and Daddy's grinding tools to enter this wood reminds her of walking off a beach covered in people and into the sea. Behind her the world hushes. Cool air softly washes her skin.

Giant trees, too high to climb, shrink her down tiny and she thinks of a girl dressed in red in her storybook. A picture of a small figure against dark trees that covers two big pages on which she tries to find every owl in the trees. But this wood is more than a picture. It's alive, murmuring, growing, yet pauses its business to watch her.

She remembers the song they sing at school about a silent night and holy night. Some of that song is in this place and something else too that makes her nervous and she understands why Archie does a poo as soon as he gets inside these trees. Anxiety wants to shake her tummy loose too. And she wants to run screaming. It's hard to breathe around her terror of getting lost and never seeing her mum and dad again. It comes up her throat like sick, though she doesn't feel ill. But her need to walk into these huge, dark halls of silence is the same as the temptation to swim, if she is standing on the ledge above the deep end of the pool at the leisure centre.

She takes a step, deeper, then another. Then a few more.

The ground squelches. An exposed root, slippery as the banisters of her nan's stairs, scoots one of her boots sideways and she nearly falls. But gradually she switches to the spongy track between the bony roots and is soon hopping over swampy puddles.

In no time at all, she's much closer to the kind lady, whose song flows around the huge legs of the trees and calls her to the hill and the standing stones. Waddles is waiting for her and soon Gracey feels as safe as if her mum and dad are with her too, holding her hands. She can't go wrong. One path in and out, to and from the hill, and kids are special guests anyway when the lady sings. The princess's voice carries this message through the stillness and the further Gracey walks the more she feels like she's having a good dream. The kind lady knows she's coming too because the birds are piping her in.

It's not far now. White flowers and onion smells thicken amidst crowds of blue flowers. Gracey recognises the tree that has fallen like a starving white man who's tripped and thrown out crooked arms to break his fall. And here are the Christmas cake bushes with shiny berries and leaves like plastic; over there are the coils of barbed-wire vines.

When she's near the hill and standing-up stones, Gracey stops walking. Now that she's so close to the wood house, she's a bit worried about who's making the smoke that she can smell and could see from her garden. It smells really funny too.

She came here for the lady and Waddles but now starts thinking of the witchy woman and the bad-breath man wearing yellow trousers. When she wonders if they will be here today, the fear she felt last time comes back, prickling her tummy. She doesn't want her flopping boots to make any sound.

A tangle of saplings and bushes fills the spaces between the trees and hides the grassy hill but there are plenty of peep-holes if you're small. Gracey creeps to a spy-hole.

Two fires on poles flicker inside the glade. The grassy mound arcs between the tiny flames.

The fires are cupped in blackened metal bowls. Sooty exhaust spirals. One fiery bowl snaps and gutters on the churchy bit with the flowers, the altar. The second bowl of fire is at the other end of the glade. That one billows with the strange smell she can taste like marzipan and lemons and something bitter as Daddy's brown beer the time he gave her a sip.

And today, the wood house is making Gracey remember a painting she saw in the museum on a school trip. A picture of little, hairy people wearing animal skins. They were as black as matchstick men and all stood around a huge bonfire. Tall stones circled the blaze too, throwing giant shadows. This painting was hanging on a wall behind a glass case with bones inside it; leg bones stuck inside rock. Everything inside the room made her afraid of time, as well as afraid of the notion that she was made of bones inside skin, and that when she died her bones would go into the ground and be stuck inside cold stones, buried under mud. It was too horrible to imagine for longer than a moment.

She's getting the dreamy feeling a bit too now, like the one she had in the garden when the lady's voice was sweetly singing inside her head. But this feeling isn't so nice this time. The lady's voice is back but sad and it makes her feel colder, and the tall trees with the black tunnels between them that disappear into big caves, the spicy perfume and red flowers, the old stones cold as ice, the hollow hill . . . all swirl about inside her head.

As if he knows something is going wrong, Archie whimpers behind Gracey. He sinks low to the earth and won't come any closer when she looks at him, which is not like Archie at all. Instead, he's looking up and nose-whistling. Gracey follows his eyes to a black lump hanging from a tree.

She closes her own eyes and can't bring herself to see *that* again; the raggedy shape with a toothy face. And as soon as she's seen it, the worst smell she's ever known drops and swamps her like an old blanket made from rotten meat. No almonds, lemons and bitter perfume now.

A deep hum of flies vibrates the air. Gracey coughs and notices tiny white things dropping onto the mud near Archie, like seeds from a tree when the wind blows hard. But unlike seeds, the white things writhe. They're the same kind of grubs that her granddaddy used for fishing. He kept them in a plastic box, inside the fridge.

A jumble of new voices starts from the hill, choking out a rough rhyme. She cannot hear the words in the rhyme and the lady of the woods isn't joining in. She's gone quiet. The birds have stopped singing too. Gracey nearly says 'Hello' so that no one jumps and gets angry when they find her spying. Because there's two things in the glade now that might, or might not, be people.

Gracey didn't see them come in but they're standing on one leg by the flames in the bowls and it's they who are making the grunty rhyme.

The rhyme makes silence fill every lightless hollow outside the ring of rocks and turns the trees to stone. It's like nothing inside the wood wants to be noticed by the two whitey things standing on one leg.

They are as still as statues until they start skipping.

Grass grows round and round the stones. An old clock telling strange times, of years and years, not minutes or hours.

Maggots curl their ribbed tails.

Gracey's mouth dries because she can't close it. All the blood runs from her face and she knows she's as white as the woodwork her daddy painted yesterday. That's who she wants with her now, her daddy. She's so scared and might be sick too, inside the cloud of flies and the stink.

Backwards the whitey ones go now, around the grassy mound. They're turning the big stone clock the wrong way and her eyes follow the backwards skipping and bulge from her face. Archie barks like he's mad and can't stop. Then he growls and she's only heard him make that noise twice before: once at the vet and once at a delivery man.

Gracey can't move her feet.

The whitey ones might be the ghosts of bad animals. That fatty one, which has dropped down and is scampering on all fours inside the grassy circle, has a scruffy black head with yellow tusks. Running backwards, it's going faster than she can run forwards. The other one is skinny with sticking-out bones like skeletons in graves.

Gracey's thoughts smash into bits and scatter like a stone has gone through a window inside her head. Only silly thoughts hang behind to try and stop her thinking about the skinny one, prancing through the gaps, so springy and up on its toes and going backwards like a horrible monkey with no fur on its cold skin.

Her whole body is shaking, she can't get air inside, her eyesight is flickering and she doesn't know what to do when a face appears on the other side of her peephole.

The skinny whitey with the black head must have stopped springing backwards and crept up to the edge of the clearing while she was watching the fatty one, because now the skinny is grinning as if to say, *It's no use at all. I can see you and I am going to get you.*

Tatty and tufted mangy fur face. Big white eyes. And are them things on its head horns? Like bulls have? The bad kind that chase people through fields? But just as soon as she looks back at it, the bumpy muzzle and bulgy eyes pull backwards. Or maybe just disappear.

Gracey moves a foot. Falls on her backside. Throws away new Waddles like it's his fault that she's gone over.

Somewhere behind her, Archie is barking and pacing and barking. When Gracey turns her head and finds him, he's not looking at her but at the two whiteys who are running again, round and round the hill, inside the ring of trees, inside the ring of stones. White legs and slapping feet going backwards, the wrong way, so her eyes go the wrong way and her thoughts bend into a circle that also turns the wrong way.

Gracey closes her eyes and struggles onto her hands and knees to stop seeing the whiteys. But sometimes, as they rush past, their black faces must be peering at her, from holes in the bushes. They know she's here. She won't look at their faces again but Archie can see them and goes crazy as the leaves rustle near her head and the horrible faces poke through.

When she opens her eyes, she's looking at the mud that has seeped wetly through her dress to freeze her front and back-bottom. Upon the soil, the grubs twist and poke eyeless faces towards where the sun must be.

Archie creeps away from her on his belly and looks more like a cat than a dog. He's going inside the ring of stones. Gracey would call him back but has no air inside her body. All that's left inside her is a swirl of the horrible things she's just seen, going up and down, round and round, like she's going round the hill with them too and saying a name to get that lady singing inside the hill again.

When she scrabbles upright, she goes all giddy and dizzy. It's like she weighs nothing and could float up to the hanging fox who is nailed to the tree and dripping grubs. There he is with his pink tongue looping black gums in a grinning mouth. His big yellow eyes are still open. His red legs are as thin as flutes. He has a white tummy. Black flies buzz about in the smell of him dead.

When Gracey opens her mouth to cry, fear sucks her distress back inside her body because the two whitey things that were running backwards around the grassy hill are now standing on top of it. And they're keeping very still. Their scruffy black heads watch the sky. Archie is up there too, climbing up the fattish one as if it has food and he's licking under the fat whitey's legs. The skinny whitey is up on its back legs and the front legs dangle and twitch. Its long mouth hiccups at the sky.

Inside her head, her own voice tells her to run.

Gracey runs.

Tears scold and blind her eyes. Branches whip her skin. Her little legs pump the earth but are never fast enough.

There's no sound in the wood. Everything here has closed its mouth and eyes.

A final peek backwards, to make sure they're not chasing her, and she sees the skinny whitey leap off the hill and out of the ring of stones. Up it goes and out of sight, like an ape with long ears, flinging itself through a forest.

She never hears it land in the branches, so maybe it can fly. But if she sees it flying, she knows the fright will stop her heart.

19

'Gracey! Gracey! Come and see your curtains. Paint's dry.' Fiona clatters off the stepladder and listens for her daughter's response from wherever she is in the house. She waits in anticipation for the thump of racing feet and the urgency of her daughter's narration about Waddles's escapades in an empty room; too many words all falling over each other in a breathless rout.

But only silence answers her call, until a muffled thud from Tom's hammer downstairs offers some sense of her not being alone in the house.

It's very rare, even when Gracey is deeply engaged in a game that consumes every molecule of her being, that the girl does not scramble for the sound of her mother's voice when called. Fiona leaves the bedroom and leans over the stairwell. 'Mate!'

'Yeah!' Tom answers from the lounge that faces the garden. A room all but finished by their predecessor. After neatly plastering four walls, he proceeded to block the windows with lengths of timber, then hang himself in the hall. Every time Fiona ascends the stepladder she thinks of *him* ascending a stepladder.

'Gracey down there with you?'

A pause, then, 'Thought she was upstairs.'

Fiona pushes herself off the banister and peers into the master bedroom. Some of her daughter's toys colour the floor. Fiona remembers her crouched there. *When was that?*

107

'Gracey-love?' Fiona's eyes skim over the mountain her daughter fashioned from tins and a dust sheet. Toy animals stand on top as if surveying their kingdom. Building blocks Stonehenge the base.

Silence.

From downstairs, she hears the shuffle of Tom's feet as he comes into the hall. Fiona hears him call, 'Graceeey!'

A call neither heeded nor answered.

Fiona walks to the window. *Walks* but is aware of moving as if she's being deafened by the continuous scream of a fire alarm.

Eagerly seeking the sight of her daughter, her vision scatters about the wasteland of garden and rests upon the dark aperture of an open gate, in the decrepit fence, at the foot of the garden. A lightless tunnel, beyond this breach in their defences, burrows into scrub and the trees. She thinks of a jetty without railings, waves lapping.

'Shit.'

They're not running but nor are they walking. Halfway between the back door of the kitchen and the garden gate, their brief anger at Gracey for wandering into the wood again dissolves into a heartburn of anxiety.

'Gonna put a lock on that,' Tom says.

Their tense, pale faces mutter vaguely reassuring remarks to each other as they stride towards the trees. Neither processes what the other has said because they are each committed to censoring the arrival of thoughts most unwelcome in these situations. And then they come to a stop at the same time and stare at the little form of their daughter that appears beyond the gate.

Baffled, they stand mute, minds reaching for words to form questions. But never having seen that expression on their daughter's face before, their hesitation is brief. Soon, they're running to her.

At the mouth of the track, Gracey's dazed gaze is more blank than dreamy and doesn't seek her parents. It's as if they've arrived too late and what's done is done.

20

*P*rone to sudden frights and swamped by terrors of dangers merely perceived? Always, like any child, but this time is different. Gracey's small bloodless face, her unusual silence and stunned eyes, prompt Tom to sink to his knees before the kitchen stool. Seeing her so pitifully reduced before him, he fears that the confidence and certainties his daughter has gained in four years have all been stripped away in a single afternoon.

A sudden recognition of her smallness and wondering innocence hits him under the solar plexus. Her beautiful green eyes don't acknowledge him, only look through him and blink as the girl's mind fathoms and ferrets for the truth of a thing; matters and concerns still unshared.

Tom can't breathe. He wants to hug their daughter, sling her under his chest and squash out the woe. But Fiona is closer and Gracey wants her mother.

Always a child who wanders off. Turn their backs in a supermarket and she's two aisles over inventing a shopping game with items from the lower shelves. As soon as she could walk, she was off across grass, frigid or dewy, abandoning him in the park with the pushchair laden with bags and bears. He can see her now, two, maybe three years old: rubber boots, like toys at the end of her stubby legs, weaving circles on the turf of recreation grounds, her breath puffing. Reckless and euphoric at the simple joy of movement, she'd always stamp in a straight line towards a horizon busy with cars. How he'd

110

scan the terrain for dangerous dogs, fast bicycles, ponds, the glitter of broken glass, turds hiding like coiled serpents. And give chase. Today, he never even saw her leave the house. The idea of her not coming back is not new but remains an idea he cannot abide.

'Get lost, my Peanut? Give yourself a fright?' Stating the obvious just reinforces his feeling of uselessness.

Fiona's shoulders and voice are loosening with relief, though a stern tone endures in her voice. 'What did Mommy say, aye? About going in there?'

She casts a sharp glance at Tom and he shies away, withered. He feels fraudulent and suddenly detached, uncoupled from these two people who hold him upright in life. He dragged them to a broken-down house with hideous neighbours, so far from school, jobs, friends and comfort.

Financial anxiety is the only electricity running through their wires now. Like a feckless politician he's sold his daughter his idea of a life amongst the trees, clean air, rabbits as friends. He's never lived in the country before. What would he know? About anything? The broadband is a trickle but was fast in the flat. Instant access to the world, to people. Another warning of how far he's led his tribe from everything familiar.

'I'll fetch Archie,' Tom says.

No one answers him.

Pressed against her mother, Gracey finally sobs. The warmth and scents accompanying her from the hospital bed and cradle overwhelm her. A memory wave, summoned by a simple fragrance of her mother, rises above every seawall erected in a lifetime. The safest place: Mommy.

Fiona *shush-shushes* and kisses Gracey's tousled head.

Tom lets himself out.

21

*D*usk ages a low, already dark sky. What light there is silts down and makes Tom feel as if he's suffering from a degenerative eye disease.

Once he's clear of the garden and amongst the roots of the old wood, the sky's dim sheen is entirely swallowed on the far western side of the woods, wherever that boundary is.

'Archie!'

Ducking under brawny branches, batting at obstructive saplings, as his paint-spattered boots slip-slide about the track, he implores the dank earth to give up the dog and Gracey's new penguin. But his vision can only strain at the murk as if he's underwater, in a canal.

Between choking scrub and pillars of trunk bound by ivy, definition blurs to blackened clumps of nothing. Nearby, one thing climbs upon another and becomes something else entirely: tree into giant, bush into wolf on two legs, bracken into a face he almost apologises to; a fallen limb transforms into a caped woman, bent in grief. Voids spread, deepen. Treetops thrust their arms upwards and grasp at the dying sun with drooping fingers.

'Archie!'

He staggers half-blind where wily things watch. Pale and warm like a trembling animal that smells of warm food and should be buried in its own burrow by now, he stumbles. His oldest instincts prickle for the pounce from behind or the side.

'Archie!'

Being here so soon after the last futile search for another lost toy, and now a dog too, heats his low spirits into exasperation. It smoulders like the onset of indigestion. Yet here he is, seeking another penguin lost at the wrong latitude in alien terrain. *Both of us stuffed.*

'Little man!'

Gracey wouldn't have strayed from the track, so the toy, at least, should be on it somewhere. Part of the toy's fur is white too. There is little opportunity to step off the rough crease grooved through the trees, maybe even by animals.

On he goes, with a stronger sense of confinement striking him as he bends and casts poorly adapted eyes about his murky feet. But he hasn't progressed more than a few hundred metres when a whiff of corruption pulls him up straight.

Wincing at the miasma that seems intent on becoming a permanent taste inside his mouth, Tom peers about his feet. Nothing is visible. He swats at something that he doesn't see but hears hiss past his ear. Then peers up and at an orbit of whining insects.

Peepholes in the canopy admit a blue, gassy light and outline a tail, limp yet bushy, hanging from a birch tree.

Tom stumbles backwards, his forearm across his mouth and nose. 'The fuck?'

At first he thinks it's a cat. But the drooping legs appear too hard and bristly to be feline. Only when a white throat is discernible below a triangular snout, which broadens to large, cocked ears, does Tom see the tortured remains of a fox.

He squints, disbelieving and weakened by horror, at the grin of sharp teeth, exposed in black gums, protruding through the shallow light and into his comprehension. A small dog frozen in the act of panting, or cleaning its mouth with a long tongue. A fox fixed against the trunk, the neck garrotted with a bracelet of dull wire. The tree turned gamekeeper.

Coughing, Tom withdraws as the carrion stench and cruel intent of this spectacle seep an unbearable dread into his thoughts.

A few days have passed since he's ventured this far inside the wood but he recognises the fallen tree stripped of bark and made bony-white; one of few things still visible close to the ground. And no animal had been throttled against a tree trunk when he was here before. He'd been scrutinising the track but would have surely smelled it and heard the flies. So this carcase was positioned. A corpse installed like a thief in a gibbet to swing above the sole ingress from his garden gate; intended to deter visitors from stepping too far inside this *old* wood. Someone local is responsible.

Little Gracey has seen the dead fox too. An animal she's only ever known as a character in cartoons, or in illustrations in tales of talking animals, twirling whiskers and wearing red coats. His child, a little girl, a lover of all baby animals, saw *this*. She can't contemplate the death of a character in a storybook, let alone a butchered animal strangled by wire, blackened by blood and boiling with flies in the very wood that he's pitched to her as magical.

This was to be a place of mystery and enchantment, surrounding a warm home that would forever glow in her mind as a place filled with love and light. Not this: impenetrable scrub as feral and depressing as their cold, sad house, in turn cursed by the trauma of a man's ghost hanging in the hall.

And into Tom's mind bursts an image of Mrs Moot's absurd head; self-importance and innate hostility etched into a face loathsome to him. He can almost hear the patronising tone, yipping out of that lined, whiskery muzzle. *Yisss?*

What had she said . . . *As a parent are you not concerned for your daughter's safety?* Then she mentioned something about Gracey's imagination, about her getting ideas in an old wood . . . *We scolded her for her own benefit . . . It is no place for children.*

And then Tom is running away from the miasma of the dead dog in the tree and his breath is strangled. Gasps and exhalations want to become screams of rage. Into the darkness he races awkwardly, punching at anything that flaps near his head or crosses his chest like arms; branches designed to increase his torment, waylaying him, making him boil.

Until . . .

A shaking of branches above him, behind him, back near the fox; verdure protesting at the passage of a thrusting body. A commotion accompanied by the determined raking of paws or hands that seize and grip.

He stops. Turns, his fire of rage transforming into a hoarfrost of terror, growing from the pores of his scalp and icing the steps of his spine. So deep does this rupture of fear tear that his testicles clench, then shrink.

Peering up, he loses his footing. Snatches a hand into nettles. Wet skin on live wires.

His vision rakes the filigree and petrified coral that webs the underside of the wood's canopy; a tatty basket weave projected by low light onto the charcoal screen of sky. Nothing moves. But any lump, any shape at all up there, might be the cause of the noise.

At ground level, a bulky form careens onto the track, dragging his eyes down. A few feet ahead of him it comes barrelling, kicking itself free of the scrub.

Monkey or monster? From the trees it came?

The impossibility of this moment slips cold fingers about his throat, to squeeze all reason out and through the top of his skull. And for a few unbearable seconds, his entire being strains itself through his horrified eyes to determine that *this* thing before him *is not possible.* He can neither move nor let loose a held breath.

Paws pad wetly. A small, shaggy shadow, black as the sky will soon be, waddles closer, crossing inky voids footing tree roots. Without a defining feature, save the low bulk and a sway to the gait, as if a heavy belly swings across wet soil, it comes. Right at him. Up to him.

Tom whimpers. Even turns sideways to brace for an impact about his legs that he expects to be terrible. He wishes he could raise both feet from the ground like a housekeeper frighted by a mouse in one of Gracey's cartoons.

And then the thing sneezes, causing a steel nametag to tinkle upon a buckled collar. One step away from his shins, the loaf-like head, with drooping bedraggled ears, finally redrafts itself into a recognisable form.

'Archie! You bastard! You nearly stopped my heart.'

His voice draws no friendly bark, nor leaping or reaching up his legs. No smile. There is only a subdued puppy here who has laboured to reach him, the stubby tail lowered, a flag in mourning.

He must have been lost. Abandoned by Gracey who fled the dead fox. Left here to mooch and get turned around, whining and snuffling for his people as the light thinned from the very air before his watery brown eyes.

Tom's heart cracks.

From incandescent rage to the petrifaction of terror, pure and white, to a joy that brings tears to his eyes, Tom is left dizzy.

'My little man.' He drops to his knees and accepts the mooching bulk and its wet nose and sodden ears. From what he can see, the pup's eyes seem sad yet grateful to find his master here. Tom picks up the spaniel and fusses it in the way he'd wanted to fuss his own child in the kitchen. But finds himself immediately inspecting Archie's face, because of the dog's constant licking of his muzzle, as if his mouth is hurt . . . until a branch snaps clean above at a cold, airy distance.

A hiss of air follows and makes Tom suffer the sense, rather than the sight, of a form much heavier than a bird or squirrel, flinging itself to another branch, high up, over his head.

Tom swivels about, his head thrust back, Archie clutched tighter to his chest. He scans the ink-blotted underside of forest roof but can distinguish nothing moving amidst the impenetrable lattice of twig, the blackened rafters of oak, elm, larch and birch. Up there, anything could become anything.

A bird? Big bird? An owl? And might it have been hunting Archie below?

Tom hesitates until the smell of Archie's wet fur fills his sinuses and reminds him of home and the girls; some vestige of warmth and togetherness.

Archie presses his head into Tom's chest and licks at his muzzle. A sick child. *Take me home, Daddy.* Tom knows the signs and wants to get out of the dreadful wood, the blinding thorns, this reek of compost and throttled carrion.

Cautiously, he moves backwards, glancing up and around himself as if wary of aerial attack, until he reaches the broken gate where the old crucifixes glimmer like dull pewter. Dim beacons reminding him he's home.

22

*T*om swings the back door shut with a foot. His heart thuds and shakes out the last drops of adrenalin but now he's indoors, at least he can detect a smidgen of a house's purpose: to provide shelter and security, or something like that – and for the first time too. He needs to bury his shock from the woods under the cushion of the kitchen lights and the comfort of the girls' presence. *Home.* This has to be home, because there isn't anywhere else for them to be now.

Boots kicked off, he plants and earths his feet on the old lino, then drifts to Gracey, holding Archie under his arm. His daughter's face remains buried in her mum's neck but at least she's stopped crying.

Tom kneels down. 'Look who I have here.'

Gracey moves her head a fraction, peering with one eye to see what her father cradles: the furry baby of the family.

Archie gazes in the direction of Gracey but can't summon the usual snuffling eagerness with which he solicits fuss. The dog remains preoccupied with licking his muzzle.

Tom nestles Archie into his basket, where the pup watches and beseeches Tom to be kept within his arms. A pathetic but heart-aching appeal for comfort, but the dog has become heavy and is a barrier between him and Gracey and what he wants to ask her.

'What a pair. Lost in the wood. You two, honestly. Frightened me and your mum half to death. Twice now. What happened, my love? You see something?' Tom thinks of the fox frozen in grinning death, black with blood and flies.

'She's in shock.' Fiona says, in shock herself at the very idea that her daughter could be traumatised.

'Why did you go in there, my Peanut?' Tom asks, ignoring Fiona's frown that communicates that this is not the time for the interrogation that she will surely expect to carry out. But Gracey is sufficiently quieted to respond and seems eager to share her horrified fascination with what she experienced. 'Lady of the woods told me to come in. For lost Waddles.'

'What lady? The lady next door?'

Gracey shakes her head: *no*. 'Lady in the trees said she's got Waddles up in the wood house wiv the stones.'

'Wait. This lady, she asked you to go into the wood? When you were in the garden?'

Gracey nods.

'Who is she?'

'She's in the trees by the hill.'

'You've seen her?'

Gracey shakes her head, her expression doleful. But intrigue has crept into her widening eyes as if she's just realised how strange it is to hear a disembodied voice from inside the wood.

'But she knows your name?'

Gracey nods.

'And when you were in there . . . you met the lady who called to you?'

Gracey shakes her head. 'She weren't there. There was white monsters by the hill and a fox in a tree they hurted.'

Tom and Fiona exchange glances. Fiona is mystified but Tom feels ill at the details contained within this simple account. He looks at the kitchen window.

Dark glass, revealing nothing but the inside of the kitchen. *Need to get blinds on that. So that nothing . . . no one can see inside.* Out there is what's left of the old fence dividing the two houses. The end panels smashed. The remnants stacked upon an overgrown lawn. Beyond that: *them*. 'Something's not right here.'

'You don't say.' Fiona is angry with him but shouldn't be. He needs to correct her. 'It's them again.'

'Not now. Chrissakes.'

Tom peers into Fiona's eyes, prospecting, sifting, seeking a hint of curiosity about what the hell just happened to Gracey, let alone him too. He sees nothing but the hard stones of his wife's disdain, walling him out.

'You heard what Gracey said,' he offers, his voice softened, a conciliatory gesture.

'Who told her the woods belonged to her?'

And then Gracey sits up, forcing herself into the exchange, compelled by the tension between her parents. 'New Waddles is lost!'

23

Fiona places the book on the littered surface of her daughter's chest of drawers. After twenty minutes reading *The Little Grey Men* to Gracey, she's been reaching the end of sentences with little idea what they were about. Thoughts of things unconnected to gnomes have drifted in and out of the story. Ghosts in her muscles continue to hang curtains and stroke a paintbrush at walls that Tom stripped and cleaned. A thick smell of emulsion has deadened her sinuses to competing scents. Even though she wore gloves, her fingertips are stained.

Gotta get them clean for work tomorrow. Iron your blouse. Gracey's uniform. Is there a clean cardy? We haven't done her home learning.

'Gnomes in the wood, Mommy? Maybe they're gonna look after New Waddles 'til Daddy finds him.'

Fiona wades from the chop and swell of her preoccupation, drifts ashore to her daughter. 'Don't even go thinking about that place. It's out of bounds.'

And then, from outside, she hears Tom's raised voice and her skin is frostbitten. He's gone next door. She asked him not to. Then told him not to. He never answered, just kept on drinking that second glass of rum. She knew he was troubled when he returned with Archie, distracted and masking what looked like fear with a nervous smile. And the way he spoke to Gracey, like he'd just witnessed an accident and was pressing another witness for details . . .

Fiona's been busy since, getting Gracey bathed in a puddle of lukewarm water, collected from the trickle the exhausted boiler drip-feeds the bath. Drying her hair, finding pyjamas, fielding requests, while Tom paced the kitchen, eventually coming to rest upon his knuckles, looming over the sink, looking at nothing. Even when she was one floor up, she knew he was doing that. His lips would have been moving too. An actor rehearsing lines for a performance. *Just getting my head straight*, he'd said, when she came down and asked him to check the air in her car's tyres.

Bastards next door put a dead fox in a tree to warn us away from going in there.

You don't know it was them, she'd said.

Bloody do!

There's no point arguing with him when he's like that.

A couple of glasses of fiery rum dissolved the last threads restraining the angry giant inside her husband. And he's next door now, the thud of his palms against the Moots' front door carrying across to her and Gracey. Tom's voice follows but sounds so far away. 'Hey! Hey! A word! Hey! I know you're in there!'

Gracey peers at her mum. Fiona looks at the curtains and bites her bottom lip, aware of the little face turned toward her, pale, as if a light is held under her chin; a small, questing mind studying her expression, probing for signs of dissonance within the harmony of Mommy, Daddy, Gracey and Archie. Fiona feels like she's holding her breath for most of each day now.

Tom from afar: 'What! Do! You! Think! You are playing at? Eh! A dead animal! To frighten a little girl! You hanged it there! You nasty, cruel, small-minded cowards!'

Gracey will have seen this mum-face before and Fiona has glimpsed this very expression herself on many reflective surfaces: the deepening of hairline fractures around her eyes and mouth into fissures. And she always winces.

But she's had good reason to worry herself sick since Tom's contract finished, following three years of steady employment, earning the salary they'd used to secure the mortgage. Another four months of sporadic employment followed in which her husband either wasn't paid what was agreed or was doing twice the work agreed but only paid for what was agreed. Even the dregs of leave cover he managed to claw up, on unfair terms and remuneration, have evaporated. His efforts since to tap old contacts and scratch a few half-chances from the air have also been in vain. And now he's desperate, trying too hard and really disliking himself when reduced to this. He's filling the gap by fixing up the house – *it's all working out if you think about it, as I'll get the house ready sooner this way* – and boring a bigger crevice into their dwindling savings, while they make do with her job at the bank.

She can cover the mortgage payments and her petrol, the food. Nothing else. They will need to pay bills, buy building materials, pay tradesmen . . . *the roof, wiring, plumbing, plastering*. He's got to cover that.

This house will never stop taking what they have. She can smell its terminal illness, the constant need of the sickness in the mildewed plaster, in the dusty air currents she hears like wheezes, dragging the dead skin of ages from beneath the floorboards and into their lungs. And this is just the start. They're not nurses, they're undertakers.

'Dad losing his shit again?'

Fiona is startled back into the room by Gracey's use of that word. She knows Gracey's acquired it from her, when she's talking on the phone to her own mother.

Fiona meets Gracey's earnest eyes and she wants to burst with laughter and tears at the same time.

When she comes into the kitchen, Tom's refilling his glass with neat rum.

'I reckon they got the message. Even if it was delivered through the bloody letter box. They were hiding. I could hear the old bastards. Like rats in the dark.'

Fiona settles upon a stool at the kitchen counter and watches her husband while waiting for a pause in his tirade, or a crinkle of doubt in his eyes, before she speaks. His blood is up.

'That's animal cruelty. They're not farmers or hunters. Can't just kill an animal and use it as some kind of territorial marker. On public land. It's mediaeval. Who the fuck do they think they are?'

She wonders if one thing has become mixed up with another thing in his mind; if he is transferring his disappointment onto the neighbours. But she won't engage with him when he's like this; even finds that she can't now, like she's had enough of him and is as bored by him as she is angry with him.

'I've work to do. That skirting won't put itself up in the front room. I've wasted enough time looking for a fucking penguin and a dog. Jesus wept.'

Fiona looks at her watch. 'It's late.'

Tom ignores her and leaves the room.

24

om watches Fiona's car pull away.

Head turned to peer over the backrest of the childseat, Gracey stares at the house itself, not at her daddy in the window upstairs. After waking subdued and fearful she's still not smiling.

His family gone for the day, Tom pads disconsolately from his daughter's room, drifts into the master bedroom. Nursing an anger hangover, his spirit is a seafront wrecked by a storm, his thoughts splintered deckchairs and beach huts. The sign for ice-cream hangs from a tree.

Reparation with next door is no longer possible. No chance of an icy atmosphere between the houses that might eventually thaw, or a meagre tolerance. That was the best-case scenario from day one. Gone now. Last night he raised a fist to their faces. *Went round their house*, like a dad in the Seventies whose child had been clipped round the ear by a neighbour.

Wincing, as if knots of twine tug tighter inside his belly, he recalls what he shouted through the letter flap. *No, no.* Too much to revisit. Recriminations lid his eyes with shame. What if they'd nothing to do with the fox?

How does Fiona do it? Stay so calm?

Tom stoops, picks up the dishevelled tongue of the duvet that laps the floor of their room and tosses it onto the bed. At the window he looks upon the cratered battlefield of his garden.

Archie has dug three holes into the overgrown lawn, pitting the land as if to further prove that it is the surface of an inhospitable planet. The grass also appears darker this morning, the colours absent as if the one saving grace of the wild flowers has vanished too; flowers that don't appear to have opened that morning. *Front faces east. Light's there.* Maybe that's all it is.

Turning to what can be seen of the neighbours', his vision switches channels from monochrome to polychrome; from anaemic black and white to an intense, bright spectrum of colour, an explosion of fecundity in bloom. Startling him, until movement at the end of the neighbours' garden catches his eye and breath: Magi and Mrs Moot, entering the garden from the tangle of woods, each carrying a basket.

Tom steps back, nerviness instigating a need to pee, as if he's just sighted two bullies idling at the school gates that he must pass through.

When Tom enters the kitchen, the pup whistles piteously. His dog is now a subdued black lump lying motionless inside a basket. Uneaten food hardens inside the dog's bowl.

The puppy's soft eyes beseech his master's. Tom squats and strokes Archie's head. 'Bit off-colour, little man? Or is this sympathy for me being in the doghouse?' Tom fondles Archie's ears as the dog licks at his muzzle. 'Hurt your mouth? I'll have a look in a bit. But take it easy today, mate.'

Out back, at the edge of the patio, Tom kneels and inspects the other sickening subjects in his newly won kingdom. He fingers a spray of hedge bindweed that threads a mop of privet; the vines extend from the skirts of the wood.

Gracey loved these horn-shaped petals, all open as if to sing like a hundred gramophone pavilions, growing along the side of their garden with no neighbours. First day, when let out the back with Archie, she'd rushed to them. But this morning, they're batwing shrouds enclosing desiccated pistils, the flowers withered into themselves like paper left in the rain.

Tom tries to remember the last time he saw the bindweed when it wasn't like this, like *dead*. *Yesterday?* No, he didn't look yesterday but within the past few days the plant wasn't in this sorry state.

The demise of the foxgloves weighs heavier upon his heart. *Fairy hats*, Gracey had called them. Characters in one of her books wear similar. Clumps in the shade of the collapsing hedge had grown higher than he'd seen before, developing an alien aesthetic: clustered speaker-horns of an unearthly vivid purple, facing down; flora from the covers of his dad's old science fiction paperbacks. A public address system on poles on Mars. But now all are wilted a dark winey hue, some growing black like gangrene in a wound, the stems rattling like corn stalks after a biblical pestilence. Considered weeds but not by Gracey. She'd entwined them around Archie's collar. From the window, he and Fiona had looked down and laughed at their 'mad hippy dog' bounding over tufts of grass behind their daughter. *Days before.*

White clover like snowfall had recently wintered this lawn too, a patch of land rewilded to scrub after years of neglect. But each and every creamy flower is now seared brown, as if scorched to carbon by a nuclear flash. The flowers look like refugees flooding from a city, overtaken and engulfed by a star's heat.

Bright yellow herds of bird's-foot trefoil had also recently flourished in the foundations of the smashed fence. Like the subject of a dreamy watercolour, the flowers had enlivened ruin. They've been wiped out too as if by the equivalent of a defoliant dropped sticky and fizzing from above.

Tom casts about the unruly grasses, searching for any survivors. But all of his flowers are drooping, closed, shrivelled.

An insistent drone of flies draws him to the apple trees. He suspects these three trees were once part of an orchard that the houses on the outskirts of the village were built over.

As he draws closer, the juvenile, unripe apples appear unhealthily dark, no longer green, their circumferences uneven. Holding an apple in his palm, like a farmer before a winter that will be bleached by hunger and need, he turns about a puckered, sappy apple-corpse. Flies orbit the trees greedily, getting their load on with cider tasting of bruises. Tom swats at one near his face.

His garden has deceased overnight, is entirely blighted by a disease that spread in twenty-four hours or less. *Impossible.*

At the end of the lawn, where the fence was broken by the neighbours, the breach now suggests the entry point of an invading army that swarmed swiftly and withdrew just as fast. Smart ornamental trees demarcate a second border on the neighbours' property, peeking over his slouching fence where it still stands. A symmetrical row of trees posturing like smug knights who've just ridden his hoary peasants down, scorching the earth before proudly cantering home to a realm of pageantry and light.

All that is visible of next door's garden is untouched by this rot. Instead, it glows luminous; a celestial aura visible to passing aircraft.

The hum of a Flymo purrs from over there. *Snick, snick.* Clippers idly prune behind the rickety fencing near the patio. His neighbours, gardening again. *What else do they do?*

His imagination swiftly prickles and cools with a suspicion they are only outside because he is in his garden. They're faking, are pretending to be busy. This is an act, a contrivance, a cover, when they're really outside to witness his reaction to a dead garden.

Did they do it? And how?

Tom scuffs over his pox-grass to the fresh holes that Archie dug in this tatty land. At the base of the first depression, he spots a dull glimmer, a drizzle of soil peppering a tarnished surface. Another lead tablet. Leaning over, reaching inside the hole, he digs the metal tile loose with fingernails that become encrusted with the ruddy-brown soil.

Another metal tile buried a foot down in his lawn?

It is lead.

As he cleans earth from the upper surface with his thumbs, markings become immediately evident.

Tablet in hand, Tom stumbles to the next hole and squats. Finishing a dog's work like a man digging his own shallow grave, he removes another lead tablet, also inscribed. Sitting on his heels he studies it, perplexed. Then rises with a groan and plods for the garden hose.

Chilly water swills soil from the tablets. He can better see the markings, the curious scratching covering one side of each dripping plate. They're worn but suggest hieroglyphs, symbols, or characters from an alphabet he doesn't recognise.

Indoors, he places the two new lead tablets on the window sill, next to the first tile that Gracey and Archie uncovered. Three now. How many more are out there? What are they and how old are they? He wishes he had someone to ask, like a friendly neighbour. Relics from some local industry perhaps? Parts of a building long razed to the ground? Something, a tradition, connected to farming?

As he worries the enigma, he catches sight of a wet smear on the kitchen lino beside the dog's basket. A small, frothing puddle of phlegm tinged pink. The dog has been sick.

Tom lowers himself beside Archie's basket. 'What you been eating, lad?'

He refreshes the dog's water bowl from the kitchen tap, though it takes a while to beg enough water from the pipes. He places the brimming bowl close to Archie's nose. Stroking the dog's head with one hand, he uses the other to dab at the frothy vomit with a handful of paper towels.

25

*T*hrough windows thrown wide to disperse the smell of the bond he's spread around the perimeter of Gracey's room and that now sticks vinyl to the floorboards, Tom hears Fiona's car turn into the lane outside.

Eager to show off the new, shiny floor of the bedroom, he skates his hands, as if feeling his way across ice, across the new surface. After wiping out the morning, and dropping four hundred quid at a garden centre (then hiding the stuff he bought in the shed), he forced himself upstairs to lay vinyl on the floor of Gracey's bedroom. And is glad that he did so.

He'd rough-laid the sheets of flooring yesterday to let the material settle and acclimatise overnight but has since cut the rubbery blankets of lino into sizes so perfect that he's surprised himself. He can no longer detect a ripple or crease under the smooth dark covering, and at a glance it looks like real timber.

The new flooring will re-seal the dross of ages, puffing up through cracks and jagged edges like black curls shorn from a dirty head; the very crevices the mice must use to access the house's interior. And at the borders of both bedrooms, he's filled every observable gap and cavity with silicone sealant.

He also found time to neatly and squarely tack a wooden trim around the foot of the walls in Gracey's room. Another barrier to what they don't want entering the house or her lungs. Completing perfection, a metal bar now gleams at the threshold of the room, where the newly hung door swings smoothly and soundlessly. He's removed at least one old groan from this building and opened a new chamber within its heart.

He'll shift their bed out tomorrow morning and lay a floor in the master bedroom. Maybe he can lay vinyl over the hall floor downstairs the day after and even floor the living room this week too. If that all goes as well as Gracey's bedroom, this is possible.

Right here, under his hands and knees, a new place is taking form; one brighter, smoother, more youthful. Purpose is being restored, the summit regained. He must remember this, recognise it, acknowledge it. And after the death of the garden, he needed this today. God, he needed it.

The sound of the front door opening punctures the house's silent inner skin; a bubble bursting at the same time as he snaps from the frowning concentration required to lay a floor.

Two pairs of feet bump the bare floorboards downstairs, Gracey's voice rising from the stamping commotion. 'Archie-bear! Look what I made for you at school!' Her small feet drum along the hallway in search of the dog that never bounded to greet her, nor scrabbled at the front door, whining with impatience to get to his Gracey.

Tom inspects his work from another view. Blots off a solitary hair with a fingertip as if inspecting the bonnet of a new car.

And then Gracey starts wailing in the kitchen.

Tom rises stiffly to his feet. She's had a long day. They really push them at that school. Followed by two hours at after-school club until Fiona got there from the bank. Then forty minutes in the car to get here. *Home.* She'll be asleep by 8.30.

When Tom fills the kitchen doorway, he's not sure what to look at first, nor whom to speak to. 'What's all this then? Aye?'

Fiona is crouching in one corner, holding Gracey. She's had a long day too. Her hair is flatter, her makeup worn off, her eyes crinkled by weariness, and now the little girl's face is buried in her chest and sobbing it sodden. Fiona's eyes are moist too. Tiny crumbs of mascara form a sediment of soot upon her cheekbones.

No one looks at Tom.

He peers around them and sees the padded basket and another puddle of the horrible pinkish foam the dog has sicked up. Inside the padded bed lies a black body: stiff and inert, head back, eyes open. White foam beards the pup's muzzle as if he's suddenly aged a full lifetime that very day, passing in his sleep like a grandfather dog at the heart of the house.

26

om closes the book, *The Little Grey Men* by BB. He and Fiona read to their daughter on alternate nights. And tonight, Gracey's in their bed. After the death of her puppy, there was no argument from him about the sleeping arrangements.

As if to evoke reassurance from the toy, Gracey peers from under the covers and into the inert pupils and glittering irises of her second new penguin that arrived by courier that morning. Tom studies his daughter's expression. Her questing eyes are framed by lashes as fine and soft as anything on the earth. They contain a vulnerability he finds near unbearable. The moment is fleeting but he feels that he only truly sees his daughter at bedtime and is granted glimpses into the wholeness of her. Once the chatter and antics subside and she rests, he is often struck by a breath-stealing recognition of the little person that he has created and must protect.

Gracey wants the best for everyone. Needs to be happy. Can only bear minor fluctuations from a condition of absolute security and contentment, or she will bruise and damage. Yet here she is, in a big, strange house echoing with black mysteries that her parents shield her from. She knows they do. Tom knows that she knows.

Out there, the old wood: a catacomb of shadows and tantalising trails boring undergrowth. An endlessly whispering sea. But into these vast spaces, these new places, death has now crept and snuffed out the warmth and companionship and love that she shared with another small life. Archie.

Tom reads all of this in his daughter's expressive face: the fast thoughts that flit across a small mind, darting like minnows in shaded depths, between concerns and revelations, to matters too awful and final to endure when so small. Children suffer and always have done. *But not mine. Not yet.* That had been the plan.

Lowering himself to Gracey, he kisses her forehead lingeringly. Her arms circle his neck.

Gracey's attention shifts to the windows.

'You're safe,' he says.

Gracey isn't convinced. 'Them trees. Frighten me.'

Tom sits back and holds one of his daughter's hands. Gracey grips her penguin tighter. Glancing over his shoulder at the doorway, he makes certain the coast is clear, then turns to his daughter. 'Your dad would never let anything happen to you. You're so precious to me.'

A small squeeze from her hand.

'But the other day, when you and Archie were in those woods. What did you see? *Mmm?* In the trees, before you turned back?'

Gracey's eyes widen with fearful excitement and enough gleeful satisfaction at being asked the question that Tom suspects he's inviting exaggeration.

'White people was goin' backwards in the wood house by the hill that was gonna be my den. Walkin' funny. They put a foxy in the tree. Hurted it.' Gracey's face creases to cry.

Tom uses all of his willpower to keep his expression neutral, to not respond with horror to these childlike details. 'Where was Archie?'

'Inna wood house wiv the white things. First he was scared and growling at the foxy, then he crawled inside the ring and went up the tiny hill. Was licking the piggy's leg.'

'These . . . the white things were people?'

134

Gracey shakes her head emphatically. 'Monsters with no clothes on.'

'They fed Archie?'

'He was licking a leg.'

'A leg?'

'Like he licks fingers.'

Outside a stair creaks. *Fiona.* 'Tom. A word.'

Tom flinches. Then kisses Gracey.

'Mommy gonna tuck me in?'

'Of course. She's right outside.'

'Daddy don't go.'

'Dad's just outside listening till he comes to bed. Then he'll be right next to you. Hall light's on.' Tom rises slowly from the side of the bed, winks at Gracey.

She clutches his fingers. 'When Archie goes in his garden bed, Daddy, take his blanket, so he's warm.'

Tom smiles and nods. His eyes moisten and he can only see the room as if it's underwater. He uses all of his will to not drown in the pity and love he feels for this small person, and to not sink before the horror that has come inside their lives today. He swallows but can hardly speak. Then he whispers, 'Promise.'

27

$\mathcal{N}$ ight's tide draws in, inking the uneven patio and desolation of the garden. Inside the kitchen, Fiona stands before the sink, her arms folded. Her skull's grim expression is mirrored in the windowpane.

Tom skirts the trapdoor of his wife's mood, gaping to his left, and heads for the depleted bottle of rum on the counter. He notices Fiona's laptop is open. The graphics of their online bank account scar the screen.

Without moving her head, Fiona speaks in a tense whisper she doesn't want carrying up the stairs. 'I don't want you encouraging her. With these . . . whatever they are. I don't want our child even thinking stuff like that.'

Tom splashes the ruby spirit into his glass and speaks in the same suppressed, terse voice. 'You think she's making it up?'

'Course she is. She don't know what she saw. Or if anyone was there. But let me guess, you don't think she's making it up?'

'Hard to define exactly what I think.' A mouthful of the spirit burns his gullet before becoming a crashing elevator, on fire, that impacts his stomach. 'But I will say this. Whatever is going on, and something is, it's connected to them.' Tom nods at the wall adjoining the neighbours. 'Chelsea Flower Show.'

As she turns, Fiona's eyes are closed but trembling and she's drawing a breath to launch a tirade at him.

Tom ploughs on. 'Archie? Gracey saw one of . . . someone in that wood feeding him. *Mmm?* The garden is now bloody dead. It wasn't a couple of days ago.' Tom lopes to the windowsill, steps into the remaining haze of Fiona's perfume. She still hasn't changed out of her work clothes. He picks up a lead tablet, his wrist straining at the weight, and raises his voice. He will be heard. 'What are these? All over the dead lawn our dead dog dug up. Makes you think. The last owner—'

'Paranoia. About them.' Fiona nods at the wall. 'You haven't stopped since we got here. As if we haven't got enough on our plate, Tom. This house? Everything that's wrong with it? We can barely afford the essentials and you've just blown four hundred quid on gardening stuff. Four hundred! A chainsaw?'

'Only a small one.'

'Real essential item.'

'For the hedges. Can't do them by hand.'

'When we've gotta be careful. With every penny. You haven't had a call in . . .'

'Gracey needs a garden she can play in.'

'She needs a dad who's . . .'

'What?'

'Just ignore those nutters next door.'

'I'm telling you, Fi'. From the beginning. One thing after another. The fence. The woods. They nailed a fucking fox to a tree to scare Gracey. To keep us out. Who else would have done it, or had any reason to? They did it. Them. Next door. Poisoning the neighbours' dog cos . . .' Tom pulls up. He hasn't told Fiona about the altercation that concluded with Archie squeezing one out on the neighbours' front lawn. 'It's possible. If not likely. Little Archie.'

'You don't know that.'

'You're not here during the day. You don't see those freaks.'

'No, cos I'm working. And it'll be overtime now too, or a second job, because we need that bloody roof repaired. While our child will be at after-school club. Living the dream, mate.'

Tom goes to Archie's basket and kneels. The dog is covered in a blanket.

'Mommy!'

Behind him, Fiona sighs.

'Mommy! There's a sound!'

Tom turns from where he's crouched. 'I'll go.'

'No, you bloody won't.' Fiona tears up and marches out, touching at an eye with a tissue. 'How'd you expect her to sleep after making her imagine all of that!'

Upstairs, Gracey starts crying. The very sound makes him feel twice as awful as he's done since they found Archie stiff with death. He can't abide Gracey or Fiona crying and will usually do and say anything to make them stop.

28

A torch balanced upon an old brick illumines Tom's sexton labours as he spades the last of the disrupted soil into the small grave. At the end of his atrophied garden, he then pats the earth flat, before reaching for the little cross he made from two fence slats. ARCHIE is written on the rough timber in white paint left over from the master bedroom. Tom sinks the stake into the soil, then buckles Archie's collar about the cross-section of the marker.

The mournful dusk inhabits Tom's heart as much as it does the sky and air. He turns the same pewter colour inside as he presses his hand against the broken ground and whispers, 'Little man.'

In days to come, his daughter will cover this ground with votive offerings. Too easily he imagines plastic bowls with daisies withering and lolling inside them. Sprigs of berries for sure; whatever she can forage to lay here while she chatters to the spent shape beneath the soil, remembering how a pup's moist, pleading eyes once filled her with a love too painful to recall.

Wiping at a cheek, Tom surveys the devastation of his land. Smashed fence panels stacked like storm wreckage. Dead plants. Wormy fruit on the apple trees ringed by drunken flies.

They've only been here a fortnight and he's already burying their dog and standing upon a blighted lawn. A four-year old's forays into the woods resulted in a mutilated fox hung from a tree.

Coincidence? Fuck right off.

Tom eyes the woods. A jagged silhouette dissolving into charcoal. Within the trees he senses gnarled and scaly shins, dew-dripping caverns, wet burrows veining scrub storing leagues of shadow, scent-peppered paths where small creatures flit and hunt each other.

A memory falls across his thoughts: a weight crashing through the canopy. Something bulky launching from one tree to another. *What was that?* Gracey's story about funny-talking white monsters walking backwards. Archie drinking from the 'piggy's leg'. He can make no sense of it. Nor the idea of a 'lady' that Gracey alleges called her into the trees to collect her toy. Could this be inspired by the stories they read to her, the cartoons she watches? They're so careful with what she's exposed to.

But their pup is now under half a metre of churned soil, about to be digested by the natural processes of a rural world in which he'd wanted his family to find happiness. This he cannot deny, spin or make good.

And has his family merely moved here to expire too, to be reduced to mere traces? Bones in soil. A legacy of half-finished rooms for new owners to inspect, mere months after his family's brief tenure. Too easily, he imagines future hearsay from an estate agent. And gossip in the village about a similar run of bad luck that dogged their predecessor, who swung from a light fitting within six months of buying the house.

Nobody could tell Tom why *he* did it, or who *he* was. That man's mark upon this place was nothing more than a couple of neatly decorated rooms, smooth floorboards, some lengths of bright new wiring, his death. Unfinished, his life and the building he renovated.

But they'll know what happened. Next door.

Tom's gaping tightens to a glare which moves to the proud lines and imperious roof of the Moots' house. A subtle gleam of woodwork in dying light fashions a predator's grin. Curtains drawn. He imagines they can see in the dark and roam through their perfect dollhouse without electricity.

Them.

They inhabit his mind.

The smirk of Magi Moot, condescension from first contact. The diminutive and strident Mrs Moot; a puppet-limbed scarecrow whittled by spite's razor. Proprietary and rude. *Bristle-cheeked witch. Playmobil hair,* he thinks unkindly and almost smiles. That's what Mrs Moot's head brings to mind: Gracey's tiny plastic people with the clip-on wigs. He wonders if Magi cuts his wife's hair with the garden shears, fashioning that henna bulb about the haggard, joyless face. The memory of her mean, diluted blue eyes mocks him.

What would make them smile? Someone else's misery.

Tom's laugh is more of a bark. Raucous, it grates the still evening like the crowing of a pitiless bird about to eat another's eggs in the wood.

Are we to be bullied?

How many incursions is he expected to tolerate? If the Moots are capable of trapping and throttling a fox with wire and poisoning a beautiful spaniel pup for taking a crap on their lawn, then what else might they do to their neighbours?

One man has already died here.

The visitors, kissing Mrs Moot's hand. Deference bent their curtseys low. The absurdity of the gestures!

Fear. They, the Moots, want to be dreaded. No one could ever like the freaks but the Moots will accept terror over affection. Fawning respect is what they crave; timorous subjugation before their impossible standards.

Not I.

You have to trust your instincts in these matters.

These people are not right. They mean his family harm. The displays of superiority, the belittling and undermining of him at every opportunity: all this is strategically wrought, concealing something more sinister that has begun to seep across the border.

They despise you. Their minds were made up about his family before they even set foot on the property. *It's not you, it's them.* And *they* won't stop. For as long as his family resides here, the torments will continue and escalate in severity.

Maybe the Moots sensed he was close to breaking and at his most vulnerable. With such a burden of responsibility upon his shoulders, they wished to hasten his fall.

At the edge of his eye, the makeshift marker on Archie's grave earths Tom, coldly. His thoughts lose their footing and stumble until all he can think of is a family member murdered. *Because that's who you were, my little man: one of us.*

Tom's jaw clamps, his bite sharpens. Before calmer thoughts gather to question the compulsion, his legs carry him to the shed. Behind him, the very trees form an audience, the wind a crowd's roar, urging him on. And with each stride a little more of the unbearable pressure of his frustration is released. He's broken the seal and this surge of rancour will become fury when it touches air.

Fucking years of it. Had enough. All of it, of everything. Fucking, fucking, fuck off!

Tom unlatches the flimsy door of his armoury, swings it wide. A man possessed by his own demon, he spits into the gloom, speckling the rubbish and rot therein. Diesel of creosote, mildew on wooden slats, the sepulchral aroma of frass: scents of the woody cave of the shed that stirred memories of his own childhood when he first opened this door. How he'd recalled hours of mooching inside his granddad's potting shed and his dad's piny hut. And for the first time in years he remembered how his own thin boy-arms used to raise heavy tools reeking of oil. Pricking his fingers on the teeth of a saw too, bleeding among the cobwebs; then building the courage to confess to having been where he should not have been. Tonight, he's where he should not be again, to collect another type of weapon.

Before him, inside the tangy, cobwebby confines of this shed – his *own* shed! – lie the rusting and mould-spotted relics abandoned by former occupants, crowding shelves and huddling in corners: brown plastic pots, blanched seed packets, a broken broom, a table more fungus than wood, two garden chairs of bleached canvas, metal frames leprous with corrosion, dust-furred paint pots. All of it connected by deep funnels of spider web, encrusted at depth with pearlescent eggs. *And a new chainsaw!* Still gleaming and shop-bright. He bends into the dross and shadow and uncoils the weapon's lead.

At a half-lit bedroom window, Fiona watches. Arms folded, face long, she turns away without Tom noticing she was there.

Tom's legs carry him to one of the kitchen sockets. From there, he unravels the cable and charts a course for the border. Across this bleak land, only he moves, striding the bumpy, holed earth, bedraggled with blight. He plays out the electric line like a fisherman lowering a crab pot, the shiny umbilical cord slapping his heels. In the crook of an elbow he cradles the long, thin blade of the saw; untested in combat but not for long. Retreating into the distance, the open shed gapes blackly, a silent mouth wide with the horror of what it's unleashed.

A quick march and Tom's before the ornamental trees overhanging the lower section of the fence, still upright by the patio. From here, he can better see exactly what was intended when the Moots planted their trees. The border on this side of his property is his responsibility but they have made it impossible for their neighbours to manage the demarcation. By planting the birch trees they have laid claim to the boundary.

Trinity College trees, he thinks, with the V-shaped thrust of branches, raising thin limbs in supplication to the sky. The foliage will inevitably umbrella onto his side. *They* knew it would: a determined force of attrition forced this fence, his fence, to buckle and break apart from the posts.

Where he can see through gaps, the ground between the base of the trees appears clear, pampered and neat. The birches are newly planted; additions that have not yet blended into the landscaped showpiece of next door's garden. Maybe the trees were installed when his house was empty, the neighbours erecting symbols of their dominance after his predecessor committed suicide? The Moots would have seen the tragedy as an opportunity to encroach upon the hated border. *Of course!* And the replacement fence they demanded of him would have required erection deeper inside his garden to allow for the pale, reaching limbs of the Moots' birches.

They even want your land.

This slender line of turf may well have been fought over for years before he moved here. The disputed terrain of the border is only a few centimetres wide, the width of a fence post. A trifling measurement that serves to both encapsulate and intensify the pettiness of the couple next door.

And these trees are watchtowers. Sentry boxes casting shade onto his property as the sun moves from east to west. From midday to early afternoon, they will keep his lawn in shadows that will lengthen as the trees grow higher. The Moots established this beachhead to occupy the soil and air of his property and to cast his family into darkness. The lower branches are jackboots, kicking his door in.

I will not allow it.

At the front line, the grunt then roar of a chainsaw obliterates the tranquillity of dusk. At this explosion of noise, at so late an hour, the trees of the wood appear overawed, subdued by shock.

Tom eases his finger from the trigger as lights flash on next door, upstairs. White lances glare around the Moots' curtains. Two pairs of eyes must be desperate to see outside.

Tom squeezes the trigger again and a grunting power shakes his hands and quakes the world to a shimmer. He feels an urge to plunge spinning teeth deep into meat and he lofts the whirring blade to the top of the sagging fence. Clumsy and staggering from the weight of the raised weapon, he places the blade upon the pale neck of the first tree.

The chainsaw blade skids about smooth bark and bounces away.

Tom clenches his fist on the handle.

When he gets the metal teeth to scrape again at the white bark of the first leafy offender, the tree quivers, even cowers.

Tom pushes the chainsaw harder until the blade grips then chews the sappy innards of the first nape. Powerful vibrations shake his bloodless hands, transmitting the machine's desperation, until it slices clean and out the other side.

Lopped at shoulder height, the bushy head of the tree topples sideways into its neighbour. Rustling as they crash together, the undamaged tree attempts to hold its butchered comrade aloft, but the fallen treetop is too cumbersome and disappears beyond the fence.

Tom moves down the line.

Papery leaves and rubbery twigs extend so far onto his property that they spike at his face, as if in some final, desperate defence against superior firepower.

It's dark and getting darker, the atmosphere seeming to judge his actions. He can hardly see what he is doing, where he is cutting. But he is bolstered by the assurance that if these had been his trees, the Moots would have cut them back. As if next door would accept a solitary frond from his garden overhanging the border! *Preposterous!*

Fiona appears at the kitchen window. Throws it wide. Her face stricken as she calls out.

Deafened by the chainsaw, Tom doesn't hear her.

Bliss now engorges his every muscle and sinew from ankle to neck. He's not felt so drunk and joyous in years. He's inebriated, reeling; the live current that powers his weapon lights up his arteries and turns his nerve endings into Christmas lights.

He cuts a swathe across the greening, sagging fence panels. Two. Three. Four. Five trees. Felled.

Thank you, my brother, the fence seems to intimate. *Reinforcements at last to release us from this burden that grows stiff along our bent backs and kicks our feet from under us.*

Tom sings along to this great outpouring, this sluicing of rage. No one can hear him. He can say anything at this defining moment, anything at all in this collision of wills at the border of his new life. And he is elated, freed and made buoyant by new vigour, compelled by the sheer ecstasy of inflicting revenge.

'Respect this fucking border!'

They never saw this coming. He'll fight fear with fear. *To the end.*

Hit them where it will hurt most.

Fiona is behind him on the grass. Maybe she has been for some time but the blizzard blowing so hard inside his skull and blinding his vision to everything save destruction makes him unsure when she appeared. There may have been a tremulous hand on his shoulder at one point. But right now, her hands are pressed onto her cheeks. She's shouting but there's only the accelerating, overheating scream of the reaper that still shakes within his arms. Anger is automated, powered beyond restraint.

One by one, the remaining birch trees go down, shaking in protest before slumping onto the neighbours' side of the fence. Groomed border guards toppled, put to the sword. At least a dozen but he's stopped counting. Decapitated unto the last man standing where the Moots smashed his fence down.

At the rear of the Moots' property, the interior lights create a misty glow about their French windows and kitchen. An opening door, out of sight, extends the lambent area further across their sunless, sleeping garden; a sanctum rudely awoken and traumatised by the sudden violence of an attack upon itself, and upon those who tend its perfection daily.

Only when the last trunk topples does exhaustion catch up with Tom. But the deed is done.

Fiona scurries along the decaying lawn, following the cable like she's chasing a twenty-pound note plucked from a hand by the wind and blown along a footpath. She disappears inside the kitchen and, moments later, the chainsaw whines down, its power gone.

As the grinding din of the chainsaw empties from Tom's numbed skull, he can do nothing but stare at the red weapon he grips. Inhaling the motor's oil, dazed as adrenalin drains from his limbs, he finds himself irritated by the chainsaw's whining to silence. He feels there was more cutting to be done. His ears ring like a cold bell tower.

I am man. But he pants like a thirsty hound.

Night has all but fallen, yet he sees more of the world now that the birch trees have been rendered into branchless poles. A bigger sky confronts him, inked by cold space and spotted with distant thermonuclear explosions.

Fiona reappears holding the plug and cord. 'You lost your bloody mind?'

Right then, the screaming starts.

Fiona and Tom turn to the sagging fence. Apertures in the fence slats catch the light pouring from the house next door, like a searchlight seeking the source of the terrible sound of woe, the hysteria unleashed in next door's garden.

It's Mrs Moot, inconsolable at the desecration of her trees. Close to the tatty boundary, close to the ground as if she is on her knees, Mrs Moot falls apart. So high is her wailing skirl, Tom is reminded of a Middle Eastern funeral lament, as well as something that might not even be human. Her mind must have snapped from the horror and disbelief of what he has done to her ornamental phalanx of birch.

Over there, out of sight, Magi Moot adds bass. As if stabbed through the side and forced to watch himself leak blackly through his prissy fingers, he groans.

The tremendous satisfaction Tom feels is momentary. And then his elation is gone and he becomes again the man of sorrow who held the weight of their dead puppy against his chest; his own heart thudding as if in some futile attempt to resuscitate the dog. A fuller sense of the wanton destruction he's just wrought leaves him nauseous.

In an attempt to revive the dying embers of his purpose, he shouts in the direction of the neighbours, to offer justification for what has been done, 'I didn't come here to bury our dog!'

After gaping wordlessly at Tom, as if she doesn't recognise her husband at all, Fiona throws down the plug and cord, turns her back on him and stamps into the house.

Tom steps away from the boundary, the cumbersome chainsaw dragging at the end of a spent arm. His coals cold, only now does disbelief begin to settle as he stares at the weapon. He doesn't want it in his hand anymore.

Across the border, he's reduced the Moots to dark lumps, huddled against the soil. He can't see much of them but can hear them, sobbing and whimpering.

Job done.

29

*B*ehind his heels, the toilet rinses more than flushes. Under the floorboards, a knocking protest ensues as if all the energy of the flush is uselessly contained between the floors and not inside the bowl where it needs to be. He'd forgotten his own rule of not flushing at night. Sometimes Gracey wakes crying in terror at the sound.

Tom shuts the door on the shaking mess but the eruption in the pipes pursues him across the landing, banging behind his heels like the fists of angry neighbours. He wearily wonders if they will soon be reduced to using a bucket filled with water to sluice the pan clean.

Wearing only his socks and underpants, he wanders inside his daughter's empty pink room. New paint gleams in low light above new flooring, its chill passing through his socks.

On the landing, his tools and decorating materials are stacked against one wall, a dust sheet folded over his workhorse bench, parked at the side of the passage.

Tom pushes the door of the master bedroom to create a narrow gap. Peers inside and sees Fiona asleep, facing the window, arms encircling Gracey. Half of that small form protrudes from the duvet, skinny legs akimbo, arms clutching another new Waddles. They look exhausted.

Tom stoops and picks up the bedding that Fiona has left outside the room for him. A sleeping bag, a pillow. As he raises the bed linen, a faint residual tremor of the chainsaw's grind shudders inside his shoulders. He turns away from his family and makes for the top of the stairs.

Propped up on their old couch before the uncurtained windows of the living room, Tom faces the garden. Dim light leaks from a lamp, angled down, at the foot of the sofa. Up to his shoulders his body is cocooned inside the sleeping bag.

He can't remember the exact details of each episode but he estimates there have been no more than three clashes, in their past, when Fiona was this angry with him. Too angry to speak. But the silence will thaw and she will unpick the stitches of his actions tonight, across the coming days, and he will feel punctured and he will sag with remorse.

Around him, an unfinished room glimmers, softening to dusk in the corners. A scent of dereliction lingers. The cold of outdoors mingling with interior damp. The mealy smell that infuses the kitchen rises in here too. He's not noticed it before. Mouse piss.

The wretchedness he feels is evident in the pallid reflection of his morose face, screened upon a dusty pane of glass in the old French windows. *Is that how I really look now? How often do I have that face?* He looks past his reflection and watches the moon instead; three quarters full, illumined as if from within. The sky around its pitted face is pitch.

Sipping rum, he considers next door. On the other side of that wall, beyond a thin skin of bricks, the Moots are probably awake and in counsel. Maybe *she* is sobbing at the kitchen table while Magi comforts her with another steaming mug of herbal tea. Both will be wrapped in dressing gowns, their old feet concealed by slippers.

Madman. Lunatic. Thug. Vandal. Bastard. He imagines the tirade levelled against him.

At least, the police remain a no-show. The nearest station is forty kilometres distant. He assumes the police have been called and that a report has been made but a neighbour lopping their trees may not warrant an emergency. But he will Google the bylaws about foliage overhanging a border before the law arrives in daylight.

Clumsily, Tom returns the empty glass to the floor beside his makeshift bed. Extinguishes the lamp. Settles down. Only sleep can save him now and put him out of this misery. For a while.

In darkness, he watches the distant moon through lidded eyes.

Water.

Water so dark he sees nothing below the surface lapping his ankle bones. Only a dim and broken reflection of his pale nakedness is reflected.

But his entire form is instantly thrilled by the cool balm of the water swishing about his feet. The cushioning sand beneath his soles and the cool black shallows kindle him with new and invigorating life. His senses immediately sharpen. So keen are they that even in such darkness he detects the motion of the others, who walk silently here but withdraw to let him pass.

A powerful, clean smell of moist rock and pure water inflates his chest. So potent is the air he inhales so deeply that the tight grip of his fear becomes feeble, loosens, is blown away along with all the pressing concerns that shape and direct his thoughts, and engage him in frantic races that have no finishing-lines. Dry leaves scattering behind his heels.

Had he not been seduced by the flame ahead, his standing in water would shock him more. But before his eyes, a sinewy column of deep orange fire pours upwards into darkness, without a flicker. He thinks it wonderful.

Silence in profound stillness around the flickering light. The hypnotic tug of the fire. A gravity like a current pulls him deeper into the flame's orbit.

So energised in every limb, so roused in spirit, he wants to roar from sheer joy. An overwhelming revelation of his true vitality is near. The closer he moves towards the nourishing, wondrous flame, the more intense the potency he draws from the water.

A fire without much heat, the height of a door, that embraces his tingling, open skin. Stepping through the fire is akin to passing through a warm waterfall.

To appear inside the cave of which the flame marks a boundary he has crossed.

A revelation, a full and complete understanding of himself and his place in the world, of the world itself and all that is below, beyond and above it, awaits inside this cavern. If this is the passage to death then he will take it without so much as a glance over his shoulder.

Naked, swallowed by this wondrous, gentle void, he submerges into nothingness. The sense of inhabiting a body falls away with the trifles of an oppressive past. Here, all of that is rendered meaningless.

The void takes new shape beyond the flame and glistens with diaphanous crystals. They speckle the walls of a cavern, the rock arcing then narrowing into an entrance. Low light issues from an oval aperture, leading to a large tunnel at the far end of the cave. From within the new passage rushes the fast-flowing music of a new body of water.

He enters the passage as if he is approaching the banks of a mighty, dark river beyond. A river that created its own bed at the dawn of time.

As he emerges from the passage and into a second cavern, he might have stepped into a vast shadow, as high as a mountain.

Such age he senses here, in this crude cathedral of stone, its true volume and distant extents remaining unclear. But the merest suggestion of the origins and purpose of this space belittles him to an insignificance that is exquisitely terrifying. If awareness dared to quest and grow here, oblivion would put a welcome end to comprehension.

Towards a new light at the far end of the cavern he continues, water soundlessly rippling his ankles, the muscular tumult of the unseen river growing, funnelling at his ears. Unto the dim smudge of light he strives, close to tears in his haste to greet the power of the promise that awaits.

A thin hush of a breeze moves through him, inspiring a deep thirst for a wonder he left in childhood and has forgotten. Its revival brings tears to his eyes. They run freely as he glides through the dark, enclosed by indistinct walls of ancient rock. The sound of the unseen underground river grows deafening.

Ahead, a second flame, identical to the one he passed through, will guide him through the next stretch of this odyssey. He knows this instinctively and onwards and deeper he ventures until an array of sigils bring him to a halt.

They gleam from rock-faces vaulting to a roof as vast as a great sky. His mind swoops and his feet stumble; he careens sideways. He will not look up for fear of falling vertically.

The signs soon entrance him, hold his stare fast. He rights himself and understands that he has encountered these markings before. Symbols that appear to him like faded and concealed memories, just beyond his reach.

Far above, he imagines flying buttresses, ribbed vaulting, a clerestory riddled with more symbols; the cavern a space hollowed and hallowed by meanings and presences he'll never understand.

He implores the sigils for their meanings. Old, weathered markings, decorating damp stone walls that dome the great flame in the vast, awesome stone nave.

Beneath his feet and beyond the walls the unseen torrent rages, tempting him closer to find its edge and the assurance of a searing, blinding ecstasy. A submersion that no soul could withstand. Yet every soul would willingly leap into the unseen onyx current, to drown in a momentary bliss bordering torment.

But the power of the single flame is even greater. Unto it he pads as if to the heart of this underworld region.

Here stands a stone plinth, from which the great smokeless flame leaps silently. A crude, weathered block. No fuel for the fire is evident but upon the rim of the dolmen, and about its foundations, red flowers with petals vivid as blood garland the stone.

Beyond the flame, firelight touches the vague outline of another solid object. A second blockish form.

A large, crude throne seemingly carved not by hand but by erosion across a span of time he cannot guess. So engulfing would be the terror of knowing how long this seat has occupied the apse before the flaming altar that to save his mind his thoughts rout.

Suffocating dread is mere preparation for what sits upon the stone. More than a glimpse might destroy his eyes and mind, smash them flat like birds' eggs pressed underfoot. Inhaling sharply, he covers his face in its presence. Naked, reduced, his wits ransacked by panic, he sinks to his knees, abject, begging not to see, or be seen.

By the figure. That wills him to look upon it. A figure mostly indistinct, save for a length of horn. Or are they vast ears, extruding from a cowled head with the features hidden? The black blades rise into darkness, their thick and bestial roots crowned with a tiara of the same red flowers that litter the altar. And are those arms at rest upon the hoary rock, or forelegs as narrow as bones peeled of flesh? The torso appears collapsed, vague within the murk of the cavern. The hem of a robe cascades to cover shrivelled legs, impressed against the garment like roots beneath topsoil.

A statue, he hopes more than he has hoped for anything. Let this only be an idol, he prays. But to what does he plead for mercy? What other god could be more powerful and fearful than *this*?

Water roars.

Tom wakes beside the sofa, on his knees. Hard floorboards burn his skin. His hands cover his face as they did at the end of the dream. Protecting him from what sat . . .

A dream . . . underground. Where it was marvellous. And so frightening. *Black water. Signs upon walls. Flames. A figure. That thing upon a stone throne* . . .

Tom peers about the room. Tentatively touches a floorboard to make certain the room is there.

What would make him see all of that? He's never had a dream like it; not even the vivid torments of the highest fever compare. This wasn't disjointed or nonsensical but a clear narrative.

He rises unsteadily and his joints crack. He stumbles to the patio doors where a bright moon glazes the long panes of glass; a lunar luminance misting vague lumps that re-form the garden after sundown. At the rim of the woods the thin light settles like vapour.

Stepping between the rickety doors, he gulps chilled night air. Eyes closed, bending over, hands upon knees, he wants the sensation of the cold patio slabs beneath his unshod feet to startle a true awareness awake.

A murmur of raised voices crosses the border from next door, the words indiscernible.

Tom straightens and stares at the newly cropped trees, the haggard silhouette of the shipwrecked fence. A boundary fought over mere hours before.

He feels his way along the wasteland of a former flower bed. As if he is walking on lumpy biscuits, clumps of soil crumple beneath his bare soles. Weeds catch between his toes. Scrub prickles and crunches in protest at his trespass, forcing him to where the foliage is thinner.

A panel split from a wormy post offers a slit. He peers into the inky void.

There's light over there, towards the end of the neighbours' garden. They're up there, at the boundary of the woods. They must be, the Moots. A torch's sabre scythes, then is doused behind obstructions, plants, the pond ornament and small trees. A second beam is trained upon the ground, in an open space, dispersing the illumination outwards, to the wood.

Tom stares about his feet, seeking clear passage to his ruined lawn. He can see nothing but steps into darkness anyway. As he tiptoes onto the bumpy earth of the dead lawn, a sharp object stabs his arch and he swallows a shriek.

Wearing a shirt and underpants and creeping up the garden at a crouch, he feels ridiculous. The cold catches at his breath now, numbs his hands, his feet, and bruises his nose and inner ears to an ache. But he must see what they are doing. He hasn't a watch, though guesses it's about three in the morning. Any later and the sky would lighten.

The upper third of his garden, where the fence is missing, opens onto the neighbours' arboretum. He's more exposed when so close to the gap the neighbours smashed into his garden, so he drops to all fours to slip forward.

Beyond the groynes of the last standing fence posts, an array of the Moots' neat shrubbery offers him fresh, unlit cover. Unless they were to walk to the very border and direct light into his garden, they won't see him there.

A childish glee compels him over the last ten metres, to the top right corner that is entirely lost to darkness. Dew splashes his inner thighs and forearms as he scampers. And where the wood surges over their fence, he is able to stand upright and concealed.

From here, he peers into the garden next door and is offered a murky view all the way to the neighbours' back door. And yet, no sooner does he strain his eyes at where the torchlight plays than he wishes that he'd stayed indoors with the French windows closed. And locked.

The landscaped miniature lawn at the top of the Moots' garden, which would look more at home on an exclusive golf course, is entirely coated white.

A few moments are necessary for him to discern, aided by the glow of the Moots' torches, the texture of the pale surface. Fabric, or cotton, because he is staring at an arrangement of white sheets. And the bushy lumps laid in a row upon the linen sheets are the tops of the trees that he lopped earlier. The severed trunks now lie in state, like the heads of royals or saints.

The toppled crowns conjure a memory of the lament that he heard earlier. Tonight, he clearly sawed through heartwood and the Moots have since gathered their dead. The trees were truly beloved and with reverence his neighbours have lined the fallen boughs upon burial shrouds.

Whoever is speaking next door is not speaking in English as they increase their murmuring to an indignant rant. As if he's been confronted by the deranged, speaking in tongues, this guttural intonation of so many crude and mangled words swamps him with revulsion. And curiosity. He rises to his toes, his vision tracking to the origin of the horrid voice.

His inquisitiveness swiftly transforms into gaping disbelief.

A lone, pale figure emerges from behind a miniature island of night-blackened flowers.

A torch is positioned on the ground like a footlight, to illumine the horrid passage of the white figure onto this strange, bright stage. The bearer of the second torch remains hidden from sight, clothed by murk and the leafy barriers of the middle garden, but the second torch adds additional illumination, a peripheral glow.

Gracey's *Whiteys*.

As it silently passes through the light, there is an insubstantial, tenuous quality to the silhouette's movement. Through the incorporeality of the atmosphere, the emerging chalky form seems to glide across the white sheets, the tread silent. When the figure turns about, as if to confront the stone imp in the pond, Tom flinches. And though the light only mists the form with a thin luminance, it reveals enough to make Tom wish the apparition had remained unlit.

Upon a seemingly bloodless body, a dark head tops bony shoulders: an absurdly oversized and grotesque headpiece, transforming the entire head of the wearer into lumpy contours. But horrible details are visible. Chiefly, a pair of bristly ears and cruel tusks that curl about an open maw. Beneath the snout, a row of doglike teeth are stained the colour of grimy sea shells. The mask either depicts, or actually is, the black and bristling head of a wild boar.

Below the misshapen head, the lithe human body is ashen from head to foot. It has been daubed or smeared with a white substance that has dried like baked mud. Myriad black cracks attribute a horrible age to the flesh.

Beast-headed but the thing is human and female, is slender-hipped with small breasts upturned to sharp nipples.

The figure raises a bare foot from the grass until the masked woman is balancing her weight upon the other stringy leg, which she keeps straight like a ballerina at the bar. She is closely mimicking the posture of the imp-statue. Flesh and stone face each other. An arm delicately unfolds from the woman's bony side and stretches outwards. A hand uncurls. Upon the end of that extremity, a single finger is stained darker than the limb. The discoloured digit solemnly points across the border, over the devastated lawn, to pick out Tom's house.

From the permanently open jaws of the animal mask, more gibberish chatters. The unrecognisable tongue is now grunted more than spoken and suggests the phlegmy croak of a toad. The tone was already coarse but this foul outburst is defined by a peculiar vitriol, a hatefulness.

Any courage and purpose carrying Tom this far evaporates. If he hears much more of this voice, he suspects his mind will unravel. He clamps his hands over his ears. But that hardly stays the horror.

With the two torches now functioning as house lights, a second form emerges from the wings to tread the stage. And upon the white sheets, a series of delicate, mincing steps soundlessly carry the new player to where the pig stands upon one leg.

Conjuring the image of a ghastly ballet dancer, prancing from the grave to court a swinish devil, the second chalky phantom possesses the sparseness of an old man's limbs and frame. But the skin is boyishly smooth and also coated white.

The second head has been transformed by a grisly headdress too, one patchily furred and elongating to a muzzle. Eye sockets as big as hen's eggs sit atop the skull. Ragged ears sprout vertically as if stricken into alertness. It's a large hare, the body skinned to smooth fat; something that could only hop through a nightmare, or through some gruesome *avante-garde* pantomime.

The terrible face of the hare also confronts the stone imp within the pond, an ornament that increasingly resembles a shrine. And though upright, this second character's elbows rest against a hairless chest so that the reedy forearms dangle like those of an animal resting upon its hindquarters. And so lifelike is the posture, the hands might even be bony paws.

Then, as if to better demonstrate the bestial qualities of its guise, the hare-thing sinks to a crouch before creeping across the white sheets to the boar. Who retains her position upon one leg and continues to point at Tom's house. When the ghastly hare reaches the pig, it lowers its long face in deference.

Before Tom can look away, the hare issues a horrible squeal of excitement. Like a lamb below its mother's belly, the hare's bumpy nose proceeds to worry at the inner thigh of the boar, before beginning an eager suckling of the teat that it finds there. Lapping and gulping sounds soon ensue until the sound of its feeding grows too noisome.

Tom sits down and presses his hands even harder against his ears. What remains of his concentration he employs to keep down the hot, sour contents of his stomach. Only when he hears the metallic chink of the neighbours' gate being unlatched does he look up and peer at the Moots' empty garden.

30

*W*armed by jeans, jumper and work boots and gripping a torch he keeps switched off, Tom returns quietly and with purpose to his garden.

He quickly moves to the thick darkness of the bordering wood.

There are voices. Out there. A murmur becoming an intonation of raised voices far away among the silent trees. A sequence of barked cries in rhythm that comes and goes.

Wariness intensifying to fear, Tom hesitates at the gate.

The Moots. It's his neighbours he can hear; people transformed into these grotesque 'whitey' things. What Gracey saw. They're mad. As mad as pale serpents that wait in the undergrowth, seeking opportunities to bite and poison.

Tom looks back to his house, drawn by the thought of Gracey and Fiona sleeping. A yearning holds him still until he returns his attention to the forbidding treeline, a pitch-black and rustling wall.

Instinct warns him to never confront the neighbours again, in any circumstances. To never risk another encounter with their sinister craziness. But he has a more compelling need: to convince himself that what he has just witnessed is nothing more than grotesque rural eccentricity. He knows that he will not rest until he knows who the Moots really are. *What* they are. *What* he has moved his family to live beside.

He should never have cut down their trees.

Regret feels like a breastplate made of lead. The shadow

of terrible consequences that he's introduced into his life, *their lives*, seems to have exposed his nerves to a new kind of static. The opportunity to turn a blind eye, as his wife sagely advised, is long gone. This dispute has passed far beyond weathering a neighbour's petty torments.

Angling the torch beam at where he places his feet, he moves as stealthily as he is able, his sight and hearing a low-powered radar, directed towards the distant chatter: two voices now, if that's what they could possibly be, calling to each other.

Along the mud path he slips and slides, head down. Attempts to smother his rapid, nervous panting only shorten his breath. An arrhythmic heartbeat disorientates him as much as the oppressive darkness; a void crowding the frail torchlight, as if the very trees are issuing the impenetrable darkness in protest at any dilution his watery beam attempts.

A few hundred metres inside and the voices are less obscured by the acres of trunk, foliage and scrub. At the limit of his hearing, the speakers' mouths might now be crammed with food, or their chattering concealed by cloth. But from what is decipherable, despite the lower registers they contrive with their vocal cords, he still recognises the speakers.

Mrs Moot, who growls as much as she speaks. 'Under the earth . . . The sow.'

Answered by Magi. 'Blessed bitch . . . The earth.'

Oh Christ. His hair feels as if it's attached to his scalp with pins.

Just preposterous. *The things that people get up to.*
Whitey things.

Tom kills the torch. Crouching, he waits for his eyes to accustom to the darkness.

At the perimeter of a clearing he slows until he's merely inching forward. There, bent over with one hand impressed into cold soil, he finds a gap sufficient for a frightened face to peer through. And within a circular arrangement of saplings, a woodland glade opens to his eyes.

A circular space, flickering amber. A place he has not seen by day, or twilight, because he's never reached this far when hunting for Gracey's penguins.

Gracey's woodland house? Where the lady spoke to her?

A sooty light clings to these trees, as if a dirty vestige of the day became trapped when night fell. But the smeared and swaying illumination is not residual: it oscillates from lit tapers, flames upon poles planted about the foliage bearding the glade.

The grassy mound is manmade. An earthwork. Spherical, as if cupped and smoothed by a potter's wet hands.

A pampered, grassy moat rings the hill like another fussed-over lawn. Such perfection strikes him as immediately incongruous amidst the tangle and leaning boughs of the wood. This place is maintained, the site is curated as if sacred, the grove groomed as precisely as the Moots' gardens. Their mania and obsession extends here.

The neighbours' warnings about the woods and their aversion to trespassers suddenly makes sense. This is a place they don't want investigated. And for good reason. *Because of this, this horrible thing that they do here.*

Movement stirs the glade. From out of an infernal tiger-stripe of shadow, Mrs Moot appears. Naked and lithe, she moves backwards. Her strut is ridiculous but horribly compelling. A drawn-out walk. A mime artist mimicking a world set to reverse.

The bristly, tusked pig mask still conceals her entire head, the bone spurs thrusting from her crude mouth. The flesh of her exposed body remains plastered and ashen but as she orbits the grassy mound, black streaks become visible. They stain her shoulders, breasts and belly.

As she passes a taper, mounted high upon an iron stave, the drying tributaries that mark her flesh gleam crimson. Glittering ruby splashes of fresh blood.

No longer the rude, imperious oddball he confronted in her garden and porch, this persona is *other*, something else. A woman transformed. She has thirty or more years on Tom but the supple power she wields in every limb excites and revolts him. Aghast, and unintentionally bowing, Tom lowers himself to the mulch of soil and leaf-fall, his jeans sodden in an instant.

Daring to raise his face, but only once *she* is concealed again behind the mound, he stills his jumping eyes to better survey as much of the visible glade as he can.

Four thick tapers on iron stands impose four markers into the grove: north, south, east, west. A crude stone dolmen serves for an altar, positioned before the flames marking north. Upon its summit a black animal is splayed, butchered. A goat or lamb, he thinks, from what he can see of the lolling head.

Closing his eyes on the tortured statement, though it cannot be unseen, he thinks of gambolling Archie, that snuffler of chins. His disbelief is usurped by his revulsion. Nor does his growing familiarity with this lunacy lessen a terror he's not encountered since infancy. And has he not seen something like this grove before? *In the dream!* Though this version of the altar is rusted by animal blood; in his nightmare, a similar stone plinth was garlanded by red flowers.

Last seen suckling betwixt the ghastly legs of his pig-wife, and still wearing the hare headpiece, a naked Magi Moot soon prances into view and draws Tom's eyes.

Light upon those bony toes, he moves the counter-clockwise route the boar trod. While still stained white and made bloodless like the dead, his narrow chest is similarly streaked crimson and black as if a recent and messy guzzling produced spills. Maddeningly white and wide, his excited eyes glimmer inside the sockets of the lumpy, oversized face that he has transplanted onto his human visage. The whiskered muzzle bobs as he moves, the tatty ears spear vertical.

When the figure dances across the spy-hole, Tom presses himself earthward as if genuflecting before this terrible sect, priesting its hideous ritual.

Mad fuckers.

Beast-headed Mrs Moot lopes out again from behind the mound and heads to the altar.

Repelled but unable to not look, Tom raises his head a fraction to better see the north of the glade, where the pig comes to a standstill and positions itself behind the stained rock.

Hands raised, palms facing the sky, the boar stands upon one leg and holds the same awful pose Mrs Moot assumed in the garden, before the stone imp of the ornamental pond. She faces the grassy mound, her petite and mired breasts rising and falling from the exertion of the backwards dance. And from the open mouth of the swinish head, a breathless but elated voice incants, 'In the room beneath the earth I saw the sow.'

Shifting in the soil, Tom glances south and locates the chalky hare. It too has stopped striding backwards and stands at the opposite side of the grove, its long feet set in the first position of ballet. Hands raised at either side, palms facing the sky as if commanding an audience to rise, Magi answers the pig's call. 'We fed the sow. Blessed bitch. Blessed virgin. Our mother of the soil.'

The pig. 'Above the room beneath the earth we are exulted.'

Call and answer, tossed across the glade between the Moots. And immediately, as if some infernal sluice has opened, a sound of running water covers the earth.

So loud and clear is the gush that Tom wouldn't be surprised to find himself lying face-down in a swiftly running stream. Desperately, he looks about himself but there is no stream here. And yet the silvery, bubbling song of a brook flows without cease, about his face and through the darkness that suffocates the ground that he can barely see.

Again, remembrance serves as curse and intensifies his fear to panic. This is the soundscape of the dream he so recently suffered. So has he transported the music of subterranean water from a sleeping vision to these woods? Or has this fountain, or spring, been startled into a cascade by the loathsome activities of the dreadful Moots? Maybe speakers are concealed out here to stream the tumult of moving water through the air of the wood.

Yes. They must have a recording that they activate when . . . doing all this. They must.

The pig's voice deepens to a register that Tom suspects is subhuman. Her words crumble to grunts. 'In the room beneath the earth I see the sow.'

The hare's voice strikes a falsetto, an animal screech. 'We fed the sow!'

Each figure then crouches to the earth in perfect synchronicity, as if enacting some grotesque performance art.

How? How did two gardening-obsessed oddballs become so deranged?

In flickers of half-light, to complement the vocal effects, the nuances of the Moots' physical bearings change again. Impossibly, the posture of his neighbours assumes an even more bestial character. The patchy form of Magi, smudged and inked by shadow, reposes upon stringy yet powerful haunches like an upright hare. Mimicking bony forelegs, his arms dangle before a torso contriving a length that it didn't possess before. His nose even sniffs at the air, as if pausing in the clopping of a crop after catching scent of a circling fox.

A swinish grunt yanks Tom's horrified scrutiny to the pig-like Mrs Moot. She, or it, now roots face-down in the soil. Before the altar she snuffles loathsomely at the leavings that have dripped from the carcase above. And, surely, too quickly for any human being that was not a trained dancer, and one that was much younger than Mrs Moot too, the pig-thing then scurries forward. Moving upon closed fists and the balls of its feet, the grotesque figure scampers, grunting, to the mound. Where the hare now sits, upon the summit, with a mangy head raised to the sky, the forelegs hanging limp.

Impossible. An illusion that the hare could move so quickly, from the ground to the mound. Equally incredible for its belly to now wisp with hair. Mere moments before, there had been no bristly disruption of the chalky daub; Magi's torso had been smooth.

The hare angles its head further back and issues a fresh scream, one that withers the parts of Tom that he's barely holding together. And it is a cry unlike any sound that human vocal cords should be capable of producing. Lonesome yet wretched with spite. A screech of malevolent woe.

Tom scuffles backwards more noisily than he'd have chosen before his wits fled. Feet catching the undergrowth, he loses balance, then rights himself and glances at the grove.

Verdure obscures the ring, the altar, the fire, yet he still sees far more than he wants to.

The ragged silhouettes of the pig and hare are both now upright, standing side by side, upon the summit of the mound. Their posture is awkward and unnatural as if they are four-legged animals trained to stand upon their hind legs to mimic people.

They're too far away for him to be certain what the eyes of the hare have picked out. But the maw of the pig mask that Mrs Moot must use as a visor confronts the scrub in which he presently flounders. Feeling no stronger nor more capable than a lost child, Tom dithers long enough to observe the hare and the pig sink to all fours.

Simultaneously and soundlessly, they crawl forward. Descending the slope of the mound, the two whitish forms slide from view. But their direction of travel throttles Tom's mind into a wordless scream of alarm.

Scrabbling to locate the torch's switch with shaky hands, his balance is shot to staggers, then a drunken wheeling. His boots may as well have trampled bubble-wrap.

At the edge of his meagre sight there is a darting motion of a long form, as the hare leaps vertically, its ears streaming like rags strung on internal wires. And as if capable of flight, the dark streak vanishes inside the canopy of this unreal night. Among the upper tiers of black boughs, the spindly form is collected with a rustle.

At ground level, the thump and scrape of determined feet soon follows. Unseen and low to the ground, the pig-thing barrels to the grove's border. A swinish bleat shatters the night's held breath, dispersing the last vestige of Tom's composure. Then a squeal, that is almost a word, precedes a hungry grunting mere feet from his position. From the scrub before his shins, the beast burrows.

Tom bolts.

Along the track. Left, right, straight ahead, the torch's frail strobe washes twists of stick and foliage charred jagged. Whispering wells of darkness sunk between limbs, stout trunks, vortexing vines, all conspire to swallow the light.

Crashing at the side of the path, the swine bellows and squeals and issues ravenous grunts. Tom falls in response to its hungry call. Regaining his feet, he staggers off the track. Then leaps onto the narrow groove heading out.

No sooner does he regain the path than the hare screams from directly above his head.

His own scream promptly answers as if he is already its prey, swooped upon from above and soon to flop from a tatty black muzzle, his neck broken and loose.

Upon a tree limb bridging the path, a murky silhouette stains the skeletal canopy. The long-eared hare, perched a considerable distance from the ground, watches him.

Tom's appalled gaping is only severed when the boar crashes the undergrowth at his ankles. And he is sure that he hears a set of yellow teeth snap together.

He drops the torch as if it is ballast that slows him. His stagger turns to a sprint that seems to place no distance between himself and the deafening screams and grunts of his pursuers. Swamped by fear, he briefly considers lying in the soil and begging for a swift dispatch. But hunted by the pack and reduced to an animal himself, his urge to flee blind is greater than his instinct to submit and he reaches a speed he's not known since a distant adolescence.

Smashing through scrub and bramble, clawing the air with raking hands, he careens along the unlit path leading to his garden. As if he's running through a crowd with its legs thrust out to trip, and many sharp fingernails raking to drag him down, his face is whipped, his chest spiked, his legs sliced. But on he goes, stumbling and leaping. His breath and heartbeats seem to lag behind his exertions as if his organs belong to another fleeing body at his heels. And when Tom hits the garden fence, he retains no sense of how long it took him to reach his property.

The palisade stands firm. His body snaps in half and gambols over the barrier. His head and shoulders strike a mess of weeds.

Like a badger run to ground by hounds, he crawls the sopping verdure of his holed lawn that stretches to the distant shape of his burrow. The faraway patio doors gape blackly and about him yawns the open grave of the garden.

Above his face, a depth of frigid air oppresses. A profound silence falls from the sky. And a colder, heavier gravity presses him down against the earth. Spent and wounded, he is an animal paralysed with shock after the hunt has passed, or relented. But so loud was the crescendo of his desperate exit from the woods, he cannot guess when the pursuit ceased.

He's not even sure that he's escaped. Not sure if the Moots had merely played with the equivalent of a harried mouse on a woodland floor; perhaps to shape a promise of what comes next to those who defy them.

31

ℋis hands seem to belong to someone else. Disembodied, they jerk as if operating seconds before his mind can understand their difficulty in securing the windows and doors.

He's also hurting all over from where the wood tore and ensnared him. A dew of lymph and speckles of blood ink his hands. Inside his jeans and hoodie, stings sing out in a chorus of small screams. Shooting blue pains streak his back and one hip from his upending over the fence.

With the door bolted, Tom slumps amidst his bedding on the sofa. Enfeebled currents in his mind fail to stir his thoughts from stasis. He can do no more than stare into space, eyes locked by horror. Only the sight of his torn jeans returns him to the room, the present, to an even greater astonishment at what he's just witnessed. *What you are living next door to.*

He longs for curtains to draw and further shut out the sense of all that has entered their airspace from next door.

Memory returns piecemeal, out of sync. Each recollection more sickening than the last.

The slowed backward striding of the counter-clockwise dance. That drapery of limp, glistening fur, the blood seeping from an animal and marbling the stone altar. Magi Moot's maniacal eyes glimmering inside the sockets of the ragged headpiece. *It, the hare, sitting like that* . . . The blare of the pig's grunt. Echoes too horrid to allow within memory. A pasty devil upon one thin leg . . . *pointing at this fucking house* . . .

169

Tom breathes unevenly. A wet rattle in one lung. What air is sucked in, slips out a wheeze. *What, what, what are they? What, what, what do I say to . . . the police?*

He recovers his phone from the floor. The police must be called. An animal was slaughtered. Two, if he counts the fox. Three, if he counts their dog, *because they poisoned him!*

This is intimidation. Some kind of . . . *witchcraft? That,* he really can't accept, even now. *Because . . . that* doesn't exist.

But all he has endured from day one is part of the Moots' design to harass and frighten their neighbours. That he'll put money on.

Why? What is the purpose of it?

To drive you out.

The neighbours are mad. Vindictive. Twisted. They have mastered some kind of . . . he doesn't know what. *Acting?* Performance trick to mimic wild animals? However they do it, they're lunatics who have somehow bypassed the criminal justice system, social services, the world, living here for decades.

Tom punches the keypad of the screen and jams the phone against his ear.

Sure, he cut down their trees but they smashed his fence.

What did that scruffy guy in the knackered car say: that they will make sure he moves out, or will wish that he did? *Something to that effect.*

How many people know about this? Them? In the village?

He doesn't know the village, or anyone there. There are no shops, nothing for them down that hill. They've only walked through it once and they never saw a soul.

Their predecessor? *Poor bastard must have been gas-lit into hanging himself by those . . . by . . .* He cannot find the words required to report his neighbours to the police. How can he reasonably and accurately describe people that daub themselves white by night and emulate pigs and hares?

How it leapt into the bloody trees! An illusion? And the pig?

Mrs Moot. A horrible sense of her authority freezes his thoughts. The commanding will beneath the beastliness. He's seen people, women, bow before her upon a front lawn. *They kissed her hand!*

'Police,' he says at the prompt from the operator.

'Please wait while I connect you.'

Another woman of the night soon appears, on duty at the nearest police station. 'Hello. How can I help you?' she asks, firmly, distractedly.

Tom stammers, his voice immediately suppressed by embarrassment before the first word is uttered. 'Neighbours. My neighbours. They're . . .'

'Sir?'

'Not right. They're doing a ritual. In the woods. They . . .'

A long pause as the police officer waits for him to finish his nonsense. He can't finish. The heat and expansion of the blood behind his face, the torrent inside his ears, derails his thoughts. Numb tongue. Throat squeezed.

'Sir, are you in danger?'

'Yes. No. Not now. Maybe. I don't know. They were . . . doing something. Mound. Round this hill in the woods at the back of our house. We just moved here. Are new here. They. Next door—'

'Sir, what is the nature of the complaint? Is it a nuisance you're reporting? If it's noise then disputes with neighbours are usually a council matter.'

'No. Worse than that. They killed an animal! And our dog. I know they did. A fox the other day. They tied it to a tree to frighten my little girl. They're savage. Sadistic. Cruel people. We're not safe here.'

'Sir, are you saying you saw your neighbours kill an animal? Your dog was it?'

Tom stares in exasperation at the phone. 'Fuck.'

'Sir? Can I remind you—'

'Sorry. I'm sorry. But . . . we don't get on. With them.

Haven't been here long but there's a dispute. About the fence, woods, noise. Back and forth. And . . . our dog is now dead. They told us we can't go into the woods. In there, this . . . like a witchcraft thing was going on. They were *dancing*.' The last syllable is a puff of breath; a weak and hopeless final note in a stream of gibberish.

'Sir, I'm not sure I understand. Can I ask if you've been drinking?'

Tom hangs up. Tosses his phone onto the sofa before the urge to smash the handset against the floor overrides his circuits. Face in hands, his scratched fingers clutch and claw his scalp. He stares into space. He rocks back and forth. And stares some more.

32

Exhausted but as mentally alert as a soldier in a foxhole amidst a continuing battle, Tom smoothes another sticking plaster over one of many scratches lining his calf. Emerging from a short dreamless rest, he was sickened at the sight of his own blood staining the sleeping bag. The fabric was stuck to his skin in three places and needed peeling off. Cotton wool balls, sodden with iodine, orbit the first-aid box on a kitchen table turned field hospital. *Stitches?* Six sticking plasters patchwork one shin alone. Another three stripe a forearm. One cheek and his hairline are scraped raw. He can't even remember incurring some of the wounds. Some lacerations probably need bandages – *do we have any?* They've bled down his leg for the two hours of the sleep he crashed into.

At the hollow boom of Gracey's feet coming down the wooden stairs, he tries to hide the stained debris he's been dabbing at the cuts.

His daughter capers into the room, dressed for school. 'Oh, Daddy! What you done?'

Desperate for Fiona to come down so he can tell her about his traumatic night, he hasn't thought of what to say to Gracey. In the glare of the morning, his experience in the woods already feels unreal. Too shocking and chaotic to process, or compare to anything else in his life, or the lives of anyone he knows. And yet, between midnight and dawn, he knows for certain that he witnessed the deranged capability of *next door.*

173

When he awoke, a horrid anticipation of some fresh terror was the worst feeling of all.

'Accident. Gardening,' he says, as Gracey picks through the first-aid kit, hoping to help.

She frowns, tries to understand why her father was gardening so early. 'There's a scratch here.' She taps her eyebrow.

Tom nods, his smile too pitiful to live more than a moment before it twists to a wince.

Fiona, dressed for work and looking sufficiently stern to make Tom's spirits plummet even further, is not long in following her daughter into the room. Her tipped heels ricochet against the floor. 'Self-harming now? Getting close myself. State of you.'

Gracey folds into Tom's arms for a snuggle. He squeezes his daughter, kisses the top of her head. 'Cut myself on some wood, Peanut. Not to worry.'

'Daddy, you have to be careful.' This is what they say to her after her mishaps. Hearing it echoed is endearing but vaguely insulting.

Fiona snatches a lunchbox from the fridge. Stuffs the plastic container into Gracey's schoolbag. Grabs a second packed lunch. Slips it inside her handbag. She shakes the sleeve of her navy blue jacket from her watch. Angles her head to the door. 'Gracey.'

Tom stands and kisses the top of Gracey's head again. He doesn't want to release her. He wants to cry into her hair.

Running late and clearly still furious about his performance with the chainsaw, his wife dashes from the room.

You don't even know the half of it, he thinks. But how can such a tale be told, or subject broached? Like a normal person, his wife was asleep in the middle of the night. Not face-down in the dirt of the woods while a freak-show danced the glade backwards, grunting and squealing, a dead animal dripping upon their altar stone.

Tom calls after her. 'Fi'. About last night.'

She ignores him and unlocks the front door.

Tom follows the girls onto the drive but soon stops to gape at the caravan parked directly outside their house. A dirty obelisk casting a shadow over the unruly lawn. They've moved it from outside their house to his. Grubby side panels now wall off the far side of the road, where empty fields hem green hills, reaching out of sight.

Gracey prances to the caravan to investigate, her rucksack dwarfing her back. Fiona unlocks her car without giving the caravan a glance.

Tom breaks from his appalled gazing at the abandoned vehicle and shuffles down the weedy drive. Uneven slabs and loose gravel jab his bare soles. Tom reaches for Fiona's elbow to prevent her ducking inside the car. 'Fi.'

She looks up. A pretty face blanched beneath the blush of cosmetics, suppressing white rage.

'Fi', this place.'

'What about it?'

'Ain't safe. Last night . . .'

Tom looks at Gracey to make sure she can't overhear. She's standing on her tiptoes, peering at a grubby window. A tatty, faded orange curtain conceals most of the glass. 'There's people inside,' she says.

Tom turns to Fiona. 'Something happened.'

'You can say that again. What were you bloody thinking?'

Across the hedge, the neighbours' garage door grinds along metal runners.

Stricken hot then icily cold by the thought of what might come leaping from that space, Tom swivels to look in the direction of the Moots' house. He hears muffled voices.

'Gracey! Come to Daddy.' The edge in his tone alarms Gracey, who sullenly obeys as if unfairly reprimanded.

Out the side of his mouth, Tom whispers at his wife, 'Not that. Afterwards. In the middle of the night. I can hardly believe it myself. They . . .'

His wife's lovely eyes search his but there is no warmth in her expression, which somehow increases her attractiveness to him, as if he is losing her and only now realising just how special she is. Her scrutiny seeks something in his expression she suspects he's hiding. Dishonesty, perhaps, or signs of madness.

'I'm not kidding, Fi'. They were doing this . . . ceremony. In the woods. Fi', they killed another animal.'

Fiona slips her elbow from his hand. Tucks herself carefully inside the car, slips off her heels. Locates her driving shoes. Thrusts her silky feet inside them.

Tom glances fearfully at the neighbours' house again. Only the upper storey is visible, the curtains closed. A mix of voices creep over the hedge, overlapping. Three, he thinks. Someone laughs. *Is that a good sign?*

Gracey climbs into her child seat and Tom rushes around the car to secure her seatbelt through the array of plastic slots. Soon as he shuts the passenger door, Fiona starts the car, releases the handbrake and rolls the car down the drive's incline. Tom follows the car, unwilling to let them go and be left on his own. 'Love you, Peanut,' he directs at Gracey.

Only at the end of the drive does he stop. At the sight of the police patrol car, parked outside the Moots' house, where the caravan was yesterday, he feels as bloodless and stiff as he knows he appears. 'Fuck.'

Fiona's window lowers with a robotic whir. 'I'll leave you to deal with the law. Criminal damage, I'm guessing.'

Before he can think of an adequate reply, her car pulls away and he's truly on his own. The realisation breaks him out in a nervous sweat. He's returned to the state that consumed him mere hours before, inside the wood: sickened and weakened by a fear that he can smell.

33

He needs an upstairs window to monitor what transpires next door and tiptoes into Gracey's room.

He'd intended to call the local police station once Fiona left, to apologise for hanging up, for being incoherent, to make a better report about the previous night's activities. But the Moots have beaten him to it.

Making sure he remains far enough inside the room and concealed from below, he sees the neighbours, now restored to their usual selves. She's dressed-down in gardening scruffs. Magi resembles an ageing keyboard player from a Seventies prog-rock band. But this reversion to the Moots' idea of normalcy does nothing to alleviate Tom's revulsion at the sight of them. Nor does it ease his horror at his memory of their other selves.

The Moots' visitor is an attractive policewoman, her blonde hair fashioned into a tight bun, which Tom can see on the back of her hatless head as the WPC bows to Mrs Moot, while clutching the crone's gloved hands to express her heartfelt gratitude. A parlay that sickens Tom with the same poignancy he felt as his neighbours stood before the imp of the pond, each balanced upon one leg; an intimation not only of lunacy but of an enemy's stored power. A connectivity they possess to this place that he merely trespasses.

Grinning, Magi watches Fiona turn the car at the end of the lane and accelerate away. A knowing, spiteful expression

177

twists his bearded face as he turns and confronts the window that Tom peers through.

Tom starts but does not flee. *How can he know I'm here?*

Still grinning, Magi moves his hands behind his gleaming pate and extends his index fingers to fashion the ears of an animal. As he does so, the very floor and the pink walls of the room judder a fraction in Tom's peripheral vision. 'Shit. Shit. Shit,' he whispers. But before he can withdraw from the window, Tom's attention is held fast by the police officer lowering herself to her knees.

Also aware of where Tom cowers, Mrs Moot turns to face Gracey's window.

Kneeling, the police officer grasps the older woman's hips and places her pretty face between Mrs Moot's buttocks. She then kisses his neighbour's arse with devotion.

'No. No. No. Please.' To his own ears, Tom's voice sounds especially frail.

Beside the grotesque display, Magi's grin broadens.

Mrs Moot's imperious expression softens with bliss.

In the silence of his old house, Tom sinks to the floor and sits still.

34

His head dipped and eyes closed, a fresh, uncapped bottle of rum and a half-filled glass on the kitchen counter, Tom hasn't moved in a while and only stares at his hands, clenched on the edge of the sink. *How long have I been here?* At least, he suspects, since the patrol car drove away. What feels like hours ago.

And once 10.30 has come and gone, according to the kitchen clock, he still finds himself incapable of much beside this sitting hunched over in the silent places of the unfinished house. Inconsequential household objects blur in his vision, barely acknowledged. Thoughts pour slow as treacle before running fast as rain-bloated rivers, overrunning reason but drowning a motivation to do anything but remain motionless and agape.

When the internal storm finally abates, he feels broken, sleepy with inertia, and his jaw aches. He's been either grinding his teeth or staring at damnation like a grinning skeleton. His vision settles upon Archie's empty basket then moves to Gracey's toy buggy. A furry pig now sits strapped inside and peers back at him, expectantly.

Unleashing a roar, Tom snatches up the glass of rum and heaves it into the wall facing the neighbours' house.

Glass explodes, a silvery grenade. A splash of rum on the wall, dripping around a dent in the plaster.

How did he get here? He's read about similar situations. And seen the television documentaries. Conflicts between neighbours that at first appeared preposterous but grew credible when investigated by journalists; hideous narratives of victimisation, narrated by talking heads with regional accents. Stories that used to make him feel blessed that he and the girls didn't live next door to the offenders.

There's always been plenty of material to fill the TV schedules too. Criminal damage against parked cars. Excrement squirted through letter flaps. Security cameras directed over fences onto windows. Exhausting wars of attrition in magistrates' courts. Social competitiveness escalating to hostility in an unequal society, in which some cannot countenance the shame of being materially inferior to those next door. Tawdry, audacious acts of status-completion against perceived rivals: tabloid fodder and, perhaps, a British speciality.

Not far from their flat in the city, a man even disposed of an elderly neighbour. Dismembered her in his bathtub, then fed her piecemeal to the attack dogs that he kept in cages round the back. The incident briefly made headlines.

Their smashing of his fence. The intimidation of Gracey. Archie's defecation on the Moots' lawn. His destruction of their trees. A spiteful war of wills. Fire exchanged in tense voices . . . Making him no better than those he has ridiculed on television. He's in the club now and saw a confirmation in Fiona's eyes last night. And this morning.

Though surely his neighbours are different. *Surely. The dream, the lead tiles, the ritual in the woods, the things that chased him . . .* All evidence of *something else* he still struggles to accept. He can't prevent himself, even now, from stubbornly striving for a rational explanation; part of him still insists the Moots have some mastery of illusion. A power to suggest *things* like the magicians that perform in Las Vegas, who make you see what is not real. *But how?*

Outside in the hall, the letter flap creaks open then slaps shut.

Tom jumps. 'Christ!'

Bewildered, he waits for his hammering heart to slow, to mallet to dull thumps. Outside, a throaty car engine roars.

Too frightened to investigate what has been posted, he lingers in the kitchen, pacing, until he has the strength to creep from the room.

Sat on the sofa in the living room, Tom inspects the envelope. Brown paper stationery with a prepaid stamp. A franked business reply envelope intended for a magazine subscription service, for a publication called *Elm, Oak & Yew*.

The envelope isn't addressed to him but to a company that distributes the periodical about trees. The business address is scored-out with marker pen. Above the crossed-out address, 'The gentleman at number 1' has been handwritten in a delicate cursive script. Tom lives at number 1, so he imagines this letter is intended for him. There is no postcode, no stamp. The letter was hand-delivered. *The sound of a car pulling away outside.*

Usually, there is little to no traffic in that lane. If things were different and they had normal neighbours, he would be delighted by a seldom used road. Now he often finds himself longing for some sign of mundane activity.

The shabby envelope and the weight of its contents – the thickness of folded paper and an item made of card – brings on an urgent, hot need to void his bowels. He fears the missive has come from one of next door's arse-kissing subjects. Irrational to think so, paranoid to suspect this, maybe, yet still a shiver sows a frosty crop in the runnel of his spine.

When he tears into the envelope, using his thumb, a soft rain of dried herbs patters over his hands. 'The fuck?'

Peeking inside the envelope, Tom sees slips of paper. Gingerly, he fingers them out. Two photocopies of newspaper clippings and a black business card. He places the card on the cushion beside him, his attention stolen by the first clipping.

'VENEFICIUM' is hand-written, in the same stylish hand that addressed the envelope, above the clipping's headline: HANGED MAN NOT FOUND FOR WEEKS. Beneath the text that Tom doesn't read is a grainy photograph of his house, taken from the front. An article dated five months before they moved in.

A second inset picture displays a photograph of the previous owner of the house, standing beside the lopsided porch. Tom has never seen him before. He looks forgettable, ordinary: thinning white hair, small and stocky, muscular hands, dressed in tired working apparel spattered with paint. A suggestion of a shrewd intent narrows hard eyes unaccustomed to mirth.

Tom glances at the second photocopied article, also clipped from a local newspaper. Another word has been handwritten at the top of the page: 'MALEFICIUM'.

Below the handwritten word, the headline blares: POPULAR LOCAL MAN FOUND DEAD AFTER KILLING WIFE. Beneath the headline is a photograph of two smiling faces. A portly middle-aged couple standing in his back garden when it didn't resemble Passchendaele.

Tom picks his phone off the seat beside him, Googles *veneficium*. He struggles to hold his eyes still, to concentrate, but he manages to extract some information from a free online dictionary: 'The preparation of poisons', 'Witchcraft' and 'Sorcery'.

In the silent room his swallow is too loud. He Googles *maleficium*. And 'Witchcraft' leaps from the screen again, as does a line of text: 'Inflicting harm upon others through acts of sorcery'.

Tom drops the phone and picks up the business card. Blows herbs from the shiny black surface.

Printed in gold lettering across the front: 'A. BLACKWOOD, PhD. Traditional Healer. Practical Magical Guidance. Magical Training. Cleansing. Tarot. Kabbalah.'

Tom's gaze drifts to the garden and to the shorn trees at the border that he cropped with the chainsaw. His attention shifts into the orbit of the dog's empty basket. Across his thoughts white figures leap; one screams, one grunts. He clenches his eyes shut and actually turns his head to the side, as if to avert his eyes from the recollection of those dancers of the fire-lit glade.

'Oh dear God. Shit, shit, shit.'

Nervously, he picks up his phone. Reading from the card he taps the onscreen keypad. Moves the phone to his ear.

The call is picked up after one ring and a sonorous voice blares from the handset. 'Are things getting desperate?'

Tom doesn't speak for a while. His mind blanks when it is required to process so much – the awful suggestions of the article, the definitions of the strange words, his vivid recollection of a policewoman sinking her face between Mrs Moot's stringy buttocks, an animal butchered upon an old stone in a night-blackened wood . . . It's all too much.

He's surprised at his own voice when it eventually comes: aged, tremulous, raspy and a cause of shame. 'Who are you?'

'This is only the beginning,' the magisterial voice intones, as if broadcasting to a theatre audience reduced to silhouettes before the footlights of an old, narrow stage. 'We should meet. Soon. I fear you've no time to waste.'

Tom's eyes move to the light fitting in the hall. The white wire is too visible; a cruel taunt left dangling within sight of a condemned man's cell.

'My address is on the reverse of the business card.'

The caller disconnects.

35

*T*om recognises the knackered car expiring on the drive of a Seventies semi. The house on a street made up of identical buildings that would have appeared clean and functional in an architectural model, fifty years before.

Yellowing nets droop behind Blackwood's windows, the panes grimy enough to filter sunlight golden-brown. No one's bothered to cut the lawn for at least a year either; something he and Blackwood have in common. Here, the contagion infects every third property in the street.

Magical Practitioner. 'Jesus wept.' Driving here for answers from a man of so eccentric and dubious an occupation now makes him glow with shame. Even more than before he left home. This time, the heat of humiliation beads his scalp with sweat. Being here is a testament to desperation; something he'll never live down if anyone were to know he'd visited a magical . . . He can't even think the word.

The thought of navigating so many narrow B-roads for an hour-twenty to get here, when he should have been working on the floors upstairs, while waiting on a builder and plumber, hangs his head lower. Every hour not spent looking for work, or improving parts of the house, is an hour pissed away.

And yet, overriding his fidgeting about money and falling behind are persistent, now insistent, questions about why his predecessor never finished the house.

This oddball knows something about his neighbours. There's a connection and a history to be unravelled. The newspaper clippings suggest something audacious and vile. This man wanted him to read them.

Tom alights from his car and slings the holdall over a shoulder. Three lead tablets weigh heavy inside the nylon bag, chinking dully as he moves up a drive sprouting more weeds than his own. He possessed enough presence of mind to bring the 'treasure' that Gracey and Archie discovered under the lawn. Lead bricks, covered in runic markings and concealed underground, have assumed a new significance in the light of the day following the night before. At the very least, Blackwood, PhD, may know a thing or two about the *artefacts*.

Before he's stepped under the cascade of unruly honeysuckle that has succeeded in pulling a lattice-work trellis off the porch canopy, the front door swings wide.

Tom's breath hitches. His impression that Blackwood was waiting behind the door, or perhaps watching for him from a window, does nothing to settle his nerves. The uncomfortable silence is instant and long. No pleasantries are exchanged as the two wary men, who assuredly have little in common beside unkempt lawns and a palsy of social discomfort, size each other up.

The man before him remains as dishevelled as Tom remembers, but his glasses are now perched upon a pallid scalp above his puffy, pale face, the ears and eyebrows long ungroomed. The same trousers he'd worn when he clashed with the Moots stop an inch too short of his ankles, exposing a sock mismatch and lace-up shoes.

Tom feels obliged to break the uncomfortable deadlock. 'I need you to tell me what the hell I am living next door to.'

In silence, Blackwood shuffles to the side and motions for Tom to enter.

185

Carpets come and go inside the magical practitioner's home, patterns changing, patterns fading. Boxes and bookcases in the cramped hall grow pelts of grey dust. A kitchen displays a step-pyramid of dirty crockery. Open packets of food and soiled dishes litter counters. And competing with the scent of a ripe bin, the sharp body odour clouding from the magical practitioner's formal shirt encourages Tom to slip a finger under his nose.

He follows Blackwood to a living room so congested he's certain he's entered the lair of a crazed shut-in, who might yet be dangerous. Little of the walls remains visible behind the bookcases. Thousands of hardback spines suck the dim electric light from the room, creating a brownish pall darkened by closed curtains. In one corner, a cluttered desk supports a computer monitor, the screen saver glowing with signs of the zodiac.

'You may need to sit down to hear what I have to say.'

Tom struggles to see any place where it might be possible to sit. No visible surface exists that isn't building towers of books, ski-slopes of paper or a tidal flotsam of clothing either awaiting the iron or being sorted for charity.

Forced to sit on one buttock on a couple of inches of the sofa, he warily glances at the vast astrological chart papering the wall from backrest to ceiling. 'What am I doing here?' He isn't sure he intended to speak aloud.

Blackwood takes up a position beside a bookcase on the opposite side of the room and adopts a professorial stance; a contrived attempt at eminence that makes Tom want to bark with derisive laughter.

'May I call you Tom?'

He nods.

'You and your family have made a very unfortunate choice about where to make a home.'

'I have my wife to remind me of that, mate. It doesn't require reinforcement.'

'She hasn't left you yet?'

'No!'

'And you can still stand the sight of her?'

'What?'

'Then we may have time. Not much. They're good. Make no mistake. The Moots are powerful.'

Half sure that he should just get up and leave, Tom raises his hands to signal mystification.

'Your neighbours are cunning folk,' Blackwood intones, as if the weighty revelation should be immediately acknowledged by his guest. But the remark simply hangs in the gloom until it too becomes as absurd as the speaker.

'That a New Age definition of cunts?'

Blackwood winces at Tom's language. 'Root-cutters. Pharmakides. Peddlers of low magic. This is what I am referring to.'

'Still none the wiser.'

'They are paid for their services. Enchantments. As were their parents. You're going up against a legacy.'

'Hang on. Parents? They're not . . . together?'

'Oh, no, they're not married. Siblings.'

'Brother and sister? But . . .' *The suckling at the pallid thigh.* And *Me Dear.* Tom heard Magi call *her* that; a term of endearment surely reserved for a spouse of some years? 'When he called her My Dear, I thought—'

'Medea. As in the tragedy. And these siblings belong to an ancient tradition. Once serving the poor as doctors and vets. A few centuries ago. But their knowledge is passed on, from one generation of practitioners to the next. My aunt inducted me.' Blackwood looks to his desk, directing Tom's eyes to a framed picture positioned beside the computer monitor. In the photograph, an elderly woman with a wild bushel of hair stands alone in a summery garden, smiling. She wears a white apron. Had the picture not been in colour, it might have been taken a hundred years before.

'Our trade offers specialist services. Charms. We cure ailments. Adjust imbalances in one's fortunes. Some of us are even blessed with the gift of divination.' And there Blackwood pauses, visibly swelling with pride.

Tom remains baffled.

'Fortune telling,' Blackwood offers as if to a slow child. 'But Magi and Medea have long diversified. Their magic is malicious. This is my point. And why I contacted you. I had a sense that things were already getting out of hand. For you. That *it* has begun.'

'What exactly are we talking about here? What are they doing? I mean, how?'

'How? I'll come to that. But the origins of what they are doing to you were established twenty years ago. At exactly the same time your home developed a revolving door. What you need to understand is that the Moots are entirely responsible. The most lucrative string to your neighbours' bow has always been the removal of curses.' Still expecting his visitor to be astonished and awed at such a Damascene moment, Blackwood takes a breath to let the weight of the remark settle.

But Tom continues to gape at the man, his pity, aversion and mirth suppressed for courtesy's sake. Until Blackwood roars, 'Only it is the Moots who have been laying the bloody curses!'

Tom jumps and something else moves inside the room, as if one of the piles of paper is as startled as he is, though he sees nothing slide or fall.

Appearing to have pulled out his own pin and set himself off, Blackwood continues to roar. 'They're out of control now!'

'Lot of it about.' Tom shifts again with embarrassment for the dishevelled, affected figure. He can do nothing but study these antics with the same horrified pity with which he would gape at a furious drunk raving in the street. He jiggles his car keys.

The sound seems to encourage Blackwood to compose himself, or attempt to, but his blood is up. Closing his eyes, he slows his breathing. 'They're effectively blackmailing their victims for tributes. To have the curses removed!'

The very thought of such a conspiracy swiftly returns the man to rage. His gestures grow wilder, adopting a curious pattern and rhythm as if his hands are performing a strange dance routine in which his legs remain static. 'I should know. I'm trying to remove one now! They're ruining me! They've wiped out all the competition in the South-West. I'm the last charmer standing. There are some who have been paying the Moots a monthly stipend for ten years! Bled dry! And worse.'

Tom leans forward, his interest finally pricked by something he can understand: the suggestion of a scam the Moots specialise in, twinned with a form of intimidation they inflict upon their neighbours. Gaslighting across the hedgerow. Tom raises a hand to enforce a pause in Blackwood's rant. 'Hang on. They're clever and underhand. Spiteful, vindictive arseholes. I get it. Seen it. And a lot of stuff I can't explain. Right now, that is. But witches? Devil worshippers, or something?'

Tom's remark annoys Blackwood more than his grievance with the Moots. 'This has nothing to do with Christianity! Or the bloody devil!'

'Okay. Okay. Right.'

Breathing unhealthily, the magical practitioner expounds, but as if to an imbecile. 'It's much older. As for that kind of witch, there's no such thing! Never was until after the Second World War. That's all a modern invention.'

'Black magic then. Curses? You said as much.'

Blackwood closes his eyes. 'If you're looking for a modern equivalent, your neighbours are priests. Magic and belief indivisible. This makes what they're doing extremely dangerous.'

Tom shrugs. 'It's all . . . a bit farfetched. Afraid I'm still lost, mate. I mean . . . magic?'

Blackwood opens his eyes, though they remain narrowed. 'Lot of it about. More than you could possibly imagine. Right next door to your home in fact. You're already seeing the results, or you wouldn't be here. Would you? But if you can't accept what I am telling you and cannot take what I am saying seriously, then you are already damned.'

Dread seeps coldly through Tom's bowels. Too vividly does he recall the streaky horrors that leaped and grunted through the night-woods, clomping and squealing at his heels. *They could have torn you apart last night.* 'What do they want? We have no bloody money.'

'They want you to leave.'

'That's impossible. We've nowhere to go. Mortgaged to our plums.'

'You say that now but they cannot abide neighbours. Doesn't matter who occupies the house next door, the story has never changed. I can't remember anyone lasting there long. Those who stuck it out, well . . . Some were destroyed more quickly than others. And those for whom the Moots reserve a particularly virulent contempt . . .' Blackwood raises an eyebrow. 'There have been eight deaths in that house since 1992. And three complete mental breakdowns resulting in institutionalisation. Legacy. And they enjoy their work. To them, their neighbours are mere sport.'

Tom recalls the specific chewing noise of his chainsaw blade, severing the Moots' trees. And he feels sick.

Blackwood folds his hands behind his back and rises onto his toes. 'You read the material I provided. Just a couple of samples. And this is your problem. Not mine. So perhaps this tiresome facade of smug scepticism can finally be retired. Mmm? What do you say?'

Tom yanks the rucksack onto the floor. 'These were buried in our garden. Maybe there's a connection to what you're talking about.'

Warily, Blackwood tiptoes forward and leans over the bag. He slides his glasses down his forehead and onto his nose to peer inside. But the instant he sees the contents, his eyes flash wide and fill the lenses of the glasses with fear. 'Don't let them touch me! Nor the floor! The bag. Keep them inside the bloody bag!' Hands weaving more of the curious patterns above his head, he speeds from the room.

Tom slowly closes the bag, rises to his feet and follows Blackwood. He presumes he's supposed to.

If ordinary people had lived at the address, this would have been a dining room. As it's Blackwood's domain, golden walls and a matching ceiling glow above bare floorboards. Two white circles, one inside another, are painted dead-centre. The circular margin is festooned with symbols that Tom assumes to be of an occult nature. They just have *that* about them.

Blackwood has taken up a position inside the circles, with a jeweller's loupe strapped to his head. One large eye blinks within the lens. Under an arm he holds three hardback books. He points at the floor just outside the outer circle. 'Put them down. There.'

Tom eases the rucksack of lead tablets to the floor, where directed.

'Now lay them out flat. Inside the bag. I need to examine the inscriptions.'

No sooner has Tom arranged the tablets for inspection than Blackwood drops to his hands and knees with a thump. Wheezing excitedly like a collector of strange pornography, he pushes his face close to the tablets.

Tom shuffles away. 'What are they?'

'Curse tablets. Directed at anyone who inhabits your home.'

'You're kidding me. How . . .' And now it is Tom who finds himself waving his hands around. 'How are they supposed to work?'

'Oh, they work. Very effectively if laid by experts. As these have been.' Blackwood raises his head. 'They came from graves. Very old graves.' The huge eye inside the lens of the loupe blinks once before the tatty head lowers again. 'I guessed as much. This is how they've managed the evictions. See! Here! This is Greek. Fifth century, I'd say. I've seen similar before in Somerset and Wiltshire. Causing illness. In livestock. Animals dying. A blight on crops.'

Tom's mind wrestles with the impossibility of what he is being told. But when he thinks of his dead garden and Archie's small hump of a grave, his struggle to accept the peculiar information lessens.

'Anything like that befallen you? Mmm?'

'Our garden—'

Blackwood doesn't pause to listen. 'Ah! Latin! This is Roman. Also common. Financial misfortune its aim. Something unforeseen, sudden, affecting a household. Usually placed close to the entrance of a building, even beneath a threshold. Outdoors, they're found near gates. The third tablet is Hebrew. I'll have to get back to you on that one. But, hazarding a guess, your dreams may soon become unbearable. You may suffer visions. Of the Underworld and so forth. Alas, the unholy trinity, you have it. Blight. Ruin. Madness.'

Removing his face from the open holdall and peering up again, Blackwood's huge eye blinks. 'Just from what I can see from an initial assessment, I personally wouldn't set foot on that property again. Let alone live in it.'

Believing his whole being to have been refashioned from equal parts confusion, despair, disbelief and exhaustion, Tom slumps on the tatty sofa, his head drooping over his knees.

To reinforce Blackwood's outrageous claims, an unbidden and frightful figure conjures its own pale form and springs through his memory. The creature shrieks at the sky from a strange earthen mound, then leaps into the treetops; no more than a few hundred metres from where he and his family sleep.

'If all this is . . . What can I do? To stop it? To protect us?'

A little too indifferent, even unsympathetic, to Tom's plight, Blackwood consults a tome upon his desk. As if merely pursuing a private fascination, he flicks pages and speaks offhandedly, without turning his head. 'You must start by finding the rest of the tablets. I suspect there will be more. You'll get no respite until you do. Your neighbours can enliven the curses any time they wish. You wouldn't even know until the roof came down on your head. Like landmines the curses will explode in your future. In all kinds of uncanny ways. At any time. Your wife may be unfaithful. That's always been popular.'

Tom checks his watch. 'Shit.' Standing up, he snatches up his bag. 'I gotta get on. I'll let you know if I find any more. And that'll be it, yeah? Once I've found them all?' And as Tom wonders exactly how he will accomplish such a task, Blackwood turns from his desk, his eyebrows arching above his spectacles.

'There is the matter of my tribute.'

Tom frowns. 'Come again?'

The man's face darkens, anger sharpening his glare. 'If your pipes burst, you call a plumber. Am I right? You would reimburse that professional for a service provided, mmm?'

If I had the money, Tom wants to say but can't speak. He's bewildered by the speed of events, the impossibility of Blackwood's claims that no longer seem preposterous. His confusion isn't helped by a new and chilling suspicion concerning the man's motives. And as he dithers, Blackwood produces a portable credit-card machine from the mess on his desk. 'Consultation is free. Diagnosis and treatment are not. I can also offer you a method of detection. Part of the package.'

Tom manages a whisper. 'How much are we talking?'

'Let me see if I still have the device. Then we'll settle up.' Blackwood darts from his desk and crosses the room. Outside the living room, he yanks opens a cupboard door and proceeds to noisily ferret under the staircase. A sloping pile of boxes, coats and old shoes slides out, amassing at his feet. 'Blast!'

Tom rises from the cramped sofa and slips his wallet from a pocket in his jacket. He selects a bank card and imagines every person that he has ever known laughing at him.

Blackwood tugs a metal detector from the cupboard. 'Earphones are in here somewhere. I know they are.'

Tom shuffles over and picks up the machine. It is old, battered, a pitiful instrument with which to undertake the task of uncovering curses. It doesn't even weigh much. He blows dust from the machine while Blackwood rummages, his voice and wheezy exhalations muffled by the confines of the storage space. 'Dust. I'll also need dust. From their property. From inside. It's vital.'

'Break in? For dust? You fucking mad?'

'Do I look it?'

Tom bites his tongue, then frowns as a penny drops. 'Would a caravan do?'

Panting, Blackwood noisily reverses from the cupboard. 'If it belongs to them. Or has contained them. Possibly. And they have one. They move it around that lane. The village. I don't know why but we can only try. Now, my fee.' Blackwood strides with an indecent eagerness to his desk and, with all the gravity of an earnest doctor writing a prescription, fills out an invoice on a jotting pad. He tears the page free and hands it to Tom. Over his tortoiseshell spectacle frames, the magical practitioner's watery eyes then peer at him, the intensity withering. *This, Sir, is a serious matter and requires my expertise.*

When Tom reads the sum he feels a need to sit down, or maybe even lie down.

36

Upon the kitchen window overlooking the garden, Fiona glimpses the ghost of her face: a reflection of a dark-eyed smudge, its features recast by worry and preoccupied by disappointment. After briefly interrogating herself on whether the expression is permanent, she angles her upper body forward to banish the apparition of the weary woman on the grimy pane. Her focus shifts to her husband in the distance, committed to a strange task before the uneven palisade of trees at the wood's untamed border. It was Tom's antics that first drew her to the window.

The lumpy surface of the garden already resembled a section of battlefield from the Great War. A scrap of land once subjected to obliterations and whistling impacts before returning to the wild; the craters and dugouts reupholstered by grasses, wild flowers and scrub. But between leaving for work that morning and returning home in the evening, hostilities have resumed and churn anew the soil of this no-man's-land. Mounds of freshly turned earth molehill what was once an approximation of a lawn. Next to the patio doors, slab-stones are stacked beside two holes. A cemetery plot more than a landscaped garden.

Attending to the garden is the last job on a swelling list of renovations. They would get to it eventually. But Tom appears intent on spending his precious time and finite energy on making the garden even more unsightly.

Earlier, the tardy plumber had finally showed to begin work on the bathroom. Tom had been out. Fiona found an abrupt note trapped inside the letter flap. She doesn't know when, or if, the unreliable tradesman will make the journey out to them again. It had taken so long to find a plumber with a good reputation at the right price. So long had they waited to be granted an audience, but Tom wasn't here, wasn't in, wasn't home to meet him.

An angry builder also called her at work. He'd driven all the way out here today too, to also find no one home. Fiona called Tom twice and left two messages. He never returned her calls. Nor has he continued with the flooring. He was going to lay vinyl in their bedroom today and assured her that he'd start on the floor of the hall or living room too. But, from what she can see, he has, in fact, done nothing to the house at all today. Instead, he is doing *this*, like some absurd hobbyist searching for Roman coins, when he swore his sole focus would be the house until someone hired him to do something that paid.

Tom is wearing headphones and pushing a metal detector over the earth.

He hasn't changed out of his soiled clothes from yesterday either. He put them back on for whatever he was doing in the middle of the night. Then slept in them.

His arms are criss-crossed with plasters, his hands are sooty with filth. The same hung-over expression slumps his face. She's been looking at that face for about a week now: sagging, greyish, scored with lines. A nasty scratch crosses one eyebrow. She can see it from here. *Stitches.*

She's more tired of looking at that face than at her own haggard visage.

One-handed, Tom glides the device near Archie's grave. If he claims he is looking for buried treasure she won't be as surprised as she should be. She is finding it harder to understand his behaviour as each day passes. Agitation gnaws his thoughts and frays his wires. He's either manic and throwing himself at the walls and floors in a frenzy of industriousness, or he is sunk into preoccupation and muttering to himself. Or, worst of all, he is immolating in outbursts about the neighbours.

His paranoia is baffling, embarrassing. He's not tuned into the present enough to address what lies before them. Her struggle for comprehension is becoming a failure of recognition.

Not sure I like him anymore. The flicker of thought she douses with a hiss.

She needs to remind herself that this is Gracey's father. Needs to scratch through her memories to the safer ground of familiarity and remind herself of who Tom is. Or was, until recently.

'Gonna help Daddy!' Gracey dashes to the back door, then bustles through it and into the garden. She's carrying her plastic spade they bought during the only seaside holiday they were able to afford, while saving for *this house*.

Feeling as if she hasn't the strength to stop her daughter, or even speak, Fiona merely watches Gracey prance across the holes and mounds to where her father frowns, so far away, before the trees.

With Gracey gone from the room, Fiona finally starts to cry to herself.

From out of a darkness that voids the world beyond the kitchen, Tom staggers inside, his hunched shape and bearded face morose with what might be despair; a hint of savagery sharpening a stare that does not seek Fiona at the table.

Wafting around him and billowing into the barely warm room drift scents of turned earth, damp grass, the evening cold that grips and holds the garden and woods still against the earth. Fragrances they never encountered in their flat in town. Scents that position their home on the border of a wilder place, at the edge of something vast and merciless and unaware of their needs.

Tom kicks off his work boots and rests the detector against the wall. At the big sink, his blackened, prehistoric hands yank on the kitchen tap. Pipes bang then shudder. Water trickles, drip-drops. On the draining board, stained soup bowls from Fiona and Gracey's tea remain unwashed.

Fiona's face is bleached by the screen of her laptop, open upon the table. She might be peering into a better house from the darkness outside a bright window. An empty glass of wine idles beside her. A relic of sophistication incongruous here. A remnant from the world they left behind.

She looks like an installation, exhibited here in the centre of a dim, frigid kitchen with its sun-faded cabinets and walls black-spotted by fungus and fly droppings; this old shell from the Seventies, eager to oppress and douse the single flicker of modernity that her glowing screen represents. She doesn't look up or greet Tom either.

'What's with the water?'

'You tell me. Like that when I came in. Plumbing's totally packed up downstairs. I couldn't cook the bloody tea. Tom, we're camping indoors.'

'I'll make some calls.'

Tom returns to the back door that he has left gaping, the thin warmth of the room already sucked out. He bends over and with an angry, tired grunt, drags a plastic crate across the peeling orange lino. Through the transparent sides of a container that, until recently, stored crockery carefully wrapped inside newspaper, a number of lead tablets are stacked like floor tiles. Wet soil and muddy sediment smears the side of the plastic box.

'Got 'em all.'

That note of satisfaction, even triumph, in his statement provokes Fiona. 'As well as ruining the garden, you spent four hundred quid today. Blackwood Magical Services?'

Tom can't meet her eye. 'I know it looks crazy.'

'No. It is crazy.'

'He's helping me. Explained why everything is going wrong. For us. Here. I know you don't want to hear it, but these . . . had to come up. It's a start.'

'Of what?'

'A process. Things have to change. Or . . . He said . . . he said they're curse tablets. Now, I don't—'

She can't stand it anymore. Her voice trembles as if she's about to cry and that weakness only makes her angrier. 'Curse tablets? That what you got there? Helping us, is it? You and me and Gracey?'

'Yes.'

'You missed the bloody plumber. And builder. You were supposed to be here. They won't come out again! Took me weeks to find them! But I'm guessing you were shopping for a metal detector instead?'

'It was included.'

'Bargain! New roof included in the four hundred you spanked?'

Tom turns and punches an index finger at the wall bordering the neighbours. 'There will be no bloody roof over our heads unless they're stopped! They killed Archie. The fucking fence. The caravan now? What Gracey saw in the woods. The fucking fox nailed to a fucking tree. Open your eyes! And what I saw last night, I . . .' He stops, lowers his voice. 'You need to listen, Fi'. This looks insane. I haven't lost my mind.'

Fiona gets up from the table and strides from the room, her fingers used as stoppers against tears that spout in warm springs. 'But you lost something else today.'

When his wife has gone, Tom slumps against a kitchen unit, wipes his mouth with a begrimed hand. He stares at the crate of lead tablets, inscribed with runes and plastered with mud, and then his eyes drift to the wall they share with the Moots. *So many.*

37

When Tom and Fiona watch Gracey sleep they are struck by the beauty of their child. They see the infant again in their child's smoothed features, a younger self recovered from a time when their anxiety for her safety was as fierce and blind as any madness. The sight of Gracey asleep touches a depth of feeling in Tom that is too unbearable to sustain moment by moment. Such an insight or vision for him must remain fleeting, like a glimpse of the divine. But tonight, Gracey's little sleeping face, when neither of her parents are looking, is troubled, sweat-peppered.

Tonight, Gracey dreams a curious dream. She dreams of walking backwards, in complete silence, round the grassy mound in the woodland glade. Round and round she goes until, bidden or controlled by another will as all are in dreams, she stops beside the altar stone.

A floral tribute wreathes the menhir and bloods the weathered sides of the crude column. Amongst flowers atop the altar, beloved Waddles lies inside the stone bowl. Torn open, his white fibrous stuffing is stained scarlet. A lone plastic eye stares at the sky but sees nothing. The second eye is missing.

'He's with the sow, Gracey,' says her mother, whom Gracey can't see but she knows is nearby in the trees that trap night beneath so heavy a canopy. Yet here, inside the grove, the air is illumined by gold dust. Under her feet and under the grass and under the earth, a stream bubbles fast and makes her feel like she's tilting forwards and about to fall into the sky at the same time.

'Archie's here too. Shall we go?' her mother asks.

An overwhelming awareness of the vivid colours, the startling definition and the detail of each leaf and blade of grass, begins to push her out of sleep.

Twisting against the force that roots her feet to the grassy earth, before the blood-mired rock, Gracey finally breaks through the membrane of dream. The clarity that her eyes never achieve in the real world suddenly dims.

And she is awake inside her pink room, the space softly frosted by the owl nightlight on her chest of drawers. Hair wet and plastered to her cheeks, her forehead grows as cold and clammy as a wet flannel. She sits bolt upright.

'We can all go down together.' Mommy again, with the voice from the dream that Gracey can still hear. Mommy's just outside the room.

'Mommy.' Swinging her little legs out of the bed, Gracey's eyes search the grubby shadows of the smelly old house. But she can see no sign of Mommy, so she flees the candy-walled room to the unlit cavern of the landing. The latest new Waddles dangles from her hand.

Into Mommy and Daddy's bedroom she flits, where her parents sleep with a chasm between them. Each dark head is sunk on opposite edges of the mattress.

'Mommy,' she calls. Her mother is fast asleep, which confounds her because she definitely heard her voice on the landing.

Bewildered, Gracey scurries to the bottom of the bed and raises the duvet in the middle. And is about to tunnel inside, between her parents, when she pauses, her attention drawn to a red luminance aglow on the bedroom windows where curtains don't hang.

The night outside is blushed red, not black. She's never seen sky like this. A window is open and the scarlet light shafts like it's coming through the stained glass of a church.

Entranced, little Gracey pads to Daddy's side of the bed and peers at a moon washed in blood. Where the clouds part, the sky is carmine and the stars are twinkling rubies. Down below, the wood is clotted with shadow, the earth blackened as if there's been a big fire.

And from the darkness, a pale visitor steps forward.

Indistinct but whitey, the thing looks like a skinny lady with a dark, lumpy head. She's showing her bosom and looks like she's fallen over and rolled in the ashes of a cold bonfire to make herself ghosty. She stands on one leg and points at the bedroom window.

From behind the lady standing on one leg, something shoots directly up into the air; as fast as a squirrel but as big as a man. Though it can't be a man because long ears are streaming behind the bumpy silhouette of the head.

Launching from the trees and gliding fast over the garden, the thing drops close to the house. Gracey only sees a dark shape fall. She doesn't want to see what has arrived down below so close to the house. She steps away from the window but not far enough to avoid hearing a thump below.

Gracey turns to get into bed with Mommy and Daddy but she's back inside the dream and can only move in slow motion as if her feet and ankles are buried in sand, and all the sound has gone from the night and the house. This must be what being deaf is like.

The room she turns to face is also empty.

There is no bed. There are no parents or furniture or dressing gowns on the rear of the door. No new shade upon the light. The walls are covered in old yellow paper and the floor is dusty boards with no rug. She's inside her house but at the wrong time and she starts to cry at the gaping absence of her parents that chills her heart so cold it aches and her breathing flaps like loose paper.

Gracey can only shut her eyes and cover them with new Waddles and maybe when she looks again she won't be dreaming.

When she opens her eyes, so many creaks and rustles that she never usually bothers with explode from a void of silence.

She jumps.

Her parents are back inside the room again, lying in the bed. They haven't moved. She can hear them breathing.

A glance at the windows can't be resisted because something was outside the house in the sleepwalking half-dream and the sky was all red and wrong.

The sky is now as black as deep night should be. But through the window crawls a noise, a scraping on bricks as something pulls itself up the wall.

At the foot of the bed, Gracey raises the duvet above her head like it's a wave about to crash and slips under. Grabbing handfuls of sheet she tunnels along the mattress until the inert bodies of her parents offer immediate warmth and a reassuring solidity. When her head appears on the pillows between Mom and Dad's oblivious heads, her eyes grope the dark.

Over by the open window comes the thump of an intruder dropping to the floor of the room.

Inside this rigid silence another has arrived, joining her mommy, her daddy and her. She can't breathe for fear. Gracey squeezes shut her eyes. Squashes Waddles into her face.

And here comes the rustle and bump of the visitor crawling the floor. Then there is silence, for a moment, as it pauses to watch them and make permanent the idea of itself, crouched and waiting.

Gracey pulls up her feet, squashes them into her bottom. Under her chin her whole body tries to become a numb, airless space that won't make a sound and attract the thing on the floor.

The terrible silence is broken by a *clack clack clack clack* and Gracey thinks of Nanny's busy knitting needles, tying tiny complicated knots that became a hat and scarf for her. The *clack clack* moves round the bottom of the bed and she can't stop her eyes peering over the duvet and she wants to scream so that her daddy can wake up and fight the monster, and the witch in the garden, while she and her mommy wait in the car.

There's no light coming through the windows because it's so dark in the country and only a misty glow from her owl nightlight next door reaches here. She can't see anything at

Dad's side of the bed, nor at the foot of the bed, nor Mum's side by the open door.

Click-clack, click-clack, snick, snick, snick. There is the knitting sound again but this time it's coming from above the bed.

The ceiling!

Her wide eyes dry out, right under the eyelids. She doesn't want to look up but does because she realises that nothing she wants to happen, or not happen, makes any difference at all.

What reaches down is more smudge than form but she's sure it's hanging by its feet, from the ceiling, like a giant, horrible bat. Its whitish length smears the wall and a bumpy head extends. Ragged ears the same size as Daddy's cricket bat, cock like horns and blade the bony head. And even the thinnest light is sufficient to unveil eyes rusted and liverish and bulging wide on either side of a narrow skull.

Her heart, Gracey is sure, has now stopped.

The *clack clack* of knitting needles closes over Gracey's head. As two shaggy limbs become visible on either side of her face, she lowers her chin and sucks air to scream. But the scream gets stuck, suspended at the back of her mouth. The front legs are skinny as a dog's and furred and smell of the wet cement of a petting zoo. Whitey claws do the *click-clacking*. One paw grips lost Waddles, whom she saw in the dream. He's hurt and bleeding. An eye is gone.

Gracey sinks her entire body under the duvet.

And SCREAMS.

And SCREAMS.

And SCREAMS.

At the same time that Tom and Fiona sit upright, a supple shadow slides over the window sill and draws Tom's shellshocked attention. It's gone before he can squint. In the darkness, he and Fiona then find each other.

'Gracey?' he asks.

Fiona scrabbles and disinters objects from the bedside table. A water glass bangs and bounces across wooden boards. A smartphone thumps the floor. A click of the table lamp's switch punctures the solemn, dense darkness with electric light.

Tom stares at Fiona, unable to shake himself from shock and his unformed questions, the compulsions without words. Fiona returns his gaping. Then, together, as if drawn to some tiny emergency beacon, they divert their gaze to the lump beneath the duvet. Tom raises the bed linen.

Gracey's bloodless face peeks back, eyes stricken wide by a terror they've never seen before.

After such an abrupt awakening, their disorientation lengthens and they can only gape at the little girl until she breaks the spell. 'Witch. Monster up on the ceiling. Hurted Waddles.'

Tom rolls out of bed as Fiona collects Gracey and holds her tight. Immediately, the girl sobs into her mum's bosom, clinging to her nightclothes for dear life.

Tom checks the open window. The garden is empty. He closes the window and backs out of the room, eyeing the wall they share with the Moots. Outside in the hall, he drags his fingers down his face to wipe away vestiges of sleep. Fumbling on light switches, he stumbles to Gracey's room on numb feet. Slaps on that light and races to the window. Planting his hands on the sill, he peers between the curtains.

The front garden is as deserted as the rear but the lumpen silhouette of the caravan is as visible as an oppressive stain. A territorial marker. A barricade. The woods fence the rear, the slovenly recreation vehicle bars the front. An open-plan garden on one side. The Moots have truly invaded. After spilling through their meagre defences they are now inside the keep, the house. *They must be. We're cornered.*

Tom raises a hand from the sill and studies his dusty palm. He then rubs his gritty fingertips together.

Tom peers into inky air, sees little of the two houses beyond their outlines. Nights this far from *anywhere* are untarnished by light pollution and not a chink of light escapes the Moots' interior. Nothing stirs out here. Silence thickens the dark. The wind-ruffled trees of the distant wood produce the only sound.

Blackwood needs dust from the sorcerers' house. Ammunition for the magical battle already raging.

His blood has carried him this far, its rise tangible; a tidal surge drawn by the full moon of his fear and revulsion for what resides next door. But now that he's alone in pitch dark, apprehension pinches his gut.

Something . . . there was something. In our room. A cat?

A suspicion that the Moots are entering not only their heads but their home now, and perhaps while transformed into the horrid personae he saw in the grove, is too horrid to dwell upon. Though the idea of the intruder being more substantial than a small animal also grows preposterous the longer he's fully awake. A window had been open, but scaling a twenty-foot elevation of smooth brick wall would surely be beyond the neighbours and what they believe themselves capable of performing when *altered*, or when believing themselves to be *other*.

Nonetheless, his notion that the neighbours somehow *got inside* the house persists. And if the neighbours' malevolent influence can truly extend so far, and physically, then why wasn't he the victim tonight? Because the night's target was sweet Gracey. The Moots' actions were calculated to hurt them by the most malicious means: through their child. An escalation that brings Tom close to panic.

He can only pray that what he and Gracey suffered were the 'hellish visions' predicted by Blackwood. Within his own eyes, had not two elderly people moved like animals too, through the woods, in pursuit of their quarry? One had even appeared to sit in a tree to observe his rout below. Impossible. *A vision?* Surely. *Please let it be.*

What he believes one moment he disbelieves the next. The very idea they command supernormal powers is often too much to accept. *And yet . . .*

Reassured that no one will see him at this distance from the houses, with the smudge of the border hedge offering additional concealment, he returns his attention to the caravan. And inhales its ancient respirations: rust, damp metal, a pervasive taint of engine oil.

He digs the screwdriver's tip between a rusty lock and a doorjamb made from sheet metal, and the blade grinds through. He uses the screwdriver as a lever, resting his weight against the handle. A metallic snap rings coldly.

And the door creaks ajar.

Tom stows the screwdriver in a pocket of his jacket. Collects the torch from near his feet. Holding his breath, he then eases open the squeaking door. Stepping from the chilly night, he enters a new darkness pungent with odours of damp fabric and mouldy linoleum. Carefully pulling the door closed, he seals himself inside the caravan.

Beneath his weight the vehicle creaks, shifts. The shuffle of his feet and his panicky exhalations amplify. Turning himself about, his knee collides with an object that produces a dull, hollow knock. 'Fuck.'

The torch soon ushers a tired interior into existence. A vintage caravan unchanged in decades: sun-faded laminate surfaces, cupboards and drawers. An old enamel cooker. Wendy House sink and taps. Dinky orange curtains strung along white elastic rails, covering portholes more than windows and maintaining a privacy that feels more like entombment.

To welcome his trespass, a gust of sewage releases from the sink area, and as he reaches the check curtain dividing the kitchen from what must be the living space, the aroma of a ripe bin forces his breath shallower.

One tug and the drape shrieks across plastic runners. 'Fuck! Fuck off. Shit.'

His torch beam drops from what hangs from the ceiling. Scattered light flashes about his feet as he scuffles a retreat.

The remainder of the cabin is obscured by the hanged figure's silhouette. Its booted feet hover a clear foot from the floor.

Tom returns the torch to it and dusty shadows recede from the horror occupying the airless space. Against the interior murk of orange and brown upholstery, the figure's arms are spread wide as if it was crucified first, then hanged. A pair of paint-spattered boots begin where the hems of a blue jumpsuit end. An overall that a garage mechanic would wear to toil beneath an open bonnet, covers the torso and limbs.

Tom's beam gropes higher. Despite a strong aversion to seeing a face, he finds himself impelled to seek just that, from near the ceiling where the form hangs by its neck.

'Dear God.'

If there was a face upon the murky, ball-shaped head, the grimacing features are shielded behind a portcullis of cross-hatched sticks. A dusty grate of bent and woven twigs, through which he too easily imagines teeth and an echo of the choking noises once rinsed from a throat.

It might be the result of his shock but the floor seems to shift beneath his feet. It's as if he's now aboard a small boat, abandoned in some foul estuary with the captain hanging from a bulkhead.

White electrical cord is knotted beneath the hanged figure's shapeless chin. A neck so squeezed by the garrotte, the woody ball of the head rests at a slant. Between the stained cuff of one sleeve and a protective glove, a network of entwined sticks suggest the fine bones, sinews and veins of a skinned wrist.

A dummy. Human-shaped, the head and hands made from willow or hawthorn twigs. The effigy's neck encircled by a tightened noose.

Why? he asks. *Why, why, why?* But he knows the answer and the answer almost turns his stomach inside-out like an upended sack. *Maleficium.* Part of a spell. Intent and invocation. This is no mere effigy hanging in a decrepit caravan. The figure was designed to impel the accursed into performing this grotesquely depicted act. This is how his neighbours rid themselves of his predecessor. They turned a recreational vehicle into a killing bottle. A trap in which the Moots rid themselves of vermin. *And you chopped down their bloody trees. This man didn't. For you, they will . . .*

Reluctant to touch the hanging basket of man-sized horror, Tom ducks around it. But clips one of the figure's idle boots and the form sways, an unpleasant creak issuing from its anchor.

Shaking off a shudder and stepping beyond the condemned twig-man, Tom enters a living area suffocated by wood-effect panels, sallow curtains, check upholstery on benches, a fold-down table the size of an ironing board.

And about that table, three more occupants draw a gasp from him. A trio of stick-figures, sitting upright, fashioned to resemble a family. Two seated adults and the smaller figure of a child, their limbs and heads woven from wicker, have been dressed like Guys destined to roar and snap atop bonfires.

'Oh Christ.'

Tom's beam shifts across a mum crowned by a wig that too easily resembles Fiona's bob, styled from shredded rags. A bearded father sits opposite her, his facial hair fashioned from an old paint brush. A little girl with a ponytail, artfully woven from straw and tied with a red ribbon, leans toward her father.

Between their stick hands, defined only as stunted extremities without fingers, a vase stands upon the table. A pot filled with cut flowers; red blooms that draw placid stares from three wooden faces as if all in this family have silently accepted their fate.

Sickened, Tom turns from the sinister tableau and drops a hand to the nearest counter top to steady himself, its surface filmed with dust. And he is reminded of his purpose for being here.

He grows frantic, tugging a Ziploc freezer bag from a jacket pocket. When the bag is open, he begins sweeping.

From the bedroom doorway, Tom beckons Fiona. He knows his eyes are wild but he can't adjust them. *Why should he?* When Fiona sees what sits around that flimsy table in the caravan, he might have to hold her upright. 'Fi'. Come with me.'

She's stroking Gracey's hair in an attempt to resettle the little girl after her fright. Fiona frowns at him. She's still confused by Gracey's outburst and now irritated with him for interrupting her thoughts.

'You have to see this. Now.'

A minute later, outside in the cold, Tom hands the torch to Fiona. Then uses a finger to pull wide the caravan's door, the panel bulging over the broken lock. 'Go and look in there. Then tell me I'm paranoid.'

Fiona takes the torch. She'll do this, go inside and see what's riled him. For now, she's sufficiently impelled and alarmed by the intensity in his eyes to play along. Wrapped in her dressing gown, her feet covered in Tom's unlaced working boots that she slipped on quickly, she steps up and inside the caravan. Ahead of her, the torch beam grows white circles on wood-effect panelling, doors, grubby lino.

Tom watches her swallowed by the innards of the grubby box the neighbours dumped outside their home. 'Brace yourself.'

'Go back inside. Gracey needs one of us.' A mother's instruction cast from the caravan's interior, rising over the scuffle of her hesitant steps.

As she bumps about, the nearest window briefly glows orange, then fades as the torch-beam crosses the curtain. From behind Tom come distant calls for 'Mommy!' from Gracey. Tears are not far away. Tom bites his lip. He'll go to her in a moment.

Head ducking through the narrow doorway, Fiona reappears. 'Shit-hole. But what am I looking for?'

'Aye?' Tom snatches the torch from his wife and squeezes past her as she steps down.

Inside the empty caravan, all is as it was when Tom was here minutes ago, minus the four twig figures.

He looks twice, turns about and wants to smash something in his frustration. Then he barges out of the confined space, the vehicle rocking and squeaking in protest as he stamps through it. When he emerges, Fiona is already jogging back to the house, drawn by the insistent, anguished cries of their daughter.

'They took them,' Tom says, uselessly, while also doubting his own thoughts and his closest memories. Bewildered, he entertains new ideas, ludicrous in any other situation; notions of a bewitchment that makes people see things that were never there.

Fiona has heard him and pauses in the crooked cape of their porch. 'What?'

'Us. The bloke who topped himself. Effigies. Made from sticks. In there just now! We were in there!'

Fiona doesn't move. She just stares at him. He can see the pale smudge of her face but cannot read her expression. He dares to hope she is taking his claim seriously. But when her hand covers her mouth, in the same way people smother guilty laughter or conceal grief, he understands that he's only convinced her of something else.

She straightens and her hand drops. She's still looking at him. He can tell. 'Tom. This stops. Now. Tonight. Or . . . Or . . .' Her distress returns and cuts off the ultimatum. Tom hears a sob and the pitiful sound of anguish his wife unleashes bruises his heart.

Fiona turns and bustles inside the house, her head lowered. He can merely watch her go. He knows what she's thinking. She no longer recognises the man she married, her friend and lover of eighteen years. The father of her only child, whoever he was, has been replaced by this adult changeling. A grown man paying a magician out of their savings to lift a curse. A man whose limbs are laced with fierce scratches, who only last night cut down his neighbours' trees with a chainsaw.

Such a train of derailing thoughts and hopes gains momentum, until something catches his eye. On the neighbours' roof.

Silhouetted against a moon-lightened sky, four black figures sit in a line at the peak. Even from below at this distance, the bulbous body and ball-shaped head of the hanged man from the caravan is immediately evident. Three thinner figures, their outlines stiff and literally wooden, sit beside the suicide. Tom can see the ponytail on the golem of Gracey, the jut of his double's beard, the mop of the Fiona doll's bob. All three members of the wicker family, artfully composed yet rigid, stare down at him with their sightless eyes.

Emerging behind the stick people, a longer form soon reveals itself. The long-eared, misshapen skull of the hare rises. The scrawny upper body widens. Powerful thighs become visible, sloping to the spindly lower legs as the thing stands upright. The tatty face moves in his direction.

Tom gapes until a fear of being reduced to the equivalent of a vole, aquiver beneath the golden eyes of a hawk, drags him from his stupor. He sprints to the open door of his home.

38

G racey studies the careworn face of her dad. The very face that startled Tom when he saw it first thing that morning: a scratched forehead, an untrimmed beard, furtive, restless eyes. He'd stumbled into the mouldy bathroom to urinate and caught sight of himself in the bathroom mirror of a new cabinet, propped at an angle against a wall.

He's also still wearing the crumpled outfit he donned a few hours after midnight, the night before last. The same clothes he wore to bolt through scrub and the spiky entanglements of a lightless wood, blind with panic, before tipping over the fence and crawling the earth, exhausted and scratched bloody. But his little girl still sees beyond the haggardness to the man he really is, her daddy. Tom can tell and reluctantly releases Gracey from a tight hug.

By the rising of the sun, the worst of her trauma from the night appears to have been soothed by time in Mom and Dad's bed. He marvels at her resilience.

Judging by his wife's lowered eyes, which will not meet his own, no matter how much he wants to attract her attention, Fiona's careful makeup barely disguises how tired she is too. He doubts she slept at all. The house, and him in it, is taking a toll.

Turning her back on him, she stuffs a lunchbox inside Gracey's school bag. A drink bottle follows, Fiona's movements quickened by anger. After they returned from the caravan, the

213

most he saw of his wife was the back of her head, turned away from him in bed but not relaxed into sleep. His whispered entreaties and explanations broke against a wall of mute indifference, until he'd slumped into his own silence.

Fiona snatches up her phone, car keys, handbag. Catching Gracey's eye, she nods at the door. 'Gracey.'

'Fi'.'

As if he isn't there, Fiona clatters from the room, her tipped heels striking the hall's floorboards. The front door is tugged open, changing the air pressure inside the house; homely traces thinning, dispersing, replaced by the mulchy scents of outdoors. A gas that triggers Tom's anxiety.

Gracey's face is alert to the tension between her parents. She looks questioningly at her father, who smiles and nods at the door. 'Go on, Peanut. Dad loves you.'

Gracey runs from the room and moments later the front door closes with force, the boom resounding until silence falls and cloaks the empty spaces of the house. Amidst the lingering fragrance of Fiona's perfume, Tom shuts his eyes.

39

With the same disbelief and fascination with which he watched Blackwood the day before, Tom has resumed a similar vigil by midday. He sits on the floor of *the temple* this time, his back against the wall. Even from that distance, as Blackwood mooches amidst old books scattered inside his magical circle of protection, his gum disease is atrocious and the man is breathing as heavily as a sex offender.

When he finally fits the jeweller's loupe into an eye socket, he swings the great mess of his grey head over a lead tablet and hovers above it. Scans it, left to right, sprinkling dandruff from collar and scalp. 'Here. I translated this last night. Roman nobles drove rivals to self-destruction with this spell.'

Things have also changed inside the temple room. New preparations and preventative measures have been made since Tom's first visit. Arranged in front of Blackwood's circle, a large black sheet has been laid like an unlit doorway in the floor, the fabric speckled with herbs. A second protective circle has been neatly painted on the floor, enclosing the black sheet. Chalk sigils have been inscribed inside the new circle's border. It all means little to Tom, though he assumes that in Blackwood's world, the meticulous safeguarding within a magical practitioner's sanctum is a response to the handling of the most hazardous magical materials. The lead curse tablets are in quarantine.

Blackwood's face descends to a few centimetres above a second tablet. 'This one took me a while. Most of the early hours. It's Chaldean. The intention here is to split a household asunder. A family, if you like. Hope we caught that one in time.' Blackwood moves to a third tablet. 'This one I didn't even have to look up. Seen it twice in Wiltshire. Once in Devon. Hellish visions.' Blackwood rears back and rests on his knees, wincing at the pain fired from an old joint under strain. 'You had any?'

Tom nods. 'I don't even know what is real anymore. Last night, I—'

Blackwood proceeds with the annoying habit of not listening to Tom's answers. 'I'm still interpreting the others. They're very old. This takes time. My Greek isn't what it was. But all of them are indicative of the power the Moots wield. And it's safe to say that you have a full house. Let's begin cleansing.'

In advance of his visit, a space has been cleared upon the cluttered surface of Blackwood's desk in the living room, perhaps for the first time in years. With Tom beside him, the old man carefully pours the dust scavenged from the caravan out of the Ziploc freezer bag and onto a strip of paper covered in writing. Latin, Tom guesses. Once the tipping of the dust is complete, Blackwood stands back. The big eye, visible inside the loupe, blinks at him.

'Now eat it.'

'You what?'

'This is a spell, from a Yahweh Hebrew cult, to remove a curse. Eleventh century. Dust from a conjurer's property and a sacred text must be consumed. Begin. You're wasting time you don't have.'

Tom stares at the dusty paper, then looks at Blackwood hoping to see a flicker of mirth, some indication that this is a joke. The man only nods, sagely.

Gingerly, Tom raises the paper and slips it between his lips. Grit and a taste of mildew fill his mouth.

Blackwood watches him keenly. 'Go on. All of it. Get it down.'

'I prepared them last night.' Blackwood opens one of two cardboard boxes on his kitchen table: a carton that once stored multiple packets of crisps at a supermarket. Still chewing the cud of paper and caravan dust, Tom peers over the raised flaps.

A collection of clay bowls, carefully packed with foam, fill the bottom of the box. Inside each uppermost bowl, sigils have been inscribed, meticulously painted.

Tom swallows the gritty residue inside his mouth. Mystified, he looks to Blackwood, seeking an explanation the man is only too eager to provide. 'Bury each one inside the cavities that held the curse tablets. One bowl for each hole. Make sure each hole receives a bowl. The charms must remain inside. They are never to be removed.'

Tom nods, then looks at the four crosses made from wooden slats, stacked in a neat pile beside the first box. The cross-spars are wrapped in twine and a symbol of the sun has been drawn on the front face of each upright.

Beyond the crosses, a second cardboard box is filled with bottles of milk, jars of honey, a loaf of black rustic bread, a silver flask. Tom passes his hand over it. 'I didn't need you to do the shopping.'

'You've a rite to perform. Something once enacted in a temple, or sacred grove.'

'I'm a graphic designer, not a bloody druid.'

'Any idiot can do it. I'll show you how. But there must be intention. You must believe in the protective power of the rite.'

Too tired to be insulted, Tom resigns himself to a weary nod of acknowledgement. 'I find myself believing a lot I didn't a few days ago. And if it'll stop them getting in, I'll try anything.'

'In?'

'And seeing them change. That was a hellish vision. You know, from the curse? They're making me see them like that?'

Blackwood turns quickly, seizes Tom's shoulders. His grip squeezes like a wooden vice. 'What did you say? You've seen them transform?'

'In the woods. In that clearing they've got. It was pitch, night time, but they did something. Became something else.'

'You actually *saw* them changed?'

'I've been trying to tell you—'

'What did you see?'

'A pig. Medea was like a pig. Magi, a hare, I think.'

Blackwood's face pales and he fidgets away from Tom, as if distancing himself from contagion.

'They wore masks. But I can't understand how they moved so quickly? I mean, at their age?'

Blackwood becomes unsteady on his feet and sits down heavily on a stool. One trembling hand paws the table. 'Why didn't you . . . Have they . . .'

'What?'

'In altered form, have they entered your home?'

'My little girl said so. Last night. One of them . . . I think *it* was in our bloody room. She says she's seen it before. In the woods. And outside, when I was getting the dust from the caravan, something was on their bloody roof. The hare. Watching me. My wife won't hear one more word about it.'

Blackwood closes his eyes. Breathes noisily through his capacious nostrils, their openings thickets of grey hair. 'This is far worse than I imagined.'

'What the fuck? What do you mean?'

Blackwood's eyes open and survey Tom with the gaze of a doctor before a terminal patient who remains clueless about the source of a discomfort. 'They never stopped with the curse tablets. This is how they've done it! There will be other charged articles. Inside your home. Markers. Gateways. They must also be found. Every last one.'

As Tom looks at the boxes and crosses, his meagre hopes dissipate like gas escaping a pressurised container. *When will it stop?* He slumps onto a neighbouring stool that oozes beneath him, three loose legs spreading.

'Careful, that stool is a death trap.'

Tom carefully returns to his feet.

Blackwood's hand slaps the table. 'The Moots must have fitted the property out between owners. They've had plenty of time to refine their techniques. Install charms and make ready their torments for any new occupants. Devils! I'll tell you where to look.'

Tom closes his eyes on it all. Outside his private darkness, his appointed shepherd, his family's guardian, holds forth with an enthusiasm he finds inappropriate. 'We need to build a bastion! Defences. On the land. Inside the building. Fortify it all! Or they'll have you where you sleep. Make no mistake.'

40

*F*iona's hardly aware of Gracey beside her, a small figure bouncing on her toes as she tries to see over the kitchen counter and through the kitchen window at what transfixes her mother. Fiona can't remember placing her hands upon her cheeks either, her fingers fanned. A pose reserved for troubled times. She briefly thinks of her own mother, who positioned her hands on her face when shocked by something on the news. A staple gesture of her childhood. A habit passed on as effortlessly as the colour of her eyes.

But Fiona doesn't want to be a mother who sucks in her breath quickly as if she's screaming in reverse, and who clasps her hands to her face when confronted by misfortune, real, imagined, or anticipated. But here she is, doing just that. When Fiona blinks again, her eyes are dry and gritty.

Out there, at the end of their Ypres of a country garden, Tom empties another jar, of what she guesses is a runny honey, into what appears to be a clay bowl; crockery of some kind she has not seen before. He's placed this container beside one of the holes that he gouged into their lawn the day before; an excavation to remove one of the lead tiles he'd located with a borrowed metal detector.

This is the last thing she wants to see after a testing day at work, followed by the drive to Gracey's after-school club in heavy traffic, followed by the long journey home. Tonight's display appals her. Yesterday, his activities at dusk and in the middle of the night perplexed and upset her. Now, she is aghast and wounded, perhaps fatally. Despite her repeated warnings that he couldn't fail to feel impacted by, and she saw the hurt in his eyes last night, he continues with *this*, whatever *this* is.

Tom discards the honey jar inside the cardboard box at his feet. Picks up a plastic bottle of milk, two litres, full-cream, from the same box. Milk that has not come from their fridge. He pours this milk into the bowl. The container is nearly empty, so she assumes the missing quantity of milk has been distributed between the other holes scattered about the garden.

As if adding a pinch of salt to a finely reduced stock, Tom taps a silver flask and sprinkles silvery splashes of water into the bowl. Kneeling, he then carefully places the brimming bowl inside the hole.

It's not only that he is defying her request to desist from his crazy, paranoid behaviour that is recklessly costing them a small fortune; her ire finds additional fuel in the very fact that he believes them cursed. As if beguiled by some crazy evangelist, he must now believe that magic and the supernatural are real and ever-present forces within their lives. *At his age*, when he has always proven himself immune to such delusions. But to suffer such a derangement now is unforgiveable, and at a time when they need him to be as steady and solid as a pillar of stone, preventing their lives from crashing down; lives that he has altered beyond recognition by insisting they buy this broken house at the edge of nowhere that has lain derelict since the last owner committed suicide just inside the front door.

'Daddy's being silly!' Gracey bolts from her side and makes for the back door, intent on investigating her father's latest antics at the bottom of the garden. Fiona jerks away from the counter and snatches her daughter's arm.

Gracey turns, her smile wiped away by the expression on her mother's face and by the shock of the sudden grab; by the grip of a maternal hand and the iron force within it, usually reserved for the roadside as they prepare to cross busy lanes. But her mother has never looked this way before.

'You're not going out there.'

Gracey, for once, doesn't argue.

When Fiona returns her glare to the garden, Tom is walking backwards around a hole. She can see his mouth moving as he incants something that she can't hear. He's reciting from a piece of paper pinched between his dirty fingers.

After the completion of the third turn, he lowers himself to the earth. Prostrates himself over the hole, face-down, his limbs forming the shape of a star.

While he lies still upon the ground, she notices that in the two corners at the top of the garden, wooden crosses have been erected. They resemble markers planted deep on frontier graves and are taller than the crucifix they flank, marking the resting place of their dead puppy.

Fiona hears Tom come in from the dark and scrape off his boots. The back door needs to be forced shut, the wood swollen in the frame. It takes him three pushes, the third firm but not hard enough to shake the wobbly pane of glass out. Like so many other features of the house, their movements are inhibited by small compromises. There are floorboards that cannot be stepped upon, windows too stiff to close that mustn't be opened, surfaces that won't take much weight, cupboards not to be opened, unless they're checking the mousetraps, because of black rashes of fungus that stain the innards. There are sharp edges, splinters, bowls beneath bulges secreting milky tears, bloated spongy panels that fingers can be pushed through, a porch they dart under in case it comes down upon their heads. She now despises this house without reservation.

Fiona stands with her back to Tom, cutting sandwiches for tomorrow's lunchboxes on a bread board. She struggles to even look at him. She had so much to say. Too much. It's all stuck like a herd of jabbering people forcing themselves through a narrow gap at the same time, individual cries forming a crescendo in which nothing is intelligible.

But as Tom tries to sneak away behind her, to escape the room she's frosted with her silence and her posture so stiff with anger and disapproval, she manages to speak. But she doesn't turn to face him because she can't bear the sight of him. Yet.

'A word.'

The shuffle of his feet pauses.

Fiona stamps to the table. Points at her laptop screen, drawing his attention to the new evidence she uncovered after putting Gracey to bed; after she'd bathed her daughter in the two inches of barely warm water the rusting boiler coughed up; after she'd fed Gracey another bowl of tinned spaghetti that she'd nervously heated on an oven ring that filled the kitchen with black smoke and the smell of melting plastic. Like the boiler, a portion of the roof, numerous window frames, the plumbing in the bathroom and kitchen, the oven needs replacing.

'We're overdrawn. A grand.'

'I'll make it back. Soon. Sometime.'

'We weren't yesterday!'

Now that she faces him, Tom appears how she imagines he would appear if she ever confronted him about an affair.

The smell of the kitchen's mildew and old rimy steel intensifies in the horrible silence expanding between them. Fiona swallows three times to rediscover her voice before grief can gag her or her despair smother her. She nods in the direction of the garden. 'It was for that? The stuff you were burying? A magical service?'

Tom looks at his baggy socks and shifts his feet about. Clears his throat. 'I know how it must look.' When he raises his eyes, he smiles, sheepishly.

Nothing she can recollect, until that moment in her life, has made her as furious. 'You really don't!' Involuntarily, the muscles of her face screw up to the first position of crying. She fans her fingers by her eyes, growls, recovers composure. 'What did you bury in those holes?'

Tom blows out a long breath in exasperation, because he knows how his answer is going to go down. 'Consecrated bowls. Look, I can see—'

Fiona holds a hand out as if she's stopping traffic. Clears her throat again. 'I looked at his website. This Blackwood. Some woo woo pirate sailing a ship of shit. And you're now paying him from our overdraft. For consecrated bowls. Correct me if I am wrong, the latter purchased to remove a curse from our house that the two mad old bastards next door laid on it?'

Silence returns even more profoundly to the peeling kitchen. It looks dead to her now; in its final moments of existence before a wrecking balls pushes through the soft walls.

As if before a creature that will turn him to stone if he continues to look at its fearsome face, Tom lowers his head. His rangy shape and grubby clothes blur as her eyes swell with tears.

'I'm doing it for us,' he says. 'Hard as it is to believe, one day you'll thank me for this.'

Fiona stalks from the room. She can't stop the tears. She wants to really hurt him. And herself. She wants to just pull the whole building down upon them.

Turning at the threshold, she lays down her own curse. 'I see anything else like this and me and Gracey are gone. I'll leave you. Make your choice. I ain't telling you again.'

41

'Shit.' Tom shuffles away from the hole he's broken before the threshold of the back door. Upon the two boards he's levered up with a crowbar, he sits and steadies himself. And listens to the house, seeking the sound of footsteps upstairs.

Nothing.

He eyes the hole. *Right where Blackwood said it would be. Blackwood, right again.*

The discovery of a rat's mealy nest, boiling with hungry young, would have been preferable to the sight of the black thing that is currently buried beneath their kitchen. The moment he saw it, he'd yanked his head from the cavity. The torch remains in the hole, emitting a yellow glow.

A mere glimpse of that thing has indelibly stained his mind. That slender form with closed eyes. What is it? Inert but stretching its front legs into the cobwebby darkness. An animal, he assumes, interred in a kitchen crypt; a cavity littered with rubble, broken shards of lathe, curls of tarpaper, nails rusted to fossils and dunes of grey dust.

When he first lowered his head into the gap and the buried shadows had fled the torchlight, retreating to their infernal origins beneath the floor, nothing living had moved down there. A small mercy. If the withered thing of the under-house had so much as twitched, he'd have suffered a stroke. But whatever was interred down there is long dead

225

and entombed in the trench running between the timber joists that support the floor.

There is no access for the creature to have crawled inside, to pant out its last breath. The corpse was planted; an unholy relic laid in unconsecrated ground. A desiccated carcass infested with a curse, dormant until activated. A plague virus to destroy a household. *His household.* And now he needs to get it out.

A deep breath and he returns his head and shoulders to the aperture. Miasmas of damp soil, stale timber, a hint of rodent urine, buffet his face. Retrieving the torch with gloved hands, he directs light through the Hades that exists beneath their feet.

The papery flanks of the corpse are illumined. Like a grave robber before a royal infant's remains, he reaches for the *thing.* And winces as its stiff limbs rod the palms of his hands. It can't weigh more than a few ounces but the crispy corpse catches on something. Even in death it claws at the dry soil, perhaps desiring that its rest remain undisturbed. When Tom forces the body free, a tinkle of dross scatters from beneath its ghastly shape.

He lowers the thing onto a sheet of newspaper.

Upon its new bed, which is immediately peppered with grave soot, he's better able to study the pitiful, sapless remains.

During mummification in the arid tomb, the animal's body sank upon itself but he thinks it was once a cat. The ears and eyes have been erased from the baked face but the mouth is open and bristling with needles, teeth whittled to fish bones. The fur is entirely absent, bleached from flesh by the lightless passage of time, leaving the shell as brittle as the bog-preserved leathers of antiquity.

Four shrivelled limbs jut from the drum-skinned torso, forever enacting a final leap into oblivion. And, bizarrely, as if embalmed by a taxidermist with a keen eye, the preserved tail arches like an idle whip.

Only then does Tom see the foreign body, lodged deep in the charcoal throat but extending between yawning jaws.

Paper. A small scroll bound in scarlet thread, the exterior mottled, watermarked and too unappealing to be touched, even with gloves. Evidence that must be taken to Blackwood's lab for a magician's forensics.

'Bastards.' The Moots probably destroyed the animal before planting its cursed remains behind the neighbours' back door. *Veneficium.* The expression on its face signals that death did not come easily.

Killers of pets. Poisoners of puppies and throttlers of foxes. He hates his neighbours enough to desire immediate physical confrontation. But quickly reminds himself of the murky silhouette of the hare and how it had stood so brazenly upon its hind legs astride the neighbouring roof.

Tom picks up Blackwood's floorplan, marked with estimations of where the other charged articles may lie.

Another crude hole in another old floor.

As if defusing an unexploded bomb, Tom gently inches his extended arms and gloved hands from the second cavity, this one forced through the floorboards of the living room by the French windows. At least *this* isn't an animal.

Sitting back on his heels, he holds the tapered object before his eyes. It's no bigger than a soft drink bottle made from lustreless glass. Bottles in this style are no longer blown but the shape suggests a container for fancy oils, or perfume. The darksome contents remain obscured; their decomposition has misted and filmed the sides.

Using the tip of a screwdriver, Tom worries the cork. It crumbles from the neck of the bottle like sand. Upending the container and gently shaking it, he scatters debris onto the newspaper beside the cat's rear paws. A little bone clatters amidst a rain of blackened fragments.

A small finger bone. Probably human and smeared with an ochre that flakes like old putty. Intricately tied scarlet thread binds the dead child's finger.

A scattering of what looks like rice fell from the bottle too. Under torchlight, Tom can make out the plates and ribs of dried larvae. Suffocated maggots.

He rests the back of a gloved hand across his mouth and nose. Bottled death and corruption. Canned pestilence. And if the bottle's latent power has been enlivened, what terrible and sickening misfortunes will arise in their lives? He feels too nauseous to contemplate the matter.

With the wooden ruler from his toolbox, Tom pushes the bone and the dead grubs back inside the neck of the bottle. Those that refuse to go back inside, he picks up like spilled beans and drops in, one by one. Then seals the bottle's mouth with a strip of electrician's tape.

His house is booby-trapped. *Maleficium*.

'Bastards.'

Tom picks up the list and seeks the next item.

But why does it have to be this floor?

He crouches beside the stairwell where the faint sound of Fiona's voice drifts down and where the crack of timber will surely bellow upwards. His wife is still reading to Gracey; probably because their daughter can't sleep, or has woken upset.

Tom looks at the hall floorboards and tries to fathom how to lever them up as quietly as he managed in the kitchen and living room. Those, he's half-pressed back into place but will need to secure with new nails in the morning. These planks are longer, heavier.

Blackwood's third instruction specifies an investigation of the house's foundations, running from the front threshold to the rear. A large area that the old magician suspects will conceal another infestation of the Moots' charms. Tom no longer possesses a single reason to disbelieve him. But the boards are two metres long, so it's going to be a big hole. A chasm.

His predecessor decorated one side of the reception walls and all of the ceiling to a high standard. And replaced the skirting with a calibre of workmanship that Tom can only envy. If the front-of-house artefact is under the boards on that side of the hall, he might have to take the skirting off too.

Shit.

The finished half of the ground floor had once given them hope, a glimpse of future possibilities. Had it not been renovated so well by the deceased vendor, they would never have purchased the house. And despite its many problems, the house, at least, had a floor downstairs before they moved in. Soon it won't even have that. Through demolition he feels himself moving backwards, rewinding beyond the ruin that he came here to reverse. But thank God he hasn't laid the new lino. It's a mercy. Albeit a small one.

The sound of his wife's distant voice reminds him of her last remark: the warning. But if she catches him searching for hexes inside the house, will she really leave him and take Gracey? She was so upset.

He doesn't know and cannot wait for tomorrow when the girls are out. This whole ordeal must be finished before the hour grows too late. The Moots entered their home last night, after midnight. Removing charms is the only means he possesses to prevent the neighbours repeating an incursion. If some hidden object beneath this floor allows the Moots access to this house, whilst transformed, then finding the object now might very well be a matter of life and death. Even for Gracey.

My little girl.

Right from Gracey's birth, if his imagination ever strayed and depicted the worst of all fates that can befall a child, he'd never been able to decide if he could continue living without her. He wants to cry.

Until an unexpected and desperate idea heats his thoughts to a higher pitch. *What if we just leave? Now? Tonight, just grab some bags and go? Put the cursed heap back on the market?*

Tom's almost on his feet, preparing to stride up the stairs and to issue orders for an immediate withdrawal. Their own Dunkirk, a Gallipoli.

No sooner does he think of this escape plan, than he suffers a sudden, unwelcome recollection of the grotesque dummies in the caravan. And his speeding train of wishful thinking derails.

Abandoning the house does not guarantee their safety. The Moots' vindictive reach will certainly extend beyond these four walls. His family could run tonight and still meet a terrible end elsewhere. The neighbours distribute charms to clients who live near and far. Their conjuring is so effective, wherever it is cast, that their customers kiss their arses in thanks, literally.

The trees, the goddamn trees.

Had he not deforested the border, fleeing might still have been an option. *The trees and the screaming of the saw, the wailing of Medea.* Her grief turning to retribution. Even Blackwood fears them. Tom can tell.

The floor.

'Shit.'

Sitting on his heels and fingering the crowbar, he looks to the stairwell. He daren't risk a hammer because, right here, the end of his marriage awaits. But if he stalls until the girls are asleep and then stealthily levers these boards up, before re-laying the disrupted section of the floor first thing tomorrow with new nails, before the girls clatter downstairs for school and work, then he might just get away with it.

The wrenching and squealing of old timber around the long nails of the first board obliterates the silence.

Enduring a near unbearable apprehension, Tom holds his breath and listens for a sign that Fiona or Gracey have woken.

Failing to detect so much as a creak from the bed upstairs, he slowly pries the first board free, joist by joist, and carefully lays it flat against the floor.

He's shattered. Sweat dries and congeals the length of his back and under his tailbone, but wasting no more time, he sinks to his knees and shines the torch inside the cavity.

Webs, timber offcuts, scattered newspaper, half a brick suddenly brightening. But nothing suspicious.

Shit.

Standing astride a second floorboard, just over half the length of the first, Tom jams the wedge end of a crowbar into the join. Puts his weight into a levering action and splinters good timber. Another three wrenches and hot spikes burn the length of his spine as the aged timber groans, then gives way a few centimetres.

Moving down its length, he addresses the other pairings of nails. Coaxes the plank free and opens a second lid on the darkness beneath the hall.

Footsteps on the stairs.

Tom freezes. Looks up.

Through the banisters Fiona's legs appear, clad in pyjamas. Then all of Fiona descends. She turns, peers up the stairs and speaks to Gracey, who is not in sight. 'Go on! Back to bed.'

Little feet run across the ceiling as Gracey does as she's told. Tom follows them with his eyes, then turns his wet and dust-speckled face to his wife. He reads sorrowful concern and a twist of pity in her expression.

She descends to the foot of the staircase. Pads into the portion of hallway that remains intact near the kitchen and living room. She peers through the doorway of the front room and sees the disrupted floor. Then she checks the kitchen floor and returns to the stairs. She sits on the bottom step but doesn't speak.

Tom drops the crowbar. Races into the kitchen and returns with the dead cat, wrapped inside the sheet of newspaper, its rigid contours indenting his arms. The witch's bottle he grips in his other hand.

Fiona leans away from him and the grotesque artefacts that her swivel-eyed spouse offers up.

Near breathless with fearful excitement, Tom glances up the stairs to make sure Gracey isn't there, then turns to Fiona. 'They were under the bloody floors. Where Blackwood said. Dead cat. Witch's bottle. Take a look.'

Instead, Fiona looks at Tom's twitching face. 'You're close to losing it all but you carry on. I cannot believe you're still . . . What don't you understand? I can't take it anymore, Tom. I just can't.'

'Fi'. It's why the last owner topped himself. Curses!'

'Oh, God. Tom. Listen to yourself. He was depressed. And you're ill too, mate. You need help. Help I can't give you anymore.' She gets up and trudges upstairs.

He feels absurdly heartened that she didn't shout.

Aware that the hour grows late, and still committed, Tom returns to the second aperture in the hall. Using the toe of his boot he nudges the shorter plank aside and across an exposed joist. Long nails protrude from the lighter underside of the timber. He kneels clear of them, lowers his head into the chasm and shines the torch inside the new hole.

Dizzy with shock, he yanks his head back out of the hole. 'God almighty.'

He might have just stared into the face of the devil himself, hollow-eyed and monstrous. Down there lies a vast skull, the pocked surface stained the colour of tea.

Tom dips back inside the cavity, his torch beam flashing against the underside of the hallway. Thrusting an arm inside to its furthest extent, he pinches the skull's flaking nasal bones and withdraws the object. A mandible clatters a joist.

'What the . . .' In the light of the hall the *memento mori* is revealed. More *reliquiae*, buried where they eat and sleep. Death's actual head. Tarred with carrion dust, the cadaverous face seems capable of laughter. A horse once, he thinks, but transformed by extinction. Then dressed by maniacs.

About the nuchal crest, knotted red twine suggests a single red horn. A Stygian unicorn. The elongated head has been bridled too. The headpiece, brow and nose bands are woven from rough twine, binding the bone muzzle. About the throatlatch and crownpiece, ugly wooden rosettes are threaded. Still a champion, even in hell.

Floorboards creak above. Whispers drift.

Tom looks up and hears Gracey's sleepy voice. 'Where, Mommy?'

'Gonna stay at Nan's till the house is fixed up.'

Footsteps on the stairs.

Fiona and Gracey appear.

Fiona is dressed in jeans, a fleece. She carries a transparent suit bag, containing her bank uniform. Like an evacuee in a bombed city, wearing slippers and a dressing gown, Gracey will travel light this night.

Taking one laboured step at a time, Fiona struggles with a case on wheels. She's been packing while he's been tunnelling the underworld beneath their lives; a realm exhaling invisible menace. The skull had lain directly beneath their predecessor's makeshift gallows too. Unto the final moment when the former owner of the house stepped into thin air, the poor bastard would have been clueless as to the real reason he'd been compelled to hang himself.

Despite his discoveries, his defusing of these terrible mines under their feet, Tom can now do no more than watch his family leaving him. Their household is split, sundered. The horror of it strikes deeper and colder than the effect of what he discovered beneath the hall floor.

He must speak. He must save himself. 'Fi'. Look at the head. Look. It was in the hole. Under here. Please. It's how they got inside. How they do it.'

Fiona looks at Tom as if she doesn't even recognise the grimy-faced paranoiac wearing soiled clothes. This man, who points at the abyss he's opened in the floor of her new home, is a stranger now.

Tom swings his gloved hand over the vandalism as if it is a trifle. 'This, I'll fix it. Once we're protected.'

She almost smiles. 'Protected? I don't feel safe here anymore. But not for the same reason as you.' Struggling with the case in the compromised space, Fiona squeezes around the hole to reach the front door.

Gracey watches her dad from the stairs. Then starts peering at the gap in the floor, the skull beside it. Tom doesn't want her to see the fleshless head's grimace, nor the way it has been bridled in anticipation of riding a greater chaos and tragedy into their lives. So he shoves the sinister boulder of bone back into its arid sepulchre.

'Fi'. This. The way you feel. Now. It's all part of the curse. Romans. Greeks. Where it all comes from. It's passed down. Been destroying people's lives for centuries.'

She's not listening. His wife doesn't want to hear another word. He was warned. 'Gracey. Say a quick goodbye to your dad.'

Tension passes from his body and his eyes fill with tears, blurring the broken world where he is soon to be abandoned and alone. He can't speak, he's too upset and sinks to his knees in resignation.

Little Gracey hops about the hole towards his arms. 'Will you go see Archie in his garden bed for me?' she asks, her expression serious yet hopeful. 'Give him flowers. Every day.'

Jaw quivering and throat stoppered by what feels like a cold pebble, Tom nods.

Gracey releases his neck, turns and runs blindly towards the front door. When her small foot slams onto a loose end of the short floorboard, time marginally decelerates. The air subtly brightens. Tom's breath hitches.

The plank plummets into the hole on one side of the exposed joist. The other end fires up like a horrible see-saw, fast as a mouse trap, too quick for his shuttering eyes to follow.

But the sound that booms inside the hall whitens him with nausea in a heartbeat. A *thunk* and hint of a squelch as if someone just popped a grape between finger and thumb.

Gracey stops running. Standing in the hole, her arms twitch at her sides. The timber floorboard doesn't fall.

Fiona screams.

Tom is paralysed.

Gracey drops backwards towards him and it is only then that he understands that the floorboard is attached to her face.

Her arms spasm into a seizure, as if all of her wires have been shorted by the puncture.

What's visible of her forehead and hair darkens, purples, then wetly streaks.

42

*I*f his mind was a pane of glass, a stone smashed it. The fragile screen between himself and catastrophe ceased to exist; the division between safety and disaster ever a flimsy partition. And when the delicate bulb of thought and feeling inside his skull found itself subjected to so vast and swift a change in temperature, it simply cracked.

Later, he found time to believe that when the floorboard struck Gracey's little face, the light of the hall also brightened to alter the very atmosphere of the house with a sudden starkness. Time itself oozed gelid and slowed to a speed best suited to hopelessness.

There were seconds of gaping when no activity or useful thoughts were possible. One shard of his fragmented consciousness developed a silly persona. *Don't panic*, it said meaninglessly. *She's going to be all right. Okay. All right. Fine*, it proclaimed unconvincingly.

Another splinter of his mind fell vertically in a most direful direction and declared that his daughter was dead. Killed outright. A message so ominous he'd become horribly weightless as if he'd been plunged through a trapdoor. Yet he'd remained riveted to a ground upon which he was vapour, instantly rendered to a ghost of who he'd been only seconds before.

The remainder of his thoughts flurried into appeals and nonsense that soon scattered, never to be recovered from the unlit places of the head.

If only he could breathe, move his feet.

Fiona's scream infiltrated the timber frame of the house. Then she was off the mark, her feet seeming to glide soundlessly over the wreckage in the hall to arrive beside her fallen child.

Gracey's face was concealed by the plank. A mask of grainy timber hid most of the horror below. But Fiona still forced a smile through an expression of fixed trauma; a smile that might soften her voice when she rediscovered it. As a mother, she'd recognised a moment in which a child required the deepest fathom of maternal kindness and reassurance. And Fiona would fake anything just to turn down Gracey's terror by one notch.

Tom had felt so grateful that his wife was there. He'd have wept with relief that she was, had there been time.

But Fiona had been afflicted with the same thoughts as Tom, he could tell. As she knelt by the small, twitching body and beheld the terrible syrupy *drip drip drip* from the little girl's head, into the foundations of that rotten building, she'd grimly confronted the possibility of their only child dying before their eyes.

Tom had little recollection of getting Gracey onto the rear seat of his car. Perhaps it was too awful to ever recall, getting out of the hall and to the car. The board was joined to their child, like an upside down stretcher. They didn't dare remove it. Until she was swept into surgery, it had remained affixed to her head. An actual floorboard. But a silent child and the plank she wore like a coffin lid, fused together by a nail, were somehow ferried by him and Fiona onto the drive and jiggled onto the back seat of his car.

Fiona was a better and quicker driver, with a newer car, but she was needed on the backseat, so Tom had to drive his clunker. Though so nervy did he become by the time he was seated, he couldn't make his hands work. Three attempts to fix his seatbelt failed. The third was a yank at the strap which locked.

As if dementia had downloaded itself in his whiteout of shock, he'd stared at the car keys and wondered what to do with them.

The simple task managed, the stereo came on, the volume and sentiment of the music inappropriate.

With jittery hands and only a residual memory of how to operate a car, he proceeded to set off the windscreen wipers and an indicator. The handbrake dragged like an anchor and stalled the car twice before he remembered that a car even had such a device.

Once they were moving more smoothly, they slid backwards into a darkness made more profound by not having the headlights switched on. He'd felt they were sinking slowly into the dying functions of his daughter's brain.

While driving, only once did he dare glance over his shoulder and at the back seat. But after what he'd *seen*, just that once, he'd nearly driven off the road.

His eyes had locked onto what was visible of Gracey – one side of her body, her skin as pale as death. Yet the small head and neck were rippled a lurid scarlet when the yellow glare of a street light flashed through the interior. Under the wood, she'd shivered, as if suffering a high fever.

A stampede of panic had surged through Tom's gullet like vomit and he'd come close to hysteria. He'd then fought for control of the car that slid sideways and glanced the grassy verge.

'What are you fucking doing!' Fiona had screamed at him and broken him back to his senses. His wife was arched over the plank, one foot in the footwell, one leg kneeling between Gracey and the backrest, one hand on the parcel shelf, the other gripping the headrest of the driving seat. She'd travelled the entire journey in that position. Forty minutes that had felt like a year.

Twice Fiona thought Gracey had gone. His wife's voice had risen strangled, throttled by anguish. Twice he'd pulled over and on filleted legs no more substantial beneath him than inner tubes, he'd clambered round the car and sunk into the dark, crowded rear to seize at Gracey's tiny wrists.

Twice a pulse was found. Small hidden beats finally distinguishable from the palpitations that boomed the bones of his own face. Twice he'd returned to the driver's seat knowing his daughter was still among the living.

At this stage of the ordeal, exhaustion mercifully blunted the sharper edges of his torment. But there was little relief because quieter thoughts turned to a grisly reasoning. Grim eventualities were entertained of missing eyes, brain damage, septicaemia, the effects of an old nail driven into a child's head. A thought process more gruelling and nauseating than he could have imagined possible.

From the rear, Fiona's words at one point, atremble and interspersed with swallowed sobs, put through a call to the hospital they drove to. But the roads elongated into forever and enforced their rules. There were so many stops at every red signal that you might only otherwise catch in a nightmare in which you never arrive at your destination.

Approaching the hospital, the night became a smear speckled with rain. Wet tarmac, an ocean. Innumerable signs blared on tiny roundabouts about where to park for the alphabetised departments; signage that might have been written in Mandarin for all the hope Tom had of interpreting them.

Eventually, the car's headlights swirled across the impossibly bright reception of Accident and Emergency. By that time he was nearly on his knees between the pedals of the footwell.

They'd carried Gracey out of the car.

Three smokers by the door of A&E turned to stone.

Fiona had screamed and screamed for help. People had stopped walking and talking and stared. Everyone shut down around them. Until a woman in blue scrubs and crocs appeared. She exuded an innate kindness that had made them both well up. They'd wept pleas for help.

Professionals took over then. Two doctors who looked as young as sixth-formers ran to meet them. Another couple of nurses appeared, carrying a stretcher. Their child was put first.

Neither he or Fiona wanted to release Gracey's little wrists and ankles, as if this family of three were at the gates of extinction. But they had to let her go, into the great, glaring white light.

Outside the theatre where emergency surgery was being performed on Gracey, Tom's agitation ratcheted up a notch and his body came close to convulsing. It was his shaking and pacing that set Fiona off.

She'd been sitting on one of the plastic chairs provided, her face in her hands, her hair draped over fingers that might have been making strawberry jam. His extreme discomposure, the bending over and exhaling, the wringing of his own stained hands, the terrible waiting for someone to come and tell them the worst . . . He knew he'd been unbearable. And by this time too, a cloak of remorse and shame for what he'd done to Fiona and Gracey had wrapped his skin from head to toe like heated towels and sweated him for the fool he was.

In the eyes of this woman with whom he'd tried to make a life, a family, a home, he'd rolled the dice on a lunatic's gamble and lost it all. He'd reduced the remainder of their lives to wretchedness and desolation, because he'd recklessly pulled up the floorboards of their home to locate and retrieve artefacts charged with *folk magic*. Items that were charmed and that had made them accursed.

Within the scrutiny of a hospital's lights – this great hall of science, this pinnacle of human progress – the thought processes that had convinced him of the necessity of such a cleansing of their home must have appeared pitiful, even abhorrent to her.

While she waited to see if her only child would survive the next hour, Fiona must have discovered an opportunity to change the tack of her thoughts. To set them a new course along an exploration of her husband's actions that day. Finally, her musing must have docked at the consequences of the aberrations that Tom had embraced – his burying bowls of milk and honey in their lawn, his ripping up of the old floorboards. And she was out of the chair and in his face with a speed that knocked the breath from him. Her plastic chair slid away like a foal on ice.

The first slap closed one of his eyes and switched his head from north to south. As he stumbled from the first strike, the second blow struck. That one wiped all sense from his mind, knocking his head from east to west.

Exploding from an ominous, patient silence, Fiona had looked especially terrible in that hospital corridor. Lit up with a sickly luminance, tears carving her cheeks, her forehead swiped and crusting with her only child's blood, she'd gone wild.

When she'd raised her stained hands to him again, he'd flinched. But that time, she'd torn at his hooded top and pulled him into her. He only remembered some of what she shouted at him but had understood the entire message.

'You! Bastard! You did this!' Her spittle had hit his face like sea spray on the bow of a cross-channel ferry.

His first reaction was to lay the blame elsewhere. Impossible for him, he found, even at such a time as that, to deny deferment of the worst thing he had ever done in his life. 'Fi'. They . . . It's a curse.'

'There is no fucking curse! It's all in your head, you stupid bastard!'

He let her hit him again and his ear had buzzed hotly for hours afterwards.

A nurse ran at them from somewhere in the distance.

He remembered the squeak of rubber soles closing on the tiled floor.

'Get away from us! Leave us alone!' Fiona had screamed at him and he'd heard two people, who were sitting ten feet away and waiting for their own terrible news to arrive, suck in their breath.

Dumbstruck and punch-drunk, Tom had watched Fiona turn and flee. She'd passed the nurse who'd run to get between them.

'I'd fuck off if I was you,' the nurse had said to Tom as he'd reeled. She'd looked at him as if he was a wife-beater and a child-abuser. She must have thought that he'd battered his own daughter. Must have thought that he'd put her in surgery. Must have thought that he would hurt a four-year-old girl. In the eyes of womanhood he was utterly despised. If he'd been on a bridge, he'd have sent himself off it and down, to shake himself away and out of this body.

He'd then sat in the car for another two hours. Cried for much of it. Went into the hospital numerous times to ask after Gracey.

She was in a critical condition, he was told the second time. Fiona was nowhere to be seen.

They were trying to save her eye, a young doctor whispered the third time he went in, while she held his elbow. That's when his legs went out from under him.

Three people got him into a chair like a drunk who'd gone face-down on a bender.

He'd needed air and had gone back outside and stood in the rain, sobbing.

Then he'd sat in the car again but in silence, so immobile he could have passed for dead. He didn't dare call Fiona.

He was cursed. No such misfortune was natural. His skull filled with images of lead tablets inscribed with ancient words, a petrified cat's silent scream, bones wound with red thread and the skull of a devil buried under his floor. He'd thought of the tiny weight of Archie's body as he'd tipped that pup into the soil.

His face had boiled and throbbed from his wife's blows. They were never coming back from this.

Finally, his mind had filled with a memory of little Gracey and he'd known, in an instant, that he was entirely forsaken. Only then, after hours and hours and hours of being sick with grief, anxiety, remorse and fear, did his rage return.

43

The mere sight of the neighbours' house stretches his nerves taut as piano wire. And makes him want to vomit.

No light escapes from the Moots' property. Tom imagines the occupants have retreated into the rear, perhaps sensing the frightful visage of white loathing that stands out front. And yet, he intuits that such petty, territorial people will also be satisfied that they have spectacularly won this round. Like some infernal power station, the dark house seems to hum with the contentment of the sadist; psychotic bullies safe in the knowledge of how impossible it would be for their crimes to be investigated by any authority.

Tom bends down. Picks up a rock from the border of a garden feature. Weighs it. Too heavy for a snap of the wrist or elbow. This will require an over-arm bowl. A toss. And without permitting another thought to interfere with what rage demands, he bowls the rock at the Moots' front door.

The missile finds its target with a deep and woody *thunk*.

Tom laughs madly at the star-dotted sky, a frigid canopy holding its frozen breath.

'I know you! I know what you are! Twisted, evil bastards! I'll fucking end you! I'll fucking burn you out! You hear, you shrivelled old gammon fuckers! Leave means leave, eh? That what you want? I'm not. I'll remain! You'll go first. I swear. You're fucked. Fucked!'

He stumbles up the drive into a deeper silence. Once his rant ebbs, the tense quietude before the locked doors and blank windows oppresses, chills. Until an owl tests the air with a scream, claiming a darkness that only a predator can keenly peer through.

An owl. *Owls and unicorns and penguins.* Gracey's favourites.

Tom falls to his knees. Now he's sobbing. Air astir with a westerly freezes his tears. Cold caps his nose.

Wearily, he gets to his feet. *Where can I go?* Back to his broken home with *her* blood upon the threshold? To the hospital where he's not wanted and can do nothing but further harm?

Oh God no, God no, not little Grace. He can't escape it, the terrible maelstrom inside his mind. Wrapping his arms about his trunk and bowing his head does nothing. Shouting, crying cannot ease the pressure. He's horror-struck and unmanned. His thoughts are frighted, bolting about their stable in a stampede. He wants to smash something sharp through his head and out the other side. Maybe that will distract him from the excruciating torment of merely existing while his baby fights for her life.

It's on you. Stupid bastard!

He pictures *her* face, *as it was.* And his breath is sucked out of him again. His thoughts blench, wiped of everything but a memory of those lively green eyes.

Eye.

They can save her. These *Witches. The cunning folk.* They can undo it all. Their magic is blackmail. They can lift the very curses they lay!

He's upon their door. Against their front door. Hands hammering. Again, again, his palms slam to muffle the noise of his grief.

'Please! Please!'

Until his hands swipe through empty space. The door has opened.

Tom peers up and there she is, Medea, her face half-lit

and transformed by an awful, triumphant sneer. From her scrawny frame a white nightgown hangs.

Tom drops to his knees and bows before the crone. 'She's lost so much blood. Her eye! The curse. Take it away. I beg you. Money, all of it. What we have. It's yours. We'll go. Leave. We'll go. Please. Not the little one. Not my Gracey. No. No. How could you? A child?'

Tom abruptly kills his sobbed entreaties. He is shocked mute by the grin that splits Medea's face and lights up her spite-filled eyes. A row of square, greyish teeth rim her lipless maw. 'An eye for a tree.'

Dumbstruck and agape at the display of inhuman callousness, Tom raises his hanged head higher but can think of nothing to say.

'Now who's *fucked?*' Medea whispers so tightly, her words hiss.

A faint squeak sounds from a hinge before the door is slammed in Tom's face.

44

ump bump bump against the back door.

Out of the darkness of the garden, beyond the windows, the lump of a head bobbed with reddish hair and streaked with earth nudges the pane in the lower half of the door. An appalling snout and a pair of pink eyes briefly press forward, then rear away as the thing at the door rises onto her hind legs.

A bristly underside swipes the glass and reveals a crop of wrinkled nubs. They surround two plump human breasts. The swine's milk is black.

Tom turns from it, his scream building like a sneeze that won't break. Only to be confronted by a second intruder, its horrid face grinning inside the house.

Shaggy with white hair and up on two legs, the stringy horror staggers before the broken stove, its brown claws scratching lino. The bumpy knuckle of its face whinnies.

They are people. They are animals.

'Look away. Don't look at them,' Tom says to Gracey. She's standing by the kitchen table, dressed in her school uniform. Behind her, where the hall once was, a black abyss with wet brick walls plummets to oblivion. Inside it, a fearful thing stamps its hooves.

Tom tries to gather his daughter into his arms to protect her from the sight of what grunts at the kitchen door and at what totters inside the kitchen, but the little girl remains out of his reach. His numb legs only manage to stump a step before paralysing.

When he looks at his feet, most of the kitchen floor is missing. Down there, in the gaps, dried-out cats slither between exposed joists.

Without eyes, Gracey can't see her daddy anyway. And her mum is no help. Fiona's going out in her best dress and highest heels and she's never looked better. From the doorway she blows a kiss to Gracey and says, 'When I get back we'll go down together. It's like a sleepover. In a cave. We won't be coming out again. It's so exciting. There'll be new mummies and daddies for you and one of them has a long tail.'

The back door clicks open.

The pig *clop-clops* into the house on all fours, soaking the air with a stench of straw soaked in urine and rich dung fresh-dropped.

Grunting and squealing, his visitors gather to him. Tom can do no more than tremble before his daughter's eyeless sockets. Gracey laughs.

Discoloured teeth break his flesh. Like breadsticks, two of his fingers snap away inside the pig's hot mouth.

Only then does he recover his ability to scream.

A rhythmic *thump-thump-thump*. Outside. Outside his closed eyes and faraway mind. *Thump-thump-thump*. Outside but slowly drawing him from this awful sleep.

Tom rises from the tugging swell of the vision. His last memory of the hell he suffered is of wet bones in a kitchen turned abattoir. But the hold of the dream is mercifully thinning. The nightmare's devouring anguish and the acute sensations of pain ease as he shivers half-awake.

Birthed by horror, his eyelids snap apart in a face tracked with salt. He's vaguely aware of being inside the bedroom.

Uncovered to the waist, dirty and depleted, he's alone, lying half on the bed. Wet sheets have lined the skin of his face like brands.

Bewilderment ensues until he can recall coming into the bedroom and drinking a lot of rum. *After* . . . After he put the skull, cat and bottle inside newspaper and carrier bags, removed them from the house and dumped them in the boot of his car. Then he came upstairs. Called Fiona. Twice. There was no answer and his calls were unreturned.

He must have dropped off.

Outside the room, sharp claws now grate brick as something pulls itself up the exterior wall. A shadow passes the window on its way to the roof. A stray foot knocks the window and produces the chink of bone on glass.

Downstairs, the back door handle is tugged up and down, frantically, from outside the kitchen.

Tom peers at the ceiling. Above it, comes a scampering across roof tiles, back and forth as if an animal scratches for access. A roof-tile dislodges and slides and only the distant smash of masonry on the patio below jerks Tom fully into his mind.

What is the time?

A swinish scream. Outside the house at ground level, a porcine monstrousness is shrieking with fury. The old handle of the kitchen door rattles, bangs down, squeals up. Up and down, up and down.

Tom's scalp shrinks like a rubber cap. He shuffles across his wife's empty side of the bed to get away from the windows. He knocks the empty bottle of rum from the side table and it rolls, drops, bumps the floor.

Above the ceiling, the thing on the roof clears its muzzle, then issues a dry cough that soon evolves into a squeal that Tom finds entirely too human in tone.

He's off the bed but swaying, then pitching sideways until his shoulder butts a wall. He's still drunk and remembers knocking back half the bottle. Blinking furiously to rid his mind of incoherence and the viscous qualities of the terrible dream, he passes to the open door and the landing. Swaying, he listens. From his workbench, he seizes a hammer.

Bang! Against the back door downstairs; a weight thrown upon the barrier. The door holds. The pig bleats in frustration. Sharp feet scrabble from one side of the roof to the other.

Tom's head whips from the direction of one noise to another. Soon, he grins and descends the staircase.

Like a warrior about to enter battle, he's ready for them. From fear, desperate courage grows. An inner heat beats his pipes like hot water. A man abandoned and alone but laughing madly, barefoot amidst holed floors, he turns round in the hall, arms extended from his sides, the hammer fisted. 'Come on, you bastards!'

At the back door, the pig must have heard his challenge. Its rampage intensifies and the bleats growl demoniacally.

Tom staggers into the kitchen. He considers unlatching the door. He needs to swing the hammer into the head of the determined swine. *Medea*: he wants her broken apart. Yet he pauses as a modicum of self-preservation pleads a case for caution. With their charms removed from the building, their access is denied, so why invite them in? 'You can't get in!'

He retreats to the hall, striding backwards to spare his ears from the pig's cacophony, until one of his feet plants itself inside the nylon seat of Gracey's toy pushchair.

The noise of plastic wheels, spinning across floorboards, accompanies his fall. He goes down hard, the hammer thrown clear, and his head strikes the floor then bounces. His mind whites to opacity.

Clutching the back of his skull, he groans and waits for the dizzy spell to recede. And only when coherence edges back, does he realise that the night has fallen silent. Beyond the back door of the kitchen and upon the roof, not so much as a muted bleat, or the scrape of a single claw, can be heard.

Raising himself, he peers about until his scrutiny lingers upon the black hole he broke into the hallway floor earlier. Around the dusty abyss, the dry petals of his daughter's blood lie scattered.

After the Moots' failed assault, Tom's thoughts inch back to the misery of Gracey. And before the last of the alcohol and adrenalin drains from his system, he knows he must call his wife.

He steadies himself and makes a silent oath. In the next few minutes, if he learns that the worst eventuality has befallen his child, he will go next door before grief obliterates him. It will be his turn to invade a home. Once inside, he will destroy anything living, in whatever form it assumes, with a selection of his tools, repurposed for murder. If he finds two old people returned to human form, they will be rent and smashed. If he comes upon them whilst conjured into their dreadful other selves, and possessing such awful strength and agility as they do, then he will wreak as much damage upon them as he can, before they end him.

Without his little Gracey in this world, his own death will be a swift mercy.

Perched upon the end of the bed, Tom grips his phone, closes his eyes and swallows.

This time Fiona answers.

'It's me. How is she? I need to know, Fi.'

The sound of his voice may have made her tearful. Or she could be forgiven for being unable to feel anything save grief at such a time. 'She's lost a lot of blood. There's an infection. They're . . . pumping her full of antibiotics. But her eye . . . gone.' Then Fiona completely breaks down.

As does Tom, many miles away from his wife.

45

Horse skull, preserved cat, witch's bottle: lying upon the black sheet within the temporary chalk markings, upon which herbs rain down and patter the artefacts; a cleansing shower within the golden womb of Blackwood's temple.

From the permanent protective circle, Blackwood finally stops mumbling and dusts his hands, sending a cascade of dry fragments upon the pile of tomes rearing beside his ankles. Raising his mangled thickets of eyebrow over his reading glasses, he directs proceedings at Tom. 'Now the salt. Sprinkle it. Evenly. All over.'

Sleep-deprived, Tom moves like an automaton, pouring rock salt from the sack provided.

'That's it. That's it. And there. Cover them as if you were pouring cement over a radioactive isotope. Good. Good. Now. The rite you observed. The boar. Did it stand before the altar?'

Tom nods.

'Which direction does that face?'

Tom considers where the sun rises at the front of the house. 'That would be north.'

As if on receipt of terrible news, Blackwood closes his eyes. His voice becomes a breathless wheeze. 'The hare. Opposite the boar in the circle?'

'Yes. At the start. That's how they were. By that hill. After their dance, or whatever the bloody hell they were doing.'

Blackwood's eyes open. 'Preceded by circumambulation in reverse?'

Tom shakes his head, confused.

'Widdershins?' Blackwood interrogates in a schoolmasterly tone.

'Widder-fuck?'

'Oh for God's sake! Did they dance backwards?'

Tom nods.

'Holy Christ.'

'You can stop them, yeah? More bowls? A spell?'

'Not this. If it's what I think it is.'

'You're starting to freak me out, if the truth be told.'

Blackwood hauls in a breath, sighs it out. 'Then you appreciate the gravity of this process. They'll have spent a lifetime on *the* vision. The vision they sustain is inner. The entire interface is inside them. The Moots are the conduit. But across the threshold they build in their minds, something far more powerful than mere elemental energy, or a spirit, is called upon. Must have been. And they have bound *it* to themselves.'

'I don't follow.'

Blackwood paces inside his chalk ring. His eyes are still puffy from the sleep Tom interrupted just after six. 'This is the oldest magic. Old as stones. The North is death. The Underworld. They've always been greedy. Spiteful, yes. But stupid? I never took Magi and Medea for stupid.'

Above the artefacts, now twinkling with salt crystals, Blackwood dismissively wafts a hand. 'These curses are trifles, child's play in comparison. The defences we have built won't hold for long. Not against this calibre of magic.' Blackwood then closes his eyes and bows his head, palms pressed together, as if in prayer.

Realising this man is starting to express far too much respect for the shits on the other side of his broken garden fence, Tom lunges. He crosses the chalk boundaries and seizes Blackwood's shirt front. Buttons pop and bounce. 'My daughter! She lost a bloody eye! There's an infection now! She could fucking die! You better—'

Blackwood seizes Tom's wrists and wrestles him back a step. Then loosens his grip because Blackwood has been forcefully reminded of what is at stake; of what Tom and Fiona stand to lose if the practitioner's interventions do not succeed. A childless old curmudgeon, perhaps; a committed or even an involuntary bachelor: Tom doesn't know, but the man's murky eyes too clearly reveal his horror at what the Moots have inflicted upon a child. He doubts that even Blackwood believed Magi and Medea would sink so low. And now that the old practitioner must second-guess a situation growing graver by the hour, he appears as winded as Tom feels. Blackwood won't meet his eye.

And perhaps there is some guilt in the man too, festering under those ungroomed bushels of eyebrow, because maybe Blackwood has worsened the situation. And knows it. The conflict has escalated, vertically. This is no longer some petty rivalry about the selling of charms in the South-West.

Gracey's only chance is Blackwood. Not antibiotics or a life-support system, no medical expertise or twenty-four-hour care with observation. None of that will matter a damn. There is only Blackwood standing between him and a casket so small, he cannot consider its pitiful dimensions for more than half a moment.

Will the Moots then kill him and Fiona? Or will their lingering in some kind of wretched half-life of perpetual mourning for a dead child please them more?

Tom's fists clench tighter upon Blackwood's lapels. 'What the fuck do I do?'

Blackwood totters where he stands. Peers down at Tom's hands as if they are covered in dog mess. 'Pictures. I need pictures. A name. A sign. Of what serves them. From what they draw their greater power. There may be a shrine. An incantation. A name recorded, inscribed . . . Indoors. When they leave the house, you must go inside. Find it.'

Despair lowers Tom's eyelids. Fear keeps them shut. When he opens his eyes, the first thing he sees is Blackwood's tatty slipper, nudging the cash-card reader across the protective circle towards him.

46

Inside the bedroom of his lightless house, his knees and ankles burning in protest, Tom peers over the windowsill. He's been crouched in the same place for eight hours. About his legs lie two empty plates, containing the stiffening corners of hastily made sandwiches, as well as three empty coffee mugs and a decorating bucket. He's used the latter to piss into during the stakeout. He's not eaten a hot meal in days but could barely stomach bread and cheese.

Outside, night has seeped from a lowering sky to leave him with only an impression of the garden next door: a few pale stones amidst a suggestion of shrubs, patches of grass glinting in what thin light mists the earth, and the chimera of the Moots' imp above obsidian water. Above it all, the filigreed silhouette of the wood's canopy.

From Blackwood's house, he went straight to the hospital, returning to the house in mid-afternoon. But not once since has he seen the Moots fussing about in their garden, which is unusual. They've stayed indoors all afternoon and evening, perhaps still recovering from the night's manoeuvres. Or preparing for a fresh onslaught.

Their traps and tunnels about the thresholds have been sprung, defused or blocked. But what other means might they employ to get access, to hunt him into a corner? Or will they force him into self-destruction? A kind of theatre of cruelty, played before a small audience of human eyes glaring from bestial faces? He can only guess, but if the Moots visit the mound in the ring of trees tonight, he must quickly cross the border where the fence is missing and gain entry to their home, through the rear. Evidence and materials for Blackwood's investigation must be gathered before the cunning folk return from a woodland sortie. He must go in tonight. The very prospect liquefies his gut.

While on stakeout, his family haven't left his thoughts. He's given Fiona ample cause to detest him and yet her wholesale rejection of him today left him stunned, wounded and disoriented. She's refusing to talk to him now. At the hospital, her mother acts as intermediary. His wife wears a face he has never seen before. Under her dismissive gaze, he'd felt like a stranger, a menace. The woman he has lain beside for eighteen years, he can no longer communicate with at all, let alone touch. She remains huddled into herself, arms folded, head down, enclosed. Her punishment of him, this banishing, is just. Her trauma is monumental. And yet, he wonders; wonders how deep the Moots' toxins poisoned them even before Gracey's accident. Perhaps from the moment they crossed the threshold, they were damned into estrangement.

Gracey is not doing well. An infection has baffled her doctors. It resists the drugs they feed her intravenously. Mercifully, she has remained unconscious since the night of the 'accident'. But the indefinable virus, surely fashioned by the Moots' malevolent, vindictive magic, continues to flourish. Tom too easily imagines the toxin as black ink, darkening his little girl's slender veins and flowing to her precious heart.

They are truly cursed. As accursed as the very building in which they wanted to make a home.

'Jesus wept.' Tom's strength disperses and he slumps against the bed.

A distant sound from across the border rouses him: the click of a lock and the shudder of a doorframe pushed outwards. With the shake of an old glass pane, the portal is then pressed closed.

Tom peeks out and immediately sees a smear of light casting a film across the grass next door, through which two indistinct figures pass hurriedly. Ashen and scrawny and unshod they scurry. Plastered chalky again, they rush purposefully, each of them carrying a woven basket. The boar leads the hare until they grow indistinct near the wood, finally melting into the void between the trees.

Knees cracking like green twigs, Tom struggles to his feet.

Black coat buttoned, black beanie hat tugged over his ears, a shoulder bag hanging loose, he's ready to go. Yet he dithers behind the back door of his house. His stomach curdled by a cluster of nerves, he feels yet another hot, urgent need to take a shit.

There's no time. He must go. *Now.*

Tom paces some more. Clutched in his fists, the screwdriver and hammer become absurdly heavy, as if he's a soldier who's been given a gun and ordered to execute prisoners of war.

He reaches out again to unlock the back door but pauses because thoughts of the screaming swine and leaping hare frolic inside his mind. 'Damn it.'

He steps back as his strength leaks away and courage deserts him; the courage that quickly melts whenever he considers the danger, the pitiful odds of success. He's been here for fifteen minutes and can't even open his back door.

Might they be outside, waiting to leap?

Will they have changed . . . taken form?

Hands upon his knees, he bends and blows the air from his lungs and tries to convince himself that with the lights doused in his house, and his car parked down the hill in the small village, the Moots may believe that his house is empty; that he and Fiona are still huddled in a bedside vigil, at the hospital, where their daughter lies stricken. After their assault the previous night, maybe they won't be expecting him to break into their home. It might be his only advantage and it's all he has to go on.

Peering up, he catches sight of a picture tacked onto the fridge door. Gracey's drawing of a bearded man. The image is childlike but was drawn in a frenzy of enthusiasm and bursts with colour. In the picture, Tom holds a paintbrush and stands beside a house with crooked walls. 'Love my daddy' is written above a heart drawn in red felt-tip ink. A small black dog leaps about his feet.

Tom's face creases, his eyes well.

Straightening, he hauls in a breath that shudders as if a wind inside his chest is fluttering about a sail. He steps over the loose floorboard to the back door in a single stride.

Twists the key.

He's outside the Moots' back door before he allows reason to return. And it didn't take him long to get here; not once he was committed and ran stooped like a soldier at an enemy position. And here is their door, neatly painted, red.

About his booted feet a variety of pots sprout fronds over spotless paving and a coiled hose pipe. Behind his heels, the patio and symmetrical soil beds yawn like open graves from which reduced but eager limbs thrust. He's sure that it is colder over here too. He feels fragile, thinner, too light on his feet. The bumps and gurgles of his heart interfere with his breathing and he's wheezing as if he's climbed a steep hill and not merely run up one garden and down another.

Get a grip.

He glances back, the way he's come, down the length of the neighbours' night-enshrouded garden, and catches sight of an eerie glimmer of stone. The pipe-playing imp, one-legged upon its pedestal. The slither of moon may have purposefully picked out that detail to strike fear into trespassers. With his thoughts becoming a circling recitation of motivational nonsense, he wasn't able to even look at the statue as he scurried past it. But should he have checked for an inscription?

A symbol? Some sign Blackwood might be able to use. The Moots revere the imp.

He'll do it on the way back. He's got to get inside their house first. *Now!*

Tom confronts the Moots' back door again, breath clouding his face like a hot shower's steam. He tries the handle.

Impossibly, the door is unlocked and he's almost disappointed to find it unsecured. But in he goes, carried on legs that don't feel as if they're all there. And immediately trips, falling as much as running three paces, into the darkness.

He regains his balance and smells them. Their odour, musty but exclusive, like fine clothes left in an airless room. A scent hovering amidst a miasma of herbs and dried leaves. Above his head comes a rustle as his hat scrapes the underside of something dry that sways in the darkness, unleashing a trace of spice.

Being blind inside here is intolerable. He recalls again, too vividly, the bellows of an enraged sow at his threshold and the sound of a hare's claws digging at the roof tiles. He fumbles out his phone from a pocket and turns it on. Activates the torch function.

He's inside a kitchen.

Tom casts a quick look over his shoulder to identify what it was that nearly brought him crashing down on entry.

A ghastly brass doorstop. A horrible leering hare statuette with mad eyes.

He looks away, following the swift beam of the phone screen that he swings in an arc.

Even a cursory glance through the thin light informs him that Blackwood's strange home was no preparation for the Moots' interior.

An iron Aga range squats like a bank vault on a tiled floor. An array of copper pans and pots hang from steel rails affixed to the ceiling, though these were put up long before such an arrangement returned to fashion. The sink and taps belong to the Edwardian wing of a museum. Burgundy walls are almost entirely concealed by hanging bushels of plants.

Drying herbs, rowan sticks, berries and limp flowers bustle from ceiling rails. An upside-down greenhouse with a harvest used for more than cooking.

Tom activates the camera app on his phone. Takes pictures. Though what he hopes Blackwood will find in the kitchen escapes him and he chides himself for wasting time and battery life, as well as risking exposure from explosions of the flash.

He creeps to a hardwood dresser used for the storing of Mason jars, bottles, ceramic pots and plastic boxes. The contents of most containers are obscured by an inner murk. He gets closer. Then pulls back.

Through the side of the first jar, the desiccated bodies of frogs stretch to leap. Bats, as curled as pork scratchings, fill the neighbouring receptacle. Elsewhere, dead newts float in greyish solutions. A baby fox condemned to sleep for ever is packed inside another watery cell. Next to it, an adder coils. Many of its scales have detached and float in the imprisoning umbra. Standing upon the shelf below, a row of jars are packed with dirt. Ash and bone fragments fill others.

Tom takes pictures, the click of his camera app the only sound.

The next ground-floor room must share the wall with his kitchen. A light has been left on inside.

At the threshold, Tom hesitates to gape at the walls upholstered with book spines, many antique, some crumbling. A glance at the nearest shelf reveals Greek and Latin titles, embossed in faded gold leaf, crammed together.

Tom takes pictures of one entire case. The jpegs will be hi-res. Blackwood can enlarge them at his leisure.

The wooden pedestal anchored under the window overlooking the Moots' garden might have been liberated from a church. Upon it sits a vast grimoire, hand-made by the look of the aged bindings. It is bound in a scaly leather with brass clasps and Tom hesitates to touch it. He ogles the pages the book has been left open at.

Neat hand-drawn symbols are etched in black ink over the faint scratching of pencil lead. An astrological chart on the recto page. Tom takes a picture.

Leafing wide, crispy pages, he reveals drawings of plants. Latin incantations abound across aged and spotted paper. More charts and woodcuts of figures prancing about thin pines and willows, though for what reason it's not clear. Another features the black disc of a woodland bog or pond, from which a humanlike figure with a heron's head rises to accept a large ball, woven from sticks. Inside the ball, a small face screams.

On other pages, brass rubbings of a language he doesn't recognise, perhaps from stone monuments, adjoin tracts of scripture cut neatly from bibles. More sketches of stone statues suggest the Egyptian or Assyrian civilisations. He's seen similar in the British Museum. He takes pictures. Page after page after page he photographs, paying most attention to those marked by leather strops, thin as slices of silverside.

Should he photograph the entire book? He's only captured one tenth of it. But there are other tomes like it, stacked beneath the table. Too much. Too much of everything. Too much to take in. He'll never understand any of it.

Until it's too late.

He feels a spurt of hate for Blackwood that heats his face like the sun. He can't be sure how much the man is playing him, to learn the secrets of his enemies, while making Tom pay for the privilege of risking his neck. What is he doing here?

This is crazy, pointless, futile.

So much here. *Where next?*

A work table, resembling furniture from a busy artist's studio. Upon it, under closer examination, he determines the scattered papers are actually padded envelopes, each addressed to the names of strangers.

Adjacent to each envelope, what might be charms are ready to be packed and sealed. Latin verses written on shreds of cloth and strips of paper. Fabric bags contain poultices.

Handcrafted horoscopes sit beside small animal skulls with incantations on paper tied to them with string. Dried roots and herbs abound.

Mail order?

He speaks aloud for company, for the shred of comfort a voice may offer a frightened man in such a place as this. 'And we bought the bloody house next door.'

He turns from the magician's table, desperately seeking the shrine Blackwood bid him find.

There isn't one. Not inside here, though this room suggests great significance to the Moots as if it is some kind of presbytery. So where is their altar?

The fevered flashing of his eyes about the dim, crowded room and its surfaces and shelves pauses upon a wooden unit, filled with tiny boxes, or pigeonholes. A honeycomb stuffed with brownish and ivory-coloured papyri.

Tom shuffles to it. Randomly pulls a few scrolls down. They're tied with string. He stuffs four inside his shoulder bag. Then picks up a small statue from a plinth between a bookcase and the pigeonholes. A small boar-headed figure, standing on one leg, playing pipes. Cast in bronze, the posture is not dissimilar to the imp in the Moots' pond, though this one has the head of a grinning pig. He replaces it and takes a couple of pictures.

And it is then that he hears the back door click open.

Pins and needles prickle and frost his entire coating of skin and one of his eyelids spasms. Tom can't move.

Casting about, he seeks a place to hide.

A dark wooden door, in the corner, ajar.

Footsteps sound outside the room. The soles of bare feet scuffle on approach.

Tom rushes for the cupboard.

With his spine near fused to the wall of a closet that reeks of Wellington boots, he waits in darkness. His breath sealed inside his chest, he can almost hear the seconds of an invisible clock, chiming the moments before his inevitable exposure. Did he even close the back door? He doesn't know and only remembers tripping and stumbling inside. And if the Moots have returned home changed and more animal than human, they'll surely detect his scent and rush grunting to his execution.

A musty curtain of Barbour coats, old raincoats and a waterproof cape drapes his body. He digs himself back through them, leaving only an oval for his bloodless face to peer out from. His legs and feet are uncovered. He can't see much else inside the closet. Dim forms hang from pegs opposite his face.

Feet scuffle outside the door.

Tom clenches his fist around the hammer's rubber handle.

A distant voice issues from somewhere deep within the building, further away than the study he's just rifled. He doesn't catch what it says but at least it sounds human.

A shadow falls across the gap between the door and frame. From directly outside the door, a voice booms. Magi Moot. 'Yes, Medea. Cup of tea. Perfect.'

The door opens.

Reddish light angles into the cupboard that now assumes the dimensions of a coffin. It falls across Tom's exposed face. Against the wall he presses his shoulders harder. His painfully contained breath expands like a balloon inside his throat. And when he sees the greater horror, of what leers grotesquely from the wall opposite the coats in which he cowers, the air trapped inside him threatens to escape in a shriek.

Two bristly faces, the eye sockets empty, hang from wooden pegs. One face is horribly tusked, the open jaws fashioning an eye-slit for the wearer. The second headpiece suggests a tatty hare, buck-toothed and bony-faced. The stuff of pure nightmare. Their hides and features are most surely cured from the flesh and hair of real animals, or worse. Tom recalls the scaly shimmer of the grimoire's binding and his gut pinches.

He believes he can even taste the leathery, sweat-blackened materials of the dreadful masks. Perhaps they actually blend and fuse with human heads during transformation. Or do they only suggest the likeness of what the human wearer will physically assume?

Dear God. Let it be over.

Below the headpieces, lying in a corner of the floor, the band of light also picks out one of Gracey's lost toys. And the small furred penguin is missing one eye.

Tom closes his own eyes to assist his body's containment of more than pain and nausea. But he is forced to open them when two ash-covered arms thrust into the cupboard's odoriferous space, passing inches from his nose.

Magi's thin arms are streaked and spattered with animal blood. From his chalky hands another pig mask droops. An artefact returned from some black-patched glade in the woods. And as if the porcine head has recently been engaged in the goring of its quarry, perhaps snuffling about a split belly with the tusks and crooked teeth flinging and scattering offal, the bristles glisten with blood not yet dry.

Could have been you.

Could be you.

The charmer's soiled hands hang the headpiece on an empty wooden peg, then withdraw.

Tom's trapped exhalation begins to seep free until the same blotched arms reappear to hang the equally hideous headpiece of a hare: blackened, moist and shrieking silently, its ears cocked to attention, the buck-teeth rusted with blood.

The dirty arms withdraw.

Four bestial faces now leer at Tom from where they hover, disembodied.

The door closes, sealing Tom inside with the masks, but at least he no longer need stare at the hollow punctures of their eye sockets. Like a man breaking the surface of water, at the point of drowning, exhausted air sluices from his body. He's just about to bend in half and grasp his knees when the door is yanked open again, wider this time.

Ruddy light comes flooding again, into the space in which Tom petrifies.

As two woven baskets are tossed inside the cupboard, his lips part to utter a cry of alarm. One basket rotates before resting against the toe of his exposed boot.

The whitened, blood-flecked arms punch through a fourth time and Tom believes the night will never end and that Magi knows exactly where he is hiding and shuddering amidst the cascade of old coats. This is all part of the torment: the build-up of anticipation until it is his blood that will tar the gaping maws of the hollow devil heads, worn by psychotics.

But Magi's smeared arms merely hang a scythe upon a peg, half a metre from the tip of Tom's nose. When his eyes lock onto the dark and evil-looking blade, he feels faint.

The door is finally slammed shut and total darkness reclaims Tom. Beyond the cupboard, the sound of unshod feet retreat.

Hours later, and only once he is sure that he heard two sets of feet ascend the stairs to the first floor, does Tom crack the door to survey the dark room outside the cupboard.

It's empty and he slips out and makes his way, one careful step at a time, to the Moots' kitchen.

Only when he gently presses the neighbours' back door shut behind himself, wincing at even the smallest sound of the lock's click, can he accept that he has evaded detection.

47

*A*s if ripped by shrapnel to expose the ground below, the fire of summer streams through the woodland canopy. Within these trees Tom can run no further and falls to his hands and knees, though such bloodless limbs as now extend from his pelvis disallow crawling. His jeans might be packed with cement. There is no feeling at all in his fingers either, save a remote tingle, the last spark of dying current.

His vision swims across scrub, coils of bramble, trunks shadow-blackened as if charred by blasts of light, and he squints to see what it is that has run him to ground.

Hopping arthritically, before rising like a man on his last legs in a famine, the tatty thing arrives in the glade first, absurdly tall and tufted with tawny fur. The long head coughs then grins at Tom with teeth unsuited to a human mouth. Until sunlight soon sears and blinds the awful form into a wasted silhouette.

Almost immediately, the other follows. A figure he prays is more woman than beast. Yet how can it be human with those bristles extending from rolls of pink flesh and with soil bearding the wet chin?

Her tottering into the glade compels him to peer at what impedes her advance. It is then that he sees the trotters and not feet.

A rope encircles his ankles and Tom is inverted, then pulled up towards a gnarly oak branch.

'Stop. Please. It doesn't have to . . .' he splutters until his throat becomes as moribund as his limbs.

The plastic bucket Tom uses for decorating is kicked under his head by the hare, before it prances away, screeching, 'We'll catch it all!'

When it returns to him, on the other side of Tom's useless body, the hare holds a scythe of black iron in one skinned hand and steadies the hanged man's swaying with a long-toed foot.

To the surface of sleep Tom rises, desperate to gulp a breath. And in a moment of bliss, he realises that he's been sleeping and is not suspended upside down in a wood, with his throat dangling over a bucket positioned to collect his lifeblood.

A waking groan and his blurred vision clears on Blackwood's face. The old practitioner's ungroomed features form one great expression of intense excitement.

'Thank God . . .' Tom says.

'Precisely!' Blackwood's hand ceases shaking his shoulder and retracts. 'You need to hear this.'

Still wearing the previous night's clothes, Tom rediscovers his body, limb by limb. He's slumped with splayed legs upon Blackwood's book and paper-strewn couch. Like the doorway into another dimension that he's about to topple through, the minutely detailed astrological chart looms upon the wall above.

Tom rubs at the stiffness of his lower back. He must have nodded off. No more than a few minutes ago, he remembers pulling his cap over his eyes. 'I was asleep.'

'For hours.'

'What? No.'

Blackwood steps away from the couch. The floor of the room is congested with open books, as is the desk. More so than usual. Papyri that Tom stole from the Moots are stretched out, their sides weighed down with various ornaments. The computer screen on Blackwood's desk displays glowing jpegs, all recovered from Tom's phone.

Nimbly dodging obstacles on the floor, Blackwood reaches his desk, bends over and grasps the mouse. 'I found something in your photographs.' An irritating pedant's gleam enlivens his eyes. 'The incantation they use originates from a Mesopotamian magician. It was then rewritten by a Roman. And again in the eleventh century by a Jewish scholar. Someone who knew Latin, Demotic Greek and Egyptian. Here. I traced it. From this page of the grimoire!' Blackwood jabs his finger at the photograph from Tom's phone, now enlarged onscreen.

Blinking, Tom leans forward. He vaguely recalls that page of the book in the Moots' study. A page filled with Latin inscriptions, embellished by symbols and what might have been calculations recorded in a chart.

Blackwood near hyperventilates. 'It all pertains to a lesser deity. A rite to animate a statue. Or take something from it. A *being*. To transfer it to another place.'

With his expression equal parts awe and terror, Blackwood turns swiftly from the desk as if to confront Tom. 'It's enough to make me shit myself.'

'Please don't.'

'Incredibly dangerous. A highly unstable process. Only the mad would even attempt it. I didn't know anyone could even do it anymore. The toll upon the Moots must be monumental. No mind could withstand it for long. So they must do this sparingly. When threatened.'

'Do what?'

Blackwood's chest rises and his expression adopts the familiar self-serious cast. 'They have a god.'

The enormity of the suggestion drains the warmth from Tom's skin.

Dazed by the magnitude of his own thoughts, Blackwood stumbles while withdrawing from the desk. 'Imprisoned, I would guess. Forced into service. The *voces magicae* are all there. The incantations. Though only the Moots will know how they must be said. The correct measures of minerals, which animal parts, the oils to accompany the spell, are all listed here. But it'd take a lifetime to find the right sequence. And that's exactly what they've had. A lifetime. Together. I imagine their parents passed on the keys.'

'You can defeat it? With what you know?'

Blackwood doesn't appear to be listening. 'This is how they've done it. For years! Incredible. It accounts for why they've been so successful. They've had a lot of help. Bastards! . . . Defeat it? Ha!' He laughs as if unhinged. 'Not an option, I'm afraid. Banish it? Maybe.'

Inappropriately joyous and elated by his discovery, Blackwood raises his arms to the ceiling, his eyes alight with maniacal glee. *Nor can the greatness of the heavenly ones be represented in the likeness of any human face. They consecrate the groves and woodland glades.* Tacitus was right! Don't you see? The heart of their power. From where they draw favours. The images they ape in transformation. What they have made beholden to them is captive. Somewhere near them. But not in their home. No. Too dangerous. The woods, I'd imagine. That barrow must be active. It's why they chased you out. Why they forbid trespass.'

'What do we do?'

'What do you do?' Blackwood's attention finally settles upon Tom, his eyes grave. 'You must enter the consecrated space. The circle. Then recover the effigy in which they have bound the god. It will be buried inside that mound.'

'Can't you, I dunno, cast a spell instead? From here? Or come with me and do an . . . exorcism? Banish it?'

'Load of bleedin' Dungeons and Dragons! Haven't you listened to a word I've said? The artefact! The idol! In the mound! Start digging. Break the seals. The effigy must be recovered. Then I'll have more to go on.'

'The neighbours? They're not going to just let me dig into that hill.'

'They'll have your throat open before you get one foot deep. So you need to deal with them first. Blind them. Hobble them. Hood them.'

'The fuck? Blind them?'

'There won't be any of that vile jelly business. Don't worry.'

'Jelly?'

'A hood. Blinkers. You must hood a shaman. Prevent the God's spirit entering. Block the conduit. Stall the transformation. Though their discomfort must be considerable, even when blind, so they cannot channel what they have compelled to serve them.' Upon his last word Blackwood breaks his stance, scurries to the cupboard under the stairs and throws open the door.

Tom slips from the sofa. 'My girl, this will save her?'

He's not sure Blackwood hears him over the noise of an avalanche from within the cupboard. And he forgets what he's just asked Blackwood when the man ducks from under the stairs holding a vintage shotgun by the barrel. 'Last resort.'

'Hold on. Hold on.'

'Afraid we're there, my friend. This is the only chance your daughter has. I cannot begin a banishment with the seals in place, protecting the effigy. That must be brought here before a very long process can even begin to dispel its presence. But you must deal with the Moots first. They will do anything, as you have seen, to protect the source of their power.'

'I can't.'

'You must. You must act and trap them outside of their temple, where they are vulnerable, before they can change again. I suggest you deal with them outdoors as they journey to the barrow. I doubt they will give you another night. My defences will almost certainly be swept aside and they will be inside with you before dawn.'

'Whoa. What are you suggesting? That I shoot them?'

'The Mantis you must take down first, the priestess. The pig! She's in control. The hare is but a footman and assassin. Get the legs. So they can't dance.'

48

Looking down the twin barrels of Blackwood's ancient shotgun, Tom drifts the sights over what he's laid upon the bed. As he does so, he wonders how the life of his daughter became dependent upon a roll of masking tape, scissors, two pillowcases and four shotgun shells.

His once carefree Gracey is in critical care, wracked with infection and blind in one eye; his marriage is ruined and his dog is dead. Even after all of that, he struggles to process this moment in which he holds a heavy, oily shotgun inside his bedroom and plans a home invasion.

His neighbours hold a god captive.

Tom lowers the barrel and places the gun on the bed. In Fiona's dressing mirror, he looks at himself, all dressed in black. Semi-tactical, or an old-fashioned burglar?

His thoughts have raced and stumbled for hours, leaving him weary. Dusk fades the newly painted walls and shadows the sanded door; renovations that are now akin to memories, discarded and irrelevant. Delusions and a source of shame.

His view since he arrived home in late afternoon has been, once again, the neighbours' garden. The Moots have remained indoors since he's been here, their property left in darkness. The woods beyond are clotting with forbidding shadows. If Blackwood is right, they will head to the mound at full dark. He must take up a position before then and lay an ambush. And unless he gets to them first, his neighbours will be inside

271

this last bastion within a few hours, with him. If they remain indoors, he must pay them a visit and either draw them out of their burrow, or hobble them inside their home. Before he starts digging.

Tom's mind drifts to his recent dreams of his fingers snapping inside the pig's hungry mouth and of his upside-down body, hung in an arboreal abattoir. Portents in sleep; his dreaming mind impregnated with a dreadful augury. Nowhere is safe outside and he's been backed into a corner, a few rooms. And yet still he struggles with the enormity of the act he has been instructed to carry out, to *execute*. A step he can never retrace on a path that will soon be lost far behind his heels.

Assault. Grievous bodily harm. The use of an illegal firearm. He'll go down for it. For a long time. If the Moots resist, it'll be even worse. He might actually . . . That doesn't bear thinking about. He daren't imagine *that*, nor how ludicrous he'll sound in court as he explains why he murdered two old boomers.

Tom uncaps and raises a new bottle of rum. After leaving Blackwood's house, he picked up fresh supplies on his way to the hospital. He never saw Fiona. She'd finally succumbed to exhaustion and was sedated inside a family room for the parents of critically ill children. Gracey's infection has worsened and can't be arrested to permit her weak immune system to recover and fight back. A solemn-faced doctor told him to prepare for the worst.

They are the conduit.

Who would do that to a child?

But why be shocked? he asks himself. Such cruelty is inflicted upon children in the wider world every day, without the embellishments of magic.

There can be no more bafflement and indecision. The neighbours must get onto their knees before the twin barrels of Blackwood's gun and allow him to bind and hood them.

Or, he must discharge this weapon into them and *disable* them. Blast away at their old legs.

As he contemplates whether he's going to throw up, he's distracted by a flicker of motion at the edge of his eye.

He peers outside but sees nothing. From the distance, above the old wood, he'd suffered a sense that a black object just shot into the air. Up and away.

A bird. Must have been.

He slugs rum. Sits on the bed. Closes his eyes. Grips his face inside hands that now smell of old metal. Thoughts circle, repeat, cut grooves. For hours.

Eventually, Tom picks up his phone and initiates a call to Fiona.

To his surprise, she picks up after two rings.

'Fi'.'

Silence.

'Fi. I have to do something tonight.' He clears his throat. 'Whatever you hear, whatever's said, I did it for Gracey. For us. I want you to know that.'

Silence. He has nothing to say that she wants to hear, or will ever believe. Still, he waits as if for an old friend's recognition.

'Us? If you were thinking of us, you'd be here now. With me and Gracey. She hasn't long left.'

'Don't say that. Please. God. Don't.'

'This is about you. It's all about you. Always has been.' Fiona's voice breaks and the sound of her anguish initiates the sensation of a landslide inside Tom's chest.

'I wanted us to have a future here, Fi'. I did. I wanted it more than I've ever wanted anything.'

'A future? With what you've become?'

'I've not been myself. I know. But once this is sorted, she will be okay. I swear, Fi'. I can finish this tonight. Make Gracey better. I can. I promise. I can.'

Silence returns to the line, tarries a while. When Fiona finally speaks again her voice is softer, sadder. She speaks to herself and allows him to listen. 'That bloody house. The dream of it drove you mad. I was as bad for believing we could have that life.'

'Fi'. We can—'

'None of it was ever going to happen. Our own home, in the country? What a sad joke. Those times have gone for people like us. But at least we had each other. Even in that shitty flat. Only we put our child, our angel, in there, in that place. Where it wasn't safe for her. In a place that made you crazy because we were so bloody skint and desperate. And now we're going to lose her too.'

Pips insistently pierce Tom's ears and shock. Buzzing phone flies that must be addressed. He looks at the screen. Another call coming in: BLACKWOOD.

Tom hesitates. Then swaps to the incoming call.

The voice that blurts through the handset shocks him even more than the sound of his wife's despair. 'They're coming! For me! I can feel them. The gun. Bring it. Come quickly!'

The call ends.

Tom stares at the screen. Fiona is holding.

He shuts down the phone, pockets the handset and reaches for the gun.

49

*B*lackwood's house is unlit, his car parked on the drive, the front door ajar. The lock has been broken inwards, the door-frame has splintered.

Tom fishes out his phone and calls Blackwood's number. A few seconds later, he hears a faint ringing inside Blackwood's home.

Not good. Shit. Shit. Shit.

Desperately hoping that he won't see a long-eared silhouette above him, Tom steps out of the porch and scans the roof, then the neighbouring roofs. Nothing leaps out. He ducks back inside the cover of the crooked porch.

Using the toe of his boot, he pushes the door and widens the gap. 'Blackwood?' he whispers. Then louder, 'Blackwood. It's me. Tom.'

Silence. But might *they* be waiting inside, grinning over Blackwood's inert form?

He tries to fathom by what supernormal sense, or conjured power, Blackwood detected the Moots' advance in the first place. He then worries why the man's own magical barriers were insufficient for home-defence.

Tom slips off the rucksack, the shotgun barrels protruding, wrapped in newspaper. The gun's weight pulls the bag down. With jittery fingers, Tom unclips the bag's clasps. Sliding the cumbersome weapon out is not easy. Losing his temper with the bag is a relief from a nauseating anxiety about what may be crouching inside this dark house and waiting for him.

The Moots could finish the war right here and get away with it. He's clueless about their range when changed, as well as for how long they can remain in bestial form. Blackwood was certain that the enlivening of their flesh into such spectacular physical alterations consumed a monumental power, from a divine source. But the old magician was also sure the process was dangerous and unstable and only to be called upon sparingly. The toll upon the body and mind of a sorcerer was withering, debilitating.

Tom discards the rucksack and unwraps the gun barrels. Grimy steel soon glimmers. Drawing the hammers, he cocks both barrels. And steps inside the house.

Inside the cramped reception, a glance up the stairs is rewarded only by darkness. Straight ahead, the living room door is closed.

Tom slaps on every light switch within reach. The hall light comes on but the light upstairs is out, the bulb dead or broken.

Stalking as quietly as he can on floorboards that give slightly below the dreary carpets, he approaches the living room. On his right, the kitchen reveals the usual disarray. But the next gaping doorway in the hall, unveils the shocking desecration that has befallen Blackwood's temple.

The four candle stands have been toppled. Books and papers lie scattered as if strewn about by the violence of a whirlwind.

Fear close to rupturing him, Tom doesn't linger and decides to not call for Blackwood again for fear of announcing his position. Outside the living room, he places his ear to the door and listens.

Silence.

He reaches down. Grips the handle and hesitates in a torment of indecision before weakly pushing open the door.

Before he even raises the shotgun into a firing position, at the very moment he peers into the living room he catches Blackwood's eye. Then both eyes. Lustreless eyes wide in abject terror and staring back at him from out of the old practitioner's head. A head no longer attached to a body.

The state of the walls and ceiling immediately demand his attention. Every surface is laced red. Blood flecked and streaked as if a leaking body has been spun at speed, in a centrifuge, spilling its liquid and patterning the walls with a macabre swirl of graffiti.

The chart has been torn down, the shelves cleared of books. They cover the sticky floor, their jackets speckled and glistening. Blackwood's papers form an additional confetti, scattered and crimson-spotted.

Feeling weightless and giddy, Tom turns away and props himself against a wall. He clamps a gloved hand to his mouth.

This has to stop. Now. Police. Call. Police. They killed him.

A terrible acidic burp delivers matter into his mouth, billowing his cheeks. He runs down the hall and bangs up the darkened stairs, desperate to kneel before toilet porcelain. As he runs, he fumbles two working lights on upstairs; one in a bedroom he's never seen before and the bathroom lights, activated by a string hanging from the ceiling.

The toilet lid is down, so he aims for the sink and lurches over it. But before he lets go of what fills his mouth, his eyes lock onto the foot filling the basin and the hairy ankle that extends from the shoe that the foot still wears. Inside the ankle joint, a red and whitey mess suggests that a tremendous force rent this extremity from Blackwood's lower leg.

Staggering to the bath, hand clamped more tightly to his bulging mouth, Tom discovers the second foot, at rest upon a rubber anti-slip mat. Similarly torn from below the shin, it is also shod in a boring black shoe.

As a milky spray escapes the sides of his mouth, Tom uselessly worries about leaving DNA at a crime scene.

After falling to his knees before the toilet, he tosses up the seat with one finger and thrusts his head over the porcelain. But the moment before his mouth explodes, he finds himself staring into the palm of one of Blackwood's hands, afloat in the bowl.

50

*A*midst trees he can barely see, Tom crouches, his feet lost in the oblivion of a wood abandoned by the sun. The distant outline of the Moots' shuttered house looms ahead. The barrel of the shotgun rests against his shoulder. A torch bulges from a thigh pocket. His rucksack clings to his back.

He's been squatting in the undergrowth at the top of the Moots' garden for two hours, shifting about to improve the circulation in his legs and to prevent his feet going numb. Sitting down has wicked the evening's moisture through the seat of his jeans, which has seeped an ache into his lower back. Despite such discomforts, he has remained in place within the peaty darkness in which three owls have periodically added shrieks to a symphony of rustlings. Grief, fear, regret and horror have only worsened the tense monotony and nervy apprehension of his vigil.

Tom peers behind himself and into darkness, before looking again at the glow of his phone-screen, under-lighting his face. In the old picture he gazes into, Fiona and Gracey are laughing. But these photos of his wife and daughter are little more than frail matches lit in a black, cold world. He looks at them to remember what must be done. But the sight of Gracey's perfect face mostly just glazes her father's with tears.

His best guess is that the Moots will come for him at home, tonight. As an enticement, he's left all of the indoor lights on and parked his car on the drive.

One, or even both of them, must have changed form to destroy poor Blackwood. Over four hours have passed since he found the remains of the magical practitioner. He can only assume that by this time his neighbours will have been compelled to return to their ordinary guises and are now at home, recovering. To deal with him, they will once again need to adopt new forms. But he knows his best guess is just that: a guess. An assumption. A hope. A gamble.

But as Blackwood suggested, it's most likely that the rite to curate their grotesque refashioning of flesh and bone will be performed at the barrow in the grove. From what he understands of the neighbours' tracks and previous routes that they'd taken to terrorise him and Gracey, the Moots have first emerged from the wood and entered the far end of his garden. If the tactic continues, then the cunning folk will leave their house from the rear to journey to the place among the trees that is so diabolically sacred to them, to transform again. They will need to pass by here first to reach the glade. And right here is where he hopes to take them.

If they remain transformed and are somewhere inside this wood, the odds of him surviving out here tonight are not so good. But if they are indoors and now returned to human form, as he so dearly hopes they are, he will wait here, even until the following day if necessary, until they venture out that back door. Or he busts it down and disables them where they sleep.

Between two and three in the morning, a distant click of a door brings an abrupt halt to Tom's preoccupations. He douses the phone and drops to his knees within the unruly verdure encroaching the Moots' garden gate.

He brings the gun about and his panicky breath mists the stock. For a few moments, he's concussed by his own nerves and too dizzy to see straight. He gulps at the air. And an instinct, competing with his terror, screams out the instruction that he must immobilise them. He needs to think clearly. *You cannot panic.*

Low light from the Moots' kitchen bronzes a few metres of patio and lawn. Through the smear of light, he catches a glimpse of chalky limbs and two dark, bulky heads. They emerge onto the path at the end of his vision. The two ghostly figures then wander up the Stygian garden towards his position.

As they draw nearer, the bestial boar and hare headpieces gain gradual definition, as do the hare's pallid arms and chest, still mired black from its work this night. Blood drying on ash.

Here goes. Now. Now!

Tom can barely feel his legs as he rises. Panting like a thirsty dog and sickened white to his marrow, he raises the shotgun, a weapon that grows heavier and more ungainly within his untrained hands as each taut moment drags and passes. He gets behind the stock until the gun sights cover the narrow path where it winds between two rockery features. When his neighbours reach the imp, he needs to issue a challenge, then shoot if there is resistance.

The spectral forms continue to glide towards him soundlessly between night-doused shrubs, in single file and mercifully returned to human form.

Until Magi the hare stops moving, just short of the imp sculpture, and raises its muzzle as if to sniff at the night air. The permanently cocked ears suggest these extremities are now alert to a predator.

Medea's silent passage also halts. Her distant pig face surveys the woods.

Muffled words pass between his neighbours but Tom can't hear what is said. They can't have seen him but who knows what finely attuned senses these people command?

The hare turns and retreats towards the house. The boar casts a final glance at the treeline before also turning on its heel.

'Fuck.' Tom breaks cover noisily. Wades from the undergrowth, pulls his legs high and clear as if wading through the sea. Feet heavy, limbs lose and shaky, he then runs at the gate. And kicks the barrier hard with the sole of his paint-spattered boot.

Wood splinters. The gate blows open.

The boar looks back. She sees him and starts running. And to Tom's immense disappointment, as he flies through their gate and into the top tier of their garden, he spots the hare almost at the back door.

He throws himself down the path in pursuit, the shotgun out in front, the stock nestled into his shoulder. 'Bastards!' His breath is near asthmatic, desperate, and fills the night. Inside his shaking vision, the garden's features and contours are blurred shapes, whizzing past him as he charges. Free of the wood, the arch of the Moots' roof better defines itself against the paler night sky. He has more light here, more space in which to commit an atrocity.

A feminine squeal escapes the pig mask. He's gaining on Medea and she knows it. The pig totters a mere ten feet away now, slowed by its heavy head and old legs.

Noises of the back door being yanked open by the hare bring Tom to a stop. He swings the gun about and aims low, at the pig's legs. Braces himself.

Then hesitates, swamped by a fear of being blinded or deafened by the old gun. He cannot squeeze the trigger.

Now she's ten, eleven . . . fourteen, at least fifteen strides further away from him again. *And getting away!*

BIT-THROUGH. The blast roars these almost-words inside his ears that immediately whine to a whistle and flood with an icy pain.

The torn air sucks up the silence of night for miles around. Sleeping flowers and lumpen bushes, drowsing ferns and pale boughs, the black pond, the back of each house, are all lit up as if by lightning.

A brief sound of grit scattering fast through leaves and the pig is felled. Blown flat, Medea goes straight onto her face.

A wet mist hovers about the back of her scrawny legs and withered buttocks.

Elation mixing with the cold horror at what he's done, Tom keeps going. With his ears ringing and eyes smarting from an acrid smoke, an inner compulsion assumes control of his legs and he charges. Without thinking much at all, he runs across the boar and pushes the black head down, into the grass.

A whimper rises from below the sole of his boot.

Springing off the pig, Tom lands near the patio at the same time the hare slams the back door behind itself. A click of a key swiftly follows and a loathsome face is soon glaring through the window at him. Magi the hare then turns away and the kitchen lights douse.

At the door, Tom yanks the handle. It doesn't budge inside the frame.

Standing back and clear, he aims the gun at the lock.
BIT-THROUGH.

Wood splinters. Glass blows inside the house, a silvery rain swept horizontal.

He empties the gun's breech. His hand withdraws from his pocket clutching two brass-bottomed shells with red plastic sheaths. He slides them inside twin barrels leaking exhaust, repeating the action he practised endlessly in the bedroom that evening. Cordite smoke spirals, stings his face. His excited breathing sucks in the fumes and they burn caustic and peppery like cigar smoke taken deep. Memories of bonfire nights from childhood flash like fireworks and extinguish in a moment.

Snap of the breech closing.

Inside the kitchen, his double barrels sweep left and right. He spots a light switch and he reaches out sideways, engages it.

Light glows in the greenhouse of a kitchen. Behind him in the garden rise the piteous cries of an old woman in terrific pain.

A noise ahead, in a room on the right. Their temple. Magi has retreated there as if to a castle keep, or a repository for weapons.

Has the hare scampered inside there to secure some aid or protection that might be invisible to him? Will he channel the god? How would he ever know until it was too late? He needs to act fast and disable the other neighbour as Blackwood instructed. It was the last thing the magical practitioner ever told him.

Hinges whine as Tom pushes the door inwards with the toe of his boot.

Book-lined walls in darkness.

Tom goes in. Flicks on the ceiling light. His eyes and the gun sights track everywhere, across pedestal and grimoire, the desk cluttered with charms, the pigeon holes filled with scrolls.

On his left is the cupboard where he hid and the door is ajar. The black slit beckons.

His brow sweats beads. His beanie hat sags and itches like a wet rag.

He wonders if it's necessary to shoot Magi. Could the man be coerced to kneel and surrender his wrists to masking tape and to offer his chalky face to a pillow case? Tom thinks of the gun's roar. He's half deaf and the volume of a firearm indoors will surely deaden what remains of his hearing. Maybe, if he just positions himself before the door and issues a challenge, then –

A scuffle from behind.

As Tom turns, his mind is obliterated by a whiteout of sickening pain. Beneath the roar of this sudden agony whisks a tiny noise of ripping cloth and an earthy thud as sharp metal is driven into meat. His meat. A cold object, one foreign and thick, has entered his shoulder.

The blow knocks him forward. He staggers and twists about-face. The rotation of his body rips the weapon from his assailant's hand.

Inside his vision a blurred, white figure silently steps away. The assassin has delivered the blade and is now in retreat to the door that's swung snug within the frame. Magi had been concealed against the wall, behind the door, waiting.

Tom's vision clears. His back is wet inside his shirt, his skin tacky as if drizzled with honey. He moves the arm and pain blanches him from scalp to sole.

A glance over his shoulder and he nearly throws up. The ancient sickle hangs from his shoulder. It's gone deep enough to self-support like a horrible bracket.

Before him, the hare's black ears are cocked forward. The toothy muzzle grins as the naked form tiptoes away like an obscene dancer. As if to push him away, it raises front paws.

Tom aims low. 'It's that time.'

BIT-THROUGH.

The hare is blown off its feet.

Walls fall and shatter, then right themselves after the cacophony. Tom's ears produce a howl of static, then whine with tone. Blue smoke reeks of a thousand struck matches.

Before silence absorbs the house.

With so much pain screaming inside his injured shoulder, Tom sinks to one knee and casts away the gun.

Before him, a childlike whimpering issues at floor-level.

Tom shakes sweat from his cold face. Reaches behind himself and clasps his fingers about the curved blade. Then cries out in pain and brings that hand before his sweat-stung eyes. His fingers are wet with blood. He roars, reaches again and grips the scythe. Eases it backwards and free.

The tool clatters against the floor.

He stays on his knees with his eyes closed and waits for the world to right itself. For a moment there, he might have been drawing the very life and soul from his body.

He tries to remember why he's here and what is supposed to happen next. *The plan.*

He shot them both. *Got them both, did them both, put them both down.* They could die from shock, from their wounds, from blood loss. It's everywhere beneath Magi.

Dear Christ. Did I do that?

One hand moving fast, the second slow and dripping blood from his shiny fingertips, Tom watches himself unclip the rucksack. Then he's taking out tape, scissors, the pillowcases.

He shuffles to the leaking hare. Unmasks Magi's terrified, tear-strewn face, the ashy makeup running into a blood-soaked beard. Frightened eyes beseech his own. Tom tugs a pillowcase over Magi's head, then lets it thump against the floor.

A shriek of masking tape. A snip of scissors. A length of sticky tape held out before noosing the cotton tight round Magi's throat. There is no resistance. Magi can only clutch at his torn legs that Tom will not look at.

Shuddering like a carthorse, Tom staggers through the hallway and kitchen.

Outside, the pig is crawling towards the end of the garden. A white form inching with great difficulty across the grass. Its legs are strewn behind, lifeless like a shredded tail. From the concealed head sobs seep, interspersed with grunts.

Tom jogs to the figure. Moving is good and switches his thoughts from the bleeding gash in his shoulder. Running keeps the rest of his blood pumping and chases away the woozy idea that he's fainting and that his limbs are fragile sticks.

Seizing a pair of bony ankles, he raises Medea's ripped legs from the grass. The boar shrieks from a mind-swelling agony.

Tom drags her back to the house.

On the floor of their temple and sanctum, shivering and shocked from blood loss, two ashen figures lie before him: his neighbours, the mighty Moots. But now so reduced, with their heads taped inside floral pillow cases, their spindly wrists bound behind their backs and their withered legs blackened by blood.

Tom swigs from a bottle of water and gasps. 'It's under that mound. In the circle.'

Each faceless form appears to stiffen and their shakes subside to tremors.

During the silence that ensues, Tom's hearing ebbs back a little and he becomes aware of their rasping breath, condensing inside the makeshift hoods.

Medea eventually gathers herself and claws back enough strength to speak. 'Don't. For your own sake.'

This encourages Magi. 'It'll destroy you.'

'You already did that.'

Even with her old legs reduced to strips of wet jerky, Medea retains enough vigour to shriek. 'Bloody idiot! It'll kill us all!'

Magi speaks from one side of his mouth, around pained gasps, and Tom worries the old boy might be succumbing to a stroke. 'It must stay in the ground. It's using you. To free itself.'

An unwelcome moment of doubt shadows his purpose, then passes. 'You'll say anything. I'm breaking the seals. Blackwood told me what to do before you murdered him. I'm breaking the chain and I am healing my daughter. You cursed her. You condemned a little girl. You're worse than the manure you toss round your roses. And if my girl doesn't survive this night, I'll behead you both, with this fucking gun.'

Medea's head rears from the floor, gasps, then drops. 'Don't break the seals. Blackwood was wrong. She used him too! She reaches . . . She plants visions.'

Magi writhes, cramps sideways in pain. 'You mustn't let her out!'

Tom spits on the floor, their floor, to clear his mouth. 'That poor bastard who lived in our house before us, you drove him to suicide. You murdered the couple before him. Blackwood now. And how many others, over the years? Anyone who displeased you, you wretched pricks. You've profited from that thing you keep up there and you have destroyed innocent lives. We were next. My daughter! You did this! You made me do this.'

Medea's muffled voice pierces her hood again. 'Fool! You should have left. We only tried to frighten you. Protect you! From her. We protect the world from what cannot be banished. You think we wanted this? This life? Here?'

Magi quickly offers his mistress some wheedling support. Until the last, he still peers from behind her skirts. 'A curse! We were born into this. Never wanted it! We've spent our lifetimes containing *her*. It's our role. Our inheritance. She cannot be dispelled or destroyed. Don't you think we've tried, you bloody idiot!'

Tom shakes his head, takes a step forward and kicks Magi's feet, producing a shriek from the defrocked hare. 'Tell you what. I'll help you. Bind your legs and give you a chance. Just tell me how I do it. How I lift the curse you put on my girl. Then this can stop. I have bandages.' He doesn't but finds that he guiltily enjoys the idea that he can say anything to them now. He wonders if he's always had this sadistic potential.

Medea's head rises again, like a horrible white serpent with its head and fangs in a bag. 'Never! Her blood is on your hands!'

The very sound of Medea's spite-filled voice assists Tom's recall and once again he sees the look in her eyes, the night she gloated about blinding a four-year-old girl.

Tom uses all of his remaining will to not blast apart Medea's writhing head. 'I'm going to dig it up. Set it free. Then whatever will be, will be, bitch.' He turns and leaves the room.

Medea's voice ascends to a thin wail. 'Don't! For the sake of all that you love, don't let her out!'

Magi's phlegm-choked voice follows him through the kitchen. 'We beg you! No! No! No!'

The black night draws Tom to the back door and into itself.

51

ithin the circle of stones, before the hallowed barrow and stained altar of rock, Tom stands alone.

Out here, the very earth, and all that extends upwards from it, is subdued. Surrounding him, the skirts of scrub are quiet and the perpetual restlessness of the trees has stilled. He wonders if time itself has paused. Perhaps the entire landscape that surrounds the sacred space of the grove has become immobile in respectful fear; receptive yet hesitant, lest any movement or sound draw the baleful attention of what lies beneath the land.

A god.

And to think, that in more innocent times, his daughter and their puppy walked nonchalantly here, thrilled by the glade's strangeness and the prospect of adventure. Tom marvels at how he'd believed this place to be a mere strip of old woodland that would bring his family closer to nature – a refuge, rescuing them from their existence in a city where the natural world had been entirely absent.

Of the age of this place, its histories, laws and character, all that it has seen and lived through and preserved, he knows so little. And yet he brought his family here. Believed they could just buy a fallen house at auction, paint a few walls and live happily ever after. He's tempted to roar with laughter at his delusions, until he suffocates.

There is no one left to guide him now. Blackwood has been eviscerated, drawn and quartered, and will eventually be found, piece by piece, once his dismal semi-detached charnel house throngs with flies.

Behind Tom, over yonder where the two houses stand and bow before this furtive and mercurial woodland, his two elderly neighbours are bound and hooded. Their cunning is sealed inside pillowcases while they slowly expire from blood loss; from the wounds he inflicted upon them with a firearm.

Tom shakes his head. His life should never have contained any of this. *What did I do to deserve it?*

But it was so easy to get drawn in, to go to war. Destruction doesn't take long, once you get started, and he would be lying if he denied that defacing his neighbours' trees and blasting them with a shotgun carried its own deep satisfactions. At least at the time.

How swiftly the Moots made him unrecognisable to himself. But there is no more time to think of that.

The torch on the grassy surface illuminates the tracks of the boar's trotters, the shotgun, the bloodstained rucksack. But Tom's attention slides to the barrow and to where he must now break ground. And he thinks of Gracey's tear-stained face, bidding him goodbye. *Little Gracey.* He sees Fiona's tired eyes too, welling with tears. The mummified cat. A candle flame in total darkness. A crude throne. Blackwood's head leaking upon his desk, the eyes open. He sees again those grubby headpieces leering from wooden pegs inside a closet. Archie stiff in his basket, the small eyes lost within ebony fur. *Misery and death.* All of that came from whatever was drawn from here: a divine draught from old stone.

Freshly gathered flowers crown the stained altar.

Tom grips the spade in one hand and wonders what will happen when he smashes the seals. Beyond scant instruction from Blackwood, and a desperate desire to reverse the curse on Gracey, he suspects, now that he stands before the barrow, that there is another gaping hole in his knowledge; an ignorance of the consequences of what he is about to do.

Will the concentration of infernal power that has been buried and stored for so long just disperse? Released, will such *veneficium* and *maleficium* as he has borne witness to no longer be directed at his daughter's destruction? *Could it be that simple?*

Blackwood said it was a god. *It is a god.* Blackwood wanted to banish the god from the enlivened effigy. *Effigy.* That is what he must dig for, though Blackwood is no longer around to dispel whatever possesses the artefact.

His thoughts divert at another sharp angle to consider the Moots' terror of what lies below. Should *it* remain in the ground, as the Moots, its guardians, pleaded? Freed, will the god wreak upon him a far worse fate than the Moots ever had in mind? After all, they remade themselves in *its* image. And that idea alone makes Tom feel faint and sick.

But then, were they simply stricken by the idea of losing the power that had sustained them for decades? And those savage and bestial custodians, who would desolate and take lives with impunity, in pursuit of favours they siphoned from this ground, must be stopped. He has a duty to end what his neighbours have been getting away with. For decades.

Yes, *it* must come out, because it remains Gracey's only chance. That matters most. His little girl. *It's why you're here.* And if he frees it, might he not ask of it a favour?

Wincing from the pain in his shoulder, Tom readies the spade; a simple tool before a force of monumental strength and unnatural power.

Better get started.

Eventually, steel kisses stone. As if digging himself a grave, lit by white torchlight, he's hacked the barrow for an hour until the chink rang out and chilled him. The blood on his back running freely with sweat and soil, he's laboured through exhaustion and his expression has remained a grimace throughout the excavation; a cramp of determination and stifled pain that has watched a pile of black soil slowly accumulate to a hump beside his boots.

Tom now stands inside a great rent in the north face of the barrow, where his eyes widen in awe. This temple's heart is hard.

Spade wielded over his head, then down with an angled blade, he furiously slices at the remnants of wet soil. Then steps away and scrabbles for the torch, eager to illumine what has just tumbled from the dirt at the base of the mound.

Amidst the clots of dark soil, bones glimmer.

On his hands and knees, he desperately rakes the disrupted earth with his gloved hands to gather the ghastly crop, until he holds a large skull aloft. Though its grotesque proportions and dirty humanlike teeth suggest an otherworldly monstrousness, he thinks it's a pig skull. One that is faintly inscribed with sigils.

And there are other skulls. One is much smaller than the first. But once his thumbs have scraped away the wet soil, he discovers the bony walls to be similarly decorated. *A hare?*

The third skull is instantly recognisable as human, also inscribed. He can only suppose that these are the seals, the remnants of what was once interred here, to serve an esoteric and ancient function.

Smaller items, pale as grubs within the moist earth, are also visible. A number of smaller bones and several flat stones that appear to have been marked or etched. He doesn't examine those. They'll tell him nothing. They speak a language he cannot understand. So he puts his tortured back into noisily cutting the remaining soil from the base of the stone that lies behind the bones.

Another ten minutes and he can barely get his back straight. His spine, shoulders, elbows, wrists and hips all scream from being worked red and steaming. But he now finds himself partially hooded inside a porch with earthen banks; a crevice that he's burrowed, a metre deep, into the northern face of the mound.

Mining so far horizontally, he's also recovered and cleared what appear to be two columns and a lintel of stone, a triolith. A doorway made from granite. And from directly before the aperture, the bones and remains had tumbled like unlocked shackles.

Between the plinths, which stand no more than a metre high, he is able to punch through the clot of soil at the top, then scrape it away from the threshold to create an imperfect hole. A black gap a man might crawl through.

A hollow, lightless space exists beyond the arch. If the patterned bones and stones before the entrance were the seals, then the effigy must be inside.

But it is nothing more than his imagination, surely, that a vague breeze is licking his face and cooling his skin, sweat-lathered and embedded with grit. And try as he might to justify the abrupt change in temperature because it's the coldest part of the night and he's stopped exerting himself with the spade, he cannot dismiss the growing stench of an old latrine and residual corruption.

Tom shoves a hand beneath his nose to block the miasma drifting from the bowels of the barrow, then scrabbles for the flashlight to illumine the hollow interior.

Mere moments after switching the torch on, the dim beam of electric light, as well as whatever thin light seeps through the cloud cover, goes out. Soundlessly, instantaneously, every vestige of light is extinguished from around him in the grove.

His own panicked breathing is all he can hear as a void swallows all, below and above him and in every direction he turns. He panics and briefly suspects blindness; yet another curse inflicted upon him by this rotten, infernal hump of earth.

A sound from below stops his fidgeting and twitching. The noise of a stream bubbling under his feet. There is a light too, over where the mound was. Or, at least, where he thinks it stands, because in this oblivion he doesn't know which direction he is now facing.

Ahead of him, distant, small and flickering like a candle flame, a solitary light grows into existence. And at once it summons a memory of a recent dream: the vision from the night he cut down the Moots' trees.

Cautiously, Tom moves towards the flame in the void. As his own hands, which he cannot see, reach out to detect obstacles, he's sure he's been through this before. He also fears that he has moved out of the glade. There is no turf beneath the rubber soles of his boots now, only stone.

His discomposure and growing disorientation are almost unbearable and he crouches as if to make himself smaller and less likely to walk into something, or to be seen.

How far away is the flame? It had seemed to be a few metres off but now seems to be a conflagration at a far greater distance.

And is he not now hearing the sounds of what must be a vast cave? A place below the world, dripping with moisture, where water torrents in the distance with the roar of a subterranean river. But he cannot have stumbled inside the barrow; the hole in the door was too small to walk through and when he reached for the torch, he could not have taken more than a few steps from where he'd been standing before the triolith. The barrow was never so huge. The grove had no stream.

Ahead, the distant flame leaps higher to illumine the crude cradle of stone from which it blazes. The distance between himself and the light is still impossible to deduce. The rock upon which it rages might still be the one that stands in the grove but enlarged to the size of a house. Or something even bigger.

Dear God, where am I?

A curious animal noise emerges to sniff about him in the darkness. No sooner does he hear the sound than a sloppy mouth sweeps the stone behind his heels.

Tom tenses rigid and gulps at the cold air to suppress his panic. Air that tastes of sewage.

Circling counter-clockwise, the beast shuffles and snuffles. Its heavy respirations suggest a monstrous size, the noise rumbling from deep inside a large throat.

Near hyperventilating with terror, Tom stumbles from the thing before it closes upon him in the dark.

Moving in the direction of the flaming stone, it doesn't take him long to suspect that he's being herded towards it. A hound is terrorising a sheep, and when a swinish grunt bleats no more than a metre behind his head, he flees blind.

The subterranean river in the darkness begins to run alongside him. It is close but never visible, nor discovered by any splashes beneath his boots.

Ahead, the great flame now dances upon an altar wreathed in scarlet flowers. It must hold what he came for. The rest is illusion. Magic, he tells himself. Some kind of defence. Hellish visions.

Approaching, he sees the throne behind the fiery shrine, and he stops running. Hacked into shape as if by blind giants, or crudely assembled from fallen dolmens to fashion a huge chair . . . He's seen this great seat before.

Or is it small, this rock upon which a wizened figure sits, like a dark monkey in a temple?

The occupant of the throne remains indistinct but in the flash and ebb of flame Tom makes out black legs, hirsute where visible and concluding in a pig's trotters. The head is hooded by a cowl. A tiara of linked flowers encircles the hood. Ears similar to a hare's, but much broader and longer, extend through the cowl, their tips lost to sight and disappearing into darkness.

Tom looks down upon something the size of a child.

Then he is looking up at it and it is vast.

The god. The prisoner of the barrow.

From behind the rough-hewn throne, a serpent-like shape rises. A long tail as blanched as a grub, whiskery and plated with scabies, rears like a blind worm. The eyeless tip prods at the air and selects him.

Tom's entire head, or maybe just his vision – it happens too quickly for him to process – is yanked forward at great speed. A tremendous magnetism pulls his awareness through space, across the divide. His sense of himself, his very consciousness, is sucked inside the cowl. And before he can scream, he's swallowed whole by the dark cave of the faceless god.

Inside the hood, he's half aware of a vast depth of freezing space, dotted by distant celestial bodies. Stars that begin to rotate counter-clockwise in a noisome whirlpool. Faster and faster, moment by moment, the rotation accelerates. He can't breathe. His last fragment of composure unravels.

Passing too fast to be counted come visions. A sense of a life rewound and unspooled.

Arriving at the house. Gracey runs to the flowers . . . Marrying Fiona . . . Gracey a swaddled babe in his arms, tiny eyes searching his own . . . Himself, younger, looking up at himself as he is now, his eyes filled with tears . . . A boy looking up . . . He remembers looking up on that very day and seeing . . . A baby peers up from a basin in a hospital . . . Red squeezing contractions inside a muscular womb, a heartbeat . . . A barren moor misted by drizzle and low cloud, a lone pillar of stone . . . A monument's silhouette, beneath stars rotating at dizzying speeds until the void descends again.

He's back before the throne. It stands no bigger than a house brick. He might just pick it up in his hands and break the small clay doll with the covered head that sits upon the rock.

A tiny voice streams from the black hole of the cowl, the vent no bigger than a fingertip. Exposed to the sound, Tom screams and drops and writhes about the wet stone floor. A seizure electrifies his nerves. His head bends to his ankles.

Vaulting thousands of metres into the mist-wreathed stars, the throne is colossal, and the vestments that fall from the occupant form a great waterfall of reeking fabric.

A void.

He's without body.

An atom of mind persists inside a roaring freeze that extends too far to be understood. His last spark rotates counter-clockwise, building to an impossible speed . . .

All of me gone.

52

Distant screams draw Tom from a warm darkness. A cocoon he misses the moment he is stirred awake. Odours of cold earth and leaf-mulch flood his nose and mouth. His slowly peeling eyes confront a night silted by murk and looming with old stones. He lies shivering upon the disturbed soil of the open barrow.

Like a survivor of a shipwreck, his limp limbs scattered upon a foreign shore, he tries to comprehend how, or why, he was spared.

Then, from afar, from the direction of the houses that sit beside each other so uncomfortably – one shabby, the other resplendent and empowered – another terrified scream slashes the black air and Tom's shaky reorientation into the world is shattered.

As he rolls onto his knees, pain familiarises him with the stab wound – a swollen mouth agape in his shoulder, now broadened to a horrible smile by his efforts with the spade.

Shirtless, besmeared and concussed from being within the presence of whatever had seeped from the mound to take him entirely within itself, he can do little for a while save watch saliva loop from his mouth.

Eventually, he forces himself to lift his hoodie with the arm that doesn't hurt and he covers himself clumsily like a child getting into wet clothes after a swim. As fabric, rougher than it ought to feel, slides over the gash, he gasps.

White with pain, he bends over and seizes the shotgun. Claws it to himself. Then stumbles along the narrow path leading *home*.

Distant yellow lights from the houses guide him. Pale squares that jump in his vision until he's leaning against one of the Moots' gateposts. There he pants from the exertion of merely dragging himself this far. And he walks no further. He remains huddled by the gate and stunned by the freakish movement that he can see inside his neighbours' house.

Straight ahead lies the lit window of a ground-floor room at the rear of the Moots': the window of their study, or temple. Through which he can see Medea, inside the room where he left her. Only, from this angle, she should be out of sight because he left her bound upon the floor.

She is not on her feet though; she is horizontal. And moving. The means of her propulsion is utterly confounding but that is definitely Medea Moot, silently spinning in mid-air, behind the window. Near the ceiling of the room, as if held aloft by invisible hands, she turns about.

Twirled like a doll, her little arms and legs kick and claw but fail to gain purchase on the furnishings. Her bindings are gone but the hood he taped about her throat still covers her head.

The speed of her horizontal rotation soon increases and round she goes, thrice more, until her covered head strikes a wall and stops her dead. At this remove, the collision is soundless, though the force of the connection, of head to wall, is still capable of making Tom wince. The lifeless form of the old woman then drops out of sight, as if discarded.

Fresh screams immediately resume, from the voice Tom heard when he woke beside the barrow. These cries issue from the garden, he thinks, but he can see no one and no movement in the darkness. Until he looks up.

In the air, a shape hovers against the sky: Magi Moot, still hooded. And like his sister indoors, he is suspended above the earth by impossible means.

Held aloft and fast by the invisible presence, Magi screams like a rabbit cornered by a stoat. The movements of his head are frantic inside the pillowcase while his stained legs hang lifelessly, the ankles still cuffed by masking tape. His arms, though, are loose and thrash the air. He must have chewed through the binding on his wrists. In the front of the pillowcase a small black rip is visible, where the man's teeth desperately gnawed through cotton to get at the parcel tape securing his hands.

But Tom's brief musings about Magi's escape attempt are quickly arrested by the sound of ripping cloth. And an arm is torn from Magi's torso, before dropping like lumber to the lawn below.

A noisome sound of twisting sinews follows. And, as if his hand is caught in spinning machinery, Magi's second arm is slowly rotated inside its socket, one full turn, before being worked looser with a crunch and then a snap that echoes inside the wood. The amputation concludes in a wet sucking *plock* as the second limb is entirely wrenched free from the levitating victim.

The discarded arm falls and lands without a sound.

Armless and bound at the ankles, the old man gargles through a pain so monumental that merely imagining it comes close to draining Tom of consciousness. And yet Magi's chalky form continues to gently rotate and leak from its armless sockets, casting vital fluids that patter over his beloved flowers, so far below.

Finally, Magi's neck is squeezed like a wet towel. Stretched and snapped by unseen hands. Twisted around twice for good measure. And when the neck has been extended to the shape and consistency of an empty sock, the head is plucked free of the torso with a loud *pock*. Hooded, it shoots away in an arc and into the woods, a popped cork trailing linen, until it drops and softly thuds out of sight.

Tom turns away and as he dry heaves over the verdure, he hears the whooshing sound of Magi's torso as it is cast away over the treetops; launched like a comet with a tail of spatters pebbling the leaves of the wood's canopy, until the lifeless trunk is also reclaimed by gravity and crashes among the sleeping trees.

Tom raises the eternal face of the fearful and oppressed. Nothing would be gained by running. And besides, he cannot even feel his legs. Shock has shut him down. His body merely hums with a current that palsies his extremities. What now serves for his awareness simply waits for a great violence; for this divine and vengeful slaughter to descend upon him. He imagines being knotted in the air and he groans.

He braces for the god's touch. Anticipates its sport.

There is not so much as a murmur or rustle about him. And yet he writhes inside at the force and intensity of the great scrutiny that has turned upon him. He can feel it like the cold pressure endured when swimming down from the tepid layers of the sea's surface to reach freezing, rippled sand.

His mind still reeling from the unravelling and ransacking it barely withstood inside the underworld of the mound, he slips to his hands and knees and lowers his head.

Finally, he is sobbing. At what must be the end, he speaks his daughter's name in an incantation of immense love. If he is permitted any shred of himself at all in this moment of certain extinction, then he will take his love for his child with him.

A great remorse and a pity for himself rises like a wave. And when it crashes, it leaves him exhausted and flat, even warm.

Now. Now. Do it now. I'm ready.

Whether the atmosphere changes, or shock and fear have finally shut him down, he'll never know, but gradually, he begins to feel alone.

Like a child that has been unbearably exposed and made vulnerable and frightened inside a room recently occupied by a stern and terrifying adult, he begins to sense that the mighty presence has left, and that the room is empty of all but himself.

Tom peers into the garden.

Darkness. Murky and indistinct shapes of plants and rockeries. Whitish posts of beheaded trees. Two silent houses.

Nothing speaks or cries or moves save a pale arm without a body, which twitches upon a patch of perfectly groomed grass.

Tom succumbs to jaw-rattling shivers all over his body. The deep trauma within his shoulder flares red.

53

*A*s he stumbles towards the kitchen of his house, the pane of glass in the top half of the back door projects Tom's reflection from out of the darkness and onto its mirrored screen.

And he is startled by this face from history, even prehistory, that confronts him. Forehead and eye sockets stained with the blood he's smeared from his hands, and smudged by the soil that was then streaked by successive torrents of sweat, he's near unrecognisable. His beard sprouts wild from cheek and chin, a ghastly crimson brush. Within it, his white teeth flash a grimace.

Indoors, he finds a wall to lean against. The injured shoulder slumps, the arm below cradled against his belly. He waits for his breath to catch up, his heart to slow. He needs water.

His eyes roam aimlessly around his feet. Archie's little bed drifts through his vision. Gracey's toy push chair. Fiona's box of fruity teas.

To think that only weeks before he'd worried himself sick about finding new work to pay a plumber. Such a concern is a luxury now. *Bedtime stories and anxieties about the school run. Getting clothes dry with the heating in such poor shape. A car service. Shopping. Parents' evening. Walking the dog . . .* Mundane dots that join up to form the silhouette of family life, his former life, now discarded; the white spaces between the dots were once coloured by unexceptional emotions, thoughts, habits, routines, absent-mindedness. But that's all sunk into history now.

'Jesus Christ.'

Now he's laughing mirthlessly. But he stops when he thinks of the awesome presence that towered over the world at the edge of the woods.

Where is it now?

An image comes to him, of an old body coming apart in the air. Then he sees himself falling into those spinning stars.

Tom bends over, shakes his head as if to cast droplets from sodden hair, to turn the horror he feels into mere tears that can be tossed out of a mind.

He slumps to the floor of the kitchen. Rifles through his shoulder bag. Finds his phone and then Fiona's number. She's called him three times in the last hour, when he was consumed underground, or wherever it was that he'd been taken.

A familiar recorded message shouts inside his ears. His wife's voice: 'Say something nice after the beep.'

Seconds soundlessly elapse into the past. His shoulder smarts and throbs hotly. Even now, all he's granted is the opportunity to leave a message to a family he's already lost.

'Gracey. My darling. It's me. If you . . . If you ever hear this, I want you to remember that no matter what people are going to say about your daddy, he never did it. He was just trying to protect us. I'll always, always love you and your mum.'

The handset shoots sharp pips into his ear. Tom checks the screen. Swipes up the image of a green telephone.

It's Fiona. She's sobbing. 'Tom. Get here. Now.'

Gracey.

'What?' His own body-weight that grounds him to earth, the very air inside him, all rises up until his sense of himself disperses, becomes intangible.

The ceiling lights seem to brighten as dread gathers him

back together. When he feels as if he's naked and standing in cold rain, he starts to sob. 'No. No. Not Gracey. I won't . . . She can't . . .'

'She's awake. She's come back. They saved her.'

54

lack fumes billow into darkness. Windows glow like oven doors. A strange sight is illumined by the fire that beats before the overgrown lawn, this portion of night engulfed by a great conflagration.

Flames eat out the old caravan, devour it, pop its bones and gristle, lick its bubbling juices, then send them hissing and diffusing into a chemical stink.

Sitting cross-legged like a warrior after battle, Tom watches the pyre. His eyes dance orange, red and black as he comes down from all he has seen and done. But only broken pieces of his former self re-form. He senses gaps where bits are missing and lost, perhaps for ever. A solitary, hunched figure with a dirty face, he's a statue painted with blood and soil and lit by the blaze that leaps from the caravan's blackened sockets.

He watches the effigy of himself, the stick father, burn inside the wreck. Crackling and seeming to nod as if unable to get to its feet and escape the blaze, the wooden man burns. And into Tom's chest the flames seem to extend their ruin. He feels them snap and twist about his heart.

Beside Tom on the cold and dewy lawn sit the not ungraceful effigies of a mother and her daughter. Family members that he carried from the vehicle before lighting the fire; a wooden daughter and wife, their limbs shaped from curving branches, faces rounded into blank expressions, backs straight. Silent companions that wait beside the traumatised and motionless father, as if offering what support they can.

Eventually, a police car's lights swirl icily about the aftermath and flicker over this curious installation of a bloodstained man, sitting beside his stick-wife and twig-child.

Car doors open and close.

For a while, no one speaks.

55

One year later

Click. Stutter. Click. Stutter. Click. Stutter. The second hand of the white clock is always moving, yet it often tricks him into believing that the thin, plastic arm is not really moving at all. That it is stuck.

Click. Stutter.

Motionless upon a single bed in a Spartan whitewashed room: a man. Anyone that looks in at him, through the window in the door, any time he's in here, will see him lying in the same position. He doesn't move so much now, nor eat. When he's inside his room, he tends to stare at the blank ceiling.

Click. Stutter.

Any exertion requires an effort that seems beyond his resources and will. But why move or do anything when your thoughts are so compelling? When so much needs to be figured out, remembered, sifted, considered? Then revisited and placed in the right order like stacked crockery? This way, he knows where all of his thoughts and feelings, random or otherwise, can be retrieved.

Click. Stutter.

His beard is much longer these days. His face careworn but usually emotionless or slumped by sadness. His eyes, most often blank from medication, only rest on standby as deeper explorations of consciousness commence.

Post-trauma world.

What can be said to the man who has lost everything and who knows things that no one will ever believe? He often thinks about this but believes the staff are sympathetic to his ideas, in their own way.

Click. Stutter.

He always fills the journal dutifully. He was given the thesaurus he asked for. Writing so many of his ideas and notions down makes him feel better, though he's not sure why.

Click. Stutter.

Simple fittings and fixtures form the fabric of the world that encases him and meet his eyes when he wakes. Blue rubber mattress. A desk and chair coloured silver birch. Reinforced glass in the windows.

Upon the desk stands a photograph of Fiona and Gracey. Pictures Gracey has drawn and sent to her father are taped to the walls. Same things he sees every day. He notices all of their details.

The faint smell of cleaning fluid he doesn't mind. Occasionally, a whiff of almonds may rise in his room but he's never found the source. Fresh flowers bloom too and cast pollen, but there are no flowers in his room. Side effects of the medication, *they* say.

Click. Stutter.

He's found that many of the other men in this facility are polite. Many are as silent as him. Some friendly overtures have even been made to him but he rebuffs them all. The other men here have done terrible things, are a danger to themselves and others, though you'd never know it by looking at them. They know about him too, that he killed his elderly neighbours and a crank called Blackwood, though nobody knows why. They're still trying to figure that part out.

The narrative of the story – his story – that he endlessly recounted to detectives and doctors and psychiatrists has never changed. But the style of its telling has evolved over time, from impassioned to reasonable to morbid to flat.

His neighbours were cunning folk who used malicious

magic to curse his home and household. The people next door were undetected serial murderers, who'd been doing away with their neighbours for years. The Moots were magicians who possessed the ability to channel the power of a captive god, a pagan deity that he has no name for, in order to transform themselves into large, vicious animals.

To protect his family and to remove the curse that manifested as an infection of the blood that was killing his daughter, he shot both neighbours in the legs with a borrowed shotgun and bound them. He confesses to that detail. But he never killed them. He let the god out and the god destroyed its jailers. That part of his story always forces his doctor to contrive to be unmoved.

Click. Stutter.

When he told Fiona about the facility and its small population, she looked at him in the way she must be looking at the strange men who now show an unwelcome interest in her. The men that alarm her. Tom just can't be sure, with any certainty, how much of the affection and love and attraction that Fiona once felt for him has survived. Some of it, he thinks. But there's nothing to rebuild and there's no going back and they're getting a divorce. He's sure she's seeing someone else.

Gracey still loves her daddy. And though his family had to relocate and start again, and now use Fiona's maiden name, his soon-to-be-ex-wife has never discouraged her daughter from loving her father. In fact, no matter what anyone else says, he knows that Fiona will always defend him around Gracey and insist that his daughter cherish her memories of her daddy. For that, Tom will always love Fiona.

It is Gracey, more than anyone or any single thing that he has ever encountered in the world within his lifetime, that he misses with all of himself. Should she abandon him, he calmly acknowledges that what's left of his life isn't worth continuing with. Though he'll never tell his daughter that, because he wouldn't want to upset her.

The lights click out.

His thoughts begin their passage through another circle.

They eventually dim and settle to sleep and again he sees a bright green glade, amidst dark trees. He's not alone here and never is. Something watches him. Always. He can turn and run through the cool groves and dart between the columns of trees, following the golden light and his sense of a presence existing just over there, or there, or ahead of him, where the wood opens and the birds sing; an array of birds he hasn't seen since childhood that orchestrate melodies to delight him until tears run down his face. But he never finds the one who watches from afar and who is everywhere around him at the same time.

Nor does he ever find the stream that runs incessantly through those woods and his dreams. It might be under the ground.

And yet, often, he and the other one of the woods talk in his dreams and all is revealed and he wakes up laughing or crying with joy, or merely smiling. But not a word of what has been said amongst those forbiddingly beautiful trees can he remember when again he finds himself on the blue rubber mattress staring at the ceiling of his room.

Tom loves to dream. When he dreams he is not alone. He feels cherished.

Side effects, *they* say. He's not so sure.

Click. Stutter.

56

Crunch of a key and the door clicks open.
Tom moves his eyes from the ceiling to see who has come into his room.

It's Rob, the nurse. 'Tom. Visitor. Solicitor.'

As Tom enters the plain white-walled visiting room, Rob tucks himself against the wall inside the door and surreptitiously slips his phone out of his trouser pocket.

The same clock upon every wall in every room here. *Click. Stutter. Click. Stutter.*

Tom draws out the plastic chair before the blank table. He sits down opposite a woman who is not his solicitor, but whom he is sure he's seen before; his dim sense of recognition flickers but offers no satisfaction. He knows her face but doesn't *know* her. It's almost there.

Almost.

Click. Stutter. Click. Stutter.

'Hello, Tom.' Without standing up, she extends a hand towards him. Her skin is pale, the fingernails blood-red.

Wary, Tom refuses the proffered hand.

'I'll be looking after you from now on.'

Tom frowns. 'I have a solicitor. My appeal was refused.'

The woman retracts her arm. 'I'm here for another matter

with the same desired outcome.' The woman smiles again and there is something inappropriate about her expression, perhaps frivolous, even sly.

Tom turns his head and looks at Rob, who stares at his phone screen. And then he remembers.

Over a year ago, before he was sectioned, he saw this tall, slender woman outside the neighbours' house. This is the smartly dressed visitor he once saw standing upon his neighbours' drive, not long after they moved in. So long ago now, but he's had plenty of time to explore those final weeks of his old life since arriving here.

This woman had a nice car. This woman kissed Medea's hand. Now, she's smiling at Tom. A smart black leather briefcase lies before her upon the table.

'It's quite simple,' she says. 'So I'll get right to the point. Bottom line. What would you like more than anything else in this world?' Her expression grows a touch salacious. She has lovely eyes and a thin nose that makes her clear, lively eyes appear even lovelier and darker. Tom can't remember ever seeing hair so black, so perfect. It is pulled tightly into a short ponytail, and the top of her head catches the institutional light and glosses.

'Who the fuck are you?'

'Someone very special owes you a very big favour. For assisting in her release.'

Tom draws back. More suspicious than baffled, he glances again at the nurse, who still peers at his phone.

Click. Stutter. Click. Stutter.

'He can't hear a word,' she says.

Click. Stutter. Click. Stutter.

'No one in here can. Don't worry about the cameras and the staff looking at the monitors. They're seeing something else.'

Click. Stutter. Click. Stutter.

Tom looks at the clock. The second hand clicks and judders but does not progress around the face of the clock. So he was right, it can happen. He watches the second hand for some time until the snap of the latch of his visitor's briefcase distracts him.

Still smiling, as if she's done something clever, she raises her elegant hands from the interior of the case and cups a concealed object upon the table surface. When she removes her hands a white mouse is revealed, sniffing at the air. Beside the little creature, an antique iron sewing pin idles incongruously, as if recently emancipated from a museum display. 'One drop of blood. Left hand. And we can begin.'

Tom swallows. As if he is a child seeking a teacher's protection, he looks again to the nurse.

Rob continues to peer, entranced, at the screen of his phone.

'Go on,' his visitor says. She uncrosses legs concealed beneath the table. They whisk. 'You won't remember but it's all been explained to you. *Promised.*'

Tom's alarm drains and he feels the strange excitement of anticipation, though is not sure why. As if compelled by a decision already pondered and made, he reaches for the pin and raises the brittle black spike from the white surface of the table. Then he looks at the woman, not sure whether he's seeking direction or a sign of trickery.

She smiles, nods. 'She's in the world now. Because of you. She's . . . so *capable.*' The woman shows him her lovely strong teeth between the scarlet of her painted mouth. 'She's wonderful. And terrible. Be grateful you are in her good graces.'

Tom winces. Then it's done. On the pad of his index finger, a drop of blood forms a shiny dome. He extends the pricked finger towards the mouse.

Across the table, the woman speaks quickly but silently, her mouth moving so fast that Tom is sure that no language could be intelligible at such a speed.

A tickle upon his finger as the white mouse feeds.

Tom looks down as the smiling woman's alabaster hands cup and cage the mouse. The creature is gathered and slipped inside her briefcase. She snaps the lid closed.

'One last thing and then you can go and see *her* whenever you like. If you do exactly what I ask.'

Tom stays quiet and watches the woman's eyes closely. She lowers them to the table and smiles wickedly, whispers, 'On your knees. Sup her wine.'

Tom watches the plain table top between the woman's lovely white hands. He imagines that his eyes would follow those hands anywhere, desperate for a caress. One of her fingers rises. A blood-red nail taps the table's laminate surface.

Knock. Knock. Knock.

Again, Tom glances at the nurse. A man oblivious, who listlessly gazes at the screen of his phone.

Lowering his head, Tom peers beneath the table.

And sees the glimmer of patent court shoes, then the woman's shapely legs, skinned in sheer black hosiery. Her ankles are set apart, her glossy knees spread wide.

Dipping his head further down, Tom peers along the underside of the table.

The visitor's pencil skirt is rucked to her waist. Amidst the erotic view of her legs, dimly shimmering to her stocking tops, the grotesque is immediately visible. Upon an inner thigh, a wrinkled nipple extends.

57

*I*nside the art room, Tom sits alone at a craft table. He's oblivious to the nurse and three inmates who sit at the other tables. Pots of paint, brushes, sheets of newspaper and offcuts of brown and black fabric crowd his elbows.

Strip after strip of newspaper that he has torn from the sheets is laid out on the table-top before him. Methodically and patiently, he places the torn lengths of paper upon the surface of a red balloon that he has lathered with white PVA glue.

He then moves the balloon carefully from side to side and methodically arranges the gummed paper over the pellucid surface. In time, soggy, darkened paper conceals every millimetre of the balloon's rubber.

Infrequently, the nurse on duty glances at Tom. But what the inmate is making is unclear to the nurse.

Now the heating has been turned off until the morning, the radiator clicks as the temperature of the steel unit and pipes drops.

Naked in the cooling air, Tom stands alone in the centre of the room and stares at the ceiling.

Inside the stiff shell of the headpiece his breathing is loud.

Sweat pebbles his scalp. The air is hot inside his homemade helmet of paper, glue, paint and fabric. His nose is filled with the scent of newsprint, the mayonnaise tang of dried glue, vestiges of rubber from the balloon that he punctured and withdrew from his creation once the gum had dried. But he'll get used to the smell. The mask must remain upon his head for some time yet.

Little light enters the mask. Some seeps through the eyeholes he fashioned, a little off-centre. A thin glow warms under his chin, coming through gaps where the stiff paper hem touches his collarbones.

Below the grotesque headpiece, the entire surface of his bare skin stiffens as the coating of paste dries. Rising from his flesh are the perfumes of the toothpaste that he has used, and of the tub of moisturiser with which he has smeared his body matt white. When he studied himself in the mirror, he looked ghastly but was reminded of the Moots, his dead neighbours, when they'd coated themselves in daub and ash.

Directly above his head, the lens of a ceiling light burns bright. Familiar cracks that he has studied for hours spiderweb from the fitting embedded in a plain white surface. He stares at the light bulb, and through it to focus on the far greater distance that exists beyond this room. At the same time, he builds within his imagination the vision that he was given in last night's dream. The flame.

The long flame must remain upright. Grow strong and high.

Below his feet, the river runs. Let it run between *there* and *here*.

He keeps all of this within his mind's sight.

In the darkness before the flame, persist until you arrive.

And say the words.

Below the light, Tom's head is raised, covered in the grotesque papier-mâché headpiece. His creation is rudimentary, accidentally sinister in appearance. Childlike too and yet, after he'd applied the last patch of tufty felt, and concealed the last chink of grey newsprint with tawny paint, he was satisfied that most people would identify his creation as a mouse's head.

Staring directly at the light above his face, inside the quiet of his thoughts, he turns the light into a flame again. Another attempt to ignite the inner fire and to keep it lit. Perhaps this is already his thirtieth attempt tonight. But no matter, he's getting better, is gradually absolving himself from this room, the facility, the world, and entering the private darkness that is accessed through the column of fire. The months he has spent prostrate and silent in this room and upon that small bed have abetted this new purpose.

Around the flame, to all points of the compass, a deep velvety darkness spreads.

Hours later, Tom continues to walk backwards in a circle beneath the ceiling light. Arms always raised, palms upturned, he goes widdershins. Until he stops and stands upon one leg.

From inside the headpiece drifts his muffled voice.

'In the room beneath the earth I saw the sow.'

58

The glow of a bedside night-light pushes the darkness away from the top of the bed and the pillows, yet thickens the shadows in the corners of the little girl's bedroom.

A unicorn looms near her head, its pink horn dipping into the soft yellow light. A shadowy doll's house leans against a wall, the small plastic household asleep. Lego structures from the little girl's imaginary daytime worlds lie abandoned, left in darkness like construction sites. Books lean haphazardly on the shelves of a solitary bookcase. Toy animals line the top of the bed, gathered like an audience around the head of the sleeping child. Directly above the pillow, a toy mouse watches over her.

In the middle of the big pillow, Gracey's head is at rest, a polka-dot eye-patch covering one eye. The other is enclosed beneath delicate skin that flickers, as if the surviving eye follows rapid movements during the girl's sleep. She smiles and shows the dark her small, square teeth.

On the wall beside her bed, next to her head, a shadow rises. From the floor, in absolute silence, the dark form grows until it is upright. Within the shadow, limbs and a body steadily grow in corporeality like a picture on a screen emerging through a blizzard of static; interference that slowly clears and leaves a dark impression of a chalky figure standing upon one leg.

The visitor's head is oversized. Long ears and even longer whiskers spear from it. A thin tail restlessly shifts through the clot of shadows concealing clawed feet.

The figure probes from the darkness of the wall, which now resembles an indistinct space that might be mistaken for a door leading from an unlit room.

The visitant's body is human, though the flesh has the appearance of being lightly furred. A long nose, extending from the large head, twitches like that of a rodent during its cautious entry into a living space.

Gracey's secret smile extends beyond her lips and lights up her face. Her eye remains closed.

'My daddy.'

Story Notes:
About This Horror

*A*s you now know, this is not a haunted house story. For sure, at the beginning, a family buy an old and decrepit house, and the property even boasts a tragic history. Sinister presences occupy spaces inside the house and even climb through the windows. The building itself works upon the minds and dreams of its inhabitants; this house profoundly affects all who decide to live beneath its roof. So readers might expect to enjoy, or endure, another haunting inside an old house. And yet this story is not a haunting and this house is not haunted. It is cursed.

Horror writers and their readers favour haunted buildings. I'd guess that, even more than zombies, vampires, werewolves and demons, the haunted house, with its ghosts and apparitions, may be the most perennially popular device in the field of horror, from the Gothic onwards. We all love a haunted house story. Long may disembodied voices and footsteps sound in supposedly empty rooms on the pages of stories. As a writer, I'm certainly not done with the setting and its ideas. And yet I'd warrant that one of the greatest horrors of all, for so many, will not be what you actually live, eat and sleep inside, and call home, but what lives next door to you. The neighbours.

So this is a horror story, a folk horror story to boot, about horrible neighbours. It's very English but I hope its ideas, themes and effects will be felt and appreciated universally.

Neighbours, eh? Easy to overlook them. Too easy to dismiss your new neighbours as an outlier, an insignificance that will have no effect on your lives and play no real part in your pursuit of contentment, comfort, security, protection, shelter, warmth, privacy and solace. We all need our homes to provide these stabilising values in our lives. Not only are these domestic attributes and qualities really important to our mental and physical well-being, and to the happiness of our families, but we probably still consider a decent home to be a human right.

We will also go to great lengths and expense to acquire the right home and to make it ours (to find our current family home, we looked at thirty-two properties in twelve months and bought number thirty-one). So, whether they're rented, or inherited, or we're mortgaged up to our plums, our homes are extremely important to us, in so many ways. Sometimes they may be all we have. We'll probably spend most of our lives inside them; will sleep most of our sleep inside them; will spend much of our income on maintaining and improving and repairing them. Our children will grow up in them, and pets will mark their territories around them; our homes may also bring us close to penury and bankruptcy. We do life in them; we go through life in them. And, in a strange way, a home can become a mother to us when we're older. Homes protect us.

Home. A word with a single note that signifies safety. From the world outside. From others. From *them*.

Given all this, whenever we move into a new home, before we even put the key in the door, why do we pay so little attention to the people who live next door? Why do they continue to be an afterthought? And if your property is semi-detached or an apartment, you will have other people, even lots of other people, occupying their own private space mere inches from where you live, sleep and eat.

You will see them. They will see you. You will hear them. They will hear you. Some of the things you do will affect them; some of the things they do will affect you.

As I see it, before moving house, you should consider that who lives next door is as important as how many rooms you're getting, or the state of the roof and plumbing.

But do estate agents even mention the neighbours to prospective buyers? Do the previous owners and tenants brief you (as they're fleeing)? Does anyone ever try and warn you about those who live over the hedge and fence, or above and below you in a block?

Do they hell. And so neighbours often get away with terrible behaviour for years. Even murder.

I'm going to get personal now. Not including halls of residence, at the time of writing I've lived in twenty flats and houses across fifty-one years. Each of those properties, or homes to me, had neighbours.

One house was burgled twice and the neighbour heard a group of intruders smash a window but never called the police. One neighbour in London wouldn't let me read my gas or electricity meters, because they were in her porch. I also lived next door to a house with a revolving door in which scores of people came and went and one was murdered as I slept. CID woke me up at 4 a.m. and asked me if I'd heard anything in the night. I said, 'Are we talking about that side?' And we exchanged a knowing look. When I left home at 6.30 for work, police tape encircled our little house. A man from forensics, wearing a white suit, was doing a fingertip search on the pavement outside the front gate. I literally stepped over him.

I've had neighbours who sat on their roof at night and sang; neighbours whose kids had a hunting bow and shot barbed arrows through the hedge into our garden; a neighbour who, without asking, parked her car on our drive, because she had three and was tired of trying to squeeze them onto her own; neighbours who smashed fences and used a front lawn as a right-of-way. I've had a great many neighbours and some of them I would only wish upon my worst enemies. The scene of the chainsaw cutting the tops off the trees is a true story – it actually happened to a friend of my dad's as well as a friend I now swim with in the sea.

So I have lived very close to the compulsively rude, provocative, unpleasant, entitled, selfish, boastful, anonymous, even murderous: they were all neighbours. I've had neighbours on my mind for years, folks.

And yet, as a child in our many family homes and at our many addresses in New Zealand and England, apart from the odd sad divorce, still deeply shocking in the Seventies, my memories of our neighbours are wholly positive. My parents exchanged Christmas cards with some of them for decades after we moved. We had neighbours who looked in on each other's sick kids, socialised together, fed pets, invited us to barbecues, loaned keys, babysat, assisted each other with DIY and gardening, dropped us off at school when it was wet. . . One neighbour even gave me my tea after school, when I was four, when my mom was ill and my dad was at work. She was lovely and looked like Cat Woman in the early Batman cartoons. Neighbours regularly welcomed us and became friends (even when my pet chickens destroyed their vegetable plots).

The concept of the 'good old days' is a slippery slope, a loaded and often misleading idea, particularly in these days of dangerous populism. But neighbours, generally, used to be better. I'm talking the Seventies, and before that too, I'd guess. That's what I think. And I've said it.

If I am right, then what happened to good neighbours? Neighbours who'd run round with a bucket of water if your house was on fire? Or, the modern equivalent, take in your package from Amazon when you're out? Where did *they* and *those* values go?

I think the breakdown of community and society, especially in the freewheeling, greed and status-obsessed Eighties, did something to the role and duty of being a neighbour. The very nature of *the neighbour* was transformed, or just ceased to exist. Neighbourliness probably went the way of a good many other things that made life easier and more pleasant. In the Seventies, the societies I lived in were less transient, more equal economically and more egalitarian in outlook; few owned much stuff. The Second World War still wasn't that far away in the rear-view mirror. Postwar, the Commonwealth countries that I knew weren't so competitive about status, or fearful of strangers, or resentful about not having enough stuff, or ashamed of a low status conferred upon them in a loaded game in which we are all pitted against each other in a futile challenge of compare and contrast. Though some poor bastards still lived next door to Fred and Rose West, and Christie, so nothing was ever perfect!

International cities may have always been exceptions too, where many homes traditionally tended to be self-contained units, and people more anonymous; where people lived next door to each other and shared the same steps, but never shared a word in years, or ever. Neighbours may even have studiously avoided each other's eyes. But in the 'burbs, towns and villages, things were different.

So it is these divisive times that we all now haul ass through, and my age and personal experience, that have contributed to my desire to write a horror novel about neighbours. I am surprised that there aren't more – I can think of just two. Yet haunted house stories are innumerable. How many of us have lived in a haunted building? Very few. How many of us have had awful neighbours? Nearly all of us, I'll wager, at one time or another. Unless you're really fortunate and never move, you will have bad neighbours in your life. The more you move, the more of them you will encounter and experience. And in these times of great division, of the dismantling and hasty rebuilding of the state, and of grotesque inequality and the absence of traditional communities, I've decided to use a microscope on two sets of very different people, who hate each other. But share a border and dividing wall.

I've shrunk the world and society down to, pretty much, two houses, two gardens, two families and a wood beyond the fence. Simple world; intense relationships. I don't even want to give the place a name; it is rural, it is British, it is regional (in the South West). The young move into an old house with people of a different generation next door. Class, age, territory, personal habits and priorities, personalities (and their disorders), differences, actions and reactions, even cultures: they are all then poured into the pot and shaken. These were the things that mattered to me aesthetically, when they collided. I then added a touch of magic. And horror.

This novel also marks a change in my approach to the form: it is adapted from my own screenplay (my second) for a feature film. The screenplay has been in development for three years and in that time I have produced five versions of the same story and attended umpteen meetings with directors and producers. One day the screenplay may even get the "trigger" and become a film. Who knows? It won't be for want of trying. But now I've completed this adaptive process back to front – film to book. So, how did this happen? And what was I thinking?

While writing my first two screenplays – or "block horrors" – I was advised by some film pros who know their onions to write films that could be financed for $3 million, in order to increase their attractiveness to backers and sales agents. Films in roughly the same vein as most horror films. But before I'd even finished the first draft of each screenplay, I also knew that these two stories would simply have to become my next two prose novels. If the films are never shot – or never shot as I intended – the stories and characters won't die. They will, at least, live on in books.

I spent months researching aspects of this story for the screenplay and probably used less than 1 per cent of my research. No matter, that's how it goes. I then wrote a very detailed treatment for myself – around sixty pages (in an industry of headlines and one-pagers, in which few seem to want to read blocks of text, this lengthy treatment was for my eyes only). This research and treatment process consumed about four months, full-time. I then wrote the screenplay in six weeks because I'd done such thorough prep for it. This disparity between prep and actual screenwriting, I have read, is not uncommon. But did having a fully thought-out story and cast make the novel easier to write?

No.

I had more of an outline for the story and plot and characters and ideas than I've ever had before starting any of my other novels (and I've always done a great deal of research for each of them). But this novel was just as difficult to write as all of the others.

Cunning Folk – the novel – required seven drafts and fourteen months to reach completion. In that time, I reduced the first draft from 110K words to 90K. So why was adapting a 110-page screenplay into a novel no easier?

Because a screenplay can't tell you how to write a novel. A screenplay is told visually, in pictures, with a little dialogue; a novel is told within the inner life of its characters and you also need to paint the sets and do hair and makeup for the cast, and FX . . . A few seconds onscreen may need an entire chapter on the page.

But the novel you've just read has barely deviated from the characters and story in my screenplay. It's an exact representation and adaptation of the film that I imagined while writing the screenplay. I also think, but then I would, that *Cunning Folk* would make a cracking little horror film. But we'll see . . . It's not down to me. But even if it never becomes a film, the story will live in this novel. Nothing was wasted. Two bites of the same dark cherry.

The other major facet, to my eye, that distinguishes this novel from my others, is that this is also my first comic horror novel. At least, in parts. Much of it isn't funny at all; the scene with Gracey and the plank is one of the most upsetting things I have ever imagined – what I call 'a permanent harm to the writer scene'. But there is a tragicomic tone to much of the story. A comic tone that was never planned; it evolved naturally within the screenplay. And then it infected the novel. But if you don't find this story humorous, no matter at all. Take the horror straight up!

So thank you all for entertaining this novelised-potential-film . . . and don't let your neighbours grind you down!

Manes exite paterni
Adam L. G. Nevill
December 2020, Devon.

Acknowledgements

My research for fiction takes many forms and chief amongst these forms and channels are secondary sources. For *Cunning Folk* Professor Ronald Hutton's encyclopaedic *The Witch* was a primary source of knowledge and inspiration. I also either read Ted Hughes's poetry or the peerless J. A. Baker early each morning before I began work on this book, to get my mind into the zone.

As I explain in the Story Notes, *Cunning Folk* began life as a screenplay, one I developed with Will Tennant, Ash Clarke and Elisa Scubla, across many meetings and phone calls. Their guidance and suggestions were invaluable.

I want to acknowledge the deep debt I owe the Ritual Limited team for producing these books. I may have gone indie but doing indie properly is not a job for one man alone. None of this would be possible without the marvellous artist Samuel Araya, for his consistently spectacular cover artwork, my long-term editor Tony Russell, Pete Marsh of Dead Good Design, Simon Nevill, Anne Nevill, Iona Nevill (who helped her daddy with the advanced reading list and for being a constant companion on our many trips to the post office together), Gill Parry for the second proofread, Peter Davis at Bluewave for my eBooks, Journalstone for the audio, TJ for my hardbacks, Ingram for the paperbacks, Amazon my primary retailer, Dave our postmaster in Paignton, Brian J. Showers, Helen McQueen and We Can Creative for my website, and Mark Dawson for always keeping me up to speed.

I do everything in my power to make my horror resonate but without reviewers and readers to boost the signal, I'd have far fewer readers and might not have continued for so long. So a big two-horn salute goes out to those reviewers and horror fiction devotees who were kind enough to give my *Wyrd and Other Derelictions* their time and who shared their thoughts about that curious collection. I'll shout-out to as many of you as I can find and recall but if I have missed anyone, apologies and I'll get you next time.

My sincerest thanks to Jim Moon at Hypnogoria, Sadie 'Mother Horror' Hartmann of Nightworms and Cemetery Dance, Dave Simms and Cemetery Dance Online, Gavin Kendall and Steve Stred at Kendall Reviews, Joe Scipioni at Horror Bound, Tony Jones at Gingernuts of Horror, Anthony Watson at Dark Musings, Michael Wilson, Bob Pastorella and Thomas Joyce at This is Horror, Janelle Janson at She Reads With Cats, Harpies in the Trees, The Sleepy Librarian, Read by Dusk, Marc's World of Books, Dead Head Reviews, Stephen Bacon, Divination Hollow Reviews, Ben Long of Reading Vicariously and Beyond the Veil, Karen Crighton at Horror DNA, Tom Adams, the ever attentive and passionate Nightworms reviewers: Undead Dad Reads, Daniel De Lost, Reads With Dogs, Kimberly Yerina, Team Red Mom, Edward Demian Stafford at Apothecaria Obscura, Ashley 'Spookish Mommy', Chandra at 'Where the Reader Grows', Ashley Ochoa, Beverley Lee, Miss Misty, Kirsten Holt, Robby Biggs, Flame Imperishable, Amanda at the Crooked House, Hollywyrd, Liz Sanchez, Pictish Dreams, Ghoulish Spirit, Life in Books, John Kealy, Ana A. J. Serrano, Jeremy Megargee, Alyson Hasson, CJH Reads, Philip Fracassi, Sameena Hussain, Eldritch Signs, Matt Hull, Diala Atat, Melissa Nowark, Paul Feeney, Patrice Hawkes-Reed, Pap3rcut, Reading Pensive, Alex J Knudson and the many other generous and avid readers of horror at Instagram.

About the Author

*A*dam L.G. Nevill was born in Birmingham, England, in 1969 and grew up in England and New Zealand. He is an author of horror fiction. Of his novels, *The Ritual, Last Days, No One Gets Out Alive* and *The Reddening* were all winners of The August Derleth Award for Best Horror Novel. He has also published three collections of short stories, with *Some Will Not Sleep* winning the British Fantasy Award for Best Collection, 2017.

Imaginarium adapted *The Ritual* and *No One Gets Out Alive* into feature films and more of his work is currently in development for the screen.

The author lives in Devon, England. More information about the author and his books is available at: www.adamlgnevill.com

More horror fiction from Adam L. G. Nevill and Ritual Limited.

The Reddening
Winner of the August Derleth Award for Best Horror Novel, 2020.

One million years of evolution didn't change our nature. Nor did it bury the horrors predating civilisation. Ancient rites, old deities and savage ways can reappear in the places you least expect.

The Reddening is an epic story of folk and prehistoric horrors, written by the author of *The Ritual, Last Days, No One Gets Out Alive* and the four times winner of The August Derleth Award for Best Horror Novel.

"Adam Nevill is a spine-chiller in the classic tradition, a writer who draws you in from the world of the familiar, eases you into the world of terror, and then locks the door behind you." Michael Koryta, *NYT* Bestselling author.

"One of the most subtle and powerful writers of dark fiction - a unique voice" Michael Marshall, *NYT* Bestselling author.

Available in eBook (and included in Kindle Unlimited) at Amazon and in paperback and audio from all major online retailers. Signed editions are available from www.adamlgnevill.com.

Some Will Not Sleep
Selected Horrors

Winner of the British Fantasy Award: Best Collection 2017.

In ghastly harmony with the nightmarish visions of the award-winning writer's novels, these stories blend a lifelong appreciation of horror culture with the grotesque fascinations and terrors that are the author's own. Adam L. G. Nevill's best early horror stories are collected here for the first time.

"Great storytelling, but across a wider palate and range of styles than you might have expected, leading to some delightfully unexpected visions and hellscapes." *Gingernuts of Horror.*

"There is not one single tale which feels less than the others, none which seem to be mere 'filler'. They are beautifully crafted, original and complete works." *This is Horror.*

"In *Some Will Not Sleep* nothing is sacred, nothing is safe, and goodness me, if you like horror fiction you're going to absolutely love every damn minute." *Pop Mythology.*

Available in eBook (and included in Kindle Unlimited) at Amazon and in paperback and audio from all major online retailers. Signed editions are available from www.adamlgnevill.com.

Hasty for the Dark
Selected Horrors

Hasty for the Dark is the second short story collection from the award-winning and widely appreciated British writer of horror fiction, Adam L. G. Nevill. The author's best horror stories from 2009 to 2015 are collected here for the first time.

"These tales are dark, starkly violent, but also subtle and ambiguous, often at the same time." *This is Horror.*

"The nine tales are cleverly varied, exhibiting varied pace, chills which deal with the supernatural in both every day and altogether freakier situations, and other curve-balls which drop feet into other genres." *Gingernuts of Horror.*

"His stories weave their way inside of your head and plant seeds of doubt and terror. He is a master of creating oppressive, creepy atmospheres and of taking your imagination to places you would rather he didn't." *The Grim Reader.*

Available in eBook (and included in Kindle Unlimited) at Amazon and in paperback and audio from all major online retailers. Signed editions are available from www.adamlgnevill.com.

Wyrd and Other Derelictions

Derelictions are horror stories told in ways you may not have encountered before. Something is missing from the silent places and worlds inside these stories. Something has been removed, taken flight, or been destroyed. Us.

Wyrd contains seven derelictions, original tales of mystery and horror from the author of *Hasty for the Dark* and *Some Will Not Sleep* (winner of The British Fantasy Award for Best Collection).

"This is a different collection, one that might remind one of Peter Straub, Thomas Ligotti, or even Robert Aickman in its exquisite weirdness. It is well worth the read. Recommended reading for any serious horror fan or for speculative fiction aficionados who crave intelligence in their weirdness." *Cemetery Dance.*

"I can't recommend this collection of stories enough. This is experimental literary horror and the experiment has exceeded all expectations. Read this and enjoy the horrific scenes Nevill has laid out for you." *Horror Bound.*

"Nevill guides us through ruined landscapes and describes the aftermath . . . then leaves it to the reader to piece together what happened. Each of these derelictions left me unsettled and I couldn't put the collection down. 5 Stars." *Deadhead Reviews.*

Available in eBook (and included in Kindle Unlimited) at Amazon and in paperback and audio from all major online retailers. Signed editions are available from www.adamlgnevill.com.

Free Ebook

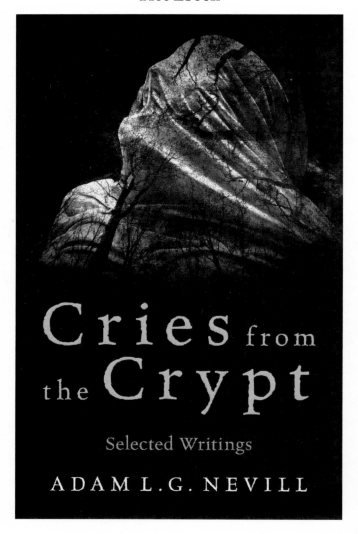

Cries from the Crypt

Selected Writings

ADAM L.G. NEVILL

If you like horror stories, missing chapters, advice for writing
horror, articles on horror fiction and films, and much more,
register at www.adamlgnevill.com to seize your Free Book today.

Made in United States
North Haven, CT
02 March 2022

16674045R00202